The Magickal Summer of Evie Edelman

HAVE YOU EVER WONDERED HOW BOOKS ARE MADE?

UCLan Publishing is an award winning independent publisher. Based at The University of Central Lancashire, this Preston-based publisher teaches MA Publishing students how to become industry professionals using the content and resources from its business; students are included at every stage of the publishing process and credited for the work that they contribute.

The business doesn't just help publishing students though. UCLan Publishing has supported the employability and real-life work skills for the University's Illustration, Acting, Translation, Animation, Photography, Film & TV students and many more. This is the beauty of books and stories; they fuel many other creative industries! The MA Publishing students are able to get involved from day one with the business and they acquire a behind the scenes experience of what it is like to work for a such a reputable independent.

The MA course was awarded a Times Higher Award (2018) for Innovation in the Arts and the business, UCLan Publishing, was awarded Best Newcomer at the Independent Publishing Guild (2019) for the ethos of teaching publishing using a commercial publishing house. As the business continues to grow, so too does the student experience upon entering this dynamic Master's course.

www.uclanpublishing.com
www.uclanpublishing.com/courses/
uclanpublishing@uclan.ac.uk

The Magickal Summer of Evie Edelman is a uclanpublishing book

First published in Great Britain in 2025 by
uclanpublishing
University of Central Lancashire
Preston, PR1 2HE, UK

978-1-916747-48-7

1 3 5 7 9 10 8 6 4 2

Set in Kingfisher by Becky Chilcott.

A CIP catalogue record for this book is available from the British Library.

Printed and bound in Great Britain by Clays Ltd, Elcograf S.p.A.

Harriett de Mesquita

The Magickal Summer of Evie Edelman

uclanpublishing

For my two grandfathers:
The Yorkshireman who left school at fourteen,
and the Rabbi's son who became an Oxford don.
For Ted and Daniel.

APRIL

Daisy – Diamond – Aries – Fire

"April brings the primrose sweet,
Scatters daisies at our feet."
SARA COLERIDGE

(She clearly did NOT live in Leeds)

I SUPPOSE THAT I SHOULD WRITE SOMETHING VERY deep and illuminating about the coming of spring, and new beginnings and such like. I think that the Spring Equinox was in March, but up here in Leeds the winter stays for longer. So this is my Spring Equinox, the beginning of this diary. The world is neither tilted away from the sun nor towards it; it faces it head on. That is what I had better do: face everything head on.

I can't start any sort of writing without Anita Brookner, it just wouldn't feel right. I doubt that she was particularly witchy, just Jewish in the same way that I would like to be: ingrained, gently cynical.

"Girls who are alone too much need not suffer in this day and age . . . and she has a little money of her own, which is no bad thing for someone without friends."

I am not quite like that, though. It isn't quite true of me. Probably not, anyway.

Horoscope for April:
Leo: Consider that self-expression may happen in many different ways. You will feel busy this month, but don't forget that while you are rushing to deal with everything at once, your true nature will reveal itself.

Erm . . . I'm not sure . . . well, all right then.

MONDAY 5TH APRIL 1982

It is very late at night for a New Beginning – almost tomorrow, but not quite. Beginning something new sounds like the crack of the spine as I opened this book, and looks like the cream square of blank paper. There is always something pleasingly spacious about a blank page. Or am I the only person who finds blankness calming? I am about to spoil it, of course, with my messy writing, and equally messy thoughts and feelings.

"New Beginning," I say to myself, pen poised, feeling very important – even though the diary wasn't my idea. It was a psychiatrist's idea, actually, but if I write out spells and press flowers and record the occasional hex, if I am cross rather than talk about 'feelings', he'll never know. My witching is the most interesting thing of the twenty-four hour blocks in which I somehow exist.

Twenty-four hours. Twenty-one years old. 'Temporarily Without Employment' is the technical term, I believe, and if you watch the news, it seems that a lot of young people are in my situation. "Filing Clerk wanted," one of my parents will read out over breakfast. "You like sorting things out, Evie – you could do that."

"Typist?" The other parent will ask, upward inflection of voice well merited.

At the very idea of going into an office, a muzzy, black crest of panic rises up inside me. "I am *gearing up* to work," I reply to Dad and Lizzie, with admirable restraint.

Anyway, New Beginnings: it all began with a bearded dragon lizard in a psychiatrist's office this morning, although of course nothing ever begins, if you think about it. Try to stick a pin in where something began and you quickly realise that one hundred things went before it, like the Russian dolls that turn out to be wooden shells with a smaller doll inside.

I suppose that I should begin my diary with a bang, rather than talking about Russian dolls and filing clerks – there should be something portentous, for posterity. Ordinarily, this would have been difficult: mooching around the house and mooching to synagogue once a week doesn't give much scope for thrills. But, fortuitously, I actually have just the event:

My Aunt Mim breathed her last on the corner of Vicar Lane and George Street, carrying a bag of oranges, last Friday. Friday 2nd April.

I underlined it for impact, you see.

She was dead instantly from a heart attack, the doctor said when he telephoned Dad. I could hear his papery voice on the line saying that she 'wouldn't have suffered, et cetera', and I wondered what precisely the 'et cetera' was. Dad had frowned: I could tell that he was thinking the same as me. That the doctor was being banal, when the important fact of the matter was that Aunt Mim had gone.

The disembodied voice of the doctor had gone on and on. Aunt Mim had been my most special person, and I realised that her death would be 'an event'. That was how I described it to myself. I suppose I meant that I would have to experience her loss in my own way. Of course, Dad, Lizzie and my brother Joe would be *sad*, but . . . I wouldn't grieve as part of a family unit. I would grieve for Aunt Mim by myself. Perhaps I should do a list of some kind?

Things to remember to mourn:

1) Aunt Mim.

Last Friday, all I could think of was that I had been lucky to live twenty-one years without having to work out how to grieve alone. Previously, it was done as a family member, or as part of the synagogue, but Aunt Mim meant something special just to me. I didn't feel lucky. I didn't feel anything. It was as if the *thought* of Aunt Mim's passing had wedged itself into my brain, without actually ripping open that gaping space that she would leave behind.

"Yes, yes. I'll come down. Identification. Yes." Dad's frown eased into a pained expression that gave me a kind of creased feeling inside. It was as if a paper bag was crumpled and crackling in the pit of my stomach, and I twisted and turned to get rid of it.

"I suppose that we'll have to put down that bloody dog," Lizzie whispered over my shoulder. "Evie, why are you jerking about like that?"

"I'll have her," I offered instantly. "I've always wanted a chihuahua."

"Have you?" Lizzie raised her eyebrows.

"Well, not really," I admitted, "but I'll take Peggy. She likes me."

"I wasn't aware that she liked anyone," said Dad. He put the phone down carefully and sighed. Lizzie went to him and put her arm around his shoulders, reaching up slightly to do it.

"I'm going to look after Peggy," I said, more confidently than I felt. I wondered what dogs ate. Would Peggy like Findus pancakes? Lizzie served a lot of those when there wasn't company. I'm not sure if anyone in the family really likes them, but, as my mother, the oven and everything that goes in it seems to be Lizzie's domain. Will I inherit dominion of the oven when I grow older? I hope not.

Lizzie sighed too. She released Dad's thin shoulders and eyed the mahogany legs of our sofas possessively from the hall. "Peggy will chew her way through the house, you know. Grief. Trauma," she added darkly.

"Well, you always say that the chesterfields are uncomfortable, too springy. You could use the opportunity to get rid of them and buy a three-piece suite," I offered. I could never distinguish between a three-piece suite and suit, but it was something that people said, a pleasant pattern of three monosyllables. Three. Piece. Sweet.

"Oh, *Evie*," said Lizzie. "How can you think about furniture at a time like this?"

There was no Special Friday Dinner that night. Instead, the three of us, Dad, Lizzie and I – there should have been four, but Joe always seemed to be with his wife nowadays, which I thought was selfish of him – went into our living room. There we sat in its sepulchral chill, shifting on the sprung sofas in a chorus of apologetic creaks as Dad, waxen from his visit to identify Aunt Mim's body, recited the tale of her demise.

I was mystified by the bag of oranges. Running my hands over the tweedy fabric of the sofa, I reflected that Aunt Mim *was* often mystifying, in a pleasant sort of way. Had been mystifying. What happened to those oranges? I imagined them rolling away, tipping off the kerb in a series of unsettling little thumps. They would have spun under car tyres, their pulp and juice dragged into a shining smear. Perhaps a kindly passer-by – a lady, I imagined, in a pale blue coat – might have stooped to pick them up to keep for Aunt Mim when she came to. It was a painful thought, that act of useless kindness.

The oranges must have been purchased at Kirkgate Market. What were they for? Aunt Mim had never been remotely feminine or Jewish about the way she approached the kitchen. Her forays could best be described as fiercely experimental. She had the air of a pugnacious explorer determined to conquer and subjugate. This undomestic approach had made itself obvious in her culinary offerings: pineapple jelly that hadn't set and became 'sweet soup'. Scones the colour of sunburnt flesh, with strawberry jam mixed into them 'to save you a step'. God knows what she had been planning with those oranges.

"I want to be cremated." I heard Aunt Mim's voice reverberating in the thick, white air of the living room, bouncing from the drinks cabinet that none of us ever opened and reflecting in the mirror above the fireplace. She wasn't really there, unfortunately – it was my memory dragging me back to the gossiping, cooking, smell-saturated aftermath of synagogue on a festival day, Aunt Mim, defiant and loud. It must have been over a decade ago, because I'd had to look up at the adults. I could see her so clearly, overflowing either side on one of the function chairs, her chubby feet planted squarely. I could even see the horrified face of the other women she was talking to. "I know we aren't supposed to want to be burnt away after . . . everything, but honestly, it's for the best. If you choose it, of course," she'd added hurriedly, as I opened my mouth.

"I wonder whether I should ring Rabbi Guld about a burial plot now?" Dad said now, looking at his watch, his voice thin.

"On a *Friday* afternoon, too," said Lizzie, shaking her head.

*

I don't want to write about Aunt Mim any more. Not today. Monday is the sort of day when pagans would worship the moon, did you know that? It is a reflective, dark, blue night without a moon. No moon, no Aunt Mim – it should be obvious to me now that she has gone. I hate writing about her in the past tense, whilst being unable to imagine the present without her.

I wonder whether I can recall my entire conversation in the psychiatrist's office this morning. I have a good memory (although I am 'young for my age', apparently. Mostly according to Lizzie).

"Are you ready to start?" said Dr Gordner.

"I suppose so," I replied. "You don't look like Carl Jung at all."

"I am sorry to be a disappointment." Dr Gordner's eyes looked as though his mouth should be laughing.

Before, I had tried so hard to imagine Dr Gordner and his office. He was a psychiatrist, Dad said, a trick cyclist. He couldn't look like Sigmund Freud because Dad looked like Sigmund Freud, right down to the round glasses, air of owlish concentration and sense of remove from the everyday. So, perhaps Dr Gordner looked like Carl Jung, I had thought. I looked up Carl Jung in my encyclopaedia and found a picture – there he was, rather friendly, his round glasses perched on top of his head as if the camera had just caught him between appointments, a twinkle in his eye. Dr Gordner must look like that, I thought, only on a bicycle, one of those old-fashioned ones with the big wheels, doing a trick. Juggling, perhaps?

But when I went into Dr Gordner's office, all I could see was the bearded dragon lizard. "Oooh!" I said, making my way to his glass cage, banging into something I hadn't noticed on the way. I found out afterwards that it is called a vivarium, not a cage. A vivarium's primary purpose isn't to contain what's inside, but to create an atmosphere in which it can survive.

"That is Sigi," came a bland but well-modulated voice from behind me.

"What is he?"

"A bearded dragon lizard."

"I should have known that," I said, cross with myself. Sigi really did look like a little dragon, sat on his branch, his eyes flicking opaquely back and forth. I stared through the glass, fascinated by his thinly stretched skin. His tiny pattern of scales bulged and warped with the smallest of movements, barely containing his toothpick bones. Sigi's 'beard' was a series of strands under his chin that looked like melted and pulled plastic, his whole body variegating shades of pale pink and grey. He seemed balanced on a tightrope between beauty and ugliness, vulnerable as he wavered, making my own skin crawl as delicately as his.

"He's twelve," came the voice. "An older man."

"An older gentleman," I corrected. Sigi had clearly never done a day's work in his life – he looked as soft and languid as a baby. "What does he eat?"

"Live insects and vegetables."

"Got it." He must be around thirty-seven centimetres, I thought, holding an imaginary ruler against Sigi's tapering body. "What are those holes at the side of his face?"

"His ears."

"Got it." Those holes were a direct opening into his body. Uncovered, unprotected, they pulsed gently. He was listening to us. I looked at him. Bearded dragon lizard, twelve-years old, name of Sigi, holes for ears, home a glass cage, diet of insects and vegetables. That all seemed satisfactory.

I turned around, assimilating the large window that let in the sight of iron-coloured clouds of early spring, the rows of cracked, peeling spines of well-worn books. The line of pot plants in brass tubs was presumably supposed to be bright and cheering, but they were coloured grey by the sky. Finally, my gaze rested on Dr Gordner. There were no round glasses, pushed to the top of his head or otherwise. He was short, balding, wearing a knitted waistcoat and staring at me with small, mild eyes. He wasn't what I imagined: mentally, I placed him at a family party in a village hall, drinking slowly and watching the young people dance. How disappointing that he wasn't the Dr Gordner I had created for myself.

"Your parents tell me that you've had a death in the family. HaMakom Yenahem Ot-cha betoch sha'ar aveilei tsiyon vi-rushalayim."

"Todah m'od." (Yes, I can speak a bit of Hebrew.)

"I am so sorry."

"Don't be sorry," I said firmly. I mean, there was absolutely no point in Dr Gordner getting upset. I wasn't upset, yet. Over the weekend, I had watched Peggy the chihuahua feeling the lack of Aunt Mim, her eyes round with anxiety, and occasionally almost convinced myself that I felt the same. I didn't want Dr Gordner to feel that at all; it wouldn't be fair on him. "The funeral will be this Thursday," I said, to close the matter, "at eleven fifteen in the morning, at the Asher Israel Synagogue."

"Now, do you prefer Eva, or Evie?" Dr Gordner was clearly getting down to business.

"Evie."

"How old are you, Evie?"

"I'll be twenty-two on the eighth of August," I said clearly. "I'm a Leo. Loyal but temperamental."

"Fine. I see. Now . . ."

But memories of Aunt Mim had invaded Dr Gordner's study. Her stout form was so unattractive that it was appealing; it gathered a sort of attractiveness because you spent longer looking. Almost a perfect square, she was dressed in one of her knitted dresses that rose and fell over the rolling contours of her body, stretching good-naturedly where it had to. She had the most beautiful eyes, Aunt Mim: large and grey, animal-like in the way that they had a soft, trusting gleam to them. Her wide mouth that curled when she talked, and a wedge-shaped nose that drew her face forwards. She was handing me a packet of Smith's bacon-flavoured crisps – I was a teenager.

Then, I could hear the sea and I was much younger. Aunt Mim had come with us on holiday to Bournemouth, the year that she had developed a mania for sea swimming. I could feel the English summer breeze that wasn't quite as warm as you would like it to be, and hear the deeply specific roar that the wind made when it pushed itself through the pine trees. Aunt Mim had struck out in the waves; Dad and I stood on the beach, watching, fascinated. We both worried that Uncle Harry, or Auntie Annette, or the children, would laugh at her, and that we'd hate them. Uncle Harry's dog, a cocker spaniel named Jet, had followed Aunt Mim into the water. Their two curl-plastered heads bobbed opposite one another, level. Then Aunt Mim turned towards us, laughing. That was how I remembered her. Aqueous, canine with her startled eyes and wet hair, ineffectually pawing the water that roared and sucked her in, enjoying kicking against nature but blissfully aware of her own limitations.

*

I am going to digress now, but it is my diary and I can do what I want. I shall tell the story of Dr Gordner being the last link in the end of a chain of events that started with Dad's friend from his university days (long, *long* ago).

I hadn't seen John for years: we had moved out of London, all the way up a left-leaning diagonal line to Leeds, when I was six. John was left behind at his university doing research. Before his visit last month, I had asked Dad, "Is John Jewish?". I didn't mean to be narrow-minded – Dad didn't mind that John was a Gentile, so why should I? But I always ask with anyone unfamiliar. It helps me place them, you see. Most people I know are Jewish. The ones that aren't seem exotically pale, their colours beige and powder blue and peach. Anything Jewish I see surrounded by bright orange and gold.

"Are you going to give your Uncle John a hug?" he had asked, hefting himself out of his beige Ford and opening his arms to me. I let myself be enfolded and smelt cigarettes. "Of course, you're too old to call me 'Uncle' now, aren't you?"

"I don't know," I'd said. "I'm not sure if it's a question of age, exactly. I mean, I would call my familial uncle 'Uncle' all my life. That is to say, all his life, as he will probably predecease me. But it is a different situation when the tie is not actually familial. I suppose it conveys a childlike trust that you are implying is now outgrown."

John had blinked.

And he'd started watching me over Lizzie's fillets of sole au vermouth from the St Michael's *Book of French Cooking*. He had begun to talk about a lady he worked with called Lorna, who published a paper last year about some condition with a German name. He talked carefully against the sounds of our knives as they slid through the fish. I thought what a romantic name Lorna was, like Lorna Doone, who had flowing, dark hair and a special necklace. I had sometimes imagined that I was like Lorna Doone, that the family I had grown up with were not really related to me, and there were better relatives waiting over the horizon. These relatives never materialised, and I had learnt over time that it is actually rather uncommon to be a beautiful, displaced heiress.

People who have this condition, said John, suddenly being careful not to look at me, have certain traits. They have social impairments, they repeat themselves, they are very singular, he had said, and they have absolutely no common sense but are very good at certain things. And would Lizzie mind passing the potatoes? This was delicious. I'd shot her a triumphant glance. Earlier that day, Lizzie had asked me to switch the oven on for the potatoes, but I was distracted by the radio and switched the washing machine on instead, so we were eating late. But surely John didn't mind, if he liked the potatoes?

John left on Sunday afternoon, squinting against the rain,

saying what a pleasant weekend he'd had and how nice it had been to see Dad and Lizzie again, and nice to see you, Evie, haven't you grown tall, and we mustn't leave it so long next time. We watched as he swung out of the drive, shivering and wrapping our arms around ourselves and then dashing back inside. He had left Dad a piece of paper with Dr Gordner's name written on it.

It turned out that Dr Gordner's youngest sister Rachel had married a tailor named Donald Rosenfeld, whose older sister Jane attended our synagogue with her husband Eli Sutton. It also happened that Dr Gordner practiced psychiatry from his flat just off Boar Street (this is what you say about psychiatrists for it to be correct, apparently. You can't 'do' psychiatry, you can only practice it, which suggests to me that you never actually get very good). Apparently, he was 'progressive', which worried Lizzie. But Boar Street was just off the Corn Exchange, whose sheer grimy magnificence marked it out as a reassuring landmark for her – she still had that southerner's distrust of The North. It was near Leeds Art Gallery too, a cultural respite beloved by Dad. These omens seemed favourable, so an appointment was made.

"What happens if she has this *thing* that John says?" Lizzie had asked last night in the next room, thinking that I couldn't hear. Her voice, though not loud, became more bell-like with anxiety, taking on a clear tone that cut through the fuddled warmth and hum of our electric heater.

"I don't know," said Dad. He never saw the point in elaborating. Neither did I.

"But . . . what do we *do*?"

"I don't know."

I heard the rasping shift of his papers, the crackle as he rearranged his grip on them, his fingers denting and crumpling what had been smooth. Dad was a historian, but 'History' conjured up images of emperors and beautiful women in velvet chokers and war. Victorian England in the Aftermath of Industrialisation – that was his speciality. History with a small 'h'. He had nothing to do with the glamourous bits. "It's Asperger's syndrome."

"What?"

"It's not a *thing*. The correct name is Asperger's syndrome," said Dad. I looked at the wall that separated us and tartly nodded my approval through it.

"Whatever it is," said Lizzie, made querulous, "whatever fancy name you give it, he kept on about autism. How's it not autism?"

"John explained," said Dad. "That it's a different disorder."

"Then why did he keep saying about autism? *Elsie's* boy had autism."

"I know."

"He ended up in an institution. She couldn't cope."

"We've coped with Evie, haven't we?"

Silence. I could only imagine Lizzie's expression. Perhaps she had given a small snort that hadn't survived the journey through the wall. I thought of the word 'Asperger's'. The emphasis was on 'asp', like a snake, the kind that killed Cleopatra. Then, 'berger's', like hamburgers. Reptiles and meat patties. The two didn't go together at all, I thought, frowning. Then I stopped thinking, as frowning prematurely ages you. I am not vain as a rule, but once you get wrinkles on your forehead you really are stuck with them.

"Well, what if . . . ?"

"Evie can look after herself," said Dad. "She's intelligent. John said that people with Asperger's are intelligent, just eccentric."

"Should we be paying this Dr Gordner to tell us that our daughter is eccentric?"

"We are *paying* him to tell us whether this particular eccentricity has the name of Asperger's or not."

"Gerry . . ."

"Look, I have to get through this marking," Dad had said, with a rustle of papers, and there was silence. I had completely forgotten what I was doing and looked down, quizzically. Oh, yes. I was cutting an article out of the paper about Peggy Flounders, the witch with a beard. The front of the paper and the next couple of pages were taken up with stories about the navy going off to try and regain the Falkland Islands, because it appeared that we lost them over the weekend. They seemed very far away – I really wondered why anyone wanted the Falklands, except to mention them in an occasional speech. A page or two after the fuss, things got interesting in the shape of this Peggy Flounders article. She seemed a very bad-tempered witch, but I supposed that you would be grumpy being a witch in the early eighteen hundreds. Constant misunderstandings, and the beard probably itched too.

*

"Evie?"

"Yes?"

"Now, I'm going to ask you some questions, about you, about

your interests, things like that. Would that be satisfactory?" said Dr Gordner.

"Yes," I said firmly. I nodded, so much that my neck hurt. It wouldn't be nice, or interesting, or amusing. But it would be satisfactory, certainly.

"The library book you picked out for me last week was very satisfactory, Evie – I always wanted to learn more about gardens . . ."

I was at the dining table, reading a letter from Aunt Mim. I could see her slanted writing at the top of the letter: *"18th April 1981"*. It was a year ago. Our dining room was a dark place, even in the morning, and the letter was written on pale cream paper that was almost translucent. Aunt Mim and I kept up a secret correspondence – well, I say secret, but nothing escaped Lizzie, of course. She acknowledged our club of two with a traditional, universal gesture of maternal resignation: the sideways glance accompanied by an inaudible sigh. Aunt Mim would write to me, sliding the letter in a post box for its journey from Chapel Allerton to Alwoodley that could be walked quicker, just to tell me things that looked better written down. I would do the same back.

". . . What do you understand Asperger's to be?" said Dr Gordner.

Ah, I thought, one of those trick cyclist questions that make you juggle your own thoughts. I suppose that Dr Gordner wants me to feel as though I am a willing participant in all of this, but if he just told me what Asperger's is then I would pull it into my mind, memorise it and be done. It doesn't matter what you think, only what you know.

"It's . . . um, where you aren't very sociable and are only good at some things?" I cut out bits of Lizzie and Dad's conversation, plus what John had said, and pasted it together. "It's like autism, but it isn't really."

"Well," Dr Gordner sounded like an underwhelmed teacher, "those are good points, Evie. You see, Asperger's wasn't really terribly well known about until last year, when a lady named Lorna Wing picked it up. People with Asperger's are not quite like other people: they start to exhibit . . . peculiarities from around the age of three, and they don't mix with others terribly well or read social signs."

Signs? Sign posts, directing me places that I couldn't go. I felt insulted – I tried, I thought. I went to school, synagogue, the Victoria Quarter to look in shops, all those places filled with other people's faces emitting signals that remained foreign, indecipherable. I socialised – I stood there, people said things to me, popping out strings of words that flew at me from various angles, and I would parry them with words of my own. Wasn't that what other people did?

"They are clumsy, impractical, repetitive and obsessive."

"I don't have much going for me, do I?"

"They are terribly literal, and lack a sense of humour . . ."

As Dr Gordner looked at me, I raised my eyebrow. He smiled, and the bands that his words had wrapped around me loosened a little. Dr Gordner was a person as well as a psychiatrist. Perhaps he played golf at weekends, although he didn't seem very athletic. What about trainspotting? That seemed more likely. "Perhaps

I have the Jewish humour gene," I offered, "and it offsets the Asperger's gene."

"Truly a mitzvah."

"Quite." Sigi had turned his head away from us, his little dark hole of an ear pulsing, still listening. I wonder whether he thought my sense of humour a blessing.

"Now, tell me, Evie, what do you do in your free time?"

"All of my time is now free," I said. Freefall – the feeling of falling that is all long 'l's and 'f's. I divided up my free time. Divide and conquer, and then feel guilty for enjoying it. Sometimes it would be nice to get free of myself.

"Ah. You don't have a job then?"

"No."

"Hmmm."

"I did, but . . . I didn't do very well. They thought it was better if I left."

"Uhm."

Dr Gordner's non-vocal expressions were reaching ever new heights, I thought. I wished that I could orchestrate them all together, all at the same time. What an odd wave of sound that would be. I imagined all that noise moving towards me and shuddered.

"Lizzie found me the job, in the office of her friend Sarah Baum's husband, helping with the accounts," I said before Dr Gordner could ask me, even though it disrupted our pattern. "But I had to go there every day, and . . ." my shoulders pulled upwards, "the filing cabinets would make this slamming noise . . ."

my chin tucked towards my chest, "and there was always a chorus. A chorus of bleeping and chirring of the phones mixed with the people's voices, which sounded feathery in comparison, tickling at me . . ." I rocked a little, held tight by invisible hands the length of my spine. Back and forth, back and forth, lulling until the noise went away.

"Uhm hmmm," said Dr Gordner. "Interesting."

Was I interesting? I am not sure that Dad, Lizzie and Joe thought that at all. Exasperating maybe, but . . .

"So, tell me about your hobbies then. What do you really enjoy doing?"

"*Don't* tell the doctor about the . . . the witchcraft thing, Evie," Lizzie had said to me at breakfast. I had a piece of toast on my plate with two thirds of a banana sliced over it. A full banana was just too much, I found. Lizzie had a grapefruit, Dad had Grape Nuts that rattled drily into the bowl and grew soft and quiet as they soaked in their milk. "If the doctor thinks that *you* think you are a witch, then we are really in trouble."

"I'm interested in witchcraft," I said now. I didn't actually tell Dr Gordner that I *was* a witch, because I didn't want us all to be in this nameless trouble of Lizzie's. The idea of trouble was always worrying because I was so bad at extricating myself from its clutches.

"Erm . . . tell me about that."

"Well, witchcraft has been around since ancient times," I said. "The stereotype of the ugly, evil witch only became prevalent with the onset of organised religion when witch hysteria took hold, and they were blamed when awful things happened, like bad harvests. They never even sat on brooms – just used them to sweep away bad spirits! Actually, witches are probably special women who are rather beautiful, like the picture of Circe by J. W. Waterhouse. Have you seen it?"

"I . . . errr . . . which gallery . . . ?"

"It's in my parents' dining room," I said. "A print. Circe is wearing a lovely dress, although a little revealing. And there's Isis – she pre-dates the bible – and Morgana Le Fay, and Anne Boleyn. Mary Bateman, Yorkshire's first serial killer, was a witch. And Ursula Southeil – better known as Mother Shipton. When we first moved to Leeds, Dad took me to Knaresborough's cave to see the Petrifying Well. He thought that it would be appealing to a child due to the word 'petrifying'. There was a carving of Mother Shipton there, and I felt that she was looking at me and smiling a bit. Witches are wise, you see. We have . . . *They* have healing hands and excellent memories and a facility for language and rhyme."

Dr Gordner opened his mouth to say something, so I hurried on. "They practice magick, only you have to spell it with a 'k' in order to differentiate between that and the tricks that magicians do on stage. They use spells and energy and crystals for healing, and hexes to cast misfortune. Would you like to hear what a hex sounds like? I can do one for you now, Dr Gordner."

"Oh, errr . . . No thanks, Evie. Not now."

*

I think that was most of what happened – I have a good memory, don't I? It is terribly discomforting sometimes.

After all that, I went into Dr Gordner's office as Evie, and I emerged Evie with Asperger's. It was official – I was given a letter and everything, which I have slipped into my diary until I can think what to do with it. Perhaps I should suggest to Dad and Lizzie that we frame it and put it in the posh drawing room? Next to Dad and Joe's degrees? PhD History, BSc Chemistry, Asperger's syndrome . . . Lizzie hates me calling the drawing room posh, by the way. But it is so posh that we never go in there.

The thing is, I feel exactly the same as before. All I want to do is indulge my witchiness and commune with nature and the supernatural realms. Aunt Mim would have understood. One of my earliest witchy memories was finding Aunt Mim a four-leaf clover from a huge patch of three-leaf clovers in her garden. "You have special sight, Evie," she had said to me, and we had pressed it together.

I want to use my witchy powers to make the world a better place, to cast spells that actually work and possibly even combat widespread unemployment. First things first, though: I am going to try cutting a bit of Lizzie's Aloe vera plant and mix it with some oil, then put it on my hair to make it less curly. The *Garden Lovers; Natural Ways* book says it should be olive oil, but Lizzie only has cooking oil, which I should think would be fine.

WEDNESDAY 7TH APRIL 1982

I thought that I conducted myself with great aplomb (a very rounded word) at the solicitor's office to discuss Aunt Mim's will today. We'd been back in the centre of Leeds, near Dr Gordner's.

"Hi, Sigi," I whispered as we drove past, and waved in his general direction.

Unfortunately, my hair still looks oily and caught in the light of the fluorescent bar in a bit of an odd way. I will keep washing it. Nearly all of the green bits of Aloe vera are out now. I hadn't realised that you take the clear jelly stuff out of the green casing and just use that. My curls look curlier than ever.

Peggy didn't mind my hair – we picked her up from Aunt Mim's disapproving next door neighbour yesterday, and she barked at me whilst I washed my hair. She barked when I played my Adam Ant record, too. I suppose it's all about acclimatisation. She was left at home today – I thought she might bark if she didn't agree with Aunt Mim's will as it was read.

No stipulation for cremation had been made in the will. Perhaps, for all her many florid acts of rebellion, Aunt Mim didn't dare flout that one Jewish tradition. Rabbi Guld has quite a gimlet eye – even Aunt Mim might have quailed. Or maybe she just forgot. Anyway, she did manage to cock a snook at Rabbi Guld by a) dying just before Shabbat began, the holy day of rest – and the Shabbat before Passover no less, and b) having entrusted her last will and testament to a lawyer with the distinctly un-Jewish name of Gavin Stephens. "I mean, he sounds almost . . . *Welsh*," Lizzie had said suspiciously.

It was to this office of Gavin Stephens that we repaired, five days after Aunt Mim died and two days after I started my new diary and visited Dr Gordner, should the three things ever be joined on a continuum.

We were 'The Family' of Aunt Mim, and it was true that we were all she had. Dad, Lizzie, myself. Joe was at work, later home to his flat in Sandton Court. He'd acquired his aforementioned wife Val last year, then a baby three months ago. It's all too much change, I think. At least, it is for me, so it must be even worse for Joe. I suppose that I should include Val and baby Tom as family too, but they are extraneous, I think, rather than core.

'The Family' waited tensely and I felt every strip of my muscles stretch like pulled elastic. I gripped hold of the wooden chair with both hands and stared at the grey filing cabinet, then at a distinctly illogical pile of folders on top of it (why aren't they *in* the cabinet? What is the point of a filing cabinet if you don't file things in it?). Why do all roads lead to filing? I don't *want* to work in an office with a watercolour of the Victoria Quarter, an imitation mahogany desk which gleams like an ice rink, and smells of carpet and stale coffee.

*

As I made my way back downstairs afterwards with Lizzie and Dad, I pondered how Dr Gordner's office could be so different to Gavin Stephens's when they were both offices. When will I learn that two things called the same thing can be different? Joe would have talked and joked and lightened the mood. We carried ourselves carefully, conspicuously silent, our coats pulled on but unbuttoned.

Emerging onto the street, we had left it too late to put our gloves and scarves on – the northerly cold had gotten us, penetrating and completely unsympathetic to our fragile states.

I felt as if the edges of us were shaken gently. One of us – me, to be precise – was now different in a way that was clinically *and* now financially quantifiable. I could feel Dad and Lizzie's concept of me shifting as they watched their feet on the stairs, then, in the biting air, looked upwards at the sky for rain.

We walked – tramped, really – to the car. I looked back at Gavin Stephens's office, its horizontal stripe of the sooty building with its high stone roof that reminded me of a French castle. Above the street-level row of shops, sharp white triangles stuck out at disconcertingly regular intervals with 'lease acquired' on them.

"What does that mean?" I asked Dad, gesturing upwards.

"It means that the lease for each of those has been purchased by a seller and then can be assumed by the buyer."

"Oh." I had lost interest before Dad finished his sentence. The signs were too sharp and pale to have anything to do with all those words. There was a ladder propped up against one of the shops, just left there forlornly. Lizzie skipped around it, but I walked under: my superstitions were not the commonplace ones. We walked past a television shop, and a clothing place called Tontos. It sounded American to me, like something out of a Western, but the same blouses and pleated skirts hung motionless in the window as any other ladies' clothing shop. A sludgy combination of a pale toffee coloured blouse and a skirt of brown, green and yellow shapes that were peculiarly formless (because shapes caught my eye) . . .

"Get in the car, Evie, before we all freeze."

"All *right*. I'm coming."

The headless blouse-and-skirt mannequins watched me as

we moved away – I kept my eyes on them until other cars got in the way and my neck couldn't turn any further. The corners of Dr Gordner's desk and the voices in the street knocked around together in my head until it ached.

I have always felt that I am too big for cars. I am certainly too tall for Dad's Ford Cortina, and far too tall for Lizzie's Ford Fiesta – her 'little car' that she 'bombs about in', which makes her driving sound far more explosive than it actually is. The trouble is that I am a little over five foot ten, although certainly not five foot ten and a half, which would be excessively tall. I can see over the head rests out on to the road if I sit up tall enough, although I usually slouch to lessen the resounding feeling that I am too long. I didn't want to watch the road today, or look out of the window. The seats were a sort of velvety beige fabric that pulled darker when you ran your hand against the grain (grain? Pile? Pile of grain?). I did this now, pushing my fingers up in an arcing shape so that it was just my palm that did the pushing, shivering a little with delight because it is the most sensitive part of me.

Lighter.

Darker.

Lighter.

Darker.

Sniff.

Lighter.

Darker.

Sniff, sniff.

What was that? It took me a few moments to realise that I

would never locate the noise of this sniffing unless I dragged my eyes away from the seat fabric. I looked up and realised: Lizzie was crying.

Lizzie was unusual for a mother – she was just so pretty. I know that in the hierarchy of adjectives, 'pretty' comes below 'beautiful', perhaps even below 'striking'. But it was unusual for us Jewish girls, us 'daughters of Israel', as Sarah Leverson used to term us when she wanted to make a point, to be pretty. We were handsome, exotic, dark, beautiful sometimes – our looks fetishized by the Gentiles that surrounded us to mean something dangerous and Eastern that drew them in.

"I know all about you Jewish girls," a man had said to me a few years ago. He had reeked of alcohol and smiled sourly.

"Come along, Eva," Lizzie had said, pulling me away.

"But you never call me Eva. . ." I could hear the man snorting with laughter behind me.

Lizzie's charm lay in the fact that she was lighter, brighter, more . . . more shiksha I suppose. Her hair was a mid-browny blonde that by some subtle tweak in shade was just superior to mouse. She had little, neat features, not much on their own but together creating a regularity of form that people loved because it was reassuring. She was slim and small, and I suppose that in some unconscious way Dad married her expecting to have a daughter in the same mould.

Unfortunately, I was what Dad ended up with. He had Joe as well, who was vaguely fair and slightly more regular, slightly more Lizzie-ish than me, but I had inherited none of Lizzie's charm.

Most of the time I am not beautiful at all; only in a dark room lit by two non-ceiling lights do I really look attractive. My hair is bobbed and somewhat bush-like – rather like Aunt Mim's actually, only at a more juvenile and manageable stage.

I could see that I was 'of Dad', just as I could vaguely comprehend that I was a 'daughter of Israel', or rather, Jewish, especially when I had to refuse bacon sandwiches and wasn't allowed to nightclubs. But I just wasn't 'of Lizzie'. I couldn't equate myself with her at all. That was why I always called Lizzie by her name, you see. Like an acquaintance rather than a mum. I just couldn't see the same blood running in our veins.

"What do we do now?" Lizzie blurted out.

Dad said nothing as we drove away from the city centre. He did this journey home every night – his almost-central university office to Alwoodley – and I wondered whether he was struck by the irony of reconstructing the diaspora of the Jewish People of Leeds in his Ford Cortina. For they had landed up in the slums right in the heart of the city, and gradually moved north towards the respectability conferred by gardens, bigger houses and golfing facilities. Their journey was an upward one, both socio-economically *and* in the car.

I watched for the sliver of Dad's cheek as he turned his head to check traffic. The bristle of his beard made my shoulders tense. I stared at his eyes in the mirror as they glanced upwards to check the road behind. A couple of times, he slid his eyes in my direction and we caught each other looking.

We skirted around the Alwoodley golf course (Dad wasn't a

member, much to Lizzie's disappointment) and onto the winding lane of green gardens, interrupted semi-regularly by enormous chunks of Victorian house, as though they had been parachuted in from a great height, squashing any unfortunate vegetation they landed on.

Our own enormous chunk of house stared down at us, ugly but indisputably substantial. I often wondered what on earth had possessed Dad and Lizzie to buy Hawthorns – it would have made an excellent dental practice or Christian retreat. The uncleaned Yorkshire stone positively glowered with grime; the three-storey square block of the house bulged by the front door in a half-hexagon shape like the pot belly of an old man. Above was a balcony, presumably a flight of fancy on behalf of the Victorian architect. But really, a balcony was completely ridiculous: who would hang around outside their bedroom just to look at our front garden? More rooms meandered either side of the main building, one concealed behind a sort of half-hearted gothic wall. I should also add that there were no hawthorns in the garden whatsoever.

"I'm going to my room," I said as soon as we got inside, banging the hall table accidentally with my hip, not stopping to glance at the painting of Thornlaw Saw Mill that I liked – the colours were too deep and rich for me today. My hip tingled delicately from the bump. Clumsy and repetitive, Dr Gordner had said.

"Evie, don't you think that we should have a discussion . . . ?"

"No."

I shook my head and shot up the stairs, taking the last two

steps on each flight together. I careered into my room, pushing the door away so that the handle crumped into the wall and the whole door reverberated back on me, making me shriek. I didn't want to be touched.

"We need to talk about Aunt Mim's will, at least . . ."

*

My room always had an 'atmosphere' after I had been away and absorbed in something else. My things seemed to blame me for abandoning them, silently accusing. Or perhaps I was just discombobulated – I should try and reason this out, I thought to myself. I'd been told that I had some sort of . . . *thing* that prevents my brain working properly, *and* I'd missed my markers between the front door and my room: look at the saw mill painting, hand on *top* of the end banister, top two steps together (that bit was all right), into bedroom left foot first. I was out of my rhythm – no wonder I was upset.

"You would have almost been a perfect square," I now said to my room (it was always a good idea to break tension with small talk, I supposed), "if the ceiling had been a little lower. Very nearly a box room," I said reassuringly, "but not quite."

The room and I looked out on to the tops of the garden trees and a sky that was streaked with patches of brightness, the light petering out before it got to my window, in a sudden change of heart. I had always wanted Joe's room at the front of the house with a far bigger window. After his wedding it had been assumed that I would move in there, but somehow, I couldn't bring myself to make that journey or let Lizzie clear away any of his discarded possessions. So, I remained in my gloomy little garret, pining vaguely like a forgotten princess for Lord knows what. Sometimes I wandered into Joe's room to pick things up and put them down again, in abject sympathy for their abandonment.

My possessions were the things that made my dim little box room bearable. There were my bookshelves, the order of books not alphabetised or organised by subject matter, but the order in which they were read. There was no deviating from that order, random because of my haphazard purchasing style, then instantly fixed on the shelf.

There was my desk, with two pictures above it of Adam Ant at an interval of 7.7cms from each other. Adam One I had torn from the front cover of *The Face* almost a year ago, red rose to his chin, yellow ribbon in his hair. "It's a bit bizarre, all this, but let's go along with it," he seemed to be saying. Adam Two is from the front cover of *Jackie*, wearing leather trousers, and his legs are shown to best advantage. I try to divide my looking time between the two Adams equally.

The left side of my desk is taken up with twelve crystals arranged in four rows of three. The rose quartz and the jade are in the centre row; they are the prettiest colours. On the windowsill there is my collection of china rabbits. They are dressed like humans used to dress – waistcoats and pie-crust collars and things – with exaggerated, shining eyes that make me feel a sharp pain in case anything should happen to them, and remind me of Peggy. Lizzie gave me the first one – it was unusually perspicacious of her. I went over and pressed my little finger into the fruit pie that one of the lady rabbits was carrying, feeling the bumps of the china fruit filling. Everything was as it should be, I supposed.

On the opposite wall to my bookcase, adjacent to both Adam Ants, I'd hung a print of Frederick Sandy's Morgana le Fay, mid-incantation, pleasantly triangular in shape due to her billowing silk dress, wrapped in a leopard skin sash. She looked a little like me, I thought – although I had tried that pose in the bathroom mirror and found it distinctly uncomfortable. She was an 'enchantress' rather than a witch, presumably because she was fabled to be rather good-looking. Perhaps that made me an enchantress too, although I really wasn't sure about the alluring aspect of the whole thing. I really, really wished that I wasn't quite so broad-shouldered and flat-chested.

I had chosen a sweatshirt that Dad had brought back from his academic Australian conference trip to wear to Gavin Stephens – it said 'G'DAY MATE!' across the bosom in red and blue on the white background. They are the national colours of Australia, you know. But there was no bodily support for the words, just billowing space where my bust should have been. It was too bad, and I was sure that Lizzie and Dad would now prefer to call me 'an Asperger's' rather than a witch.

G'day mate? I wasn't having a good day.

*

I pulled my diary off the desk onto my lap – it feels cosy with the diary closer to me – when Dr Gordner's letter fell out and swished slowly to the floor, light as a feather. I'd forgotten about the letter, but suddenly I was picking it up, and then I was reading it. I felt fierce about it for a moment; the letter was mine in essence but probably something that Dad and Lizzie would want to squirrel away in Dad's filing cabinet. But would not get. Smoothing out the paper, I caught my breath when I saw that some of the creases had tarnished the lettering, making it cracked and pale. My skin prickled along my arms as though I was afraid.

Confirmation of Psychiatric Assessment: I have diagnosed Miss E.R. Edelman with Asperger's Syndrome.

On mental status examination, there is a tendency towards repetitive and clumsy action, slight rocking, etc, and notable reduced eye-to-eye contact...

Where did Dr Gordner expect his patients to look if he stationed a bearded dragon lizard behind his desk? Suddenly, I didn't want the letter. It was a grey letter, I decided, concrete blocks of words that bricked me up into a narrow space. So, I opened the window (wincing – rain had started on a diagonal slant, and it fell on me in a pattern of cold dashes) and threw it away.

Dr Gordner and my parents didn't know *everything*, I decided, flopping onto my bed and looking at my blue ceiling. The walls were white, but I had insisted on blue for the ceiling, like the sky, although the sky in Alwoodley hardly ever matched my ceiling.

"Healing hands, language and rhyme, memory, hearing," I chanted to myself. Those were the witchy powers that I liked the best after much research in my encyclopaedia *and* in the local library, no less. The library had smelt funny and echoed and its books were spattered with matte fingerprints on the clouded plastic covers. I wrote to Aunt Mim about each book; as I edged my way closer to discovering my own witchiness, she had always been there, rotund and encouraging.

"Healing hands, language and rhyme, memory, hearing." I got off the bed and stretched.

"Healing hands, language and rhyme, memory, hearing." I went to the window again.

A figure trotted across the lawn and Lizzie's voice called out. She stood on tiptoe, craning over the hedge, her little hands reaching out to grasp something cream and fluttering that Mauri, next door's gardener, was offering.

"Oh, thanks so much, Mauri."

"There we go, love. Got it, have you?"

"Yes, thank you—" The space was where 'love' should have been inserted, but Lizzie never called anyone 'love'. She couldn't bring herself to. She called people she was very fond of 'darling', but I suppose she thought that Mauri might get ideas if she called him that.

"We need this," she said to him, tucking my diagnosis letter under her jumper to keep the rain off. "It's very important."

"Not to me," I said, my breath misting the window.

What was Asperger's, I wondered? What category of thing? 'Is Psychology the New Religion?' Lizzie's women's magazines asked. They twittered about 'symptoms' and 'the mind'. Had symptoms replaced God, or the Devil? Was I ill? I didn't feel ill. I was just arriving at adulthood, at the prime of life, and yet I was out of my time too. Nobody wanted to say the word 'witch' – I wouldn't have minded. But they have to come up with a new name that turns out to be even more insulting than the old one.

There was something else that had been important though, written on a piece of paper: Aunt Mim's will.

*

Gavin Stephens the solicitor had cleared his throat and brought the sheaf of papers closer to him, whilst we had all tried to take the edge off our sense of anticipation. Personally, I had thought about biscuits due to the smell of coffee in his office, overtaken with a sudden longing for a biscuit, any biscuit, when normally it is Jammie Dodgers or nothing.

"*I, Miriam Ana Rachel Edelman, being of sound mind and body...*"

I could almost feel Lizzie's eyebrows raising without even looking at her. She was of the opinion, expressed most often after an Advocaat on Christmas Eve or towards the end of a dinner party, that Aunt Mim was thoroughly eccentric. Gavin Stephens seemed seized by a sudden fit of impatience.

"*. . . etc, etc. Leave the gift of ten thousand pounds to my brother, Gerald Isaac Edelman* (that's Dad) *and the same to his son, Joseph Gerald Edelman. I also leave five thousand pounds to the British Chihuahua Society, to carry on their sterling work...*"

Was Gavin Stephens Welsh, I wondered, and could I ask him? He did seem to have a slight accent. I hummed quietly to myself, trying to match it to the voices I had heard at the Criccieth Country Hotel that summer when I was ten. Lizzie glanced at me and nudged me sharply, right in the ribs. I glared at her.

Gavin Stephens had paused then, one could only assume for dramatic effect. There was some general looking around amongst

The Family, an air of mild bemusement. I felt a quivering sensation in the pit of my stomach. It would be unbearable if I thought that Aunt Mim had not thought me worthy of a mention.

". . . the remainder of my estate I leave to my niece, Eva Raphaella Edelman, in the knowledge that she will care for Peggy and take my Alpine Sunbeam to the car wash at Chapel Allerton, where the man knows its ways, once a fortnight."

There was a stunned silence. When Dad spoke, his voice sounded as though he was being held by the neck.

"The remainder of the estate?" said Dad. "Mr Stephens, how much . . . how much does my sister's estate . . . ?"

Don't think about it, Evie. Just don't think. But . . . how could Aunt Mim have left me so much money? I tried to imagine the amount in a sort of pile of notes, each one fastened with a paper band like the wads of cash that are stolen in films during bank robberies.

No. Perhaps it was some awful mistake? I didn't want Aunt Mim's money, I thought, and my eyes pricked with tears. I didn't want Asperger's either. Asperger's was *their* word for me; all of the notes grouped with paper bands were Aunt Mim's. If I took her money, then Aunt Mim was definitely gone.

"Ah." Gavin Stephens rubbed his forehead hard with his middle finger. "When all's said and done, counting the sale of the house, the pictures, as well as those rather fortuitous investments, I should imagine . . . that we are looking at around five hundred and fifty to six hundred thousand."

"I see," Dad had said, very, very quietly.

Aunt Mim wasn't here, I realised. Peggy toddled into my room instead, jumped up on my bed and curled into a dormouse shape. If I didn't take all of those horrible papery notes, then they would disintegrate in the bank. They would grow translucent and crumble away, just like Aunt Mim, and it would all be useless. Was this grieving? A bubbling up under the flat surface of my everyday me – the line of routine, patterns of conversation, the feel of familiar belongings – suddenly a little dark blue spike inside that pushed above those things, like a little spring of water? I started to cry. I was finally grieving!

"Excellent!" I said loudly. Now, I must find a handkerchief somewhere before I cry on my diary.

THURSDAY 8TH APRIL 1982

The eighth is by far my favourite day: eight is such a round, warm, orangey number, as well as the pagan symbol for balance between heaven and Earth. Plus, it's my birthday date. So, I suppose that it was some sort of cosmic alignment to hold the funeral on the eighth. After all, Aunt Mim was round, and warm, and carrying those mysterious oranges. Dad said that the eighth was the nearest time Rabbi Guld could fit us in, as he was attending a conference on 'Judaic Healing after Shoahs through Time' for the first half of this week. *I* say that the universe is one enormous pattern.

Aren't funerals awful? I felt very grown-up writing that. That is what you are supposed to say, isn't it? There is an unwritten handbook for funerals I have never read, stating how to look and when to cry and what to say. But the more I forced myself to feel things, the harder it really was. I felt like a wrung-out cloth, desperate for a drop of something to come out of me and twisting harder and harder until my fibres were all distorted and stretched.

Trying to think of what I felt makes me frown with effort – I can feel my forehead wrinkling. The crying yesterday only lasted a little while. Unfortunately, I was then perfectly all right and surprisingly hungry.

I remember Rabbi Guld's face as close as I have ever seen it as he pinned my black ribbon on before we went into the synagogue. I could hear the concentration in his steady breath; the pin grazed me a little and I continued to feel the straight line it made in the fabric of my coat. His expression was peculiarly impersonal, I felt at the time – I wasn't Evie, I was a congregant, he seemed to be saying. It stopped raining for a bit this morning; I could see the bright patches behind the cloud when I looked up, feel the breeze that was cutting and refreshing.

"It's a nice day for it at least," Sarah Leverson had said in the car park, squeezing Lizzie's arm. Lizzie had nodded bravely and was wearing a lovely hat – black straw with a triangular brim and an enormous black velvet ribbon around the crown that crinkled invitingly. Joe had winked at me behind Sarah Leverson's back.

"Miriam is sheltering beneath the wings of God's presence," announced Rabbi Guld, which is what he was supposed to say – it wasn't a flight of fancy on his part. I thought of the painting of Icarus, fallen with his burnt wings that crowded to the edges of the canvas, and I thought of Emily Dickinson's feathered *Hope*, and then I got a little confused, about wings and feathers. Either way, I supposed that God's presence must be pretty large in order to shelter Aunt Mim. "Shall we start the procession?"

We nodded as one. "It's a nice day for it," I had said loudly, causing a moment's silence, as if we were a film that somebody had paused. Then we made our way out of the lobby, the randomly pinned notices on the noticeboard about coffee and flower arranging fluttering at us like birds, towards the burial ground.

"You all right, Sis?" Uncle Harry put his arm around Lizzie. He'd had a cigarette just before the funeral – the smell was greyish-black and clogged my nose. "What are you going to do about . . . ?"

Lizzie murmured something unintelligible.

"Very sad," said Auntie Annette. She opened her patent handbag with a loud, unspiritual click and fished out a conveniently placed hanky. "She was a lovely lady, wasn't she, Harry?"

"Oh, yes. No one else like Mim, was there? She drank me under the table, I can tell you!"

"Harry!"

"Oh, yes. Very sad day," he reiterated. I noticed that there was no shocked pause when Uncle Harry repeated somebody else's words.

". . . bombing about in that *hideous* yellow car," came the voice of Sarah Leverson, pushed forwards from the back of the procession on the wind. "All very odd."

"Wasn't it true that she got involved in all that miners' business?" I could almost hear Sarah Baum's eyes widening.

"You know why, don't you?"

"*No.*"

"Uh hmm. Married, they said. Worked at one of the pits near Barnsley."

"Was he . . . I mean?"

"Course not! Eh, you're daft, Sarah. Whoever heard of a *Jewish* miner?"

I glanced at Dad and Lizzie, who didn't seem to have heard anything. Dad's face was set – the funeral had had to be squeezed in *and* necessitated a day off from industrialisation and Victorian looms. Several terse conversations with Rabbi Guld had been had. If our telephone could talk . . .

"You remember Evie and Joe's Auntie Mim, don't you, kids?" My cousins Dave, Becky and Nicola – younger than me, befuddled by the long drive from Barnett and battered by the unforgiving April clime in Leeds – looked confused and slightly sour. They drew together, unconsciously forming a herd, pulling their shoulders up like roosting owls against the cold.

"*I* don't remember her," said Dave sullenly.

"You *must* remember her," I said. "You asked her why she was so fat that summer we were all together in Bournemouth, and she replied that in a post-feminist world the onus should be on the man questioning the physical appearance of a woman to explain himself, not on the woman to excuse her own body."

"I don't remember that," he said.

"I do."

"Well, you're a weirdo."

We had arrived at the graveside. I checked anxiously to make sure that it wasn't larger than any of the other plots on account of Aunt Mim's size, as I felt that would be rude. Satisfied, I went and stood by Dad. He doesn't have a large, scattered family like Lizzie that produce unsympathetic cousins like Dave – a point in Dad's favour.

But Dad didn't stay near me for long – he quickly moved away and stood at the front, facing us all, to give a speech. "My sister Miriam was born in 1927, in Frankfurt," Dad began, his voice carefully controlled – 'not too fast', I could hear him thinking to himself, 'annunciate clearly'. "You could say that she was born into a different world. And yet, she very much became a modern woman. She espoused many political causes; she gave freely to charity..." (I had told Dad to mention the British Chihuahua Society explicitly here, but he had seemed reluctant) "... she followed me up from London to Leeds, a 'blow in', as I believe the expression goes, but she retained her independence, her love of life. She may not have been an exactly *regular* attendee of this synagogue..."

"Ahem," coughed Sarah Leverson discreetly, towards Sarah Baum. They were staunch synagogue regulars, 'friends' of Lizzie's, although friendship seemed to comprise of being disapproving of each other.

"... but she was a deeply spiritual woman..."

"Who, Aunt Mim?" Auntie Annette murmured to Lizzie.

"Aunt Mim?" I had asked, with the inflection of a child preparing her for the gravity of my statement. It was years ago – I looked up at Aunt Mim, rather than down, my child's eyes taking in the breath of her and finding it wonderful.

"Yup?"

"I don't think that I believe in God."

"No? Here we go." Aunt Mim took a record out of its cover, dark and gleaming. She had drawn the curtains earlier, just a little, to block out the cold yellow of the early autumn sunlight. In other people's houses, I normally counted the time until I could safely go home, but not at Aunt Mim's. The books, possessions, informal collections of tat interspersed with beautiful things sat silently, coated in dust and insulating us from the outside world. Her house seemed to bulge pleasantly, it smelt of incense and oven shelves encrusted with food. Peggy snored on a cushion next to me, emitting a smell of meat and warm hair that assailed me in waves. "You have to listen to this song." She stopped and looked at me. "I don't believe in God either."

"Is it . . . I mean, is it allowed?"

"Only if you don't say as much," said Aunt Mim. She put the record on and a woman's voice – anonymous, a deep, husky, unknowable sound – filled the room. Aunt Mim heaved herself down on the sofa and looked at me as I battled not to look away – her eyes were too large and clear. "Can I give you some advice?"

"Yes."

"You have to learn to cultivate two faces, Evie. Women like us do. Don't be too honest about what you think – your opinion is going to be different to everybody else's."

"But how do I know whether what I think will be different to what everybody else thinks?"

"Stop tryin' to beee someone new," sang the woman, rolling over

the word 'be', her voice seeming to grow. *"You be youuu."* She sounded so desperate, I thought, as though she was trying so hard to reach the man she loved, but Aunt Mim and I were just getting in the way.

Aunt Mim sighed, not unkindly. "Time," she said. "Given time, you will learn when to hide and when to reveal. You'll also learn to hide more often than not."

*

"I don't think that Mim would have wanted us to mourn – as Jews, we celebrate life when we endure a death . . ." We watched Dad, and he watched us back as he talked on, blobs of reflected sun on his glasses obscuring his eyes. He hadn't mentioned their parents, I realised, but then, they no longer existed. Opa Otto had sent his wife, Dad and Aunt Mim here in 1933 with money and some diamond jewellery. It had proved an insightful plan that entirely neglected his own safety, and Opa Otto never made it over to England to join his family. Oma Mitzi removed the last 'n' from 'Edelmann' in order to blend in, settled in St John's Wood and tapestried cushions with fearsome speed and single-mindedness. She had a heart attack in 1971, just like Aunt Mim, only in the more decorous surroundings of the Royal Court Theatre foyer. It was during a matinee; I never discovered which play, but I imagined it to be some kitchen sink drama that she was probably not enjoying all that much. That left Dad and Aunt Mim to their own devices, and this wasn't unusual: the generation above my parents was depleted across the community, precious due to their scarcity, brittle because they were the ones who survived.

Just Lizzie, Joe and me (Val had stayed at home with the baby) were left now. Dad was surveying the Edelman survivors. Sarahs Baum and Leverson, plus Uncle Harry and his gang, had come to stand on the outside and look in – they were looking at us, as Aunt Mim was no longer there to be looked at. We embodied the notion of parting, because we were the ones left behind.

It was then, I recall now, that I felt something. Dad was trying to be reassuring but sounding as though he was delivering a lecture and about to mention the mechanised loom rather than Aunt Mim. Hardly any of us were there to listen – those feelings started spinning in my head, round and round until they blurred. I opened my mouth to try and catch my breath, but the gasping feeling was followed by the most horrible swelling inside of me. It pushed against invisible membranes in my stomach and throat, unstoppable, coloured yellow mottled with green and blue. Slowly it rose through my windpipe, disgorging itself in a silent roar. It pushed against my face, making my eyes bulge and burn along the lower rims, filling my cheeks and pouring out of my mouth silently. There I was amidst other people, seeming human myself but warped and distorted inside by the wave of feeling that was so unbearable that I turned in on myself, my mouth pulling backwards towards my tonsils in an inverted scream. Lizzie sniffed beside me. Why can't I just cry? I thought. Why can't I just cry like her? The shame of it made me hot; my skin prickled.

I was sad. I suppose that I could have just written that. It is accurate, I presume.

*

After the funeral, I sheltered in my room, grateful that Becky and Nicola were distracting everyone with their noise, fluttering like two little birds. I could hear them even with my bedroom door shut, their voices chiming with the deeper tones of Uncle Harry and Joe. Sometimes they all laughed, which seemed callous from the floor above but was perhaps justified in person.

I lit a candle and watched the flame flicker, watched the wax fall smoothy away in a small circle around the wick. After a couple of minutes of hypnotic staring, I prepared Mim's envelope – her letter, the sage for immortality and rosemary for remembrance (dried from the kitchen spice rack, not fresh – where was I supposed to get fresh herbs from?). The letter was one I had begun a few days before her death.

> Dear Aunt Mim,
>
> I hope you are feeling very well indeed, because I am. I thought that I should tell you that I have found a book in the library entitled The Magick Almanac, and I was thinking of copying some things out and making my own almanac. I know that you like my drawings. Apparently, winter to spring brings new energies, as the Dark Goddess ends her reign and Light returns. Do you feel a change in your energies? I think you must, because the last time I saw you, you were in that new green skirt that you found off Kirkgate Market . . .

On impulse, I had added at the bottom: *Now you can be*

immortal, Aunt Mim. You always were, anyway. I will look after Peggy.

I folded the envelope up, put it under my jumper and sneaked downstairs. Peggy trotted swiftly and silently at my heels, almost interlacing herself between my ankles. Getting out into the garden was the hardest part, but I pretended to be going into the kitchen, fiddled stealthily with the kettle and then snuck out through the pantry, scullery and boot room. The Victorians had a mania for dividing a house into purposeful little back rooms, I thought. When I had my own house, I would have a witchcraft room, an Adam Ant room and a Lycra leggings room.

"Dig, Peggy," I commanded, when we arrived at a suitable flower bed.

She stared at me.

"Dig."

Peggy eyed the cold earth and sniffed at it delicately. She looked back up at me, bemused.

"Oh, all right." I dug ineffectually with a stick and buried the letter less deeply than I should have done. It might resurface, I thought, and I would be strangely pleased if it did. It was altogether too final, this pagan burial of Aunt Mim.

FRIDAY 9TH APRIL 1982

Mourning for Aunt Mim, Shabbat, studying my *Magick Almanac*, trying to avoid Lizzie's hints about Sarah Leverson's sister-in-law needing a new assistant in her hairdressing salon ('Chic Sets for Ladies' – the horror): the obligations have been rolling down on top of me 'like rolling cheeses down a hill', as Glenda Jackson said when she played Elizabeth I. I loved watching that on the telly. Why do I feel as though the cheeses are rolling on top of me and squashing me flat?

Anyway, we are in Shiva now – the traditional mourning period for Jewish people. Why do I always assume that my reader is Gentile? Or indeed that I have a reader? Perhaps it is because I am naturally didactic – great word, a little like an animal that is almost extinct.

Shiva means seven, for the seven days that it lasts. On the one hand, Shiva is quite relaxing: lots of black and reflection and everything. On the other, we're supposed to talk of Aunt Mim and, more broadly, of family – never relaxing.

Here are my seven stories for seven days – my diary is turning out to be useful.

DAY ONE

Which actually should have been yesterday because Shiva starts on the day of burial, but I am starting today because the funeral was enough. Sorry. Long title. So, today. Right.

I had the most vivid dream – I mean, prophesy. I must start calling them that, I really must. It was as if I woke up and half of me was still in that other place. It was raining, but there was so much bright green around me – huge flat leaves piled on top of one another, dripping rain that made a song. Alex Ishkowitz was there beside me, but we weren't looking at one another.

"The tyre's OK, I think," I had said, my voice clear as a bell, and we had both known that I had meant something completely different. Then I woke up.

Sounds silly, I know, but in my dream, there was a confusion inside me – more than the usual confusion – as though something had happened. Not something actual, not a thing, but more of a shift that happens between two people that both know it.

I had stayed in bed for a while, allowing myself to think of Alex, staring at the Artex swirls on my ceiling. It was a luxury that I didn't normally allow, but I told myself that Alex was a kind of ghost. He still existed, but no longer existed for me – he belonged to somebody else now.

Then I wandered into Joe's room and watched the minutiae of Dad leaving for work, manoeuvring the Ford Escort in a manner that can only be described as punctilious into position to swing out of the drive. He went to work during Shiva, and didn't wear a black tie. I missed him as he left, then wandered back into my room and turned my attention to Peggy, Adam Ant, my books, the crystals – all those little pieces of living that I did.

I thought about Alex all that day, and some of the night.

DAY TWO – SATURDAY 10TH

Shabbat. The holy day rolled around again, and Lizzie's cry of "You can't wear a *tracksuit* to synagogue!" rang through the house. I didn't want to go to synagogue, and Dad didn't want to go to synagogue, but Lizzie said that we had to show our faces because it was so soon after Aunt Mim's funeral, and there didn't seem to be any arguing with that.

"We aren't Jewish enough to go *every week*!" Dad said, exasperated.

It must *seem* as though I am terribly Jewish, what with all these festivals and synagogue and observances and stuff. The reality is that we don't normally go to synagogue regularly but, like people of every religion, we think about God more when we want something from Him.

I hung back a little as Dad and Lizzie made their way across the car park, wondering why my body never felt like my own in the Asher Israel Synagogue, from the moment we crunched into the car park to the monosyllabic journey home. I could feel the very edges of myself in a sort of nervy tingle, like someone had drawn a very soft outline of me that itched. But the rest of me, the actual substance, everything inside, was numb. It was as though the substance of me stopped existing.

I should also add that I was wearing a dress. A navy-blue dress with white spots, a collar and a stiff silk bow at the neck. That bow looked so beautiful *before* I put it on, then it bunched out in front of me like a goitre once I was inside, flapping around and distracting me. This was my 'occasion dress', the thing I was corralled into in order to convince people that I was generically female. I had chosen it specifically because the way it hung, tunic-like, in knife pleats from my underarms made it seem low-maintenance. How foolish I was, how sartorially innocent: in reality, each concertinaed strip of fabric took on a life of its own, swinging this way and that, crashing and bunching with its neighbours or stretching in folds until I felt that I had a hundred clamouring children hanging off me.

Allowing a little time for the breeze to desist in its harassment of my pleated dress, I listened to my parents talking to the Cohens outside the open doors of the synagogue entrance, gaping to swallow its flock.

"And how are you, Gerald?"

"Well," Dad frowned, his eyes downward cast and unseeing. "I am having dreadful trouble with the faculty – any little change in the lecture programme worries them, you see, but I really feel that more time should be devoted to Cotton Production and the Young Workforce as a catalyst . . ."

"I think that Marjorie meant about Miriam, Gerry."

"What? Oh, yes." Dad looked. "Yes," he repeated pensively.

"He's got a lot on at the moment," said Lizzie apologetically.

"Of course he has, and he does such important work at the university, doesn't he, Eric?"

"Oh yes," said Mr Cohen. "Must be distracting, thinking about cotton and . . . things. Having to read all those books."

"And write them, too . . ."

"Admiring the view, are you, love?" That was Mr Abrams, clapping me on the back. The Abrams were simultaneously 'a bit common', because they lived in a council flat outside Alwoodley, and one of the oldest families in the congregation. They were eyed by our fellow well-heeled congregants as something redolent of their less salubrious pasts.

"So many of us," he said, sticking his chest and belly out towards the little clots of families making their way inside. He arched proudly, like a fish trying to reach the air. "Lovely sight, isn't it?"

The constant but irregular stream of people converging into one place seemed horrific to me. I tensed my shoulders and neck to control the fear.

"Yes," I said.

"Well, Shabbat shalom, love. Good news about all that brass, in't it?"

"Shabbat shalom, Mr Abrams." I waited a few moments and then began a slow scuttle forwards; the synagogue having the disconcerting habit of getting larger as I did so.

"Evie? Hello love, don't be shy."

"Hello, Mrs Cohen."

"I was just talking to your mam and dad."

"Yes, I saw."

"You should've come over, standing by yourself like that – you're a big girl now."

I nodded.

"Well." Mrs Cohen smiled at me and went inside. I followed miserably behind. The babble of voices, suddenly unable to float on the fresh air, flattened out and rebounded against themselves. They turned a dark, muddy yellow colour as they bumped against the varnished wooden walls of the synagogue and wrapped their way around the bannisters of Rabbi Guld's dais, which always looked like a giant playpen to me. Kehillah – community. This was what community sounded like, a discordant struggle of sounds under the yellow of the artificial lights. A horizontal stripe of crowd, faces and bodies milling, and another horizontal stripe of high ceiling filled with their noise.

Something told me that I was being looked at more than usual. I supposed that I would have to take up the mantel of Aunt Mim, I thought. After all, there was only one unusual woman left in the entire congregation now: Sarah Baum's Aunt Jemima, who had 'become artistic' in her older years. A potter's wheel had been duly installed in her garden shed and she wore a beret, which old Mrs Isaacs insisted upon calling 'a berry'.

"There's our little heiress," said Sarah Leverson, gliding towards me, her green glass earrings glinting dangerously. I backed away and bumped into the end of one of the wooden benches. "What a stroke of luck, Evie."

"Well, not really luck," I said, "as I was fonder of Aunt Mim than anybody else and our souls communed together, and I liked her dog. It's hardly surprising that she left me some money when you look at it that way."

Sarah Leverson *and* her bust stiffened. "In my day, a young girl would be grateful for such an inheritance," she said.

"I suppose that I am grateful. It just doesn't seem very real at the moment," I offered.

"Well." Sarah Leverson's earrings were turned fixedly away. "You'll have to get her married, Lizzie," she said. "They'll be queueing up for her *now*."

There was a snort from two rows back. I turned to see Susie

Leverson, Susie Ishkowitz, Sue Davis and Susie Altschul watching me, eyebrows raised, their lipstick curled into variants of a smirk. My contemporaries, daughters of the Sarahs . . . I had as much in common with them as I did Sigi the lizard.

"They'd still have to live with her," said Susie Altschul, towards their ringleader. Susie Leverson bestowed a smile upon her follower. She had long hair that she flicked contemptuously over her shoulders and sometimes wore a jumpsuit to synagogue. You were supposed to wear skirts, but nobody said anything because Susie Leverson was sharp, gave the best parties and had a very good-looking older brother who was, as yet, unmarried.

"What an *interesting* choice, Evie," said Sue Davis. "Tennis shoes and a dress."

"I chose the tennis shoes for comfort," I said. "I have wide feet, unusually so."

"You don't say."

"Yes. I prefer comfort over style, in general."

"We would never have guessed." The Susans laughed and I nodded, glad to have made them laugh properly, with their teeth – they spend a lot of time looking as attractive as possible in case other people are looking at them, but they don't seem to laugh a lot. Susie Ishkowitz didn't laugh, she just smiled vaguely and turned her head so that her bob tilted and caught the light. I supposed that being married to Alex Ishkowitz was a serious business, and stared in wonderment at her two-piece suit in red – the belt made such a tiny circle at the waist that she seemed to stop existing in her mid-section.

"Can you not get the will overturned, Lizzie?" Another Sarah – Mrs Halpern, as I didn't know her well – materialised behind Sarah Leverson.

"Now that she has this illness, this *thing*, what is it? Oh, don't look like that, Lizzie, we're all friends here. Val told Sue who told my Susie. Aspe. . .as. . . ?"

"Asperger's," said Dad clearly. "A syndrome, actually. Not an illness."

In order to be polite and allow for more freedom whilst they were discussing me, I turned away. Looking round, my gaze rested upon Alex, completely by accident. He sat with his friend David Kessel, and they were talking intently. Kessel must have been Kessler, I decided, and they changed it to blend in. But Ishkowitz, that was a shtetl name if ever there was one, and the family had kept it. I said 'Ishkowitz' a few times in my head, liking its swish.

What is in a name? Perhaps if I hadn't been christened Eva Raphaella then I could have been as confident as the Susans. Susan, from Shoshana in Hebrew, meaning lily of the valley. Very fashionable, as well as being very Jewish. If you were my age, you were called Susan, just as you were called Sarah if you were Lizzie's age. Even Valerie or Karen would have done me. But there I was: Eva. A garrulous, cascading name like a frilled eiderdown. Very Jewish, but not very fashionable.

"Sounds like 'asparagus'," said Mrs Halpern. "They come up with such odd things nowadays, don't they?"

"Go and say hello to your friends, Evie," said Lizzie. "Look, there's Val over there."

Val was talking with Sue Davis. They were joined by Susan Baum and Karen Halpern, both with their babies. I stared at Susie Leverson, trying to distil her negative energy and extract it (witches are supposed to be able to do that). Only, she caught me staring and raised her eyebrows before turning to her friends and rolling her eyes. I turned back to Dad and Lizzie.

"Do you have to take tablets, Evie? For the aspara . . . Asperger's?"

"Oh, leave the poor girl alone," said Mrs Ishkowitz from the row behind, serene and lovely in a pearl necklace. "Doctors aren't always right, anyway. They can't see inside people's heads as much as they think."

"Probably just a fad," agreed Mrs Altschul, the synagogue busybody. "Do you think Israel stand a chance?"

"What?"

"Of winning? Eurovision?"

"I just don't know who to support, England or Israel."

"Whoever wins, of course."

"I doubt either of them will win."

"Sarah, that's bordering on blasphemy."

"Ha ha!" Sarah Leverson laughed and her earrings trembled.

"I need to go outside for a moment," I said, walking stiffly away. I tried to hold my head exactly on top of my spine and pull my shoulders back. I had a fear of being thought of as masculine and loping, you see – largely because I was.

In the lobby, a hand plucked delicately at my sleeve. I turned and looked down at Sarah Baum. "Congratulations on your inheritance, Evie," she said. "How nice."

"Sarah," Sarah Leverson called down the aisle, "come and sit with us, get a move on!" Sarah Baum smiled at me, and scurried in.

DAY THREE – SUNDAY 11TH

We had visitors: Mrs Golder came round with a casserole and her deepest sympathies. Mrs Golder's maiden name was O'Casey – she 'married into' Jewishness because she fell so crazily in love with Mr Golder, who is very short with a large forehead. Mrs Golder looked a little like a horse, with big, crowded teeth and a tuft of a ponytail, but despite her endearing appearance, she often got things wrong.

After Mrs Golder had left, we stood in a semi-circle examining the casserole intensely. Lizzie was adamant (Adam Ant – 'adamant' should be my favourite word, but instead my favourite word is 'initially') that it smelt as though bacon had been added *initially* and then taken out. Dad wasn't sure. I could smell the bacon as though it was sizzling in a pan in front of me – Mrs Golder had definitely put a bit in, realised her mistake and then taken it out. But I didn't say anything because I was hungry.

DAY FOUR – MONDAY 12TH

I swung into the dining room, feeling as though the birds were singing and the sky was blue, even though they empirically weren't and it objectively wasn't. Ready for my two-thirds of a banana on toast, I generously overlooked the lack of heating and the swirled carpet because I was not in the mood for a fight. Unfortunately, Lizzie *was* in the mood for a fight.

"Evie . . . ?"

"Yes?" I hadn't even sat down.

"Dad and I have been talking."

I raised my eyebrows at Dad, who determinedly studied his *Financial Times*. He seemed to spend even longer than usual over the newspaper at the moment, his interest in stocks and shares rekindled after Aunt Mim's surprising gift to me.

"Gerry?"

"Hmmm?"

"*Help* me, please!" Lizzie hissed.

"Ah." Dad cleared his throat and appeared to be about to give a seminar. "Your mother and I . . ."

"I get it, Dad," I said. "You and Lizzie, Lizzie and you, some kind of double-act thing. What is the long and the short of it?"

"We think that you should let us take care of Mim's money for you, Evie."

"No." I wanted to have my two-thirds of a banana, not talk about money.

"We can invest it for you . . ."

"No." The banana was there, in the fruit bowl. I couldn't imagine all that money.

"You can buy a little car," offered Lizzie, as though dangling a particularly juicy carrot in front of a donkey.

"I have to have Aunt Mim's Alpine Sunbeam! I *have* to."

"Don't shout," said Lizzie.

"It's a completely impractical car," said Dad. "That nauseating primrose yellow."

"A *little* car . . ."

"I don't want a little car," I said. "No."

Dad and Lizzie blurred, turning into a series of brown and red blocks that were building in front of my eyes, blocking what was really there. I felt as though someone was churning my throat with a rusty iron pole.

"You wouldn't know what to do with all that money, Evie. It's dangerous! I mean, Sarah Leverson's other sister-in-law is going to set up a secretarial agency, and they need girls . . . it would be a good little job, until, you know . . ."

"Perhaps one day, when you are older . . ."

"I'm old now!" I suddenly felt old, or rather weary, exhausted at trying to say something that couldn't be put into words. I hadn't wanted Aunt Mim's money, but it was the remainder of her, and I suddenly realised that I wanted anything that she had left behind.

"When the time comes, you can get a little flat . . ."

"Why does everything have to be *little*?" I yelled. "Why can't it just be *normal* size? Why can't I have a flat, or a car?" My words petered out into the chasm that separated me from Lizzie and Dad, floating for a second and then falling, sucked downwards never to be seen again.

"Why don't we go and see Gavin Stephens?" said Dad. "I could book an appointment."

"I'm not going to go!"

"Evie, will you please stop shouting? Dad will book an appointment. Why don't you have your toast?"

"I don't want my toast; it isn't mine because I haven't taken it out of the toast rack yet!" I screamed, and flummocked (sorry to make up words, but at least it is onomatopoeic) out of the room, my legs working like pistons but the carpet always further away than I imagined. I may have knocked something off somewhere – I heard a crash as I stumbled through the kitchen, pantry and boot room, as though working my way through a maze, and slammed the back door. Then Peggy scratched and whined from inside, so I opened it with elaborate care and let her out. Elaborate care – that was what Peggy deserved, I thought. She was grieving. We both were.

We took up residence on the garden bench; it was too cold just to be wearing purple leggings, a knitted cricket jumper of Joe's and a pair of Dad's old slipper socks. The bench was sideways to the house, so I felt very self-conscious on one side of my face, trying to cultivate an expression of wounded dignity. Warm little bubbles frothed and exploded in my throat now, and I felt shivery in my fingers and toes – emotional upheaval does this to me.

I thought about The Evolution of Life, or at least the expected evolution for girls like me. A little job in a noisy clacking office, followed by marriage to a man who wasn't Alex Ishkowitz and yet would miraculously find me attractive *and* be Jewish. No magick. That was the trouble, I thought. The life I wanted was full of nature and flowers and spells, and the life Dad and Lizzie were trying to create for me felt like being bundled into a concrete tunnel. Life seemed unmagickal.

After a little time, the back door opened and disgorged Dad. I waited for him, listening to his steps on the lawn, which was just starting to recover from the assault of winter. He sat beside me, his spare frame seeming to fold itself like a picnic table. Silence except for the breeze, the rustle of the hedges.

"Are you coming in? I believe . . . I believe that there is a particularly nice banana in the fruit bowl this morning."

"You're trying to entice me with a banana."

"Indeed."

"What was in the *FT*?"

"Oh, this and that."

I had a sudden thought. "Are we going to be economically affected by the Falklands? I mean, if we don't own them any more and the Argentinians do? Won't it be bad for British people?" I thought of the miners – perhaps they would lose out. If so, I would have to find Aunt Mim's special married miner and warn him.

Dad put his hand across his chin and rubbed his beard, making my shoulders wiggle at the crisp little sound of disturbed stubble. "I should think, given the amount of military deployment, they will actually make money for armament. And it could be a boon for British fishing. So, all in all," said Dad with a deep sigh, "we could come out of it rather well."

"What does war cost, Dad?"

"Millions. Billions perhaps, nowadays."

"Goodness. Much more than Aunt Mim left me."

"Much more. And there are other costs, Evie. Hidden costs. It never does to fight, really, unless the gains really do outweigh the costs. It just isn't worth it."

"Oh."

"Come back inside?"

"All right."

With Dad, it never really felt familial. We had what I thought of as flashes – moments, conversations during walks, a look shared at a party – where he was just a person, I was just a person, and we happened to get on. I enjoyed those times, that fitting together of our personalities without any other bind.

I followed him back into the tense air of the dining room, where Lizzie seemed far more focused on pouring coffee than on either of us. She began a conversation with Dad about the petrol prices at the local garage, and they moved on from there to whether they really needed a dozen eggs a week or whether a half dozen would do.

DAY FIVE – TUESDAY 13TH

Two days to wait until the mirrors downstairs are due to be uncovered. Their black hangings are part of Shiva, a symbol of the fact that death has made us forget our vanity (although I have been thinking about that red two-piece that Susan Ishkowitz wore to synagogue, wondering if it would make me look a bit of a beacon and then not sure quite what I mean by that).

I must have come downstairs unusually quietly this morning because I saw Lizzie carefully pinching the black cover of the hall mirror between her finger and thumb, drawing it back and flicking nervously at her fringe.

"Caught you!"

"What?" She let the cover go and it swung back.

"You were looking at yourself."

"Was I?"

"Don't try that, I *saw* you!"

"Well, you said that it was a silly idea to cover them in the first place."

I shrugged. "They're your rules, not mine," I said.

"I won't tell if you won't." She smiled at me. It was as if the dining room argument yesterday hadn't happened at all, or as if it had happened and she had somehow breezed onwards, as though it didn't matter.

"All right," I said awkwardly.

"Our dirty secret," said Lizzie, laughing. "What a life we lead!"

DAY SIX – WEDNESDAY 14TH

Why do the days have to get longer?

I had designated that atmospheric point in a winter mid-afternoon when it starts getting dark as the time for my magicking. But this afternoon was still light, the sky still clear. I felt short-changed by spring as I carved Susie's name into a candle. I was thinking about Susie Leverson and her unkind remarks about my tennis shoes, plus I had rearranged my crystal collection. The more I thought about it, the more I decided that I could hex Susie

Leverson's negative energy. It would be a guilty pleasure, as Lizzie said when she bought a new lipstick. The guilt threatened to overtake the pleasure, but I reminded myself sternly that Mother Shipton would not have felt guilty, and she had predicted the horseless carriage for heaven's sake!

Purpose restored, I rolled up my photo of Susie Leverson (torn from a synagogue newsletter and a bit grainy. She had her arm around Susie Altshcul and Susan Baum, but I generously tore them away. I also carved 'Susie L' on the candle, so as to be very clear).

"Powers that be, remove Susie Leverson's negative energy," I said my spell three times as the candle fluttered, trying to think about Susie instead of the fact that the rhyme didn't scan. Magick was always a work in progress, I thought, before making my way listlessly downstairs and trying to draw an owl.

"What are you drawing, darling?" Lizzie peered over my shoulder.

"An owl."

"Oh, yes. It *looks* like an owl."

Dad arrived home, bringing a draft of fresh, cold air and the dry smell of his tweed jacket. "Evie, come and help me sort through some papers," he said.

"I was just doing this."

"You look bored to me. Clive has the flu, so I need someone to give me a hand. What's the point of a PhD student if he gets flu? Come on, you can draw parrots another time."

DAY SEVEN – THURSDAY 15TH

I'd dragged Peggy on her walk to Alwoodley Golf Course. She was a distinctly unathletic dog, but it would have been hypocritical for me to hold that against her, as I was an unathletic human. We had bumped into old and young Mrs Isaacs, also looking distinctly unathletic.

"I hear that you have The Asperger's, Evie."

"Yes, Mrs Isaacs."

"Can you take tablets for it?"

"I . . . I don't think so."

"What a shame."

"Yes."

"Your poor mam and dad."

I looked over at Ruthie Isaacs, normally as humourless as they come, trying not to laugh. She didn't look at me, though. She looked away, as if both me *and* Old Mrs Isaacs were the joke.

Mrs Ishkowitz was passing on the other side of the street and waved cheerily at us. I plastered a smile on my face and hoped that she would come over, but she strode on. Everybody stood a little straighter when Mrs Ishkowitz was around, behaved a little more as if they were posh. Mrs Ishkowitz had an aura, I thought, or a 'presence', as Sarah Leverson said disapprovingly. She had beautifully square cheekbones and green eyes, and always did everything a little more elegantly than other people. I wondered whether she would have wanted me for Alex now, wished I hadn't given up . . . but there was no point in thinking about that. The very action of calling her only son Alexander made her even more special – it was my favourite name. Alex had been named after his Russian grandfather.

"It should be Aleksandr then," I had said the first time I met him, "with a 'k' and an 'r'. Is that how you spell it?"

"Don't be daft," he'd said, and laughed at me, his green eyes narrowing into beautiful long lines. There was a general feeling that Alexander was not quite the right name, not quite Judaic, I suppose. But I loved the way that its Hellenic sereness sailed on for more syllables that it should.

"That Alexander of hers is doing ever so well," said Old Mrs Isaacs. "Promoted."

"He's really found his feet at that estate agents," agreed her daughter-in-law. "Practically running the place, I hear."

They both looked at me expectantly. "I suppose that I shouldn't have left him then," I offered, and watched their faces as their eyes and mouths gaped. Wrong thing to say – I should have known. It had seemed logical in my head and then been wrong in real life. Luckily, Peggy spotted the hump of a leftover sandwich further down the path and dragged me towards it. She really is most useful, if a little feral and disgusting. The sandwich was tuna, and I allowed her one miniscule nibble as a reward before pulling her away.

Almost pleased to see Hawthorns again, I got inside and eagerly divested myself of coat, waistcoat, scarf, gloves, hat and earmuffs, realising that I was a tad overheated. I looked at the picture of Thornlaw Saw Mill over the hall table. It sounded terrible, half rhyming as it did – I think that I would never have built a saw mill near a place that ended in 'law', just because of the vocals. But someone had, and later on someone had painted it too. I supposed that I liked the colours of the place: bulbous little patches of land and feathery trees that were all olive greens and gold. The little saw mill itself, playing second fiddle to a waterfall that spurted over the rock in a pleasingly rounded way, seemed to be constructed of pale-yellow stone. It reminded me of the drawings in my *Faerytales* book. There was a lot of green and gold there too, the colours of nature, of rebirth to pagans.

"Rebirth," I said to myself meditatively. "Starting again." There was a smooth rock perfectly centred in the waterfall that parted the water like long hair before it flowed its way back into a homogenous mass again. The mill wheel, only half visible and then lost to an unexplained shadowy patch, was not quite a perfect circle.

"I always said that you wouldn't find yourself unless you got out of here," said Aunt Mim. She was wearing her green skirt. It didn't suit her at all, being a horrible, arsenic type of green that was neither light nor dark and reminded one of hospital corridors. The stretched tube of the skirt aside, she looked very well, I thought.

"Did you say that? I don't remember it."

"Well, perhaps not exactly. But I bloody well meant it often enough."

I nodded.

"We don't blossom if we're squashed, Evie."

"I do remember you saying something like it. I hope you said it in spring – it's springlike in imagery."

"In imagery, yes; the vision is eternal."

I laughed.

"Evie, who are you talking to?" Lizzie materialised on the landing.

"Oh . . ." I looked at myself in the oval mirror next to Thornlaw Saw Mill. The black covering had fallen down, and by tacit agreement, none of us had bothered to replace it. "I was just . . ."

I was just talking to Aunt Mim, I realised. Not my memory of Aunt Mim, not something that had happened years ago and suddenly come back to life in my head. Aunt Mim was *here*. She was back.

I laughed again. No wonder I hadn't been able to manage protracted grief – Aunt Mim had never really left, and I must have known on some level that I would be seeing her soon. Yes, that must be it. More cosmic, universal stuff. I really was getting good at witching.

"I thought I heard you laughing, Evie? We're supposed to be in mourning . . ."

Lizzie went back upstairs before I could reply, seemingly unaware of the fact that Aunt Mim was standing directly behind me. I had the beginnings of an idea and looked over at Aunt Mim, who winked. I wanted to ask why she was visiting when I had buried her with the sage and rosemary, and why she hadn't changed her skirt, but I didn't want to be too forward. After all, she'd had a trying fortnight.

FRIDAY 23RD APRIL 1982

"Waaaah! Gaaaah!"

This is the exact noise that little Tom, my baby nephew, makes when he yells. The epithet, 'little', clearly does not apply to his lungs. Well, that sound has been recorded in my diary now, For Posterity. If I were Tom, I'd be embarrassed.

Joe arrived today for a visit. I challenged him to check his bedroom to make sure I hadn't moved anything (I had moved some things, but Joe isn't observant). He seemed peculiarly disinterested. He brought Val with him, and the baby, which I thought was a pity but seemed to please Lizzie, who called the baby Thomas Joseph, because the Joseph part was in honour of her father as well as Joe. Everyone else called the baby Tom. Coming into my room without knocking, Joe had taken a light, well-aimed leap onto my bed and watched me write my diary. I pretended to be very absorbed, so that he wouldn't ask me to go down and see Val.

"Do you feel different?"

"No. Why?"

"Well, now you have this Aspie-whatsit thing?"

"I had it before," I said. "It didn't come as a surprise, exactly. One doesn't go and see a psychiatrist if one thinks there is nothing wrong."

"Doesn't one?"

"No, one doesn't."

"Thank one for enlightening one."

"Oh shut up, Joe!"

"You shut up," he said pleasantly, and threw a pillow at my head. I ducked and it landed on the floor like a lilac cotton mountain. Peggy approached it gingerly and sniffed. I was not surprised at her cautious approach: the pillow was significantly larger than her.

"Get off my bed!" I screamed, watching the duvet deflate and crack into hundreds of little geometric shapes around him.

"Shan't," he said. I stared pointedly at his trainers until he moved his feet off the covers and onto the footboard. He did me that courtesy, at least. "What's going on then?"

"Nothing." I glanced at my Adam Ants. "Did you buy 'Cat People'?"

"Hmmm? No."

"What d'you mean, no?" I wheeled around to face him. "It's *David Bowie*!"

"I have other things to think about, Evie."

"Like what?"

"Like a baby? I've got a family of my own now, and about twenty people after my job if I don't put in the overtime that Mr Green wants."

"Mr Green wouldn't sack you," I said, "Lizzie helps Mrs Green with her coffee mornings."

"Yes, well there are various other helpers and attendees at Mrs Green's coffee mornings with sons of employable age," said Joe darkly.

"You don't even *care* about David Bowie any more," I said. "What was the last single of his you bought?"

"'Under Pressure', ironically enough."

"That was last November!"

"It wasn't as long ago as that."

"It was." My insides turned. We'd bought 'Ashes to Ashes' and 'Fashion' together on trips to the record shop, travelling into the city centre on the bus as solemnly as pilgrims. Now I had to be dropped off by Lizzie, who didn't like me taking the bus on my own. When Adam and the Ants disbanded last month, I had rung Joe and he hadn't even cared. He'd been holding Tom, whose piercing wails resounded down the phone. Joe had no consideration for others, I thought. Gradually, I became aware of an intake of breath from Joe, the beginning of an as yet unasked question. He was pausing, which meant that he was unsure – quite a novelty.

"Lizzie sent you up here to talk to me, didn't she?"

"Why can't you just call her 'Mum', like normal people do?"

"I'm not normal," I said, with just a hint of triumph. "I would have thought that was obvious after the whole Dr Gordner thing."

Joe started laughing.

"What *now*?" I wheeled around to look at him.

"I was just thinking," he wheezed, "what if your doctor-psychiatrist bloke had been in Harrogate and you'd had to drive over there? You, Mum and Dad might have been mistaken for Eurovision backing dancers – competition's tomorrow!"

"It's not that funny . . ."

"It is, though. Dad could whip you and Mum's skirts off like Bucks Fizz."

"Eugh." I turned to look at him. "*Making your mind UP!*" we both sang, upward inflection and crescendo both heartily present. One person has so many angles if you know them really well, I thought. Or hooks, rather than angles, catching you unexpectedly and pulling you back in towards them. Joe was cocky and selfish. He didn't even like David Bowie any more. He made me laugh and I loved him.

"Better get back downstairs." Joe got off the bed. "Do you know how rich you are, now?"

"Not really," I said truthfully. "I mean, what did Aunt Mim want me to *do*?"

"Well, if you have any cash going spare and want to send it my way . . ."

"I will," I said absentmindedly. I was back to trying to count the wads of notes in paper bands in my head again. "Oh, and you're getting a belly, just a little one, but a jiggly one," I noted.

"Thanks, beanpole. Well, I told Mum that I would discuss your Asparagus thingy, and I have, so . . ."

Val and Tom were waiting for him downstairs, that was what Joe meant. Val was the same age as me, but she went to the hairdressers for a set. She had taken me and her nasty friend Susan – who tittered frequently for no reason – all the way to 'Feminine She' in Ripon for our bridesmaids' dresses.

"Tiffany, in the pêche colourway. *All* the rage, this design," the assistant had said, taking a firm hold of the material around my hips and fluffing it to make the skirt even more enormous. "Lovely for an early spring wedding. Fresh. Youthful."

"Do you think that Lady Di's bridesmaids'll be in something like this?" Val's eyes had taken on a peculiar sheen.

"Bound to be, I would think."

"And you recommend the peach? I mean, *pêche*?"

"Oh, yes. Suits all body types, too." The assistant had given a brief, darting glance at my bony ankles, visible in a non-erogenous way at the premature end of the skirt.

Susan had twirled and tittered. "I feel like a fairy princess," she'd said breathily.

I'd looked at the skirt that hung as stiffly as a severed limb, at the puff sleeves that made my already broad shoulders stretch to inhuman widths.

"How do you feel, Evie?"

"I feel like a very odd-shaped table covered by a tablecloth that was a gift that no one actually likes," I'd said. "I look bloody awful."

There had been a brief pause.

"I think we'll go with these, please," Val had said brightly.

"Excellent choice, Madam."

*

I watched Joe pull the waistband of his jeans up and head for my bedroom door. He looked tired; I could see that from the back of him. Val and Tom must be rather a lot, I realised. I wouldn't want to live with either of them. "Joe?"

"Hmmm?"

"How do you . . . feel?"

"Like a bag of hammers," he said succinctly, and went downstairs.

SUNDAY 25TH APRIL 1982

Sunday is rather a perplexing day if you are Jewish and British. It's the Day of Rest, except that we have already had our Day of Rest on Saturday. Roast Dinner, but we had ours yesterday. Church Bells, which sound nice but foreign, even if I have lived here all my life. So, Sunday becomes a sort of uneasy, half-resting day. Or am I supposed to rest in a holy sort of way on Saturday, and a secular way on Sunday? I suppose that this is the idea of a weekend, except that Gentiles swap the holiness of the days around.

I loped upstairs after Sunday lunch (top stairs two at a time, left foot first into the bedroom – beautifully in sequence today), having decided to pass a pleasant half hour reading this diary thus far. I can't report any witchy doings, because frankly I haven't felt in the mood. I had expected to be titillated, absorbed, flattered by my on-page presence. Instead, Dr Gordner's voice floated through my head, and I remembered a bit of conversation that I'd left out:

"Would you describe yourself as an emotional sort of person, Evie?"

"What do you mean?"

"Well, do you often feel very distinctly happy, or very sad, or angry?"

"I don't know really."

"Ah."

"Is that wrong?"

"It is certainly abnormal. You see, most people know what they are feeling."

"You mean, most people organise their emotions?"

"Exactly so, yes."

"Like in a filing cabinet? But I organise everything else. I thought you mentioned that people with Asperger's love putting things in lists and boxes and categories. It seems like everyone has emotional Asperger's but me then. I think that you should write to the man who invented it and ask him to have a think about that."

"Haaaaaaah."

That last bit was Dr Gordner sighing, a soft noise that built in intensity. The long and the short of it (two pieces of string; I always see two pieces of string when I hear that expression, or indeed use it) was that Dr Gordner had advised me to keep a diary, recording my feelings about events. I told him that I really didn't see the point in separating my emotions from each other like the tangled sleeves of woollen jumpers out of the wash, because *then* what did you do with them?

I don't like feelings very much. Almost three weeks of diarying (goodness, a new verb) and I still don't. But I like writing, probably because I am writing about myself. My hand flies over the pages, the spine doesn't creak half as much when I turn a page, and there is nobody to tell me that my handwriting resembles 'the remains of a squashed fly', as one teacher did, who I will magnanimously not name.

There was another, more youthful, diary, of course. I burnt it in a fit of self-awareness, sneaking it on to one of next-door's autumnal bonfires. We only have electric heaters in the house and, frustratingly, you can't burn papers on a pile of plastic logs. It was a sad, angry, adolescent affair. Some of the girls at school had started picking on me, you see. Laughing at me, hiding things of mine. Stealing, really. I told Lizzie that we should call the police, and that a custodial sentence would probably be forthcoming. She had countered with the fact that 'they were only fourteen'. *I* was fourteen too, I had wanted to point out, and in considerable distress.

Still, all Water Under The Bridge now, rather like the water flowing past Thornlaw Saw Mill. I had grown up, I supposed that I was all right now, and that the girls had just been ignorant. People changed, apparently. I found that hard to believe – but I had to believe it, especially as one of the girls was so close to home.

Further back, before being picked on, there was my poetry book. Poetry about the miners, I believe. They had captured my imagination in '72. I think that I equated them with some enchanted species; all that toiling nobly underground. I'd been walking home from school once and seen a truck full of them, surprisingly solid for mythical beings, their pickets stuck awkwardly out of the back. 'STOP! NUM protest!', the pickets had said, so I stopped on the kerb and waited. One of the miners waved to me, and the others followed suit – men with tough skin and small eyes, totally unlike Dad, yet smiling at me in a sort of paternal way. I felt pathetically grateful that they hadn't been able to speak to me, thus forcing me to unveil my posh accent like an uninvited guest at a party. I had waved until they were out of sight and returned home, where Lizzie informed me that it would have to be cheese salad again and to take the hot water bottles upstairs now before the blackout started. In my own eyes, I became a kind of mascot to the miners.

But instead of being titillated by my current outpourings, I found myself thinking how young I still sound. It was all rather adolescent for a twenty-one-year-old. My mature, poised self-image toppled like a statue into the dust; I even blushed a bit. I have some worries on technique now, as I am anxious to avoid a repeat of the old diary in terms of bad poetry and allegiance to political causes because I liked the faces of the protesters. How honest should one be in a diary? Have I already said too much, disclosing my matrimonial plans with Adam Ant? People tend to laugh at me when I say things that I really mean.

If I was smart, I would see this as an opportunity to tell you whatever I wanted about myself. I would invent . . . a *persona* (a word that delicately wafts like perfume and should only really be used at odd, adult times of day, like dusk). I could tell you that I was like Lorna Doone after all, a beautiful orphan whose parents died tragically and left her free, or I could tell you that I wasn't really Jewish at all, or that I lived in Italy in the Villa Rotunda – a beautiful yet stark example of Palladian architecture that I saw in a magazine. I still have a picture of it somewhere, with a floor plan so that you can see how symmetrical it all is.

Anyone can say anything, can't they? But then I get a sneaking feeling that moves horizontally along the bottom of my stomach, telling me that I shouldn't tell stories. I will have to concentrate on emotions instead, cataloguing them like Clive, Dad's PhD student, when he helps him with research.

My stories will just have to be restricted to things that actually happen to me. Sorry.

FRIDAY 30TH APRIL 1982

Thank goodness it has finally got dark. I was so looking forward to looking forward to the new dawn, if that makes sense. For Beltane begins at midnight, the celebration of the beginning of summer. I thought that Dad and Lizzie would have gone to sleep by now, and it would just be me, all alone in a quiet house, a thought which still sends little thrills of happiness along my spine.

As it is, Dad and Lizzie have indeed gone to bed, but the fire brigade have also left, and alongside the little thrills of happiness, I also possess a sore throat from the smoke and a deep-seated sense of shame.

To be perfectly fair, I had been feeling strange – well, stranger than usual perhaps – all day. You see, I'd had a dream about looking out of a window at night, somewhere open and old, filled with dark blocks of nighttime fields, watching the silhouette of a tall man walk down the road away from me, whistling. I wanted to call to him, but you know what dreams are like – all I could do was watch.

Strange is an erroneous description too: choked, maybe. This is my *home*. But I am avoiding Dad and Lizzie, who insist upon wanting to put me in my little box, and waiting for Aunt Mim to come again. I want more and more to get out . . . somewhere, and do . . . something. Something that doesn't have the word 'little' in front of it and involve filing, typing or setting hair.

I decided this morning – the whistling man still in my mind – that I hadn't been doing myself any witchy favours of late. Consulting my *Magick Almanac*, I realised that I had not only missed the Festival of the Dark Moon earlier in the month, but also the opportunity to 'consider personal boundaries' at the beginning of the month. I am not quite sure how one does that – I have a vivid mental image of roadblocks and fencing when I think of boundaries – however, my point is that witchcraft was taking a back seat to being fed up. I wouldn't let Beltane pass me by, I vowed to my blue bedroom ceiling. I would reclaim my witching. I would mark this beginning of summer and its ensuing heat, love and lust (I know – I blush just writing that. I mean – in *Alwoodley*?).

The first thing to do was to make an altar, so that when May arrived tomorrow and Beltane began, I would have an offering to make. The mahogany sideboard in the dining room seemed perfectly altar-like to me, once I had cleared away the toast rack and the doilies. I then assembled:

- Fruit. Well, plastic fruit that Lizzie keeps in the sitting room fruit bowl and dusts once a week. I used to love squeezing the plastic grapes between my fingers as a child, because they made a squeak rather like someone breaking wind.

- Candles. Well, the Shabbat candles were there, so I didn't technically assemble them.

- A chalice. Dad's very large earthenware coffee mug that he brought back from a historian-event-thing in Preston.

- Decorative wreaths of flowers. The garden didn't have a lot to offer, so I augmented my decorative wreath with some twigs from Dad's bonfire pile, and some pink silk roses from one of Lizzie's hats. Luckily, she had a dentist's appointment this afternoon.

I was pleased with my altar. 'Don't Move – witching in progress!!', I wrote on a sheet of paper and placed in front of the candles, underlined for emphasis. Then, I lit the Shabbat candles. Just to see what it would all look like – a preview, I supposed.

"Very nice." Aunt Mim nodded her approval beside me.

"Thanks. You're here again!"

"Course. Better not show your mother."

"Evie?" Lizzie whirled into the house, pink-cheeked and buoyant despite what I later discovered was the aftermath of a small filling at the dentist's, clutching a bouquet of daffodils. I met her in the hall, hastily closing the dining room door.

"What have you been . . . ?"

"Nothing. Don't go in there."

"I . . . oh, all right. Listen, make yourself useful and go and pick me some rosemary from the garden, will you? I need to marinate the Shabbat chicken tonight."

"Rosemary signifies remembrance," I said promptly. "Did you know that?" Lizzie just looked at me. "I'm going," I said, Peggy trotting after me. I picked a few woody stalks and did an impromptu tour of the garden, explaining certain plants as though I was giving a guided tour.

Aunt Mim waited for me by the back door.

"Remembrance!" I said, gesticulating with the rosemary.

"Yes, but . . . Evie dear, what did you forget?" Aunt Mim raised an eyebrow.

"Smells like smoke," I said. "Of course, for Beltane you are supposed to light a bonfire, but . . . oh God, I lit the candles and. . ."

"Forgot to blow them out," Aunt Mim finished.

*

It turned out that one of the two Shabbat candles had fallen over, creating a sort of pagan bonfire that comprised of the warning piece of paper going up in flames, which in turn sent up Lizzie's silk hat roses. The heat of all this melted the plastic fruit, its plasticky dribble adhering to the sideboard and then dripping down onto the carpet. The Shabbat candles are part of a Judaic tradition celebrating the miracle of light. I could only surmise that, in this case, I had created an inverse miracle. Quite an achievement, if you think about it, but I didn't say that to Lizzie as she swept up the debris in furious silence, or to Dad as he arrived home from work to be greeted by a burly firefighter uttering the immortal words: "Quite safe to go in now, sir. Although, I would advise against worshipping Satan with plastic fruit in future."

*

"Take this and put it in the dustbin." Lizzie thrust a deformed, plastic butter dish at me that had not been at a safe enough distance.

"All right. It was a nice wreath, you know." I couldn't resist some form of defence. Everyone has the right to self-defence, don't they? I am sure that Aunt Mim had told me that once. "I did put a lot of effort into it," I added.

Lizzie took a deep breath, her mouth thinning into a straight line that was frankly terrifying. "If you put as much *effort* into finding a nice job, or getting a nice boyfriend, or just being a *nice, normal* young lady . . ."

"I just want to practice witchcraft," I said.

"Lizzie, do you think that we could use your kitchen cabinet cleaner on the wallpaper in here?" Dad came in brandishing a plastic bottle of detergent, the only time I had ever seen him handle a household cleaning product. "It says 'works on the most stubborn stains' – would soot count?"

"*Why?*" Lizzie positively screamed. "Why are you trying to practice witchcraft?"

"Because I am a witch," I said. Really, I know that Lizzie was upset, but it seemed obvious.

"You are *not* a witch, Evie. You have Asperger's, there is something . . . something not right . . ." Lizzie dissolved into tears. Asperger's seemed to have that effect on her.

"There's nothing *wrong* with me," I protested. "Asperger's is just witchiness, with all the fun taken out to sound more serious. If I lived in Mother Shipton's time . . ."

"Oh." Lizzie sniffed. "It's a disease, Sarah Leverson was right . . ."

"It isn't, actually," said Dad mildly. "It is a condition, which is different."

"Normal people don't have conditions, do they?"

"Well . . . let's just call it neurological," said Dad. "Can we not compromise on 'neurological' and turn our attention to the wallpaper?"

"Yes, let's," I said, and suddenly started crying.

*

It must be midnight by now, I've been writing for so long. But no, my watch says eleven twenty-three. It has been a horrible day but, without wishing to use Christian terminology, I did have an epiphany of sorts.

Wallpaper be damned, I thought earlier, shuffling out of the dining room, my tears hotly uncomfortable as they ran down my face. Thornlaw Saw Mill swam into focus in the hall and I suddenly, sobbingly, slightly snottily, made sense of everything.

The first time I had seen Aunt Mim again, wasn't she standing by the picture and speaking about being free? *That* was what all that money was for, I suddenly understood. Aunt Mim wanted to free me from a little life, from forcing myself into the patterns and habits of other people, from slowly suffocating in Alwoodley to the sound of golfers on the course and Lizzie banging the oven door open and Rabbi Guld's sermons.

I don't have to stay here, I realised, and happiness coursed through me, liquid and yellow as molten gold.

As Dad and Lizzie sat down to a sombre and much delayed supper (in the kitchen), I had tiptoed to the phone and made a telephone call. I rung Gavin Stephens. I'd memorised his number the first time he called and Dad had taken it down.

"Could I speak to Gavin Stephens, please? It is Aunt Mim's niece." I waited, listening to the sound of my own breathing in the mouthpiece. Gavin Stephens came to the phone surprisingly quickly.

"What a pleasure to hear from you, Miss Edelman . . ."

I had rarely been called 'Miss Edelman' seriously before, only by sarcastic teachers or overbearing shop assistants. I reminded myself that I was almost twenty-two – how old I was getting! "I wondered if you had gone home to your supper," I said.

"You are in luck; I am working late, as is my indefatigable secretary, Joyce . . ."

"The thing is, do I have to live at home any more?"

"Excuse me?"

I looked towards the kitchen door nervously and lowered my voice. "What I mean is, can't I move out now?"

"Well . . . yes, if you like."

"I want to get as far away as possible."

"Ah, well there are property agents who specialise in overseas sales, I believe . . ."

"Oh, I meant as far away as possible within Yorkshire, of course," I whispered into the receiver.

"Ah."

"But *how* does one do that?"

"Would you excuse me a moment, Miss Edelman?"

"Yes, all right," I said, bewildered. What was I supposed to be excusing? Was he about to hang up the phone? I heard the click of a button.

"Joyce – forget that paperwork for now, would you?" I heard Gavin Stephens say. "I have some business with a very valued client to attend to right away."

MAY

Lily of the Valley – Emerald – Taurus – Earth

**"May brings flocks of pretty lambs,
Skipping by their fleecy dams."**
SARA COLERIDGE

I AM WRITING LISTS, BECAUSE IT MAKES ME FEEL VERY grown-up and important, which of course I am now, because I am entering A New Phase of Life.

List of things to take with me when I move:
- Crystals
- China rabbits
- Many sweatshirts (the country is colder)
- Books
- Stolen books
- Borrowed books
- Candles
- Some furniture

To-do list:

- Find suitcases
- Pack suitcases
- Ask Lizzie if I can take the microwave

Actually, making lists just highlights how disorganised and immature I am in bullet-point format, which is no good at all. I feel a bit useless now.

Horoscope for May:

Leo: A project that needs accomplishing? Now is the time to put your mind to it, Leo! Don't allow yourself to be distracted by temptation.

Right, well . . . the stars have spoken, I suppose.

TUESDAY 4TH MAY 1982

"Faithful Cottage," it said. *"Freehold, chain free. Asking price: £11,250. This characterful cottage in the picturesque village of Thornlaw (amenities: post office, village shop, Barnsley 4.5 miles) comprises of a lounge/diner and kitchen with small pantry, upstairs two bedrooms and bathroom. Period charm throughout, in need of renovation. Outbuilding. Pretty garden with rural views, fully grown apple and quince trees."*

That was what started it all – just a grainy advert in the back of the newspaper. After I'd read it a sixth time, I came to the conclusion that there was something about Faithful Cottage. I thought (and I know that this sounds ridiculous, but it was the weekend and I was on my own in the house after turning down Lizzie's invite to go blouse shopping) that perhaps, it was waiting for me?

Alwoodley today has felt dull and unnatural after my little fact-finding jaunt to Thornlaw yesterday.

I'd worked it all out, and Alwoodley to Thornlaw is about thirty miles. Twenty-nine point eight, if we are going to quibble. I like to quibble – lovely word. My mission to Thornlaw was planned with military precision and various encouraging nods from Aunt Mim. I had driven the Alpine Sunbeam for the first time, terrified, blood pumping through my veins and roaring in my ears, to the point where I'd had to pull over somewhere outside Midgeley and calm myself down. Peggy thought that it was all a great adventure. Dad was at work. Lizzie was spending the day with her friend Harriet, who had moved to York and was reeling in a south-to-north way that Lizzie could identify with only too well. So, I made myself some Marmite sandwiches and drove downwards, past the city centre into the moor towns. I was a 'young woman travelling alone', scandalous in Jane Austen's time, and also in modern-day Alwoodley. I felt pleasantly wicked.

The road sort of segued into Thornlaw, curving gently onwards from the fields, its sides framed in budding green hedgerows. I could see the church tower and I smelt the freshness in the air, blossom and mud, and woodsmoke as a faint afterthought. I liked the place instantly, smiling at the blackened cottages sticking out of the ground like bad teeth. Arriving in the village was one of the few times that I had felt anything like an approximation of a Yorkshire woman, and I had an idea that this could be my normality. I felt soothed by the fields that were always just in view, cheered by the breeze and the clumps of flowers and grass that sprouted over the walls . . .

Now I'm back in Alwoodley again, in Hawthorns, writing this, squinting under my desk lamp and trying not to be annoyed as Lizzie clatters up and downstairs humming 'My Camera Never Lies'.

It is odd spending so much time in a place and still not fitting it. Being at Hawthorns isn't properly *being*. It is a cage as opposed to a vivarium, I suppose. It contains me, rather than providing me with the right conditions to thrive. I can't really describe myself as living here, not properly. Hawthorns has always overpowered me and left me feeling squashed, conferring a kind of respectability on me that I don't want or deserve. Before that, there had been London, my memories of it sun-drenched and treat-filled, but I could hardly call it home.

Thornlaw seems like the right place, I think.

WEDNESDAY 12TH MAY 1982

I haven't been dreaming recently – about Alex Ishkowitz, whistling men or anyone else. Just a sudden awaKevinng with the thought that these are the last of the old days, and immediate excitement mixed with a little fear as the filtered, dark orange sun makes its way through my curtains. I have almost been able to believe myself capable of a summer of love and lust, especially when so much opportunity is close but still slightly, comfortingly distant.

Normally, a piano chord would start plonking regularly in my mind. "Wake up, get up, one leg out first, maybe another nine minutes or so in bed would be acceptable . . ." That was my normal morning, a song of silent instructions and bargains with myself.

First goal was accomplished: I was upright. The imaginary piano plonked on. "Pick up my clothes from my desk chair and some new underwear from the drawer. Then, ready to go to the bathroom, which I do by walking out of my room and along the corridor . . ." on and on the instructions went.

But the voice inside my head was saying something quite different these days:

"*Faithful Cottage*," it said this morning. "*Freehold, chain free. Asking price: £11,250. This characterful cottage . . .*"

"Where do I live? Oh, Faithful Cottage," I tried experimentally. "Welcome to Faithful Cottage. Yes, this is my . . . my *home*."

The sun shone fiercely behind the curtains, desperate to push through. I watched the slub of the curtain fabric, its criss-cross of fibres darker and lighter than usual, the bouquets of roses that I usually despised for their irregularity picked out and warmly coloured.

The last month, I thought, as I drew the curtains so hard that the plastic rings rattled. My Wheel of the Year for witches seemed to be wheeling forward of its own accord, gathering pace. I could barely wait for Litha, or Midsommar, as you might say. The last month of this incarnation of Evie. I would sign the paperwork that Gavin Stephens would "send through", and then I would be

Evie of Faithful Cottage. I'd celebrate Midsommar surrounded by full-grown apple and quince trees. Leaning my forehead against the window pane, my mind grew blank, almost free.

Our lawn is not impressive compared to next door's, where Mauri has mown it closely enough to resemble a mini-Wimbledon. There is an overgrown buddleia in one corner that froths over the lawn like a wave, its beautiful smell almost overpowering enough to make you forget what a sadistic conqueror it is. There is the bench with the flaking paint that only began blistering on the left-hand side. The big house beyond us, and the big house to the side, and the other side.

Peggy, who had woken up so quietly that I hadn't even been aware of her, now sent a yipping bark tearing through the air towards me. She hated it when I ignored her, which I frequently did. Loving someone was not a matter of constant attention, I felt – how could it be? Turning now, I laughed and hurried over to her as her barks became so urgent that they lifted her body up and down. She stood imperious and ridiculous on my bed, her eyes shining with anxiety, her little paws and half her skinny legs lost in the duvet.

"Let's go out," I said. "Would you like that?" A jump up to lick the tip of my nose was affirmative. "Your breath smells of rotting mushrooms, and I love you," I added.

"Evie, where are you going?" Lizzie stood on the landing, an impressionist's dream of wet hair and pale shoulders catching the light. She had on her skirt and a lacey bra, a damp peach towel in her hand.

"Out," I said incredulously, indicating Peggy. I was quite surprised at the questions Lizzie asked sometimes. Surely standing beside an open front door was a clue?

"Don't you want to get dressed first? You're in your pyjamas!"

"Am I?" I looked down at the expanse of billowing cotton. "Oh, yes. Well, I forgot to get dressed."

"When will you be back?"

"I don't *know,* do I? You're always telling me that I should go out more, now you're fixated on me coming back!"

"Oh, *Evie.* Why do you have to be so awkward?"

"I really don't know," I said, and left.

*

"Oh, Evie, *just* the person I wanted to see." Mrs Halpern looked down at my spotted pyjama bottoms with horror, and then quickly (not quite quickly enough) recomposed her face to a smile. "D'you know, I *really* was hoping to see you?"

I had been reciting Faithful Cottage's details to myself as Peggy and I trotted towards the golf course, and was just starting over for the fourth time when I'd turned a corner and careered into Mrs Halpern.

"Were you, Mrs Halpern?" I couldn't think why. It felt odd talking to Lizzie's friends by myself; as though I was supposed to become a blend of both of us, to grow up and talk to these women on their own terms but still not use their first names.

"Yes, now, my nephew Abe is coming over from Manchester next month."

"Is he?" I said, into a silence that I found perplexing.

"You remember my nephew Abe, don't you?"

"Yes." Of course, I didn't remember his face. I can't remember faces at all – they blur out of my mind as they disappear from sight. Seeing someone again is relearning their face –people seem familiar, but only vaguely, as if I had seen a very fleeting glance of them in another life. But I try again to commit their face to memory in constant endeavour with no hope of success.

Mrs Halpern's little eyes creased even further with pleasure. "I just *knew* you would," she said. "He remembers you, you know, from when you met at Sarah Leverson's Shavuot party a couple of years ago?"

Oh yes: Abe Halpern. A doughy sort of person with wide, feminine hips and a fatal conviction of his own intellectual brilliance. He lectured me on gothic architecture, and I was so grateful to be discussing something other than Sarah Leverson's new kitchen tiles that I had gone along with it.

"He's still not married, you know," Mrs Halpern said now. She had inclined her head downwards and looked at me significantly.

"Do you know," I said hurriedly, "that I never understand why people think that someone who is unmarried is always just on the cusp of meeting someone and *getting* married? It's as if, the longer you stay unmarried, the more likely you are to *get* married. Whereas, surely, it's the other way round?"

There was a moment. Then Mrs Halpern decided to plough on regardless.

"You think about things so much, Evie. So does Abe. Between you and me," Mrs Halpern leant closer, and I stepped backwards, "he needs someone special, not run-of-the-mill. He's so clever."

"It's good news about the *Belgrano*, isn't it, Mrs Halpern," I blundered on desperately – it felt as though *I* was sinking. "I mean, not good news about an entire ship going down, but, you know, in terms of what it symbolises . . ."

Now it was Mrs Halpern's time to take a step back. "Oh, you're clever, Evie," she said, after a moment. "All the things you think about. Just like Abe."

I let Peggy pull me away, calling various incoherent goodbyes that clashed with hers. As I marched along, the piano plonked in my head again, each chord something I would do before June: sort out my clothes, fold them up, work out whether I needed a sofa for the cottage or whether it was extraneous to requirements. As I brushed against the clipped hedges that contained the rolling expanse of golf course, a crescendo was growing in my head and I embraced the thudding of the invisible keys excitely.

THURSDAY 13TH MAY 1982

I have been wondering for some days now, should I take my china rabbit collection to Thornlaw with me? I have signed some papers and paid some money (I hope Gavin Stephens will buy Joyce something nice with his fee), so thoughts like this are perfectly natural.

I will take my diary, of course. This old thing, with the spidery writing and the faint smell of smoke that emanates from it after the Beltane Incident. The diary isn't really new any more, and I am not sure that Dr Gordner would entirely approve of some of the entries, but I have a sort of need for writing now that has gone far beyond him. The diary is mine. A friend who never judges.

But the china rabbits? That thought reoccurred as I'd turned each one slowly around on my windowsill, watching their changing texture and colour in the politely optimistic spring sunshine.

"Evie, oh *God,* you aren't even dressed! Have you forgotten?"

"Forgotten what?"

"The Jewish Ladies League event for the relief of poverty-stricken young mothers? At Sarah Leverson's?"

I hadn't forgotten: each time I had walked past the calendar and seen "Lunch w/SL – Charity Ideas!", the accompanying dread charred my insides until they crumbled. I had merely hoped that some terrible apocalypse would happen, or at least that Lizzie would forget. These lunches-cum-charitable-works were strictly invite-only. The hand was extended to Lizzie very occasionally, on the unspoken understanding that she would leave me at home. But the tide had changed recently, I couldn't quite work out why. People sought me out, looked at me keenly, invited me to things. It was all so tiresome. "Aren't you going to congratulate me, about Faithful Cottage?"

"Get dressed *now*," Lizzie hissed.

"I don't want to go," I said suddenly, as though I had only just thought of it. "I hate all this stuff, why does everyone want me all of a sudden?"

Lizzie crossed the threshold of my room. She made to sit on my bed but hearing me catch my breath she leant against my desk instead, gingerly. "You should take advantage of all this," she said, in a voice so soft that it made me shiver.

"But I just want to go away. Or them to go away. Either. Either, really."

"And what if they go away and don't come back?" She looked upwards, searching for the right phrases to float down to her. "There's a sort of window, you know, when people are interested, but eventually they move on to somebody else. And you don't want to have regrets, do you?"

"Do you mean that if I don't go to Sarah Leverson's lunch now then I might regret it later, when she doesn't ask me?"

"Exactly! You never know what might come of these things."

I honestly can't see what would come of lunch at Sarah Leverson's. I suppose that if Susie was there, then I could see if she contained less negative energy. But what if she didn't? I clutched my arms around myself and rocked a little bit. Opportunities were so frightening – a window into something completely unknown that made you wonder why you were *supposed* to want it.

"You might enjoy it."

"They're so smug," I said.

"Well," said Lizzie, "wouldn't you be? They're women of a certain age; they've earnt their stripes. They must have been like you once."

"They're the same age as you," I pointed out. "You talk as if you're not one of them."

Lizzie sighed. "I suppose, in my head, I am still about twenty-one," she admitted, and I thought of our greengrocer who always told Lizzie that 'we didn't look so alike for sisters' and would watch avidly as Lizzie laughed.

"Susie Leverson is smug too, and she is my age. Were you ever like me?"

Lizzie opened her mouth and closed it again. "We'll be late," she said.

I looked towards my wardrobe. Inside was a new blazer, mid-green, slightly fluffed check, with gold buttons. I thought of it with a mixture of awe and disgust, my arms prickling already at the thought of its texture.

"You know, all of this is a load of bollocks," said Aunt Mim.

"I know," I said.

"What?" Lizzie paused at my door.

I seized the moment. "Aren't you happy that I am moving? It's all arranged."

"You know, you could still change your mind, Evie."

"But . . ."

"Living at home isn't *so* bad, is it? I was thinking, we could take drawing classes in Leeds . . ."

"I . . ."

". . . or go on a trip to Rome in August? You said you found the pantheon pleasantly round, once."

"Well . . ."

"You could have your own drawer in the kitchen to keep crisps and bananas, and a double bed in your room."

"I put my signature on the bit of paper," I said. "And a double bed wouldn't even fit in here."

Lizzie sighed and retreated. I just couldn't understand why Lizzie didn't *think* properly.

*

"Well, this is nice," said Sarah Leverson, to a dubious silence. I looked at the table – there was rice salad interspersed with sweetcorn and red pepper cubes ('jewelled', Sarah Leverson had called it). I supposed that I could try and pick out the red pepper surreptitiously; I hated the crunch of peppers and their taste of sour water. In the kitchen, there were baked apples, wrinkled in rows like little old women at a bingo hall. I'd gone in there to check if there was pudding, in order to calibrate my consumption of main course.

Two Sarahs and Lizzie were at one end of the table, some Susans (Susie Leverson and Susan Baum) and I were at the other end.

"Now." Sarah Leverson looked over at Sarah Baum, who picked up a spiral bound notepad, its ripped ends rustling between the iron spirals. I raised my shoulders and let them fall, hating their constriction in my blazer. "Are we agreeing about the split of the proceeds?"

Sarah Baum put her hand to the garnet brooch at her neck and ran the tips of her fingers over the smooth stones. She was effacing enough to be Sarah Leverson's second-in-command, just as her daughter Susan deferred to Susie Leverson in all things.

"That's new, isn't it?" Susie Leverson raised a plucked eyebrow at my blazer. I twisted, feeling the silk lining pressing across my back. I could almost feel the sewn seam that divided it into two halves.

"Half to the young wives of the Jewish unemployed, half to the children's home. I thought we'd agreed," said Sarah Leverson.

"It's quite nice, actually." Susie's hand hovered over the hard-boiled eggs, the unbitten ovals of her nails gleaming in the sunshine, painted lilac. She changed her mind, withdrawing her fingers delicately like a retreating spider. "*I'd* wear it, if it wasn't for the colour."

"I would have bought it in violet," I said confidingly. "I like violets. But I like green. It represents new beginnings and life and the earth."

"Shouldn't it be brown, if it represents the earth?"

Susan Baum paused mid-spread of chopped liver onto a piece of toast. I watched the greyish smear of it and felt a little sick.

"It doesn't mean earth *literally*, more, sort of, Mother Nature and plants and stuff."

"I suppose you can afford to buy things like that now, can't you?" Susie Leverson's eyes were as round and blue as the glass eyes of a doll. She looked distinctly un-hexed, I thought, and looked away. "It's like you're a different person. You can buy all the new beginnings that you want."

"I was just wondering about the unmarried mothers."

"Well, we don't need to concern ourselves with *those*, Sarah Baum."

"I suppose not . . ."

"I mean, if people think that we're throwing parties with drinking and dancing and a nice band in order to fund the products of . . ." Sarah Leverson paused mid-tirade and cast a cautious glance at us, 'the girls', as we'd been referred to. "Of unmarried *licentiousness*, well, we'd give ourselves a reputation. People simply wouldn't come!"

"No ..."

"No matter how much Babycham you put out and how much paper bunting!"

"Susie Ishkowitz had a *gorgeous* outfit when I saw her on Monday," said Susie Leverson. "Did I tell you that I bumped into her, Susan? In the Victoria Quarter."

"Oh, well, she can afford to shop there, can't she?" Susan Baum replied distractedly. "All the money that Alex is making."

"Yes, but she always looks so *elegant*. She had on a trouser suit, navy it was, and the neckline of the jacket had a little corded rope in gold around it – isn't that clever?"

"Sounds lovely." Susan pulled her cardigan closer around her middle.

I watched the sunlight catch segments of Susie Leverson's eyes, turning them from blue to clear like diamonds. The heater hummed, stuffing the dining room with artificial warmth.

"I mean," pondered Lizzie aloud, "we could add another cause, couldn't we?"

There was a sharp, inserted silence.

"What were you thinking, Lizzie?"

"There's the children's wing of the new psychiatric centre, isn't there?"

"Oh, yes," said Sarah Baum. "Isn't that where the Strausslers' daughter ended up? The one who was funny in the head?"

"I wouldn't have thought that your Auntie Miriam had so much money, Evie," said Susan in a solicitous but effete sort of way, as though she was talking about the weather or the price of tomatoes. I saw Susie Leverson smile out of the corner of my eye.

"What was wrong with the Straussler girl, did anyone ever know?" Sarah Leverson demanded an answer from her friends, fishing the serving spoon out of the rice and digging it in again.

"They said she was disturbed, talked to herself and all sorts," offered Sarah Baum.

"Away with the fairies." Sarah Leverson snorted. "I can't even remember her name, what was it now? Rebecca, Rachel? Something beginning with R . . ."

"Rose?" Lizzie suggested.

"Naomi," said Sarah Baum.

"That was it."

"Mim didn't *appear* rich at all," said Susie Leverson. "Not from the look of her." She glanced at me, a few grains of rice tumbling off her fork.

"I always liked the way that Aunt Mim looked," I said, "because she looked like her."

The smiles faded from Susie and Susan's faces.

"Evie?"

"Hmmm?"

Sarah Leverson was eyeing me, setting me in her sights. "Daniel said that he might pop in on his lunch break today. You remember Daniel, Susie's older brother?"

"Yes," I said, trying not to sound too dejected. I had an excellent memory – why was everyone so concerned that I remember their male relatives?

"Good. What decorations do we have?" Sarah Leverson snapped back into action, sending Sarah Baum's gaze scuttling anxiously over her notepad. I was dismissed, it seemed.

Thornlaw, I said in my head. *Thornlaw*. I tried to remember the smell of the air and the lovely old post office with the red door.

"There are the blue-and-white ones . . ."

"Oh, *Sarah*!"

"What's wrong with them? We're going to use them for Yom Yerushalayim . . ."

"That's the trouble," said Lizzie. "We need new ones; we can't just cart the same old things out every time."

I listened to Susie and Susan chatting, their words slipped over themselves in a steady stream until there was no sense in them, only sound and rhythm. I thought of the painting of the saw mill, the rock dividing the flow of the water. *Faithful Cottage, Freehold, chain free. Asking price: £11,250. This characterful cottage in the picturesque village of Thornlaw (amenities: post office, village shop . . .).*

"And besides, blue and white, it's so . . . so . . ."

"It's too *Jewish*," said Sarah Leverson. She laughed in a rattle; I lifted my shoulders again and pushed them against the pads of the blazer, wishing they would tear. "Oh Dan, there you are! You remember Evie, don't you?"

I looked up at Daniel, at his fleshy features that were entirely his mother's, at his dark blond hair. He was the stereotype of a good-looking man, as if someone had made being handsome a crime and put together a composite picture. Rumour had it that he was going out with a Gentile girl named Julie whom he'd met in a club in the city centre, but my mind was drifting back to Thornlaw...

"Village shop," I said clearly.

There was a horrified silence where we all seemed to freeze. I could feel Lizzie's gaze the most clearly – it seemed to bore into me. I started to blush, pushed my chair back and somehow managed to get into the kitchen without knocking anything over.

The voices slowly took up again, tentatively at first, then gushing more strongly. Evidently, they were relieved that I was not there. I stood at the worktop, pressing my fingertips over the piece of Formica where the checked pattern had been rubbed out. If I covered that one spot, then the counter looked whole; there was no break in the order. Then I looked distastefully at the apples, and stuck my finger into the leathery skin hard enough to send a pulpy white ooze of flesh rolling down its side.

"Are you all right, dear?" Mrs Leverson came briskly in, avoiding my eye.

"Yes, thank you. I was just about to get myself some more water." I hadn't brought my glass in with me. *Why* hadn't I remembered to bring my glass in with me?

"Aren't you going to go out and have a chat with Daniel?"

"I don't think so," I said, trying to copy the briskness of Sarah Leverson's tone. "Not today."

Sarah Leverson took a glass and filled it from the tap. "You know, Evie, most girls would kill for a man like my Daniel. He's got his own business, and surely even you can see that he's a good-looking boy. They were all after him, you know, even Susie Ishkowitz had an eye for him at one time. So, you could do worse, young lady."

"But you wouldn't kill to have me as a daughter-in-law, would you?" It was best to be honest, I thought, and suddenly I felt very calm.

"I . . ." I will never know what Sarah Leverson was going to say, because the words petered out somewhere inside her throat.

"What's the point," I said softly, "of you having to put up with me and me having to put up with you? If Daniel's that much of a catch, then he doesn't need me, does he?"

I finally dared to look at Sarah Leverson; it had all been so easy to say when I was addressing the Formica. I saw her eyes were round, almost as round as Susie's. The genuine shock on her face made her seem oddly vulnerable. It can't have been the first time that someone had spoken their mind to her, I thought, and then immediately realised that it probably was. I almost wanted to reach out and touch her, this bastion of Jewish matriarchy suddenly made flesh, just a disappointed older woman who couldn't procure a life of wealth and luxury for her son.

"I'm off Mam, all right?" Daniel appeared in the kitchen door and winked at me. Impervious though I was to the thought of matrimony, I blushed nevertheless – bright red circles burning my cheeks.

"All right," Sarah Leverson and I said as one.

*

As I am writing, my bedroom is running with strands of conversation and leftover noise from Sarah Leverson's. These second-hand voices float in the air, gold and orange like the middle stripes of a rainbow. The artificial heat of the Leversons' has followed me home. Even in the coolness after the sunset, I feel hot and slightly giddy. Aunt Mim is luckily leaving me alone; I suppose she knows I've had a difficult day. Lizzie is leaving me alone too; I presume because her day has been trying and that it is all my fault.

The blazer is hung on my wardrobe knob, seeming innocuous from a safe distance, its leaf-green colour still bright in the dusk. I doubt that I will ever wear it again.

My favourite time of day and year is early autumn afternoons, when the sky fades and then deepens again, blazing that beautiful coral pink, and it is sometimes still mild enough to be warmed by the air as the light leaves. Spring evenings seem an inverted form of those times; a bastardisation of everything I love. The delicacy had been in the daytime, the increasing confidence of the sun that had reached me occasionally at odd angles in the Leversons' house suddenly disappeared, leaving a coolness and unfriendliness.

I haven't yet closed the curtains; my crystals emitting an eerie glow as the light fades completely. Clear quartz and black tourmaline, those were the ones I had needed to stand my ground about Thornlaw, Daniel Leverson, double beds, the Pantheon . . . everything. Reaching out my hand towards them, I remembered Susie Leverson looking at me. I could see exactly what she was thinking – that I was peculiar, stupid, that I didn't understand her and she didn't understand me, but that the lack of understanding on her part was natural and therefore all right. Those blue eyes of hers, sometimes as pale as my aquamarine crystal, other times darKevinng in the shadows thrown by her eyelashes, had pierced me like white sun, making me turn away.

Witchcraft is a work in progress, I thought, saying it to myself a few times. A well-balanced sentence with those monosyllables in the middle; it sounded pleasant, although I doubted whether it was true. I had to admit to myself that I was not doing my best work, but how could I? Looking out of the window at the barely visible garden, its formless soft grey stretching indefinitely, I remembered Mother Shipton had predicted that York would one day have an underground water system. Yet here I was, bothering with Susie Leverson. I wanted to be like Mother Shipton, only marginally better looking and not living in a cave. I wondered if I was focusing my magick in the wrong quarter. Then I wondered what the other three quarters were?

"*Pretty garden with rural views, fully grown apple and quince trees,*" I said to myself.

I took my newest favourite possession out of the drawer, a large book with a mottled pink cover the colour of cold flesh. *Selected Writings of Opal Whiteley.* I had found it in the library when I was looking in the nature-writing section and seen it the wrong way up on its shelf. I had been sauntering past it for a couple of weeks – no one put the poor thing the right way up. So I concluded that it was clearly not a loved book, and stole it. I say stole it – I mean that I took it out and will take it to Thornlaw with me. Nobody will miss it. And, to make amends, I smuggled in my *Faery Tales* book under my sweatshirt and put it in its place. The library is welcome to it; I won't need folk tales when I am in Thornlaw and can make my own stories.

Did you know that Opal Whiteley could memorise and recite whole categories of plants and trees? She was famous for her roses and fauna knowledge. I am going to follow in Opal Whiteley's footsteps; I'll be able to name every category – nature broken down into neat sections, a series of words that will reel off my tongue like dances. And everyone will be astounded at my genius, like the Maharaja that took Opal in as his guest. Except that I am not a child; I have passed the age where a precocious memory is attractive, I suppose. I wondered whether I could claim that I was the orphan child of a French prince like Opal, but decided regretfully that I wouldn't be able to pull it off.

"Evie? Supper!"

Lizzie's voice. A strangely unaromatic yet savoury smell floated up the stairs – I guessed that it was Findus crispy pancakes. Lizzie had two meals that she cooked for company or celebrations from the St Michael's *Book of French Cooking*: roast chicken on noodles with fried onions followed by poached pears, or fillets of sole au vermouth with buttered green beans followed by blancmange. The rest of the time, we managed on a surprising amount of processed food. I would catch Lizzie looking with wonderment at the recipe for duck in a cream sauce with grapes, sometimes. But it wasn't kosher – and she didn't dare.

"Evie? SUPPER!"

Dad had arrived home twelve minutes earlier, and it took him over two minutes to take his coat off and leave the hallway – I'd watched the clock. I suddenly thought that I wouldn't be able to call this 'home' any more; that Dad would be coming to *his* home and I would be somewhere else. In my dark room, this gave me a gnawing feeling of terror that I quickly smothered. No point in being scared, because then Dad and Lizzie would be right and I would be wrong.

"Faithful Cottage, Freehold, chain free. Asking price: £11,250. This characterful cottage in the picturesque village of Thornlaw . . ." I repeated to myself, my slippered feet on the stairs beating out the rhythm as I marched downwards to the kitchen. "No," I suddenly said to myself, "because it isn't an advert any more. I've bought it. It is mine."

Faithful Cottage was a home again, and a base for my exciting new job: I was going to be a full-time witch. It would be hard at first, I thought, as my last post was purely secretarial, but I was looking forward to my new career.

After all, villages have to have a friendly witch, don't they?

FRIDAY 21ST MAY 1982

"I don't even know why I have to buy a washing machine," I huffed. I pulled my winter coat on and plucked my tam-o'-shanter off the top of the coat stand with angry fingers, ramming it on top of my head. (My thick hair immediately made it raise and hover. Honestly, I must be allergic to headgear.)

"You'll be too hot in that, Evie."

"I'm not hot," I said. "It's still dark outside . . ."

"Well, I have to be back by twelve to start my casserole, and your dad has a lecture at half ten . . ."

"Yes, all right," I huffed again. It was a dark day, I thought, both literally and in a sort of psychological way. Lizzie was Imposing Her Presence upon lovely Faithful Cottage, which was now technically mine. She couldn't stop me moving there in a few days, so her tactic was to fill it with feminine, practical things like flower vases, coat hangers, and – most intrusively – washing machines. Well, just one, to be fair. "Why do I need a bloody washing machine?"

"Language, Evie!" Lizzie was scandalised. "You won't make any nice friends in Thorn . . . Thorn . . ."

"Thorn*law*."

"Yes, if you go around using blue language, will she, Dad?"

Dad, to his credit, appeared to develop a sudden mania for studying the contents of his briefcase. Lizzie, it seemed, was off, buttoning her jacket, fingering her earrings to check they were in place, and making my life a misery at the same time.

"You'll have to get better at cooking, you know."

"Hmmm."

"And what happens if the Sunbeam breaks down?"

"I'll take it to a garage."

"Where?" Lizzie snorted. "And what if Peggy . . . ?"

She made off down the path, a litany of hypothetical issues wafting behind her like chiffon.

"Evie . . . you know that you don't have to . . ."

I turned to face Dad. "I'm becoming <u>independent</u>, Dad," (underlined here to represent vocal emphasis) "remember?"

I was about to follow Lizzie, when Dad caught at my sleeve. I stared at his clawlike hand, then up into his eyes, rounded in surprise, caught by the fact that he had intended to blurt something out, something emotional probably, but been completely incapable. I was sorry for him – I suffered the same problem, my words often got stuck somewhere.

Stepping outside, I realised at once that Lizzie was right: I would be far too hot. I could only hope that she wasn't right about everything else, and at that thought, my stomach gave a creak like a squeaking gate.

JUNE

Rose – Pearl – Gemini – Air

"June brings tulips, lillies, roses,
Fills the children's hands with posies."
SARA COLERIDGE

(I had tried picking garden roses in June when I was a child: Lizzie had shouted at me.)

I AM NO LONGER ME, I FEEL: EVEN MY OWN NAME, Evie Edelman, seems far too metropolitan, cosmopolitan, all that, to apply to me now. I am a countrywoman, and I write it proudly. I feel the absence of city noise, I watch my skin for signs of browning from being out in the fresh air, I tentatively examine my fruit trees and think about the crop. This is now, *The Diary of a Provincial Witch*.

"Potatoes are very interesting folks. I think they must see a lot of what is going on in the earth; they have so many eyes."
OPAL WHITELEY

Isn't that lovely? Although I don't care much for potatoes and certainly won't grow them. I will grow rhubarb because I like the enormous leaves, like old-fashioned ladies' fans when they went dancing. Is it too late to plant rhubarb?

To-do list for the month:
- Do something in the garden.
- Learn more about trees.
- Have at least one vision.
- Help at least one struggling villager.
- Find a coven.

Horoscope for June:
Leo: This summer will be a perplexing one for you, especially as Leo is usually so single-minded. Beware a kindred spirit that you can't spot, and a familiar face who isn't kind.

WEDNESDAY 2ND JUNE 1982

There wasn't a specific point of realisation that I was in Thornlaw when I opened my eyes this morning. It was more a collating of images and sounds in blue and grey that tipped my mind away from my old room, my old life, and into my new bedroom.

The ceiling is so much lower here; it seemed to be leaning in towards me in a friendly way. The window is smaller too, but the room is lighter and the light itself stronger as we rolled towards midsummer. Yesterday, I painted precisely one and a quarter walls in sugarplum-pink in a fit of hyperactivity. Don't ask me why I picked that shade, I am not a sugarplum-pink kind of person, but I suppose that it was the opposite to my old blue-and-white room – a sort of dividing line in paint. Alwoodley seemed a long way in the past: the zoom of cars driving past, the brown, involved swirls of the dining room carpet were fading. In reality, I had been a resident of Thornlaw (a Thornlawyer?) for almost forty-eight hours.

I kicked my feet into the tunnel of bedsheets. Peggy, whose slinky back I could see curled at my feet, harumphed and kicked back petulantly. There were no curtains. The quarter of sugarplum pink wall petered out in a feathery, undulating line of impatient brush strokes. Should I paint the ceiling pink as well, I wondered? Or would that be gilding the lily?

Here I was, thinking about paint and completely forgetting to do my witchy phrase: this was something of my own devising, a phrase to start the day with, seven of them, one for every day of the week. I had already memorised them. Today was Wednesday, so . . . oh, yes.

"Magick flows through me, as it has flowed through each witch in time," I announced loudly to the ceiling. The ceiling remained impassive.

The remaining magnolia three-quarters of the walls still belonged to Mrs Sullivan, my predecessor at Faithful Cottage. She had quite literally predeceased me: "Dropped dead in the lounge, didn't she, Vernon? Hadn't taken her milk in, and I had this *feeling* . . ." Dot next door had recounted with relish as her husband Vernon looked on disapprovingly. Mrs Sullivan still made her presence felt in the scuffs and marks and scratches on the walls – a set of mementoes to her physical existence. She had chosen green carpet – I had rolled it up in a cloud of dust and it now stood to attention against the outbuilding, stiffly offended and slightly taller than me.

"Shall we get up?" I asked Peggy rhetorically. Of course we were getting up – I had decided to always get up with the light, partially to be closer to Mother Nature, partially to make a point to Lizzie, who was trying to organise a trip to Laura Ashley for curtains that I didn't want.

"Morning. Morning."

My two Adam Ants were stuck on my wall, towards the corner so that I could see them at all times, and they had travelled down from Alwoodley in my handbag so that they didn't get bashed. I had angled them so they did not see me in bed, however. I was sure that I snored, and my mouth gaped open.

It felt so odd having two bedrooms. Having a whole house, in fact. Even though it was only seven hundred and fifty-six square feet (I had asked the estate agent), it took some getting used to. I kept having to remind myself that there was no space allotted to anybody else; I didn't have to stay out of a room or go upstairs when I wanted to be alone. Every molecule of air in this place belonged to me.

There were so many things not to think about, too: living alone seemed to remove several hurdles from my day. I wouldn't need to have a bath, I wouldn't need to have breakfast. They were things that other people did. This is what *I* would do, I thought, trailing into the second bedroom (currently a heap of my clothes and not much else): I would finally make an offering for the house. I would get to know my house spirits, as I was too sweaty and dusty before, and covered with splotches of pink paint. I was always shifting something, unpacking something, and probably disturbing them. But now, they would introduce themselves to me, Peggy and the Adam Ants. We would be like a family. My new family. Perhaps, I thought, the strength of the morning light making me optimistic, I hadn't really needed Dad and Lizzie at all, although they were helpful with bringing in boxes.

I rummaged for something to wear, whilst ruminating that silence did in fact have a sound, and thought it perspicacious of Simon and Garfunkel to have written a song about it. Silence fizzed and hummed and rustled like leaves. It had a presence that was faint but reassuring to those who were lucky enough to hear it.

As soon as I was dressed, I would head outside, even if the phone rang – which it often did, being Lizzie. She claims to be worried about me, but really I think that she is just checking that I haven't set fire to anything. That's why I haven't made an offering to the house as of yet. I am not scared of a fire, you understand. Just a bit cautious.

WEDNESDAY 9TH JUNE 1982

I have made many new discoveries on my exploratory wanderings.

Charity Cottage, home of the aforementioned Dot and Vernon, was the first to be passed when Peggy and I left the house. Then there was Honest Cottage, which I felt should have been mine really. I'm always honest, or, as other people describe it, 'blunt'. But Edith and Peter live there, and I can't imagine either of them dropping dead in their lounge any time soon.

That was the end of my little terrace: fields behind us and to the side. To the front, an overreaching rhododendron, property of Margaret and her as yet unnamed husband in the house at the end of the lane. Things got a little busier once I turned out of the lane, but the grainy façade of the houses was softened as I got to know the people in them. I had already told Lizzie about Vernon and Dot, and Edith and Peter, and Margaret and Whatshisname.

"You see?" I had said. "I am making friends, and *you* said that I would be lonely."

"Hmmm," Lizzie had said when she telephoned yesterday. "Neighbours aren't friends."

"You are friends with Mrs Halpern and the Isaacs, and they are sort of our neighbours. In fact, pretty much everyone we know lives in Alwoodley."

"That's different," Lizzie had said darkly.

I had wished that it was Thursday, because Thursday's witchy phrase is "I belong to a community of strong, spiritual women". Aunt Mim would have liked that, I thought. I had wanted to have a chat with Aunt Mim, tell her all about my new job as a village witch, and all the good things I would do once I got the lie of the land. Luckily, she walked part of the way with me.

"You're good with her," said Aunt Mim, as I set off between a gap in the low stone wall, pausing for Peggy to race though. I grazed my calves a little, misjudging the narrowness of the space, and offered Aunt Mim my hand. "No, I'm all right," she said, the rolls of flab compressing and then tumbling out again as she got through. We walked in the shirring grass together.

"Peggy's turned into such a little explorer."

"So have I. It's funny, isn't it, how I never wanted to go anywhere back in Alwoodley, whereas here I want to go everywhere?"

"But you can see where you're going here," said Aunt Mim, gesturing over the fields and hills. "You can see your path."

"Peggy can barely see in front of her, the grass is so tall. She's like a friend really, rather than a dog. She's a companion." The warm weather with a little hint of crispness was making me talkative. "I suppose that she doesn't sit in judgement on me."

"Oh, but she *does* sit in judgement," said Aunt Mim. "She just decides in your favour."

"I hadn't thought of it like that before."

"Aren't these little things beautiful? I think that they have to be pyramidal orchids, don't you? Or is it the wrong time of year? Or the wrong place, even?"

I watched Aunt Mim's inelegant little sausage fingers trail over the tiny lilac petals. Conversation with Aunt Mim was always like a spinning roulette wheel, I thought – an ever-changing parade of subjects moving at lightning speed, so that if you thought a prior conversation ended too rapidly, you just had to wait for it to come back around again. I wanted her to tell me more about Peggy's attachment to me, but Peggy barked at a windswept section of grass that moved too vigorously for her liking, and I stumbled over a large stone set deep into the earth. When I recovered my balance, I was alone again.

Still, at least Aunt Mim had sampled some fresh air and wasn't just confined to Faithful Cottage. She got about. "Here, there and everywhere," I said loudly to myself, turning and heading back, the church spire on its slight promontory sharp and clear, pinning Thornlaw in its place. I took the long route, emerging from the fields into the village.

"*Kevin!* Don't do *that!*"

How odd – my name wasn't Kevin. The door to one of houses was open and a lady stood there in her dressing gown with a plastic watering can. She appeared to be addressing thin air – a spirit, perhaps? Maybe I was drawing near a fellow witch . . .

She saw me and waved.

"Mornin'," I said, trying to take the southern shortness out of my 'o's.

"Morning, love."

"I'm Evie," I said, emboldened. "I've just moved in to . . ."

"To Faithful Cottage, oh, I know. Nice to have some young people about; most of them have left to find work."

"Oh. I'm painting my bedroom walls sugarplum-p—"

"Damp, is it?"

"It, erm . . . doesn't seem to be."

"She never did a thing to it, you know."

"Errr, no."

"Garden run wild, it did."

"I rather like—"

"Are you going to put in a patio?"

"Well, I—"

"I know, they're expensive, aren't they? Still, you could save up."

"Yes. I should really—"

"Nice to meet you, Evie."

"The pleasure's all mine."

"You *do* talk posh," she said, laughing at me in a good-natured sort of way. "I wondered for a second whether you were the one who'd bought Fielden Place, but when I saw you walking this way, and Dot'd said about the dog . . ."

"Fielden Place?"

"The nice house on the edge of Fielden Park. Grand, but homely too, not like the big house. Maureen up the road used to clean for the old couple. New ones are young, like you. Have a foreign name too – Polish, it sounds, or summat. I hope they'll speak English!"

"Hmmmm."

"I'm Margery, Derek's indoors, and my son's Kevin. Kevin, stop *mucking* about and come and say hello to the lady." Kevin materialised with as much poise and stealth as Aunt Mim. Also in his dressing gown, clutching a plastic action figure, he squinted up at me idly. I kept a fixed smile on my face – I hate children, and the feeling seemed to be mutual. We stared at one another. Then Margery plodded back inside, bouncing on the soles of her padded slippers.

I wonder what I could do to help Margery with my witchcraft? Shuddering even now at the thought of Kevin's malevolent stare and dirty dressing gown, I thought perhaps a spell to drive out demon spirits . . . I digress.

An elderly man had stared at me from the other end of the road, arms hanging limply in his black leather jacket, a baseball cap overshadowing his eyes. I waved, trying to make it as confident as possible. He stared at me but remained stock still, cowboy-style, just before they pull a pistol on you. He was Old Bernard. After our first meeting on Monday, I knew the following: his auntie had left him the forge cottage, his mother fell down the stairs when he was nine and broke her neck. He had also shown a dogged interest in discovering my surname. My heart had sunk: I had learnt that with a certain generation, there is only one thing worse than a Jewish name – a German Jewish name. "Edelman," I had mumbled.

"Edelman?" Old Bernard's eyes had widened in disbelief. "Where's that from then?"

"Frankfurt," I had said. "But we had to leave because of the Nazis," I'd added wildly, and suddenly wanted to cry.

"Closed the pits," he said.

"Really?"

"Oh, yes. Closed the one at Criggle-Ash." Old Bernard made a sweeping arc with his hands towards the fields. "Closed that in '79. Now, Cuthfoote – closed that in the sixties." He turned a little to point beyond the houses to some invisible place and then looked back at me, his eyes as melancholy as a bloodhound's. I had nodded and squinted into the distance, towards this faraway spot that was currently unseeable.

"My grandad was down the pit, you know."

"Oh?"

"There was an explosion," he said, in the same way that a child would say 'there's a spider over there'. "In June . . . May? June. 1872, it was."

"Was it?" I asked, doing some frantic calculations in my head. How old must Old Bernard *be*, I wondered? Was he really a hundred, like those old soothsayers and sages? "So, your grandfather . . ."

"He was ten."

"Goodness," I had said, not to be polite – I meant it.

"He survived."

"Oh." My family in Frankfurt didn't, I thought. Most of them didn't.

Just as I turned away now, resigned to the fact that Old Bernard would not be forthcoming on the wave front, he lifted his hand in a hieroglyphic way, his palm long and slender.

"Settling in all right, are you?" Margaret's head emerged from the open window as I walked past her rhododendron.

"Yes, I've just been for a walk."

"I saw you talking to Margery just now." Margaret leant – somewhat precariously, I thought – further out of the window towards me. "I wouldn't listen to her too much, love. She gets the wrong idea, you know? I mean, she's obsessed with the idea that we've got foreign spies or some such coming to Fielden Place. When Terry and Mae got their new double glazing, she put it about that they'd had a government grant for it. I mean! As if Mrs

Thatcher is bothered about the state of Terry and Mae's windows!" Margaret's laugh sounded like a piece of machinery boring into a piece of metal, I thought, and I shifted from one foot to the other. "Still," she carried on, "it is good that you are meeting people."

"Yes, it is, isn't it?" I heartily agreed with Margaret.

"You know Vernon and Dot now, and Margery and her lot, and Edith and Peter. Then there's me and Paul, of course. Down the road, further down there, there's Marlene and Martin, and opposite there's Pauline and John . . ."

So many couples, I thought. Pair upon pair, enclosed in their own little space, the syllables of their names forming a pattern together that others were used to repeating.

". . . And Joanie, of course! You *must* meet Joanie. She's like you . . ." Margaret tailed off for a second. "She's a woman on her own. She needs the company, between you and me – you should go and see her, in Brambledene."

"Is she, I mean, is Joanie interested in nature and . . ." *Don't say spells*, shouted Lizzie's voice in my head, *for* God's *sake, don't mention magic*, ". . . things?" I finished lamely. I was getting excited, but was too nervous to actually ask whether I would find a kindred spirit.

"Oh, no! She likes crochet, and *Little House on the Prairie* – that's her favourite on the telly – and she used to be married to Jack, but now they're going through a *divorce*." Margaret mouthed the word. "The last time that Jack and Joanie were seen together, she was chasing him past the post office brandishing an umbrella!

You didn't hear that from me, mind. Listen," she said, looking at me shrewdly, the tortoiseshell frames of her glasses catching the sun. "That really helped the other day, when you massaged my fingers for me – you've got healing hands."

"Yes, I have," I said proudly. "I suppose it's part of the job description really, of a w—"

"Well, they teach all sorts now," said Margaret in wonderment. "I suppose you did one of those massage courses, did you? At a polytechnic? Must be such a nice job. *I'd* like to do a course. Only Paul," she thumbed behind her, "he's as helpless as a baby. Couldn't get his own lunch or tea."

"Is Paul ill?"

"No, no, he's just . . . you know what men are like. And, of course, they're expensive these things, aren't they? Well, all credit to you for setting up here, I'll spread the word around about your healing hands."

"I can come in and see you, if you like? When your hands are stiff."

"Oh, that's very kind, love. Let me know what you charge."

Unbeknownst to Margaret, I had already drawn a pentagon, held it under the light (no candles – not yet. I am working up to candles again) and thought healing thoughts towards Margaret's hands. Pentagons tend to alarm people, so I haven't told her that I am supplementing the hand massaging with spells. I will exercise self-restraint, until the neighbours get to know my witching ways, and then pentagons will be all right.

'Exercise self-restraint' makes me feel very mature when I write it down. I am already independent, you see? Lizzie doesn't need to ring me all the time.

The cottage wasn't quite home yet, although I thought that my pace quickened a tiny bit in anticipation of getting back – only to run into Dot getting her milk in, her squat figure more rotund than ever in a fleecy pullover. She looked a little like a friendly sheep, I thought.

"Getting on all right, Evelyn?"

"There's no work, y'know," Vernon supplied darkly from the porch.

"No, no." There was plenty of work, I thought, surprised. All those hedgerows to forage and trees to learn the names of, not to mention Communing with Nature and the Spirits. But, come to think of it, I hadn't seen any offices about, which is probably what he meant.

"There's no work anywhere, is there, love?" Dot came to my rescue, and I shot her a grateful look. "No wonder you can't find something."

I nodded.

"Right," said Dot. "Mind how you go. Bye then, Lullabelle! Oh," she laughed, tickling Peggy under the chin whilst Peggy gazed up at her with mild affrontery, "aren't you a little *poppet*."

"Bye." I summoned up all my courage to address Vernon. "Bye, Vernon!"

"Bye, love," he said, pleasantly enough, and rambled back indoors.

I suppose that it *was* a bit odd that someone my age would want to live here, I thought to myself. Young people were supposed to want to live in cities, discovering themselves by taking drugs and experimenting with hair dye. I should think up a story, I thought, perhaps something about not being able to find a job, just until people realise that I'm a witch. I don't want people to think that I'm odd: a lot of things I do might look odd, but I only realise that after I've done them.

THURSDAY 10TH JUNE 1982

Did you know that sycamore trees can adapt to any habitat, including waste ground? That they put their roots down and grow anywhere, including our soil, which is non-native to them? I do. It was four-eighteen in the afternoon, and my interest in those great tall trees was starting to fade (they can grow over a hundred feet tall, in case you were wondering).

I decided to have lunch: a packet of Walkers crisps (cheese and onion, the most superior of the flavours in my opinion) and an apple that hadn't ripened enough and wrinkled the inside of my mouth with its tartness. After that, I didn't have the heart to return to sycamore trees. I stared at my painting of Thornlaw Saw Mill, now in its true habitat (well, hung above my fireplace, anyway), and then thought that I would walk to the church: it sounded such a grown-up thing to do.

*

The church tower had looked so picturesque from afar, like the quaint paintings on gift boxes of fudge. But you had to walk uphill to get to it, so you arrived a little flustered. I arrived just as the sun went in, the church casting a surprisingly cool shadow.

I had been in a few churches in my time, for reasons of architectural interest. Dad and I would wander around exclaiming, "Oh, look at the carving around that font", etc., in respectfully hushed tones, as befitted travellers in a foreign place. Thornlaw church was no different: it smelt of dust settling into stone and wood. Light from a huge window at the far end was soaked up quickly and greedily by the stone walls, so it was dark again towards the back pews. I stepped over memorial stones on the way to the altar, already worn smooth by countless shoes and barely legible. A wooden Jesus on the cross greeted me, his head bowed, and I felt embarrassed. I supposed that I had entered His house uninvited.

"Good afternoon?"

"Oh, hi!" I turned and saw the dog collar first, followed by the crablike face unfurling out of it: wide forehead, high cheekbones, and narrow eyes that glittered with . . . something. Religious fervour, I supposed. He looked about forty. Nearer fifty, perhaps – impossible to tell with his paper thin, almost translucent, skin. "You're Reverend Rishangles, aren't you?"

"I see that my reputation precedes me." He waited to see if I would come up with anything more original.

"Not really. I was looking at that, you see," I explained, pointing to the framed list entitled, in black italics, *Vicars of this Parish*.

Reverend Rishangles smiled faintly.

"I'm Evie, I live at Faithful Cottage."

"Welcome." The Reverend eyed me with a hint of suspicion. "Are you a churchgoer, Evie?"

"Only like this," I said instantly. In the ensuing silence, both the Reverend and I worked out what I meant – that the quietly deserted church full of memorials rather than people was the only incarnation of it I would ever know.

"It is a peaceful place," he said mildly.

"What's that over there?" I moved across a pew to look at a wooden panel, painted a long time ago with etiolated, pale figures, some of which were erased in peeled patches.

"Ah, good old Doomsday. A carving discovered, having nearly been destroyed by Cromwell's men. These are the dammed souls here." Reverend Rishangles stood beside me, shorter than me, his shoulders narrow as blades. His was a wispy presence, I decided, like smoke – lingering but strangely difficult to grasp.

"Why have those ones got no clothes on?" I looked at the prim expanse of white, hairless bodies, bellies rounded in a perfect circle.

"*They* are the fallen women," said the vicar.

"It doesn't seem very fair that the fallen *men* get to keep their clothes on. Still, it's very … errr … very nice? Very nice Doomsday."

"*I* think," said the Reverend clearly, "that Cromwell's men should have finished the job."

"Well, I … I like that rainbow that this gentleman is sitting on."

"You mean Jesus?"

"Oh, is that who he is? Well, that's quite a good bit. Only I don't like the women with no clothes on. It's gratuitous," I announced.

"They probably hadn't really done anything wrong anyway, just coveted a chicken or something."

"And yet they face eternal damnation. It's amazing, isn't it? How many stories were created simply to scare you girls into behaving yourselves?" Reverend Rishangles slid away from me towards another visitor who had just entered the church. I thought I saw him smiling.

When I got home, I found a note through my door in Lizzie's writing.

"Dad and I popped by to see you," it read, *"but you were out. I hope you are all right? Didn't you get my postcard telling you we would come down? Dad just wanted to check on the washing machine – sometimes the new ones can be skittish, apparently. Went next door but the lady there just waved at us through the window. Well, I'll ring you tonight. Love, Lizzie and Dad."*

I sighed, and picked up my smarter pair of trainers and an old handkerchief that had fallen out of my pocket onto the doormat – a gesture of house-pride in case Lizzie could see me from Alwoodley. Under the hanky was a postcard.

"Hello, Evie, just thought we'd let you know that Dad and I will be driving this way on Thursday. We'd love to pop in and see you, and the washing machine. Four-thirty all right? Love, Lizzie and Dad."

Thank goodness they had been 'popping in' to see the washing machine, I thought. If they'd only wanted to see me, I would have felt terrible. And the washing machine would be there next time. As would I, I suppose. When they rang tonight, I could just tell them that I had been busy.

FRIDAY 11TH JUNE 1982

It has been a day full of *men,* and I am not sure that I approve.

Firstly, I was woken up quite rudely this morning by whistling. Whistling is uncouth, I think, and it makes my skin crawl with its flutey noise. Cross, I tore myself out of bed and stuck my head out of the open window. I saw the silhouette of a man, a dark-haired man, jauntily tripping down the road, his whistled tune still reaching back to me. Where had he come from? Had he materialised, like Aunt Mim? I opened my mouth to call out to him, but he was too far away. Stuck in my cottagey garret, I merely watched him.

Secondly, at about ten in the morning (a civilised hour, at least), Alex Ishkowitz stood outside my window. He was talking to someone that I couldn't see, squinting in the sunshine, wearing a green shirt, a paler shade of his eyes, sleeves rolled up, laughing in that ostentatious way that men of business do.

I'd taken a breath in and forgotten to breathe out. His voice was distorted through the window pane, but it was unmistakably his: warm, but not particularly deep. Finally, he caught me moving and we looked at one another, our eyes widening and then creasing as we smiled. For the over-imaginative, it is deeply surprising when something imaginative actually happens in real life. Not quite able to believe it and feeling slightly hysterical, I darted outside.

"Evie? God, they said you'd moved somewhere down here. Is *this* where you're living now?"

I touched each side of my door frame possessively, and nodded. "What are *you* doing here?"

"What *aren't* I doing here?" He laughed. "That's the question. I thought I hadn't seen you in schul for ages, they said you'd gone off."

"Gone off my head, you mean?"

"Hah! They meant it more prosaically, but I think there might have been some inferences about your sanity, yes."

Alex was always honest with me. Occasionally this was painful, as though someone was gouging at my ego with a sharp instrument. But most of the time, I found it pleasant in a way that I wasn't supposed to. I stared at him, at his already shiny slicked black hair, at his wide, wry mouth. He had a heavy presence; not tall but stocky. His calf muscles were thick and always tight against whatever trousers he wore. He would command attention but then hold back when he wanted to, and let other people clamber towards him. Typical Jewish boy – I knew many people must think that when they watched him talk, dark and voluble, hands describing their own language. Trouble to look beyond that, and Alex wasn't as confident as he made out.

"They must be so bloody relieved that I'm not there any more, or is it a shame that the girls don't have anyone to laugh at? Sorry, I sounded bitter then, didn't I?"

"You did a bit." He smiled.

"I've just painted my kitchen ceiling red."

"Have you? Why?"

"Because my old *bedroom* ceiling was painted blue, obviously."

Alex looked perplexed.

"Opposites? For opposite places?"

"If you say so. You can take over from here, can't you, Dave?"

"Yup." A hovering man, also in shirt sleeves, nodded. "Only been here five minutes, *cherchez la femme* already, eh, Ishy?"

"Come on," Alex said to me. "Show me around."

"It still smells a bit of paint in here, the chemicals might interfere with your brain function."

"Show me around the *village*, you idiot, not your house."

"Oh."

"I don't actually think you're an idiot."

"I know. Be good, Peggy," I called over my shoulder and slammed the door shut.

"Behave yourselves, you two!" the shirt-sleeved one called.

"Who's he?" I whispered.

"Dave."

"He's a bit forward, isn't he?"

"Oh no," said Alex quickly. "That's how men like that talk. I haven't even had a chance to look around yet. You know that I've bought a place here? Literally a 'place': Fielden Place, at the other end of the village that borders on the estate. I don't know," he carried on, "you up here, me down there – we've scattered to the winds!"

"Quite the diaspora." My feet mechanically took it in turns to move forwards, one two, one two, so we chatted back and forth in a pattern. It was almost easy. I should have known it was Alex who had bought Fielden Place; it all made sense in a queasy sort of way. Alex was Margery's foreign name, the spy. In my mind, I had a hazy picture of him outside my house that I wanted to solidify whilst the news sunk in. "So, what were you doing in the lane?"

"Well, strictly *entre-nous*, they are talking about development, and if some new houses go up then I want to be first in there to sell them."

"In my back field?" I had a sharply defined vision of my fruit trees being thrown into permanent shade by looming high-rises.

"No, not the one behind you, the one further up."

"But there's nothing there!"

"That's the point, isn't it? There might end up *being* something there, though."

"But . . ." I thought of Vernon as I floundered. "There's no work here, you know!"

"People don't mind that: Barnsley's just over the way."

"But the unemployed . . ."

"The unemployed can get a job in Barnsley and then buy a flat."

I remembered Old Mrs Isaac's friend, Jane Solomons – her son had bought a bungalow in Barnsley and moved her in with him. This was held as the pinnacle of filial devotion for some time at the synagogue. "Bungalow in Barnsley," I said. I was suddenly pulled back into a little pocket of my old life, suddenly pressed with deep colours and voices chattering.

"What?"

"Nothing."

"Listen, what are the people like? Anyone round here like us?"

"Jewish, you mean?"

"No, Evie. I'm an optimistic man, but I'm not stupid. I mean, you know." He made vague gestures with his hands at our outfits. He was professionally attired, and I was in leggings and an aquamarine sweatshirt with 'Wissette Winery – Cheers to Thirty Years!' emblazoned across the chest. I failed to grasp his meaning.

"I think that you are about to find out what the people are like," I said, as Old Bernard made his way towards us, sombre as the spectre at the feast. "Good morning, Bernard!" I called with patently false cheeriness.

"Cold out," said Old Bernard, squinting distrustfully at the sun. "Cold for June. Warmest month, June. No . . . July. July, it is."

"This is my friend, Alex."

Alex held out his hand, and I felt time slow down as it stayed there, proffered but not taken. Old Bernard's gaze took in Alex's green shirt, the high-waisted chinos with his thick, brown leather belt and brown shoes. Everything about Alex seemed shiny and new this morning, from his hair to his feet. "Where're you from, boy?" he asked.

"I'm down from Leeds, Mister . . . ?"

"Bernard's my name," he said, before turning abruptly to me. "My uncle had the forge, didn't he?"

"Yes," I said.

"My Uncle Alfie."

"Yes, well . . ."

"And my mam fell down the stairs. It was her milk what drove 'er mad, they said." Old Bernard looked surprised, jolted from a daydream. He frowned at Alex, thrust his hands in his pockets and marched off.

Alex and I continued in the opposite direction. I looked at him with a smile itching at the corners of my mouth, ready to laugh at Old Bernard together, but Alex kept his gaze ahead. I realised that Old Bernard had unnerved him – Alex doesn't like it when he can't impress people.

"He didn't mean anything," I said.

"What?"

"Nothing. What's going on then? Back in Alwoodley?"

"Oh. The war caused quite a lot of clucking."

"I think we're going to win," I said. "The Argentinians can't hold out for ever."

"I meant the Israeli war: didn't you know? Operation Peace for Galilee? They do have newspapers outside of Leeds, you know, Evie."

"Not the *Jewish Chronicle*. What are they doing, exactly?"

"What are *we* doing, you mean?" Alex side-eyed me, good-humour seemingly restored, and I laughed. "We are driving back the Palestinians by around twenty-five miles."

"How are we doing that?"

"We are invading Lebanon."

"It doesn't sound very peaceful to me."

"No, well I suppose it *will* bring peace to Galilee – it all depends on how you look at it."

"So, we're at war on two sides, Argentina and Lebanon?"

"I suppose so, and we'll probably win them both. And before you get too side-tracked by the little things, the *big* news is that Mrs Halpern has got that awful prat of a nephew staying with her – Abe – and is insisting on dragging him about. Even to Mrs Leverson's dance, where he refused to bop with Susie Leverson."

"Oh, my *God*!" I cried. It was so much more fun to look in from the outside, I realised. They didn't call it a bird's-eye view for nothing: I could look down at the function room, see the new bunting and hear the band's music – a flattened blare as it reverberated off the smooth walls. I could see Susie Leverson, probably in something lilac that fit as close as cling film, sulking. "Mrs Halpern was very anxious for me to meet him again," I said.

The sun was behind me, so Alex squinted as he looked. His skin shone a little, the beginnings of sweat that was still attractive. His five o'clock shadow had come early, black bristle easy to pick out on his cheeks. "You weren't flattered, were you?" He patted me on the head, something my wiry hair resisted instantly, sending his hand springing away.

"What do you mean?"

"Oh, come on, Evie. He's far worse than I was! You couldn't marry Abe Halpern."

"No," I admitted, wrapping my arms tight around me. "And where are we?" I didn't recognise the street.

"I parked just down here."

"Hello? Helloooo?" A voice floated on the breeze. I caught Alex's look and gave a minute shrug of my shoulders. "Oh, you must be the new people, I thought I'd come over and say hello!" The lady glided to a well-judged halt about three feet from us and smiled, delighted with her own enterprise. I opened my mouth, but she hurried on.

"I'm *Joanie*, Margaret has told me ever so much about you – apparently you do massage and eastern medicine and things. Well, I could do with some of that. I once visited Japan, you know, with my husband, when we were together, for we are now separated. It was a long time ago, of course, although Margaret said that you're on your own too? Hello," she said, turning to Alex, "I'm *Joanie*."

"How . . . how do you do," said Alex. He mastered his bemusement and flashed her a charming smile.

"Of course, we came to live here for the quiet life. Used to live in Barnsley when we were first married, but we were married, oh, fifteen years ago! Oakdale Drive, do you know it? We were number four. My husband, ex-husband soon-to-be, that is, I can never get used to it, said to me, 'Joan, it's time for a change', and, of course, we got an extra bedroom for our money, not that we have children, but I've got a nephew, George, he's ever such a sweet boy. Anyway . . . he's back in Barnsley now. But I like it here, I do . . ."

Once I realised that responses were not required, I moved my head to one side, in an attitude that I hoped indicated intense interest, and had a good look at Joanie. Forty, I supposed, if she married at twenty-five. It was rather a treat in a way, to be able to stare openly at someone so closely. She seemed delicate, her eyelashes short and pale as they caught the sun. Joanie's skin grew mottled pink as she talked, her hair thin, light and pulled backwards into in an odd fan shape at the nape of the neck. She wore an orange silk scarf that drained her face even further and had a small hole at one end.

Silence. Joanie had stopped speaking and was now looking

at us eagerly, rather like that way Peggy looks at me, eyes gently gleaming, when she wants me to feed her.

"Always a pleasure to meet a friendly face," said Alex, catching Joanie's chubby little hand and giving his matinee-idol smile. "I am sure that we will see each other again soon."

"Yes, yes, I am sure we will. At the coffee morning perhaps, or at a WI meeting. The village fete has already been and gone, but . . ."

Alex and I were backing away, waving and nodding. We gave a last valedictory wave and turned our backs, walking away briskly in silence.

"Where are you parked?"

"Village Hall. Hurry, before we're ambushed again."

The Gentlemen's Banjo Club met on a Friday morning at the hall – the softly plucked tonelessness of 'na-na-naaa's floated through the air. I could see Peter through the slightly open door, his long, equine face strangely peaceful, nodding slightly to keep time as he played. We stood, fascinated, beside the double doors. The foxgloves and hollyhocks planted outside were dressed for summer in their yellow, lilac and pink flowers, waving at us. Alex's black sports car stood out in the car park, smooth and glistening like a beetle.

"TR7," said Alex proudly, unlocking it and motioning me inside. "Got it second-hand off a bloke in Liverpool. Hardly any miles on the clock."

"Oh. Does Joanie remind you of Monserrat Caballé?" Dad used to play Monserrat Caballé records sometimes in the evening. The room would fill with the undulations of her voice like concertinaed grosgrain ribbon. Her face on the records used to fascinate me: the regal beauty of that overblown woman, her eyes almost devoured by her face. Her coy, warm smile asked me to admire her, and I did. "It must be awful to have a beautiful face on an ugly body," I mused aloud.

"Or to have a beautiful body with an ugly face?" Alex suggested.

"No, I don't think that's as bad. The first impression is still good with a beautiful body because it is in the majority. Whereas, when you see a pretty face and then it stretches into nothing of the rest of you, it's unattractive. I knew a girl like that once, at school," I said. "She had olive skin and green eyes and wide cheekbones that were so pretty . . ." just like Alex, I thought, and realised why I had always liked her, "but then she had no neck, and was sort of square shaped."

"*I'm* sort of square shaped," said Alex. "I have no illusions about my looks, which is rather attractive in itself, don't you agree?" He smoothed his hair with the flat of his hand.

"Is that why you have a sports car, to make up for your squareness?"

"Watch it. Calves like Mussolini, I thought. Maybe Joanie's a love child of the two."

"Of Monserrat Caballé and Mussolini?"

"Uh hmm!"

"Alex!"

"Oh, don't pretend to be shocked. It makes you seem like other girls." Alex listened to the undiscernible banjo dirge still wafting out of the hall. "I'm not often driven to acts of homicide, but . . .

could we reverse into the Gentlemen's Banjo Club at speed, do you think? The doors are open a bit anyway. It would be a crime, I know, but . . ."

"But a service to music as an art form."

"Exactly." Alex started the engine with a low roar, and I clutched the side of the seat. I felt dazed, the sun pouring white across the windscreen. I closed my eyes and saw dark spots and jagged shapes in brown and red. "Can you believe that we're actually here?" I asked.

"Not really."

"It's very far away from where we normally are. And what we normally are."

"You're right. What tune are they even playing, can you tell?" We listened in strained silence.

"I . . . I think it might be 'Kumbaya'."

"Christ alive, Evie," Alex said, turning to look at me. "What are we getting ourselves into?"

*

I had to wait until the sun went down in order to feel more witchy, but after an exciting day that verged upon the discombobulating, I decided to practice another spell. After all, it was my career now – I was a career witch, fulfilling Aunt Mim's dying wishes and so on.

Edith had told me yesterday morning that she couldn't keep away from the biscuit jar. "Not very healthful," she had said ruefully.

"Yes," I had replied instantly, earning me a bit of a funny look from her. "You are almost as big as Aunt Mim . . ." It was hard to focus on Edith's words, given the magnificently lacquered and hennaed hairstyle she sported, that gleamed like a mahogany cabinet.

"Who's that, love?"

"Oh, nobody," I said hastily. "Nobody very big." Edith had only looked partially reassured.

So here I was, being selfless, drawing a pentacle once again on my shopping list notepad (it could be a cross if one preferred, but being Jewish, one didn't prefer). I went down to the living room and stood on the pentagon, which promptly ripped a little, but I pretended not to notice.

"Edith's Biscuit Jar, be invisible to her, fruit is what she'd prefer. The pentagon I see, so the spell *will* be." I intoned it three times, trying to be more and more emphatic. It was my own spell – rather natty, don't you think?

All the talk of biscuits had made me hungry, though. I took the torn and crumpled pentagon notelet with me into the kitchen to throw away, just keeping the scrap on the back where I had written, 'the whistling man with the lovely black hair'. I'd been trying to think about him, you see, wondering who he was. Then, I had written, 'Alex' underneath, purely by accident.

I opened a jar of honey and dipped my finger in it. As I watched the shiny trail ripple back into the pot, my fingers curled in delight, and I dropped the scrap of paper with the men written on it into the honey.

"Oh!" I pushed all of my fingers into the jar to extract it, and of course just pushed it further in. The paper slowly seeped, growing dark and mottled, the names blurring. I had just cast a *love* spell:

you write the name of the man you love and dip it in honey, everyone knows that. And I had written two, which seemed both greedy and completely unrealistic.

I sighed and extracted my fingers from the pot with a sucking sound. It was Friday, too: the best day for casting love spells (something to do with Venus – I forget the details). What had I done?

I'd have a bath – yes, that would make everything better. But before I went upstairs, I hesitated and took the honey with me. Pouring a little of the honey in your bath made the spell more likely to come true, which is good, isn't it? Even if the spell started as an accident, surely I should see it through.

The Adam Ants didn't have to know.

SUNDAY 13TH JUNE 1982

Lizzie was completely wrong, you know, about people losing interest in you if you shut yourself away. I found quite the opposite, in fact: as soon as I shut myself away in the country, everyone suddenly developed a burning desire to communicate with me.

Lizzie herself is a prime example: she phoned me today, and ... well, I was almost glad to hear from her, because it was Sunday and very quiet and I was beginning to realise that I would actually have to live here every day by myself and the thought made my insides feel a little gouged out.

"I don't want to disturb you, because I know you are 'busy'," she had begun. I am sure that 'busy' was in inverted commas, but really I felt that I had a lot going on now that I was an independent, working witch. "Are you putting sheets down when you paint?"

"No."

"Don't you want us to come and help you? We could drive down next weekend?"

"No."

"Are you eating properly?"

"No."

"Oh, *Evie* . . ."

Lizzie had petered out into silence. I had defeated her, which should have been a happy occasion but always made me feel guilty. "Alex is here," I blurted out. "Alex Ishkowitz. I suppose that Susie must be here as well. They've bought a country house."

"*Well*," breathed Lizzie, defeat all but forgotten. "I knew that he was doing well in Leeds. How nice for you to see an old friend. Well, old friends, I mean – Susie is very nice. I mean . . ."

"You mean that Alex and I could have been living in a country house together?"

"It was your choice," said Lizzie, with a sudden surge of loyalty. "I always liked Alex; your dad wasn't so keen, but then he doesn't understand people who aren't interested in Victorian looms. Perhaps one day you could buy a bigger country house, Evie."

"Suppose."

"You could afford it. Although, it might look a bit odd, you living there alone."

"I'd have to source a husband somewhere," I agreed. "Perhaps Joe will buy a country house one day."

"Not with his salary at the moment." Lizzie sighed.

"And he'd have to take Val to live in it."

"Oh, *Evie*... Val's really very nice, you know. Why, she said only the other day that you could hardly tell about . . . about all your neurology. She has grown up a lot since school, people change . . ."

"Yes, I know. People change and it's All Water Under the Bridge," I said, suddenly bored.

I had hung up after that, and tried not to think about Val. She couldn't get to me in Thornlaw, surely? It was a haven, a place of benevolent neutrality, a little like Switzerland. Today was the first quarter of the moon, and I wouldn't think about the past – I would make plans instead. What was my phrase for Sunday? Oh, yes: "I feel empathy and compassion for all living things." I had pronounced that loudly on my walk this morning.

"That's nice, love," Margaret had said, popping up from weeding her front garden. I now supposed that 'all living things' included Val.

I was about to describe Faithful Cottage, as I never got round to that, did I? I've planned a guided tour with a little help from the estate agent's written and verbal blurb.

Going downstairs of a morning, I wander into the lounge/diner. Perhaps it would be called the Front Room if that didn't make Lizzie wince – or, as I call it, my Main Room. Here, I learn about horticulture whilst Peggy dozes. I listen to the radio, flicking it off impatiently if there is a song I don't like, hanging on through the adverts if there is something promised that I want to hear. The room has a 'dual aspect' apparently, which means that there is a window either end, turning it into a tunnel for whatever light there is.

I can look out on my garden, although not without some feeling of guilt at the moment: it was Shavuot last week, the dairy festival, when Lizzie doesn't mind if we buy frozen cheesecake. It is customary to decorate an outside structure in the garden, reliving the time when our ancestors were travelling through the desert to the land of milk and honey. But I had just moved, so the only outside structures were cardboard boxes piled outside the door. Shavuot had been and gone, and I hadn't even noticed. Guilt has always seemed rather a Catholic concept to me – I am learning now that it can pop up at any given time.

So, quickly turning my head to the other side, I see my lane, resplendently bumpy and slightly leaning uphill, the hedgerows on the other side . . . where Alex Ishkowitz had been outside my window.

Oh dear. Alex Ishkowitz to me is becoming rather like biscuits are to Edith. I just can't leave him alone; one thought is never enough.

MONDAY 14TH JUNE 1982

I pride myself on never being lonely, but tonight I went to the window, watched the sun go in for the night, and wondered if I was wrong. Maybe I have always been lonely but just not recognised it. Maybe I am lonely now. Does loneliness feel a bit like a white, silent hole in your stomach?

The beginning and the end of the day is when I feel completely ... not lonely, perhaps. Let's say *self-contained*. Village life seems to entail people presenting themselves to be spoken to and chatted with during the day, then silence at night.

For example, I'd had my second – no less voluble – encounter with Joanie earlier today, outside the village shop. I had decided to get there early, estimating the time it would take me to walk there by measuring my strides with a tape measure through the main room. It was better to be accurate about these things, I thought. I arrived twenty minutes before opening time.

Passing the time, hopping from one foot to the other, trying to work out exactly what the air smelt of and peering in between the slats of the window shutters, Joanie had crept up behind me.

"Well, it *is* nice to see you again!"

I nodded, unsure of whether I could assimilate Joanie's chatter this early in the morning. But it turned out that her babbling had a strangely soporific effect. It seemed to gush around me like a pleasant stream.

"Eccles cakes," she was saying. "I am so partial. I mean, I shouldn't be . . ." she stared at her stomach fondly, "but really, I used to make them all the time back home, in Barnsley. They were very popular. I was *known* for my Eccles cakes."

"Really?" I wondered what Eccles cakes were – the pancakey things? Or was that lardy cake? Lizzie and Dad didn't really go in for cakes.

". . . so, I thought, why not make some?" Joanie suddenly looked anxious. "I expect that they'll have all the fruit, wouldn't you say? I have some raisins left from the cake I made Margaret for her stall last year, although there were so many cakes, she didn't have room to put it out and it stayed under the counter for quite some time. Not that I minded, of course. It's all for charity. There were donkeys, too, at the fête. I just hope that they have sultanas..."

"At the fête?"

Joanie giggled. "No, *silly*. In the shop." Despite the warmth, she was wearing leather gloves of deep pink, the colour of fuchsias. She began plucking nervously at the seamed edges around her wrist.

"Oh."

"So much better than currants. I do hope they have them. You can never tell. In Barnsley..."

I pressed my face to the window and narrowed my eyes, trying to glimpse the shelves through the spaces in the shutters. "There's the dried fruit, over there. I can see ... oh, that's desiccated coconut."

Joanie pressed her nose next to mine. "Oh, what are those?"

"Dried apricots, I think."

"Oh dear." We spent a surprisingly companiable moment, side by side, noses to the glass, intent upon a packet of sultanas. Mrs Grimes began to move about inside the shop, putting on her apron and straightening various packets. She caught sight of us and raised a dangerously plucked eyebrow. Joanie and I stepped back as one, and I opened my mouth to remark upon the fine weather.

"I suppose that we should be very English and talk about

the weather, because we are in a queue, but I always think that there are so many other things to talk about, don't you?" said Joanie.

"Oh, yes," I replied, my mind a complete blank.

"Words, for instance. I think that people don't use enough words nowadays."

"Umm . . ."

"I am getting very fond of wordsearches; do you do them? No, I suppose you are too young to enjoy it," said Joanie wistfully. "But you see, each wordsearch is themed. You know, all sorts of themes. Elvis Presley, for example, or gardening. It really is absorbing."

"So, you collect the words."

"Exactly. Well, you have to find them." Joanie looked at me intently, and I went all red. "I think that you would be good at finding words, Evie. You *look* like that sort of person."

"I do collect words," I said. "But in my head, rather than in magazines."

"Oh, I should try and do that! I could start my own collection. Now . . . what would my first word be . . .? Let me think . . ."

Mrs Grimes opened the shop door with a sharp wrench and impeccable timing. We filed guiltily in. There were no sultanas.

*

Talking with Joanie, I felt as though I was being so sociable and normal. "Look at me," the voice in my head crowed. Then, evening drew in, people retreated into private, divided worlds, and I was left alone. My thoughts started to somersault over themselves, undistracted now by faces and countryside and sun. They developed a life of their own, becoming coloured and garishly real inside my mind. I hated Susie Leverson, I realised. I couldn't control Aunt Mim's visits, and what had happened to those oranges she was carrying? I missed Dad, Lizzie and Joe – an ache as voluptuous as a woman in a Lely painting. I had gone through a Lely phase, you see, perhaps because I am so angular and admire what I shall never have.

I thought of witches: Strega Nonna, Mother Shipton, Peggy Flounders. And I wondered whether I would know somehow if I was dark or light in my witching, and if my life would make a sudden leap forward or whether I would remain locked inside myself, as stuck in my new life as the old.

I thought of Alex, and I wondered why my collision with him now seemed such a high point. He was something from the Past, with a capital P, so why was I pleased to see him? We had gone for a drive. The weather had turned and we had pointed out funny-shaped rain clouds to one another. I had pointed out some trees too, but I hadn't been able to see any poplars.

"Do you want to know some facts about sycamores?" I had asked him.

"Not in the slightest. Do you remember the first time we met?" Alex had asked me.

I had thought about him all weekend.

Then, I had found a postcard through my door today, on one side of the doormat, being sniffed by Peggy.

"Great to see you, Evie – what shall we do next time? It'd be good to see one another before Susie comes up and before Malcolm arrives and

it all goes to hell. He gets things moving, does Malcolm. A xx"

How exciting, I had thought. And who was Malcolm?

WEDNESDAY 16TH JUNE 1982

Another postcard, this time from Dad. He had slipped it in with my Opal Whiteley book, on the page about the flowering horse chestnut tree, which he knows is my absolute favourite tree. It had taken me all this time to find it.

"Take care of yourself, Evie, and pleasant studying! Your Dad. P.S. Shouldn't this book be back in the library now? P.P.S. I think that you should put up some more shelves in the living room – get someone in the village to help you, shelving is not my forte. P.P.P.S. For HEAVEN'S SAKE, be careful of that bathroom light pull – it isn't strong, so do NOT be vehement!!"

I had sobbed, whispering "Dad," quite pathetically over and over. Then, I had dried my eyes and gone to the village coffee morning.

The village hall smells strange when you go inside: floor wax and cobwebs, layered over with coffee. A serving hatch opened up onto the sound of footsteps and chinking china. Floor wax and feet – they all pressed together but never became a smooth whole, more of a bundle of kicking arms and legs. Still, Wednesdays are Coffee Morning Wednesdays in Thornlaw and I, Evie Edelman, was attending.

"Magick flows through me, as it has flowed through each witch in time," I muttered to myself. Technically, one went to these coffee mornings for society and buns, but I was going with the nefarious intent of finding myself a coven. I had spent too long tramping about on my own, getting lost and watching the bluish woodsmoke from bonfires and chimneys settle across the fields in a horizontal line. Woodsmoke always makes me feel nervous – I know that it is how Yorkshire smells, but it just makes me think of burning.

"Morning, nice out, in't it? Morning, Terry. Morning, Mae." Margaret bustled in.

"Hello, Margaret. Mild, in't it? I could wear my bikini!"

"So could I."

"Terry!" Margaret and Mae were scandalised.

Vernon and Dot came in. I waved at Dot but she immediately turned to Terry and began plucking at his shoulders. "Let me get this coat off you – you shouldn't have even worn it today . . ."

"I'm all right. Leave it!"

"The Jewish woman is a queen in her own kitchen – and not always a benevolent ruler." Mr Abrams had chuckled and nudged me. "Anything I can help with, ladies?"

I was back in Alwoodley, hanging around outside the synagogue kitchen, listening to the tinny crinkle of foil as it was taken off the trays.

"Charlie Abrams, stay out!" That was Sarah Leverson, rolled-up sleeves, clip-on earrings of imitation pearls. She looked at me, eyes sparkling with irritation. "And you, Evie – you'd better stay out as well."

"Hold on out there, I'm coming." Now, Edith wheeled a trolley piled with a tea urn, cups, saucers and a plateful of very yellow bouncy sponge squares cut with a thin line of jam. The trolley made a sing-song of shivering crockery as it rolled, one of its wheels flaring out and in. Edith kept to her course, hunched and determinedly steering her path.

"You are wearing green, like when I saw you the other day," I noted.

"It's me colour." Edith patted her hair. "Redheads should always wear green. Sometimes I add a *hint* of purple."

"Edith, are those sponges handmade?" Joanie appeared behind me noiselessly, just as I had been about to ask Edith whether that rule applied even with dyed red hair.

"Well, I didn't make them with my feet," she answered tartly.

"Edith, I thought about bringing biscuits," I began experimentally.

"Oh *no*, love," said Edith, wrinkling up her face, and I realised then and there that my spell had worked. How thrilling!

"Let me go . . ." Joanie was struggling with the buttons of her coat as frowningly as a child, elbows wide, "in the kitchen, I can help . . ."

"Oh *no*, love." Edith shot me a look. "You stay out 'ere and enjoy yourself. Have a chat with Evie, here."

"Are you going to have tea, Edith?"

"Oh, just a glass of water, thanks. I really couldn't manage anything else."

"They said you were foreign," said Terry, seizing a sponge square.

"Only a bit foreign," I replied, trying to sound reassuring rather than surprised. Was I foreign? Being Jewish, I wasn't really sure. I had a British passport of course, but there was more to it than that. Sometimes I felt pulled in different directions, rather like a rubber band that eventually turns colourless and snaps.

"Not an *Argie*, are you?"

"Oh, no."

"Bastards sunk the *Sheffield*, you know." Terry narrowed his eyes at me suspiciously, as though I might have known the perpetrators.

"Yes, I know." There wasn't much else to say, I thought. "What do you do for a living?" Always a safe bet with men, I thought – ask them about their work. I had watched Lizzie doing that often enough.

There was a strange pause, during which I had to look away from Terry's level, expressionless gaze. "Not a lot, since they closed the pits," he said.

"Listen," said Margaret, "have you all heard? About Flatt Field?"

Vernon harrumphed his assent. Mae nodded. I realised that I had not yet heard her voice.

"Developers! Going to build an estate."

"Oh no!" Dot gaped in disbelief. "We don't want any of *that* round here!"

"Drugs," said Edith sagely.

"It's not safe," Dot wailed.

"Don't be daft, woman," said Vernon. "It won't get built, will it?

151

I mean, there's no jobs, no nothing. Look at 'er," – I realised to my surprise that he was indicating me – "unemployed. No prospects round 'ere, is there?"

"Err . . . well, no," I said. "I suppose not."

"Bloody woman." My heart did a cold skip of fear, but it appeared that Vernon was not referring to me this time. "Thatcher," he qualified.

"D'you know, I think that if my mam and dad could have seen into the future, they would have christened me something else," said Margaret.

"Paul not with you, Margaret?" Terry asked suddenly.

"No, you know what 'e's like."

"It's nice that we get so many men coming along," said Edith.

"Only us old codgers," said Terry. "The young ones are too embarrassed to be seen knocking about in the middle of the day."

"Morning, all!" Margery barrelled in, Kevin following in a Superman costume. He ran straight up to the trolley, took a sponge cake in his fat fingers and squeezed it until the yellow debris erupted out of his hand and fell onto the other slices. "Kevin, don't do that, love. Here," she turned to me and I prepared myself for another onslaught, looking at the open door behind her longingly, "I saw you talking to that developer bloke – he looked a right one! Fancy shoes and everything. What did he say about the field?"

"Oh, that's Al— Mr Ishkowitz," I said. "He's not a developer; he's the one that's bought Fielden Place."

"Well, he won't like it out 'ere," said Margery with disapproval.

"Not with 'is fancy clothes and winkle-pickers. Very young to buy somewhere like that. Where do they get their money from?"

"Drugs?" Edith hazarded, slightly less sagely than before.

Margaret squinted at me, as though seeing me all over again.

"You two *did* look friendly . . ."

"I'm going to get some more cake from the kitchen. Lend us a hand, love," Edith said.

"Those *developers*, putting up their Jerry-built houses that folks can't afford – they're the devil," said Terry darkly.

I followed Edith to the kitchen, taking advantage of the coiffed back of her head to recover from all the faces, all those eyes trained on me. *Alex?* It was a silent clarion call.

"That Margery," Edith said sotto voce when we were inside, our shoes squeaking on the linoleum. "Always something or other. First it was foreign spies at Fielden Place, or the KGB or whatnot, now she has him down as your Prince Charming." She looked at me shrewdly, her set curls stiff and unyielding. "If you've come here to get a fresh start, you know, after a broken engagement or something, then I won't say a word. It happens more and more with you young people – men going off and suchlike . . . look at Joanie, even." She sighed.

Margaret came in, followed by a wave of Joanie's voluble chatter and then, a split second later, Joanie herself.

"You know, Evie, you should have told everyone about your massage and things," said Margaret, setting down a tray with a remonstrating slap on the counter and piling napkins and spoons onto it. "You shouldn't be shy, love."

"Margaret, do you like the smell of burning wood?" I suddenly asked her.

"What an odd thing . . ." Margaret looked away and began laying out more tea things. "Well, no, as it happens. You see, I always think . . . Edith, there's not enough saucers."

"There never is."

"I could bring some saucers with me next time," offered Joanie quickly. "I've got this tea set you see, it belonged to my late mother-in-law and then she gave it to us, well, anyway . . ."

A general air of listlessness set in as Joanie began. I wondered whether this was an offer that Joanie made frequently, as she ploughed onwards. ". . . lovely autumn leaves around the edge in a pattern, although of course the cups were different shapes compared to these ones, so the indentation bit might be a bit small. It was always too showy for us, and now . . ." The enthusiasm in Joanie's voice died.

Was Joanie witchy like me, I wondered? I couldn't imagine her pausing her own chaos long enough to do a spell or a hex.

"Well, whatever you think is best, Joan," said Edith firmly.

"I must be going," said Margaret. "I've left Paul on his own long enough – I promised him I'd only look in but I wouldn't be gone too long."

"What's wrong with Paul?" I asked after Margaret had left, tying on a headscarf in spite of the milky sun.

"Depression, I think, after he got laid off," said Joanie.

"Nonsense, men don't get things like that," said Edith. "There's really now't wrong with Paul except in Margaret's head. Fills her days, you see, fussing over him. You're young and healthy," she said, looking at me almost accusingly, "you wouldn't understand."

"Edith, now, do we put more cups on the trolley and then the cake plates on *top*? Or do we put the cakes on a level with the cups and then just do two trips?" Joanie looked up at us. "I mean, would the cakes stay on if they were on top, or would they wobble about . . ."

"They wouldn't wobble unless you were planning to run the Grand National with that bloody trolley, Joan. Oh, do it however you like."

"I just assumed that this was the best way." Joanie put a hand pensively to her chin, reminding me of Rodin's *The Thinker*. "It's better to do things right, isn't it?"

I thought that I would prefer to have got it wrong rather than go through all that.

*

Exit stage left, pursued by . . . something. That's Shakespeare, isn't it? One of the plays we didn't study at school. I exited the coffee morning through the double doors at the front, edging around the swelling number of little groups, pursued by a motley collection of words and phrases.

". . . son-in-law, ever such a nice . . . prefer them without the icing . . . still no luck . . . dole . . . more milk . . . clouding over now." I freed Peggy from the luxurious prison of the Alpine Sunbeam and we got walking, in the opposite direction to Faithful Cottage. I wasn't ready to go home just yet.

I had expected the village to be deserted on coffee morning

day, like a ghost town in a cowboy film, the gathering inside lured by the promise of sponge slices. But I saw people on the opposite side of the street, cars driving past, even a couple of ramblers looking hot and uncomfortable in their thick trousers and boots. Life clearly continued outside the confines of the village hall, and I was no closer to finding my coven.

For a while I just walked, but there came a point where I could pretend to be aimless no longer.

"Fielden Place," I said to myself. I had never seen it, only heard it said proudly by Alex and casually by the villagers.

The Fielden Place of my mind had taken shape as a red brick, square Queen Anne house (I wasn't quite sure of the salient points of Queen Anne architecture, so I just made things very symmetrical and then blurred the details). There was a topiary garden at the front – just a little one – and a lavender bush either side of the gate, tamed into perfect circles. I had better go along now, I thought, while the house was empty, and get an impression of reality to blend into my imaginary version.

The village started to thin out as it reached the edge of the Fielden Estate – green pouring into the increasing space, the houses becoming outliers. Whatever weak sunshine there was had vanished, leaving nothing much behind – a pale sky and an absence of heat or cold. I stepped onto Fielden land and felt as though I was trespassing.

I knew Fielden Place as soon as I saw it, although it was different from the house I had imagined. It was Yorkshire stone after all, as it always would have been, with very attractive

Georgian windows and an ash tree (Latin name *fraxinus*, related to olive and lilac trees) throwing a round shadow over the front lawn. I could see the back of a pelmet across the top of the largest window but nothing much more, so I went closer. And by closer, I mean leaning my forehead against the windowpane.

I hadn't expected to see anything much through the warp of the old glass, but there was Alex, a horizontal stack of books in his hand, searching for a place on the alcove shelves to put them. I drew back, but he hadn't seen me, so I watched him for a second that grew longer and longer. Finally, feeling wrong, I turned and trudged down the path. What was so guilt-inducing about watching other people, I wondered?

"Evie?"

"Oh, hi."

So he had caught sight of me. I wondered if he was regretting that immediate impulse to say hello, as I often did. It trapped you, that initial greeting, committing you to something more that you couldn't deliver.

"What are you doing here, Evie?"

"I was thinking of developing that field over there behind your house, building some high-rises . . . Only joking."

"Very bloody funny. Come in, then."

"Can I? Can Peggy come in too?" It wasn't my house, my land, my part of the village. The hall behind Alex looked dark, the windows seemed opaque and staring.

"Course." He beckoned me inside.

"Are you going to give me the grand tour? I showed you round the village last week."

"Oh, all right then. Hall."

I nodded.

"Bedrooms and bathrooms upstairs – five bedrooms, if you count the box room, which of course nobody does, and here is the drawing room." Alex ushered me into a long room. It was corniced, scalloped and dadoed to the point of being vaguely ridiculous, like a museum squashed into somebody's home. Its lower half was green, deep and pale at the same time, its upper regions wallpapered and flecked with pink sprays of botanically incorrect flowers. The whole room was preternaturally dim, waiting patiently for its furniture and carpet.

"It's so big and . . . and grown-up," I said, with wonderment.

"You could have bought this, you know. Didn't you ever think of making an investment, Evie? You probably could have bought Fielden Hall if you'd wanted to."

"Why would I want to?" I watched him, trying to relearn his face that looked different in the poor light. Alex was too far away to be able to know what he smelt like – sweat, maybe, or aftershave that was the equivalent of bright, aqua blue. "You're in jeans," I added.

"Well spotted. You're in jeans, too."

"It was coffee morning," I said, by way of explanation.

Alex smiled maddeningly and shook his head.

"What?"

"We're going to get some people over for a housewarming soon; you should come to that. Then you can meet some proper people."

I didn't think this was a house that could ever be warm. "Aren't you going to offer me a cup of tea and a sponge slice?"

"I wasn't planning on it. I was going to ask if you would help me with these books, if you must know."

For a while, there was nothing but the gentle, satisfying thud of books being placed on the shelves in twos and threes. Peggy had settled disconsolately on the parquet. Then, Alex started singing to himself. "Her name is Magic, and she dances in your hand," he mumbled tunelessly, to the tune of 'Rio' by Duran Duran. Had he forgotten that I was there? I could never have forgotten myself in front of him, I was always aware of his dark shape in the corner of my eye, his breath getting shorter as he reached the higher shelves.

"Margaret Drabble," I said, almost to myself.

"Hmmm?"

"Oh, and Margeret Kennedy too . . . Doris Lessing . . ."

"For heaven's sake, you sound like a teacher ticking off her school register."

"Have you got any Anita Brookner?"

"Erm . . . no. You can take a book, if you like?" He offered suddenly.

"No thanks," I said, offended. "I have my own books, why would I want one of yours?" Lizzie's voice yammered in my head, telling me to ask after Susie. But it was too late to appear anything other than unnatural if I asked now, even if I had wanted to. "You read a lot of lady novelists," I said instead.

"I'll let you into a secret: these books are my mother's. I couldn't have empty bookshelves – I mean, a lot of people do, but it wouldn't look right in a Jewish house, would it?"

"Is this a Jewish house?"

Alex laughed. "It is now."

"Carting your mother's books over here – I think that's cheating."

"We can't all be bookworms. How many books do you get through a month?"

"Well, I read thirty pages a day, so . . ."

"Huh?"

"Sometimes twenty-five, if I'm busy."

"But what happens if there's something really exciting going on and you get to page thirty-one or twenty-six?"

"Then it waits until tomorrow."

"I couldn't wait."

"You lack willpower," I said sternly.

"Better to be weak-willed than casually insulting."

We looked at one another – there was a space in which to do something and nothing was done. We could have kissed, but we didn't, and neither of us seemed quite sure why we held back. So we stood and watched one another. Sometimes Alex was the boy I had known for years and his familiarity made me affectionate, but then he would become a man – someone foreign who led a life away from me. Our differences separated us once again, the wall between us with little gaps through which we could only partially see one another. I thought about the sticky piece of paper with his name blurring as it steeped in honey.

Alex handed me a book with a pungent smell of disintegration emanating from it – the edges of the pages were curled and discoloured. "Here," he said, "you had better take this one, it looks just right for you."

I studied the blurb. It seemed that a respectable woman left her respectable life behind in order to move to the country and pursue her calling as a witch.

"It doesn't sound like me at all," I said, with a mirthless little laugh.

"Silly Evie. Why are you here really?"

"I'm . . . I'm finding myself, I suppose," I answered.

"How very American of you."

"I don't really mean it in an American way."

"Oh, good. You had me worried for a second."

"Always so facetious."

"Now you sound like my mother."

"I practice witchcraft here," I said suddenly.

"Now you sound like a madwoman."

"Would you mind if I was mad?"

"I don't mind," Alex said. "You are mad in such a pleasant way. Quite harmless, really."

"You make me sound like a poodle." Madness, witchcraft, Asperger's – sometimes, in my darker moments, I wondered which label fit me best. Were they mutually exclusive, or the same thing? Did I choose one of the selection like a chocolate out of a box, or was the whole point that I couldn't choose?

I opened my mouth to ask what Alex was doing in Thornlaw, but it seemed to have such an odd inevitability about it that I didn't really need to ask. I felt so comfortable beside him, unpacking, talking without having to look.

It was starting to get dark when Peggy and I finally left, our feet scrunching over the gravel. The first time I had seen Alex in Thornlaw – sunny, green and gold – he'd walked beside me and said, "Do you know that I've bought a place here?" He hadn't said 'we', I thought, not ever. Perhaps, I thought, my stomach fluttering and flickering like a weak flame, Susie would never come. Perhaps it would only ever be Alex's house.

SUNDAY 20TH JUNE 1982

I think that I have had a brush with Satanic powers.

I'd wandered into an anonymous field and sat down in the middle of the grass before I really knew what I was doing. I was lost, you see, before that – perhaps in both its meanings.

Alex had been following me around Faithful Cottage ever since I saw him post-coffee morning last week. He hadn't telephoned, but I kept seeing his black hair, surrounded by the arsenic-green of his painted walls. In the end, in the fading light this evening, I couldn't stand sharing my cottage with him anymore. I took Peggy for a kind of desperate walk – I didn't care where I ended up.

In the anonymous field that I found, Peggy instantly clambered onto my lap and sat there, her warmth balancing the cold ground beneath me. Even there, Alex pushed any logical train of thought away.

I lifted my head back into the fading light, looking up at the hills that imposed themselves upon the sky. Alex was hard to fathom, which of course made him endlessly fascinating to me. He was capable of saying something clever and thoughtful in the middle of a sentence bookended by chatter about the housing market. He had a streak of pretentiousness about him that forced him to conceal effort behind seemingly casual gestures, such as handing one a work of fiction about oneself. But then he sometimes went to great effort to conceal his shallowness too. I never knew which way round he really was.

The dark fell suddenly. I had thought that I could see Thornlaw in the distance but the soft mass of shapes could be anything. Then, it started to rain. A light, insinuating drizzle cooled the evening and made me lonely.

Satan must have invented drizzle, I thought to myself. Drizzle and coffee mornings. When you think about it, lots of things in life seemed to be the work of the Devil. There was poverty, suffering, disgusting carpets, iceberg lettuce that went flaccid too quickly . . . All sorts of things. Then I realised that this was rather a dark thought, even for me. I had a brief vision of Rabbi Guld, and tried to think no more about it.

Nevertheless, as I tucked Peggy and the witchy, disintegrating book Alex had insisted I take underneath my shirt, I had to admit that I was having a sort of reverse-epiphany: I had an Alpine Sunbeam parked at the village hall that really still belonged to Aunt Mim, and was embarking upon a journey of discovery and magick that a character in a novel had embarked upon a full sixty years before me. There were probably more disheartening things than a lack of originality, but at the moment I couldn't think of any. I stumbled in what I hoped was the right direction.

Could one die in the wilds of Yorkshire? There were tears threatening along the lower rims of my eyes and a steady assault of drizzle on my face. I felt peculiarly one-dimensional, as though I didn't really exist properly, as though the rain could make me buckle and melt me down into pulp. If I touched my own body now, hands claw-like, searching for something concrete, my fingers would have closed around air.

A low wall came out of nowhere, I scraped my shins against the jagged little edges of its stones and reeled away, heading towards a dark mass that may or may not have been my village. Somewhere in my childhood, I thought, I would have had a nightmare about this. My feet hurt, a sudden breeze whipped the rain around and behind me, pushing me forwards. I could feel my damp shirt clinging to my back in folds and tendrils of hair sticking to my forehead.

"You haven't even found a coven, just a bunch of old women with sponge slices," I said to myself, my voice both petulant and quavering at the same time. "You haven't even memorised the poplar category yet – you're supposed to know all about bloody trees and bloody plants and everything."

I was a failed witch, it seemed. Or a dark witch? My thoughts were dark, suddenly, and my Saturday phrase about healing rather than harming wanted to invert itself.

Stumbling, clutching reflexively at the bundle of Peggy under my shirt, I lost my temper. "Shit, bugger, fuck!" I yelled. They were the worst words I knew. "And where are you, Satan?" I screamed into the sky for good measure.

"You all right? I heard you calling."

I turned and squinted against a circle of light that beamed at me and refracted in all directions. For a moment it seemed to be hovering in mid-air, but then I could make out horn-rimmed spectacles underneath it, a white collar, a tie and . . . was that the head of a biro clipped onto his shirt pocket?

"Are you . . . Him?" I asked tentatively. Peggy stuck her head out of my shirt and yipped savagely in his direction.

"I don't know, am I? My name's Malcolm."

What an odd name for the Devil in human form, I thought. Still, I suppose that he thought it would make him blend in. There was an odd lilt to his voice that made me run through a list of accents in my head – Irish, was it, or Scottish? Perhaps even Scouse? No, Geordie. Malcolm was a Geordie, with a short nose that made him look impish. I wavered physically, reaching slightly towards him until a stab of pain stretching over the ball of my ankle sent my weight back onto the other foot.

"Oh, you're hurt, aren't you? I'm not surprised, out here," he said. "Here, lean on me. I'll see you home."

I snaked my arm around his shoulders, noting the slight sheen of his thick, black hair with approval. As we made our way gingerly off, he began whistling.

MONDAY 21ST JUNE 1982:
MIDSOMMAR (VERY IMPORTANT)

I can't write much this evening, being a little out of breath from all the dancing. At the same time, it would feel odd not to write on the Summer Solstice. A diary is truly like a friend, isn't it? All fun at first, everything voluntary, then comes the compunction. It is Midsommar, so record I must.

Anyway, Midsommar: the highlight of any self-respecting witch's calendar. Any white witch, that is – I am not a dark witch, not really, in spite of Satan appearing in human form the other night. No, I am all about the rituals of the solstice – outside feasting and celebrating light and warmth. I had my evening sandwich outside in the garden, put an Adam Ant record on in my head, and bopped. Susie Leverson would have been impressed. But I mustn't think about Susie Leverson, or Alex. Alex has nothing to do with my witching and therefore isn't important, I suppose. I mustn't think about Malcolm either.

If this was romantic fiction, having rescued the fair maiden, Malcom would have called round the next day with a bunch of flowers to check on her ankle, and love would have blossomed. But it has been a whole day since Malcolm dropped me off, refused the offer of an (admittedly rather threadbare) towel, looked guardedly at Peggy whose yipping had resumed, and went quickly on his way. He hadn't even crossed the threshold of Faithful Cottage.

This morning, feeling less damp and fairly rested, I realised that I should have expected some words of wisdom from Malcolm. I mean, what was the point of Him manifesting otherwise? He *did* tell me that showers were forecast for the next couple of days, but that wasn't really the type of wisdom I was hoping for.

Oh, there seems an awful lot of people not to think of. Still, I managed for a while. "How lucky," I kept telling myself, "that I have a job that takes me into the fresh air rather than being stuck in an office. People who aren't career witches have no idea what they are missing."

Then I got my hair caught in a low branch of the quince tree. I had to snap it off, go inside and untangle it.

TUESDAY 22ND JUNE 1982

I feel duty-bound to report that my magick progresses, Satanic appearances aside. Margaret popped by because the rain had made her fingers swell. I massaged them in the main room, whilst she said that she was glad her son took that job in the stationer's rather than going in the army because of all this Argentinian Business, although they've surrendered now so it's all sorted out for the best.

Mae's cat went missing and I found her. She is silver-grey and as difficult to hold as a slinky toy, but I carried her round to Mae's little house.

Mae said, "She never lets anyone she doesn't know hold her; you must have something about you." I just nodded – better not to go into specifics.

Her house was ever so cold, but she said that she never has the heating on in the day – too expensive. Mae ended by giving me a new twenty-pence piece and I held it pressed in my palm all the way home: my first wage as a witch!

A lady called Rhoda also called in because she heard that I have healing hands, and she wants me to do her feet. She lives with her mum, Vi, who apparently is terrifically old and doesn't leave the house.

Such a sudden interest in me – perhaps Malcolm has materialised to work his own magick on my behalf? Perhaps my magick isn't aside from him at all. What a terrifying thought – it makes me shimmer with excitement.

FRIDAY 25TH JUNE 1982

Is it all right to make a cassette with the same song at the beginning and end? 'Kings of the Wild Frontier' had sort of bookended the tape, and seemed to describe me and Alex. I had asked both my Adam Ants and they'd just looked ahead with a hint of stoniness – I had been neglecting them, you see, for real men. Sometimes, I hummed the chorus of 'Rio' over and over, and smiled. It didn't matter that I hadn't seen Alex for ages, I reckoned, as we were just friends now. Old friends. Acquaintances, even – kings of a wild frontier. The tape was just a friendly gift. For old times. I thought of beaches, golden colours, as I hummed, but suddenly the golden sand would be obscured by the white light of a torch and I thought of Malcolm instead, pleasantly black and white.

The days sometimes slowed down at odd hours in the middle of the morning or afternoon, as if time was getting lazy for a second. I could almost hear the dragging hand of an invisible clock. Then, something always distracts me and time speeds up again. Can witches do that or is Malcolm pushing and then pulling me, controlling my days?

There was a knock at the door. I just got there in time to see Joanie scurrying down the path furtively, hand over her face as if she was a film star avoiding the paparazzi. I called to her, but she pretended not to hear. On the doorstep was a Tupperware container filled with some rather dank-looking beige discs, and a note sellotaped to the top.

> *Dear Evie,*
>
> *I do hope that you don't mind, but I finally got around to making some Eccles cakes and of course thought of you. It took me ages to find sultanas, and in the end I didn't have enough raisins either!!! Goodness, I am out of the habit of cooking – well, when you're on your own. Anyway, I forgot to check whether you actually like Eccles cakes, and if you don't then please do throw them away – I really, really won't be offended. Honestly, you don't have to eat them. But I just thought that you'd like some, possibly.*
>
> *Yours, Joanie*
>
> *P.S. Could the first word on my list be jacaranda, do you think? Or is it silly?*

There was a disapproving intake of breath behind me. "Well," said Aunt Mim. "I'm no expert, but I really don't think that the texture of the pastry is supposed to look like that."

"Has dying made you a culinary expert?" I asked innocently.

"Don't be cheeky. It . . . it gives you a new perspective at least," replied Aunt Mim.

SATURDAY 26TH JUNE 1982

The tape for Alex is nearly done. It was by a series of slow turns of cogs in a wheel that I realised I missed Alex; each little realisation made me sad. I was wondering whether to include 'Prince Charming' on the cassette tape, but decided not, as my stomach felt oddly chilled every time I thought about it.

Then I heard a car breaking to a decorous halt outside the cottage. Looking out, I saw my parents' beige Ford transplanted to Thornlaw as if it had travelled from another realm. Lizzie was nearest me, in the passenger seat. She got out without looking at the house, lips set together. Then, Dad: I watched his top quarter above the car and felt peculiarly as though I was looking at myself in a mirror. I had missed him, but I hadn't known that until he appeared in front of me.

"Debonair and carefree hostess, Evie," I muttered to myself as I sauntered to the door and opened it. I watched with growing comprehension as Dad opened the boot and laboriously dragged out a small lawnmower. They had come *to interfere*.

"What are you *doing* here?" I shouted, shattering the rustling

Saturday peace. Debonair and carefree could wait until another time.

"We thought we'd come and visit," said Lizzie cheerfully. She was wearing magenta lipstick – her voice sounded as bright as the colour. There was an air of missionary zeal about her this morning that wasn't terribly Jewish.

"I'm going to mow your lawn," announced Dad, and marched around to the side gate.

"Did you drive down here just to come and mow my lawn?" I called after him.

"*Yes,*" he said thunderously, and marched away.

"You weren't busy, were you?" Lizzie followed me into the living room, and I suddenly supposed that I should have cleared the books and newspapers that were scattered over the sofa. I could have changed the wildflowers I'd picked, too – they were now brown-stemmed and careering downwards, their petals dried and delicate as the cobwebs on the windowsill. My living room had never looked fusty or untidy before Lizzie stood in the middle of it.

"I was making a cassette tape, actually. *Don't* touch them, it goes the other way round," I said, a distinctly adolescent note creeping back into my voice as Lizzie absent-mindedly turned one of my porcelain rabbits on the mantelpiece to a different angle.

"We haven't seen you for ages, Evie . . ."

"Do you want some crisps?"

"What? No. Do you know, I saw a *very* odd-looking woman coming out of the cottage two doors down. Bright red hair, lacquered like a helmet! And bright green nails. I mean, she was well over fifty . . ."

"That's Edith," I said with mild surprise. "And why are you lowering your voice like that? It's only you and me in the lounge."

"*Lounge?* Who taught you to say that?"

"Margaret calls it the lounge," I said.

There was a moment's silence. "Now," Lizzie rummaged in her bag, excited and imbued with purpose. She pulled out a fat wodge of paper. "I've got this *catalogue* – lots of lovely ideas for curtains and cushions and things, and I thought that you and I could have a look and then go on a trip to Laura Ashley one day . . . Does Peggy always jump up like this?"

"Hmmm? No, she's just being friendly."

"Oh. Well, anyway, looking at this, I really think that we ought to go either for green or pale pink in here." Lizzie's eyes gave a critical sweep of the main room. The sun on one side of her hair made it look falsely golden. "It's all the rage at the moment, green and pink, and they are sort of country colours, aren't they? So, they'd suit it . . . out here. Look, isn't it pretty?"

I tried and failed to take in a sort of spiralling affair with pink splodges of flower before glazing over. "Look," I said, "I don't want any of that stuff."

"Well . . . if you don't like the pink, how about this?"

"I don't like green on a *wall*."

"What about . . . ?"

"I hate pink and wallpaper and I don't like cushions and . . . I just don't really care." I looked at Lizzie's face and my throat clogged as I realised that I had hurt her feelings. I could tell from the way her pupils flared open and then retracted, just before her gaze lowered. Hurting Lizzie's feelings was such a familiar, nasty catch in my windpipe; an oddly burnt-orange coloured feeling that tasted of crumbling things.

Lizzie stared down at the catalogue, at the picture of the bedroom with the pink wallpaper. "I just thought . . . it would look nice," she said, and I could think of no riposte. How does one argue with the concept of nice? The room filled with regret.

"It would look nice in your house," I said, "but not in mine. Actually," I added, reviving, "my bedroom is pink, remember? Sugarplum."

"Will you be able to sleep in that?"

"I should think I'd be able to."

It was a shame, I thought, that Lizzie didn't have a daughter to do the things she liked with. Perhaps the situation would have been mitigated by a little tact on my part: I shouldn't have said what I thought – Aunt Mim was right about that. The trouble was that when people asked me things, I usually said what I thought – it came as naturally as breathing. I could have tried to say something tactful to Lizzie right now, but it suddenly became as difficult as moving around in a dark room without bumping into furniture. Instead, I looked out of the back window as Dad humped the lawnmower into place and switched it on.

"He mowed ours on Thursday, and I said to him, get Mauri to do it . . ."

"But he's mowing the long grass around the trees! I don't *want* it like that!" I loved the way that the long grass curled around the trunks of the trees – it made me certain that I wasn't in Alwoodley any more. It rustled very faintly sometimes when I was out in the garden, bustling to prepare itself for the dropping of the fruit in autumn. "He's doing it *all wrong*!" I screamed, and ran outside.

Anger and fear were a propelling force inside me that burst outwards into my limbs. I could feel my arms flapping, tensing and releasing as the energy of the emotion coursed along. I could vaguely hear Lizzie calling me back, but the world had turned black and yellow, streaking like paint across my line of vision. I charged out to the garden, the dull but deafening vibrations of the mower drilling into the confusion.

"Stop, stop!" I screamed at Dad. He immediately switched off the mower, looking at me as the noise puttered away.

"What is it?" He looked at the base of my quince tree as though expecting to see something deadly, and took a couple of preparatory steps back.

"Don't," I panted, the colours in front of me fading. "I . . . don't. I don't like it like that. You're *spoiling* everything."

"What?" Dad looked around him at the blue sky scattered by sweeping birds, at the winding stretch of my lawn and the swaying branches of my trees.

"I . . . I don't want you to do anything. Just . . ." I was about to say what I thought again, I knew it, and I couldn't stop myself. "Just go. I just want . . . would *like* it if you went. Sorry."

"Are you telling me," Dad said with stony politeness that

brought the black and yellow flooding back in, "that you do *not* wish me to finish mowing your lawn?"

I faced him square on. "Yes," I almost hissed. My father raised his eyebrows. With as much wounded dignity as lugging a lawnmower would allow, he made his way to the gate. I turned back to the house and watched Lizzie quickly move away from the window. I walked in a trance to the front of the cottage. "Thanks for coming," I said dully, aware at how preposterous I was being but unable to be anything different. I watched in silence as Lizzie and Dad loaded the bag with the catalogue and the lawnmower respectively into the car.

Just then, the door to Charity Cottage opened carefully. Dot and Vernon insinuated themselves into their front garden, making their way towards my parents with nervous half-smiles.

"Hello, we . . ."

"Came to introduce ourselves. I'm Vernon, this is the wife, Dot."

Dad stood and stared meditatively; Lizzie rushed into the void. "Nice to meet you," she said, almost fluttering her eyelashes.

"We just wanted to say what a nice girl your Evelyn is."

"Oh, well . . ." said Lizzie, tailing off and not looking at me.

"So nice to have some young people about."

"I'm sure."

"Well, we'll let you get on," said Vernon. "Don't stand about gassing," he admonished Dot.

"Just saying hello. You've been helping her out, have you? Very nice of you to give up your Saturday"

My stomach at this point had dropped to somewhere around my knees. Dot trundled on. "Must be quite a drive for you. Mind you, young people need help nowadays, don't they? No jobs, no jobs at all."

"I told her," Vernon said, pausing at the threshold.

"Hopefully she'll find something soon."

Dad and Lizzie stared down at Dot's compact little figure. Dad cleared his throat. "That's really . . . very kind," he said.

"Come on, Dot."

"Bye, then," called Dot.

I watched Dad and Lizzie get into the car, Dad adjusting his rear mirror, Lizzie looking at me in the wing mirror, ready to smile and wave as they pulled off. I waved too, smiling stiffly. What would count more, I wondered, the final smile or the argument?

Back inside, there was a little pile of goods on my coffee table: a box of Twilight chocolate mints, a coconut Boost, a bottle of orange squash and a magazine. On top of the magazine was a postcard, a J. W. Waterhouse – not the one I liked of Circe, but a long-haired girl ruminating into the distance against a background of cherry blossom trees.

"Dear Evie – We thought that you would like these as you settle into your new home! Lots of Love, Mum and Dad xx"

Peggy and I looked at each other. I knew that I was going to cry again and felt absurdly embarrassed for breaking down in front of a chihuahua.

SUNDAY 27TH JUNE 1982

I've just got off the phone with Joe. I'd broken the habit of a lifetime and telephoned him for two reasons. Firstly, I wanted to know whether he was part of this parental Machiavellian scheme to invade my rural idyll. Secondly, if he was, then Joe was the sort of person you could get cross with and know that he wouldn't mind too much.

"Hello?" His voice sounded furry and very distant.

"Hi. God, you sound awful."

"Still hungover from Friday."

"Why?"

"Football," said Joe, his voice clearing slightly with incredulity. "It was the *football*."

"Oh, who was playing?"

"Friday? Northern Ireland versus Spain."

"Oh. And who . . . ?"

"Northern Ireland."

"Oh. Is that . . . ?"

"Good? *Yes.* You really don't have a clue, do you? Mind you, being in the arse end of nowhere, I suppose that you don't follow current events."

"Football isn't a current event," I said. "Anyway, it is *my* job to be lofty, not yours," I added loftily. "Did you know that Dad and Lizzie came to see me yesterday?"

"Nah. Did they?"

"Yes, they just turned up and nagged me and stuff. And gave me Twilight mints," I added, in the spirit of fairness.

"Well, I think they miss you."

"*Do* they? How odd. I wouldn't miss me."

"Neither would I."

"Thanks."

"Whatever. Does everyone in your village have three heads?"

"Course not."

"Are they all related? I bet . . . what? Yes. No, it's Evie." It took me a while to work out that Joe was talking to someone out of shot, as it were – I could only talk on the phone by imagining Joe as a picture – the disconnected voice didn't seem real otherwise. "Yes, I'll ask her – *yes*. God."

"Val?"

"Yup."

"What are you asking her?"

"No, I'm asking *you* . . ."

"Oh, are you?"

"Yes."

"Right." There was a silence, and I thought how difficult the entire telephone situation was. How was anyone supposed to cope with it? Alexander Graham Bell had genuinely thought that his invention could be classed as human progress. It seemed that the rest of the world agreed with him – I most emphatically didn't. "I thought that you were asking me something?"

"I was about to." Joe took an audibly deep breath. "Listen, Evie . . ."

"I'm listening."

"It was a figure of speech."

"Got it." I had a vivid image of a statue in a garden, of a woman, my eyes taking in every stone curve. *That* was a figure; I wasn't sure where speech came into it.

"The thing is, Val and I were thinking that the flat is getting a bit pokey for us, what with Tom and the possibility of . . . you know, of another one. We were thinking of trying to get somewhere bigger, perhaps still a bungalow, on one of the modern cul-de-sacs on the edge of Alwoodley. It'd be a stretch, so we'd need a bit of help with the mortgage."

"You could ask Dad, I suppose. Or do you want me to ask Dad, is that it? I am not sure he's speaking to me after the lawnmower incident . . ."

"No, I'm asking *you*, Evie! You've got all this money just sitting around, more than you'll ever need."

"Aunt Mim gave *me* the money." I began to picture Aunt Mim's money. It was green, like dollar bills, and it rose up in a tubular shape until it resembled Aunt Mim herself, in her green dress. How could I take chunks off her and give it away?

"She was my aunt too, you know."

"Yes, but . . ."

"But what?"

But you didn't love her, said the voice inside my head. I managed not to say it out loud. "I don't think that I should lend you any money," I actually said.

"Why not?"

"Look, Joe . . ." How to explain this to a person closed to the Supernatural Way of Life? "Aunt Mim specifically gave me the money so that I could follow the natural way of things. It isn't for the manmade. It isn't for filing cabinets and cul-de-sacs and . . . and ordinary things. Anyway, I don't want to give you a loan or a donation – it sounds too businesslike. Don't they say, 'never mix business with pleasure'? It's a saying, Joe. Like 'It's All Water Under the Bridge'."

"Seriously?"

"Yes."

"Well, thanks a fucking bunch, Evie."

Joe hung up. I was left listening to the gentle buzz of the line. Replacing the receiver carefully, I felt as though a door had been shut in my face. After a second or two, I had the distinct, creeping sensation that I had done something wrong and wearily added it to my list.

"That didn't work," I said out loud to myself. It was all my fault: I had rung Joe and, however circuitously, expected reassurance. Instead, I felt even worse.

Dejected, I went to sit on my sofa, tapping the space beside me hopefully at Peggy. She remained in her armchair, resolutely uninterested in cuddles. My head jumped from one incident to another. Dad, Lizzie and Joe had made me miserable, but I was the only common denominator – *I* was the problem. It was only logical.

In Thornlaw, I had shaken off the ties that bound us claustrophobically together. When I could be alone, I wasn't a problem to anyone. Then they had invaded, because they were family and were allowed, were supposed to do that, and now I was caught up inside with them all over again.

The sun shone in through the windows, illuminating oblong patches on the walls and furniture. Margaret had gone to Derby to see her eldest son this weekend, she had told me. I imagined Margery taking little Kevin to some playground or other in his pyjamas so that he could make a joyful nuisance of himself. Everyone would've had a lovely weekend, and I was stuck inside my own head, replaying arguments.

MONDAY 28TH JUNE 1982

Alex's cassette was on the coffee table. I picked it up, my fingers tingling, as though I had never felt plastic before. I could hear the humming of the fridge and Peggy's irregular snores making arhythmic music. If I took the tape to Alex, I reasoned slowly, painfully, then I would put it in his hand, touch his skin. He would talk to me. I could take it now, to Fielden Place, leave the house, put one foot in front of the other even though it seemed that I was held back by something and would never walk or speak again.

"You're very focused on this young man," said Aunt Mim. She shifted in the armchair, Peggy snuffling in her lap. She looked like the bastardisation of a queen on her throne in that horrible leather chair, the pattern of fields outside the window an ornate backdrop framing the scene. The sun slanted on her; it turned her soft, jowly skin pure white, the crevices between her nose and the corners of her mouth became deep, black lines. The expanse of her pale green dress rolled, stretched and tucked over her body, forming a fascinating pattern out of the plain fabric.

I turned the cassette over in my hand. "Am I?"

"Yes," said Aunt Mim patiently, her voice carefully dispassionate.

"Do you remember him? Alex Ishkowitz."

"The dark-haired, stocky boy? I seem to recall that you thought you loved him," said Aunt Mim. "And then you broke it all off, apparently."

"What do you mean, 'apparently'?"

Aunt Mim shrugged. Normally so animated, her face was expressionless as she gazed at me. The beauty – whatever questionable beauty Aunt Mim had ever possessed – was in the sparkle of her eyes, her constantly moving mouth. Her features were plastic; they pulled and stretched and you watched her emotions emerging as she spoke and thought. Devoid of expression, she was any older woman, watching, waiting until the right thing was said, her whole personality on hiatus. I felt oddly cold on that warm day, shivering as she looked at me.

"I'm going," I said. "Come on, Peggy." But Peggy stayed where she was, asleep, eyes tightly shut.

*

I had pushed myself out of the house, down into the village, then up again to Fielden Place.

"Up Hill and Down Dale," I said to myself. The gravel on the drive crunched under my feet, announcing my arrival with icy politeness. I knocked on the door, realising how elegant its panels were and how thick it was – thick enough to keep out any unwanted intruders, however pretty its panels.

Susie Ishkowitz answered the door. We found each other out of the usual place, far away from Alwoodley and the synagogue. She tilted her head on one side; her shiny bobbed hair listed gently, so uniformly reddish-brown. Her dress was deep blue, and she wore turquoise earrings.

"You look lovely." There was something so tapering and elegant about Susie Ishkowitz, I thought, glad that my impulsive opening sally had been a compliment. I looked at her thin ankles, one crossed over the other like royalty when they sit down.

"Thanks." Susie looked gratifyingly surprised, but a little as though I had said something vulgar. She lowered her eyes as she fingered the deep blue material at her neck, and I looked at the pale, almond shape of her eyelids.

"I always think of one of those old-fashioned chair legs when I think of you," I said. Had that sounded right? No, quite obviously not. "I mean, they sort of curve and . . . have fancy bits on them. Your dress is nice," I added desperately.

"I got it at Next."

"Next?"

"Yes," she explained, coolly and patiently. "I went down to London, shopping. There's a new shop there called Next."

"Really?" Next what, I wondered? It sounded as though one was always moving on, which is surely the last thing a shop would want.

"Yes. Their ladies' stuff is very good."

"Oh." I realised that I would have to come up with an excuse for my presence on the doorstep that was now Susie's rather than

Alex's. Even worse, I would have to look as though I was telling the truth. "Erm," I said, into the excruciating silence.

"It was nice of you to be neighbourly – Alex mentioned that he'd seen you in the village. Would you like to see the house?" Susie asked me.

"That would be lovely," I replied in desperation, thinking that this was what Lizzie would say. "This is very nice," I said. "Goodness, look at the cornicing." I admired it as though it was my first time. Late Georgian, Alex had told me. "Is it Late Georgian?"

"I suppose so," said Susie. "Here's the drawing room."

"Of course, Susie has her own money, doesn't she?" Sarah Leverson's jarring voice reached me, carrying from a synagogue service months ago. "Her grandfather imported ostrich feathers for ladies' hats. Made a bloody fortune, apparently."

I stalked into the drawing room, determined to get away from that penetrating voice.

The drawing room was now inhabited – there were two stuffed, chintz sofas standing opposite one another, and a table covered in the same fabric topped with a circle of glass. The books were no longer the only things absorbing the subdued, north light. One didn't pay them as much attention now that the room was home to other things. There was a chest of drawers in one corner topped with three porcelain ladies, trailing frozen baskets of roses along. I thought of my china rabbits at home with a fierce longing. Above the drawers were two watercolour landscapes, so fine that they seemed washed of colour. The landscape on the left was around a quarter of an inch higher than the other, I noticed.

"The armchairs are coming; it took a little longer to get them made."

"Are you going to redecorate?" I thought of Lizzie and her catalogues.

Susie cleared her throat delicately. "We already have," she said, as though she was sorry rather than embarrassed.

"Green and pink," I said, "it's all the rage at the moment. Perfect for the country . . . for out here."

Susie didn't look at me – she gazed at her drawing room, giving a slight smile as though we were at a cocktail party. There was a bouquet of pale pink roses in a cut-glass vase on the side table. I opened my mouth to say how lovely they looked, their petals so dense and opaque that they were almost like paper, when I realised that they were given rather than bought. There was a card angled away from me, tucked into the neck of the vase: Alex had bought those flowers for Susie. He had bought flowers for his wife. I felt as though a ball of air was pushing against the back of my mouth, cutting off my throat. The reverential dimness of the room darkened even more.

"I should get going," I said, my hand going to the pocket of my tracksuit bottoms, checking that the rectangle of the cassette tape was still there. Susie looked at me. "I . . . I just stopped by because when I bumped into Alex he said that I should come and see you . . ." My breath ran out with my words. I stood there, almost panting, in the green and rose-pink room.

"Can I make you a cup of tea?"

"No, no, it's fine. Well, it was nice to see you and . . . yes."

I tumbled out of the drawing room, the hall, down the gravel driveway as though my legs were boneless. My back felt hot, as though Susie was watching me from the long window, and the fact that I knew she was far too polite to do anything like that made me hotter. There was a car parked tight against the corner of the drive – a Hyundai, whatever that was. Susie's little car, no doubt.

I felt slightly duped: why had I thought that Susie and I had ever had anything in common? We belonged to the same community, I supposed, but out here we were on our own . . . Was that the real definition of a community – a group of people who are supposed to have things in common? If you took away the Judaism, then that only left Alex between Susie and me. I didn't like to think about that.

I looked around me as I tramped through the village, hoping that I would see someone I knew to break the spell that was walling me up inside, covering me in creeper like a gawky Sleeping Beauty so that I was hidden from the world.

I saw nobody that I knew, only the half-homely hills and gradating rows of stone houses as they rose and fell. When I got home and went inside, I shut the world out. The stillness was immediate – it felt like a veil falling plumb on top of my head, its folds instantly cloaking me.

If Aunt Mim had been waiting at Faithful Cottage to tell me "I told you so", I don't think I could have stood it.

TUESDAY 29TH JUNE 1982

"I will use my power to create". That was Tuesday's phrase. I am not sure whether this counts as 'creating', but I took a Citrine stone to Margery and pressed it into her hand. It stands for energy, you see, and she always seems exhausted.

"Energy and Abundance," I had said.

Margery had looked at Kevin. "I could do without the abundance, love," she'd said.

Right now, I am enjoying the silence created by the World Cup match. I am grateful for football: it creates so much silence elsewhere. It draws people into groups, concentrates their presence and noise, and allows me to be apart from them. I enjoy it, as I have always enjoyed the sounds of parties in the distance. I love other people's enjoyment when I am far enough away.

The village is eerily quiet, as if it is holding its breath. I suppose it is never that noisy. Peggy and I walked past the church this morning when we went to see Margery, and saw Joanie over the other side of the road.

"Jacaranda?" She called over. I gave her the thumbs up. "How about 'flowing'?"

I made a so-so movement with my hand.

"Adamant!" I yelled – well, any excuse to say the name of my beloved. I think Joanie and I both felt that we were making rather a row, and were proud of ourselves.

I hope that England win, and advance as far as possible – I would enjoy some more evenings like this. Vernon had gone to the pub for the match – I watched his slow, deliberate steps down the lane and wondered for a brief second what Dot would do with her freedom. I had images of her dancing in a feather boa or doing nude callisthenics in the garden. Then, through the wall, came the muted shriek of the carpet cleaner being put round.

In the thick, warm, summery silence I can recover from the events of today. I feel as though the air is packed tight – I can almost hear how dense it is. It is pale yellow with the fading light, like butter or cheese; I could almost slice it.

As I breakfasted upon my customary two-thirds of a banana this morning, the postman pushed two cards through my door. They didn't look like bills, and weren't written in Lizzie's handwriting, so my first thought was that they must be for next door. But they said my name, so I tore in.

The first was an invitation from Susie Ishkowitz. It made her suddenly seem very near, as though she was standing in my cottage and staring at me in her usual cool way.

"*Come to dinner,*" she had written, on notecards with her address at the top, all very grand. "*Seven-thirty for eight, RSVP.*"

Only grown-ups received dinner invitations, I thought. Did she really want me for dinner? Had Alex made her ask me? I thought that people usually went to dinner parties in pairs. It all seemed a bit mature, and we were still quite young, weren't we?

The second envelope was rather squishy. I opened it and found a little enamel brooch wrapped in paper. It was a bunch of violets, the colours painted and the glaze worn away around the edges. Oddly fragile, clearly unloved. It was from Alex.

"*Saw this and thought of you – don't know why.*" He had written

– nothing more.

I looked at the brooch nestling in my cupped hand, the prick of the pin needling at my skin a little. "Sweet violets," I sung to myself. Didn't Alex know that violets are the flower of February and the sign Aquarius? We didn't have any connection to the winter, did we? But Aquarians were adventurers – perhaps Alex and I were too, striking out into the unknown environs of Thornlaw.

My hand hovered uncertainly for a full two minutes while I tried to decide if I should wear it out. In the end, I ran upstairs with it and carefully – as though it were treasure – placed it beside my bed, on the floor.

I really must get a bedside table.

WEDNESDAY 30TH JUNE 1982

"Let's sit over here," said Margaret, gesturing to the little dining table and chairs by the window, where we always sat. Paul was in his armchair, cleaved to its curve, watching television. The windows were hermetically sealed against the sunshine and there was a not-unpleasant smell of washing-up liquid and furniture polish.

"Hello, Paul."

He nodded, eyes on the screen.

"Did we win the football, then?" I had already seen the head-lines.

"One-nil." His gaze followed a presenter on the TV as she crossed the studio floor in her turquoise suit.

"Oh."

"Germany today."

"Is it? Which bit?"

"Not the red bit, the West."

"I always get confused which one it is." Margaret sighed.

"East Germany didn't even qualify," said Paul scornfully.

"Ought to take that wall down."

"No, they bloody shouldn't," said Paul. "Keeps the commies out."

"He watches a lot of news," said Margaret proudly, "on account of him not being well."

"I reckon Margaret Thatcher would agree with you, Paul. I would imagine that it suits her to isolate the East," I said.

There was a short silence. "I don't hold with 'er," he said.

"Oh, but she's very popular," I said. "She's got a fifty-one per cent approval rating, I read it in *The Telegraph*."

"Don't believe everything you read," said Paul darkly. I nodded, and thought that perhaps he didn't know very much about politics. He might have only watched the news for the sport at the end – some men did that, apparently.

Our conversation seemed to be at a close. I took Margaret's hands and started massaging them, feeling delicately for the denseness around the joints, starting to apply a little pressure. I looked at Paul's hand on the arm of his chair, the skin smooth and pale. There was something breathless about Margaret and Paul's lounge. The sun leant a sparkle to the odd little particles of dust that settled on the table in front of us; I had a feeling that the conversation about the Berlin Wall was one that Margaret and

Paul had perfected, rehearsing it for company. I felt oddly self-conscious, as though I was an interloper to their domesticity – a welcome one, but a stranger that didn't quite fit.

"Been to see Rhoda, have you?"

"Yes, I went yesterday."

"I told her all about you, about your little business. Did you see Vi?"

"She was upstairs, I just peeped around the door. Rhoda said that she is pretty much bed-bound now."

"Did you hear that, Paul?"

"Hmmm?"

"Rhoda says that Vi is bed-bound."

"Hmmm."

"Well, we haven't seen her about, have we?" Margaret turned back to me. "That *is* a shame. I remember Vi when we first moved here – she was a glamorous woman, you know. Always had a set, and her nails done. Speaking of which, do you know what Edith said the other day?"

"No?" I was tackling the joint of Margaret's thumb, which I always saved until last with a mixture of apprehension and fascination.

"She said that she thought you'd come here to get away from a man. Said she thought you might even have been married – or lost someone."

"Oh, did she?"

"Nonsense, isn't it? She's getting ideas, like Margery. You're far too young."

I nodded.

"And some people prefer a quiet life, don't they?"

I nodded.

"I mean, Leeds isn't for everyone. I don't think that Peter pays Edith much attention, that's the trouble, and she reads those silly books about women running off with someone tall, dark and handsome who just happens to be passing. There was even talk that years ago . . . well, that she'd, you know." With simultaneous women's intuition, we both glanced over at Paul. "How's Rhoda?"

"She's all right." I hadn't really attributed a psychological state to Rhoda. She was a peaceful-seeming woman, with round eyes and a slight bovine look. I had 'done her feet' and also promised to make up a potion for Jumbo, her dog, who apparently had a constantly upset stomach. He spent my entire visit snoring in his pungently hairy basket. Ginger would do, I thought, and turmeric. Maybe some nuts to bind it all together, and dried fruit for sweetness?

"Still got that awful china basket of fruit on the mantelpiece, has she?"

"Yes."

"I can't abide things like that," said Margaret, and sniffed.

"I'd better get going now."

"Where're you off to then?" Margaret's eyes flashed with possibilities.

"Just to meet Joanie at the museum," I said, feeling anti-climactic.

"I see. Well, I suppose it is a good thing that you have each other to do things with."

The Princess Louise Museum was in the centre of the village, an odd abridgement of houses with a Victorian gothic door at the top of steep stone steps. Opposite, stood the pub, hung with its Union Jack bunting that flapped and tangled in the breeze. The publican, tidying his front garden, looked at me looking at him. Joanie was waiting, fingering the strap of her handbag. She greeted me by telling me that the museum had been opened by Princess Louise herself, which I had really felt was suggested in the name.

"There's a picture of her, as you walk in . . . oh!" Joanie gasped as we made our way up the steps and stopped, clutching her chest.

"Are you all right?"

"Oh, *yes*," she panted, grabbing at my arm with her little hand so that I felt I was being mauled by a tenacious squirrel.

"You can lean on me," I offered, resisting the urge to pull away.

"I'll be . . . just . . . fine . . . just a few more . . . I have a . . . a thing," she said, motioning to her heart, whilst I nodded and tried to look sensitive. Is this really what a broken heart looks like, I wondered? It is strange that there is so much heavy breathing. Perhaps she would faint away altogether in true romantic heroine style, although I wasn't sure that I could catch her.

We scaled the stair mountain, two of our steps to every stair. There was a recurring dream of my childhood in which I had to climb a massive staircase and knew at the beginning that I would never reach the top. I was feeling distinctly that way now. I should have come on my own, I thought miserably. According to my guidebook (a moving present from Dad), the museum was 'full of oddities and curios'. Joanie and I would fit right in, I thought.

"Good job coffee morning was cancelled today, wasn't it?"

"Oh, yes."

A bored-looking middle-aged woman manned the desk and put on a polite smile as we entered. She attempted to give us each a leaflet, but Joanie – presumably afraid that her new-found role of tour guide was about to be usurped – firmly turned them down and pulled me onwards.

We wandered for a moment, looking at the tall, glass frames and slanting information boards as though they were the exhibits in themselves. I measured the length and breadth of the place, noting the two other rooms, calculating the time it would take for us to do the tour. It was so small; I could see the end before we had really begun. Joanie might have been thinking the same. As if by consent, our footsteps shortened, making more ground for ourselves. We could hear the tip-tap echo of our feet sounding light and insubstantial. I took a deep breath in, smelling the ingrained dust and the lack of habitation and the slight tang of footsteps from outside trodden into the floor.

"There's Princess Louise!" Joanie turned underneath a rather smudgy oil painting and smiled at me hopefully. "Don't be disappointed that I brought you here," her watery eyes seemed to add, and I hastened towards her, jolted into a smile.

"She was pretty," I said.

"I *do* like her dress, don't you?"

"It's very fluffy . . . rather like a wedding dress. They all looked as though they were just about to get married in those days though, didn't they?" I had thought it an excellent plan to ask Joanie about her wedding dress – she seemed the type of woman who would talk about fittings and satin and bridesmaids' colours for minutes at a time, relishing the day that she was a special kind of object. Just in time, I remembered her divorce. "I mean, Louise looks rather like Lily Langtry, although I am not sure that she would have approved of the likeness. I think it was what painters did in those days when girls had rather heavy faces, they sort of nipped them in and made them lighter."

"But she looks innocent, doesn't she? With her pearls around her neck." Joanie sighed girlishly.

"They are diamonds, aren't they?"

"Oh, yes."

"And look, here's an actual photo of Princess Louise. Definitely jowlier," I remarked. Looking closer at that young girl, I wondered whether she watched the visitors looking at her painting and making personal comments, then followed them with her long eyes around the room. What would she think of me, in my 'Let's Sweat It!' sweatshirt, my hair doing its best impression of a bird's nest? I had been a bit rude, I thought. After all, Princess Louise was better looking. Fifty-two years ago she had died, and yet people like me were still picking her over. "Sorry," I said to Joanie. "I . . . I like to deconstruct everything, you see, and then sometimes I can't put it back together and I spoil things for people."

"You would rather *know*," said Joanie affectionately. "It's all right. I prefer to keep my illusions. We're all different."

"According to the information board, she was a 'shy and

retiring girl'," I said. "Perhaps she was a dreamer."

"Or just shy, like you," said Joanie. "Margaret always says what a shy girl you are, and Margaret is an *excellent* judge of character. It's quite amazing sometimes, how she hits the nail on the head."

I marvelled at the dearth between self-image and other people's understanding of you. At the same time, I was a little flattered at the thought of being imbued with such a feminine quality. Shyness didn't fit me, I thought, but so many people thought it did. Shyness implied a demureness and modesty – one held back. I never held back, or never intended to – I just stopped, as though I ran out of road.

Satisfied with one another, Joanie and I wandered apart a little, companions across the deserted space over and around the relics. 'Relics' was the only word to use, I thought, peering into a glass case containing an assegai and shield, abutted by another case with a complete set of Meissen dinnerware. I looked at the regular little sprays of flowers across the dinner plates, roses the colour of sugarplums with their frilled outer petals that looked strangely human, like curled hair. Someone had once said "oh, isn't it lovely/unusual/old-fashioned, it's too good to throw, you should keep it" about everything in this place, and it had duly been kept, collected by someone with a kind heart and no sense. It was a room full of the useless, a museum for things that should be preserved but were not wanted. I found myself wondering if such a place should really exist, and I wasn't sure.

"Evie, come and look at this."

I clip-clopped over to Joanie like a genteel shire horse. There was a letter in a glass case, the writing sprawled in barely straight lines. "A letter from the German Ambassador, thanking Mayor of Thornlaw Jeremiah Claybrooke for his hospitality during a storm on the way to an official visit in Leeds," I read.

"Good to know that we aren't the only Germans here," chuckled Joanie.

"Are you?"

"My maiden name was Konrad," said Joanie. "My father ended up in a prisoner-of-war camp over here and never left."

"Goodness," I said. I was not really German, in my mind – my ancestors were cordoned off from anything too Germanic by their Jewishness. But I supposed that other people didn't know that. If Joanie was German, then she must have known that Edelman was a Jewish name, and yet she acted as though we were on the same side. Looking at Joanie, I realised that we actually were on the same side: it was us against them, the village suddenly solidifying into a stone-coloured mass, us safe in this little haven of oddities.

"A dress!" Joanie almost clapped her hands with joy, although she must have seen it so many times before. Whatever girlishness I had (and I did not have much) was piqued, until I realised with disappointment that the Victorian dress was built to such small, stout proportions that it was impossible to imagine myself wearing it.

"Look at the boning," I said. I had not even realised that I knew of boning, much less had ever used it in a sentence. Thornlaw was certainly bringing out hidden depths, or new peculiarities at least. My fingers ran along the glass case, tracing the stiff arch of whalebone in the bodice that stretched the blue-watered silk stiff. It looked as though a stream had been frozen.

Joanie cocked her head on one side and gazed avidly. The window nearest us darkened, and Malcolm appeared from the waist up, staring at me in a manner that can only be described as devilish. Slowly, he winked.

I gasped in a very ladylike way and turned to Joanie, but she hadn't seen. "Come in," I motioned with the hand nearest the window.

"Can't," he mouthed. I supposed that tea sets and silk dresses did rather do something to repel The Dark Side.

"I wonder if I would have had a waist like that if I had lived in those times? My husband . . . ex-husband, used to say that I had a lovely figure." Joanie patted the convexity of her stomach proudly.

"It would hurt to wear that," I said.

"Don't you like it?"

"It's just . . ." I turned to the window again, and Malcolm had disappeared.

"Oh, are you going to tear this apart? No," said Joanie laughing, "I won't let you; it is too pretty! Anyway, if you tear this dress to pieces you will end up flailing about in a riot of blue silk and muslin. You would just make things worse for yourself." She giggled.

"Silk, muslin and whalebone," I pointed out. "It is a cage, underneath all the blue and white. It just makes me feel that . . . I don't know . . . that it means something separated and extraneous to be a woman, like in a restaurant when the waiter brings you something on the side on its own little plate." Then it means something else to be a Jewish woman, I added to myself, and then something else on top of that to be a woman with Asperger's, presumably. Were there any others like me, I wondered, sending out a mental howl into the wilderness and listening to it die away? All those layers building up, making something more interesting or just more opaque to other people?

Joanie said nothing to my rumination – I wondered whether I had even spoken out loud. Only her breathing could be heard, emanating higher than her lungs, sounding precariously as though it was rasping and catching around her collar bone.

"Are you all right?"

"Oh yes." The words sailed out on a short breath, cut off before they were intended to be. "It's just, you know . . ." That gesture again, the fluttering hand to her breast.

"Your heart?"

She nodded. "My heart."

*

It was the warmest part of the day as I left Joanie and walked home. The heat of previous hours had lingered, waiting and admiring its effects on the countryside. It had been too much: Margaret's disfigured hands, Joanie's face, swam in front of me and became indistinguishable, crinkling in the heat and melting into shields and sugarplum roses painted on china. I combed through everything that Joanie had said, searching for signs of fellow witchiness, and found nothing. I had meant to ask searching questions like, "Do you feel at one with nature?" and "Do your fingers get all tingly because they are so sensitive?" Frustratingly, we had talked about other things, and I had found it interesting and been diverted.

But I could no longer enjoy anything beautiful that surrounded me – it was too bright; the sounds of the village were too loud. I seemed unable to withstand other people – Thornlaw's beauty was yet another stressor to every sense and fibre and pore as I closed in on myself. The leaves rustled and the birds sang as I walked past. Was I suspended in liquid, like a specimen in a jar, I asked myself? It felt as though I was looking at Thornlaw but unable to see it properly.

The church seemed peaceful and cool. Through the gate, I chose a bench opposite an upstanding grave. A tree had grown around it, the trunk split in half, wedging and twisting around the stone. It looked to me as though the grave itself had grown inside the tree – there was something organic and wildly miscalculated about it. A figure moved amongst the shadows – someone else was in the churchyard, putting flowers on one of the oldest graves, it's copperplate rubbed out by years and rain.

This was village life, I thought. There was still family to mourn you, a connection to place that spanned hundreds of years. I thought of Aunt Mim buried in Alwoodley, and Oma buried in London, and it made me lonely. Graves were for the living, I thought; they were a kind of reassurance.

I closed my eyes against the sunshine, which was just beginning to falter from yellow to gold. The first thing I saw against the dark of my eyelids was Alex. He seemed to exist in my mind *and* in reality with equal vividness. I started to wonder what I could have done for things to be different: our relation to each other was like wandering a hall of mirrors, infinitely playing out different versions of what was really going on, all of which seemed completely arbitrary. Was it a year I had been Alex-less? More, in fact. One year, four months . . . how many days? But Alex still provoked insecurity inside me; raised the idea that perhaps I was hopelessly wrong in all the ways that other people were right.

Dragging my hands down my face, marginally less dejected by the familiar touch of my own fingers, I opened my eyes to see the flame-red of Edith's hair. She was walking past, watching me. I thought of Maureen O'Hara – there was something about Edith's hairdo "redolent of a bygone era", as the estate agent had said when we were squeezing up the stairs of Faithful Cottage. If Edith was cosseting an image of me as a forlorn, abandoned woman, then discovering me in a graveyard with my head in my hands was grist to her mill. She pretended not to see me, so that I could continue my silent lament for The Man I Had Lost.

Whilst I was in a spirit of self-examination, I realised that I should probably not be seen with Joanie too often if I truly wished to avoid being named an abandoned woman. I chaffed against this pairing of Joanie and me, particularly as Joanie herself seemed to welcome it so desperately. But after our visit, I realised slightly shame-facedly that I liked Joanie. It was not a linear, smooth kind of like, more like peaks of kindly, sudden impulses and troughs of annoyance. There was nothing steady about it, but I had realised that she was intelligent and sensitive, and deserved more than pity.

Joanie had confided in me about her husband, and no wonder her heart was hurting – she was like a Victorian heroine, I thought, destroyed by love. Her quavering voice filled the churchyard now.

"He just changed. I know that men do sometimes change when they reach a certain . . . a certain time in life, but it was like living with somebody new. Then, he left and I was alone, he moved in with her and now he thinks that we should divide the money equally, but he spends so much of it! He never spent so much on me, and I would never have asked him to. She doesn't let me speak to him, of course, but sometimes he rings up to ask me for money. My mother had an inheritance, you see – nothing big, but . . . we were once better off than we are now. Lawyers are so expensive; I don't think that there'll be anything left. And he draws it out deliberately to make me unhappy, arranging a date with the lawyers and then cancelling it at the last moment. Sometimes . . . sometimes I think it is almost better that we never had children. What could I have given them now? Soon there'll be nothing left at all, and he knows that but he still pushes on . . ."

"Miss Edelman?"

"Oh hello, Reverend Rishangles." I squinted against the sun to see the vicar's delicate outline. His voice was as soft and mocking as the breeze.

"Here for some religious contemplation?"

"Here for some peace," I said. I started to laugh.

"What is amusing you?"

"I was just thinking what my rabbi would say if he could see me here now, talking to a vicar and sitting in a churchyard."

"I imagine that he would be furious," said Reverend Rishangles pleasantly. "We like to keep a firm hold of our respective flocks."

"When I said 'my' rabbi, I didn't really mean it to sound as though he possessed me," I said.

"Well, he is your spiritual leader, I suppose. Don't you feel as though you belong to your Jewish brethren?"

"I don't feel as though I belong to anyone."

The lady tending the graveside had left; I had thought that the Reverend and I were alone. But then I saw another figure moving in between the light and the cast shadows. I sat up straighter to check that I had seen right: it was Malcolm.

He moved through the churchyard silently but with purpose. I watched him, the back of his dark head and his tightly held, slim shoulders, walk right to the boundary wall. In a second, he vaulted upwards and over it, and disappeared.

"Look!"

"What is it?"

"Over there, didn't you see him?"

Reverend Rishangles peered carefully into the gloam cast by the round, feathered yew trees. "I'm afraid that I can't see anyone," he said. "I don't think there is anyone there."

JULY

Larkspur – Ruby – Cancer – Water

"Hot July brings cooling showers,
Apricots and gilly flowers."
SARA COLERIDGE

"Almost, she was happy . . . all one needed was a pretext.
If there were no pretext, one needed an analogue."
ANITA BROOKNER

THANK YOU, ANITA BROOKNER, FOR BEING CLEVER.
I have the strongest feeling that Anita Brookner wouldn't
like Susie Ishkowitz. It is all right to dislike other people as long
as you are demonstrably cleverer than them, I suppose.

"But these backwaters of existence sometimes breed, in
their sluggish depths, strange acuities of emotion . . ."
EDITH WARTON

Why did I get a very vivid image of Edith's lacquered hair when

I first read that, before that shivering feeling when I got to the emotional acuity bit?

> **Horoscope for July:**
> **Leo:** *You are reaping the benefits of your new-found stability, Leo. Enjoy it! But remember that chaos is always just around the corner . . .*

SATURDAY 3RD JULY 1982

6.43 p.m.: Aunt Mim and I examined my polka-dot synagogue dress critically in the mirror. There was silence except for the hum of the electric lightbulb – it wasn't dark yet, but I had decided that the clothes should be as illuminated as possible in order to be able to make an informed choice. I dipped my head a little against the low ceilings; Aunt Mim was perhaps a little too wide for the room, and I was too tall – we filled the place in different directions.

"It's not an evening dress, is it?"

"Not really."

"I suppose that I could dress it up with. . . something . . ." Aunt Mim raised an eyebrow "Or put my hair back with grips? That might look grander."

"What about that green jacket thing you wore to the Leversons'?"

"I didn't bring it with me. I didn't think I'd be needing it."

"Oy." Aunt Mim sighed.

"Anyway, what would I have worn with it?"

Aunt Mim compressed her lips and raised both eyebrows this time.

"Have you really not got anything else?"

"Nope. I . . . I thought that ghosts didn't appear in a mirror."

Aunt Mim shrugged. We stared at one another hopelessly.

"I'm not the best person to help you with this, am I?"

"No." I smiled at her to show that I was still glad of her presence.

"If I was alive, I would have lent you one of my kaftans."

*

7.36 p.m.: "Hello, again!"

I was wearing the dotty synagogue dress, Alex's violet brooch pinned to the collar, and a pair of black pumps that seemed formal to me by sheer dint of the fact that they weren't trainers. Pausing on the driveway of Fielden Place, I turned around to see Malcolm behind me, holding a bottle of wine by the neck. He had a long upper lip after a short nose, I noted, but strangely enough, it disposed me towards him.

"You!"

"The very same."

"Have you come to wreak havoc?"

"I thought I'd come for dinner with the estate agent who's going to sell my new houses, and his lovely wife. Havoc sounds fun though."

"I thought that I saw you . . ."

"Yes?"

"In the churchyard, flying over a wall. After the museum . . ."

Malcolm laughed, showing very even, white teeth that glinted like a row of pearls in the setting sun. "I get everywhere," he said.

"And you know Alex . . ."

"It's business."

Of course, Alex would have business with a devil like Malcolm.

Reaching the door, we each waited for the other to knock then took the plunge at the same time, our dry hands bumping into one another and then pulling away.

Susie Ishkowitz opened the door in a calf-length chiffon affair of pale pink, with bell sleeves and a sash that tied around the waist in a large, floppy bow. She wore coral earrings that looked like the stamens of a wild rose, the layers of her dress petals. I always pictured Susie in blue; she matched its coolness. Now I felt an unattractive little pang when I realised how pretty she looked in anything. I seemed to grow taller, the sheer bulk of me increasing against Susie's willowy figure.

"What a *lovely* dress," Susie said to me.

*

9.10 p.m.: Susie had served Lizzie's coveted roast duck dish from the M&S cookbook, the one with bacon. I had inwardly crowed with triumph at knowing where the recipe came from, and wiggled delightedly in my Laura Ashley farmhouse-style chair.

"Oh, look at that, Suse! Just what every Jew wants on a Saturday!" Alex had laughed, and I joined in nervously with him.

"Aren't we awful Jews?" David Kessel said. "I can almost feel the beady eye of Rabbi Guld; the back of my neck is tickling."

"He probably does see all, rather like some sort of dark, avenging angel," said Alex.

"You make him sound diabolical." Malcolm poured himself some more wine.

"Stop it, all of you," Susie said calmly, and handed Alex the carving knife.

Alex had not noticed my brooch – he hadn't mentioned it, anyway. He'd kissed me on the cheek when we arrived, smelling of aftershave and rum. He was mixing cocktails on the terrace, he told me, and walked me through with his hand supposedly in the small of my back, but actually clutching at the voluminous folds of my dress.

I only looked at my watch occasionally, enjoying as I was the feeling that time had slowed and become as yellow as the lights in the dining room. The sound of talking and laughing swirled like wine in a glass, making me feel dizzy. This was how I would live if I wasn't a witch, I thought. This was what normal people did, and the feeling of knowing that I was doing something I *should* was satisfying, as though I was another version of myself.

I had mostly made peace with the fact that I'd been asked to make up the numbers. Malcolm, David – they had needed a single woman – and there I was, at Faithful Cottage, just waiting to be included (that was sarcasm, by the way . . . although it was probably true, as well). We were eight in total: Rose, an elderly friend of Susie's parents, obviously gentile and very earnest about 'the unemployed' (I suppose that Vernon and Dot counted me in their number) plus George and Priscilla Cuthbert, the Lord and Lady of Fielden Hall, the poshest dinner guests it was possible to get round here, I imagine. Then David Kessel, Malcolm –

resolutely metropolitan in his smart, dark suit – and me trailing behind.

I had been seated between David Kessel and Alex, who sat at the head of the table but seemed very far away. He sent proprietorial glances around the room; he laughed every time someone tried to be amusing. He sent little marital smiles and nods the length of the table to Susie, which pierced my heart horribly. But we all played our role – there was an air of satisfaction with each other, rather as though we were children behaving ourselves, watching our parents beaming at us from the corner of our eye. The young hosts, the appreciative guests, the forward-thinking mix of religion and class – all these ingredients savoured.

David Kessel was that most dangerous thing: a single, nice-looking Jewish man with a good job. I looked at his pleasant, rather fawn-like face and beautiful wavy chestnut hair and a part of me thrilled to him, even if the overwhelming majority of me was rather disgusted with his availability. Back in Alwoodley, I had always averted my eyes from him, shuffling away when we danced in groups, been a little curt or looked out of the window when I caught his eye. I found his eligibility unattractive.

I must stop being like this, I thought. He can't help being conventionally suitable, and being unconventional for its own sake is fairly pointless. So, I smiled at him.

"I really wanted to see whether I *could* write, that was why I went to the short story classes," Rose was saying in her insubstantial voice. She patted her hair in place. "And I *can*. I *can* write. So, I have bought an exercise book . . ."

George Cuthbert nodded at her with polite appreciation.

"A lot of charity work for the area . . ." Priscilla was leaning in towards Susie with an air of girlish collusion.

"Pricing might be difficult," David was saying to Malcolm.

"If you don't try it high then you'll never know. And people are desperate for flats."

This was my moment of reprieve from conversation; there had come one of those brief moments when nothing was required of me, except perhaps to eavesdrop on the fragments of other people's talk.

"What are you thinking about?" David turned to me, smiling back.

"I was thinking how odd it is, making conversation," I said. "It reminds me of one of those wooden board games where you slide the pieces around, trying to form a picture."

"Do you want me to help you?"

"If you like."

"Well . . . how are your parents?"

"Oh, don't let's talk about *them*," I said, so vehemently that David laughed. I didn't want to think of the square I made with Lizzie, Dad and Joe, each of us in our corner. The lawnmower incident was still fresh and painful.

"Right, well . . . I am afraid I'm at a loss then."

"Goodness, your store of small talk must be even worse than mine."

David looked over at Susie and gave a rather charming shrug.

"David," she said, "why don't you see if Evie would like any more potatoes?"

9.29 p.m.: George Cuthbert shook his head. "It was blowing a bloody gale from the end of September. I checked the weather forecast every day but we never really got going." He was a colourless but handsome man. I could imagine his large, heavy features repeated in various ancestral portraits at Fielden Hall.

"I'd love to start," said Alex. "You can count me in when September rolls around."

"No point *then*, too early. Season doesn't start until October."

"Oh."

"Shooting is rather like bird-watching, isn't it?" I asked, to be met with a silence I shortly identified as incredulity.

Malcolm laughed. "It's a little more vicious," he pointed out.

"But, I mean, you need similar conditions, don't you, so there's no need to laugh at me. I mean, you couldn't bird-watch in a gale either, so . . ."

I looked towards Alex, but he seemed to be very interested in his napkin ring.

". . . so there's no need to laugh at me," I said to Malcolm, without looking at him.

"Evie is from London," said Susie to George Cuthbert, apology evident in her voice. "And she's quite the bohemian."

"Do you write?" enquired Rose eagerly, as I struggled to work out whether I liked Susie's description of me or not.

"No," I said. It was always insulting when someone you were jealous of tried to describe you, I thought. It nearly always seemed to miss the mark because of your own churlishness.

"Where's my purse?" Rose suddenly twisted behind her in agitation. "I was sure that I brought it in here with me."

"I believe that you are sitting on it," said Susie gently.

"Oh!" Rose gave a weak little laugh. "What would I do without you, Susie? Isn't she *wonderful*, Alex?"

"She certainly is." Alex gave Susie a very long, slow smile – I was sure he meant it to ridicule Rose for being so soppy.

Susie merely said, "Alex, tell everyone the story of your mother's hat."

"Well," Alex settled back into his chair, expansive. "Talking of sitting on things: my mother had bought a new hat for Passover, you see. It was a sort of straw affair with flowers on, you know, the sort of thing that girls have . . ."

I frowned at him and looked to Susie for support, but she was smiling.

". . . and she put it to rest for the night on a chair in the bedroom. Anyway, my father is an inveterate night-wanderer and decided at some point to have a sit down, and the cushion beneath him felt rather uncomfortable . . . anyway, you can guess. My poor mother woke up with an indent of my father's behind in her straw hat, and her dreams in tatters."

David, Malcolm and I laughed, although privately I felt rather sorry for Mrs Ishkowitz. She wasn't the type of woman you could bear to be embarrassed – it was painful to think of.

"So . . . did she go to the synagogue? In the end?" Priscilla asked anxiously.

"I had a lovely straw hat with flowers on – poppies and

cornflowers," said Rose, eyes glazed dreamily.

"Thought they all wore wigs, or scarves," said George Cuthbert.

I attempted to send Susie another look, and to my surprise, she was already looking at me. But Susie could look at you whilst communicating nothing, her eyes so blue that they were unseeing.

"I think that she just wore another hat," said Alex, deflated.

"Dad always says that we aren't really *that* Jewish," I said. "He normally says it on a Saturday morning, because he'd rather think about looms than go to synagogue. I suppose that's why we're all trying to be less Jewish now, isn't it? Because we'd rather eat bacon."

Another silence, this one mixed like balls of wool that Aunt Mim knitted terrible jumpers with, different strands of colour woven into the same thread.

"Evie's father is an academic at the university," said Susie.

"Oh," said Priscilla.

*

10.15 p.m.: The pale pink roses had been replaced, I noted, as we repaired to the sitting room (odd phrase; I mean, we aren't mending anything). The roses must have withered, I thought to myself maliciously.

Susie handed around little chocolates dusted in cocoa. They looked delicious, but nobody wanted them after such a heavy meal. The sky through the French doors was a luxurious navy blue, but Susie and Alex quickly turned on the lights.

"The books look different now, don't they?" I said to Alex, looking affectionately at the bumpy rows sheltering in their alcoves.

"Hmmm?"

"From before."

"Shhh."

"What? Oh, I see."

"Alex isn't much of a reader," said Susie.

Alex shrugged and looked annoyed. "Not like you or Evie," he said.

"I've just finished reading *A is for Alibi* – I couldn't put it down! What are you reading?" Susie's hand smoothed out her skirt over her knees.

"*Germinal* by Zola."

"Goodness," she said politely, as though I had just said something rude.

"You'll have to trust me on this, George," Malcolm was saying.

"Really? People really want to live stacked on top of one another like that?"

"It's aspirational."

"Yes, but outside of Leeds or York . . ."

"And it pays for you and the buyers."

"Well," George leant forwards laboriously towards his glass of brandy, "I suppose that I should trust you, Malcolm – you seem to know your stuff."

"Should you?" I wondered to myself, and then realised that I had said it aloud.

"You are very cynical for your years, young lady," said George, guffawing at his own remark.

"Evie doesn't trust anyone," said Alex. He had sat on the opposite sofa to Susie.

"That isn't true . . ."

"Well, you don't trust me."

"Or me," said Malcolm. "You go so far as to wonder out loud at my trustworthiness."

"I . . ." I looked at Alex in the lamplight. *Why* did he have to look so like Louis Jourdan in *Letter from an Unknown Woman*? It just wasn't fair. "I *did* trust you. You do talk . . . some of the things you say . . ."

"And I suppose that you always mean what you say?"

"Yes," I said instantly, "otherwise, what's the point?"

"I think that trustworthiness can depend upon a lot of things; a lot of extraneous things," said Rose hurriedly.

"*I* think that the older I get, the more I disappoint people," said David.

"We all do," said Susie unexpectedly.

*

10.32 p.m.: "But everyone deserves an equal chance, don't they?" Rose looked around, eyes shining. "Every human being deserves opportunity?" Susie quietly closed the French doors.

There was a thunderous silence from the men. Finally, George leant forwards. "Well, that sounds like a lovely idea, Rose . . ."

"It *is* a lovely idea," I said.

"Not a very practical idea," said Alex.

"It *is* practical, isn't it? Because everyone does deserve a chance, but not everybody will take it. Some people aren't built to seize what they want . . ."

"Oh, you can't say that, Malcolm," said Rose.

"You can't, because . . ."

"You can't because – sorry, Alex – but you can't be all right to advocate equal opportunities but still admit that it won't work?"

"So, hold on a second," I said. "Malcolm, are you for equal opportunities or not?"

Malcolm gave me a look that seemed to slow everything down. He shrugged. "I'm just playing devil's advocate."

"It would mean socialism," said George. "Every Tom, Dick or Harry being trained up and found a place whether they could do the bloody work or not."

Alex nodded knowingly, which I found as irritating as an itch. "But what about the ones that are actually really good?" I asked.

"What about the one's that aren't?"

"What about women and the disabled?!" Rose chipped in.

"People are different," Alex said – his air of reproachful finality almost palpable.

"They would be less different if they were given the chance," I said.

"It'll take us back into recession," said Alex darkly.

"You can't just divvy it up: a certain percentage of working-class people per organisation, that would . . ."

"Why not, George? Just playing devil's advocate again." Malcolm smiled.

George frowned.

"I think . . ."

"What if you're aristocratic but penniless?" I'd interrupted David, and the men bristled a little, but I'd listened mutely enough to Priscilla and Rose's earlier discussion about using hot water for hydrangeas in flower arrangements.

"Or working class made good?" Malcolm pitched in. He had moved to the floor, sprawling by the empty fireplace.

"Or . . . I can't think of another," I said.

"Have you two quite finished?" Alex lit a cigarette. "You must go down a bomb in the metropolis that is Thornlaw."

"My popularity is growing in Thornlaw," I said, feathers ruffled.

"Did you tell them about that whacking great inheritance of yours?"

"No, I mean, it never comes up."

"We were agreeing with you basically, like the good little Thatcherites that we are," said Malcolm. "But sorry for the interruption of us uneducated types, Alex . . . actually, I'm not sorry at all."

"Neither am I," I said.

"God almighty." Alex ran his hands through his hair. "My point is that any company, whether it's an estate agency or whatever, only has so much time and energy to train these types of people, ergo, you can't have too many boys off a council estate, or . . ."

"Or girls. How many people do any of you employ with Asperger's?" It was as though someone's hand had reached inside my throat and pulled someone else's words out. I must be drunk, I realised.

"What?" George Cuthbert raised his eyebrows.

"What on earth is that?" Priscilla laughed. "Is it a person?"

"It's a sort of disease . . ." began Alex, looking warily at me.

"Ill people can't work, as a rule," said George. "Is it contagious?" Susie's lips curled into an involuntary smile.

"It isn't an illness, exactly. It's something you have. A difference."

"What difference? We're all different to each other, aren't we?" Priscilla looked around her at the other guests, who seemed to demonstrate her point. I could feel a mixture of embarrassment and pity emanating from David, Alex and Susie, all of whom, I realised, must have known about the Asperger's thing for weeks.

"It's more . . . more than a little difference," I said. I could have mentioned autism, I suppose – that would have made Alex choke on his cigarette and George spit out his brandy. But I already seemed to have a talent to shock – no need to abuse it, and hadn't Dr Gordner said it was different? Autism was probably something awful that happened to other people's children, as far as my fellow guests were concerned. Why, I wondered hopelessly, couldn't I explain what I was? Employing the word 'witch' seemed out of the question in Susie's sitting room, but Asperger's was almost as bad.

"I don't think that we have any . . . any 'Aspergers' on the estate, do we, Prisca?"

"No."

"Not many in estate agency either," said Alex, laughing.

I clenched the muscles in my arms and legs, tensing them against the pushing feeling inside me. "I'm going to go and look at the garden," I said.

As I stepped outside into the cool, I wrapped my arms around myself, fingers irritated by the feel of my crepe sleeves, and indulged in some pure misery. Somebody came and stood nearby – not beside me, exactly, but alongside. They kept a respectful or wary distance – I couldn't decide. "Alex?"

"Try again."

"Malcolm."

"I thought I'd come and rescue you. Again."

"From a topiary garden? I don't think that I am in any immediate danger."

"You know what I mean."

I turned towards his voice, my eyes growing used to the dark, watching the gleam off his glasses, the faint, square line of his cheek. His eyes were hidden, but I had glanced at him often enough through dinner to know that they were dark also, sparkling but curiously without expression. He took two steps closer; I wished it had been three – three was my luckiest number. "You really are a lovely looking girl," he said.

"Yes, I look my best in the pitch black," I said.

"I feel as though we don't suit meeting in daylight. Darkness is easier, isn't it?"

"Desirable, even." I laughed and then reminded myself that compliments, however odd, should always be repaid. It was my turn: "I think that a Geordie accent is prettier than a Yorkshire one. It swings about all over the place," I ventured.

"I see."

"Yes."

Malcolm walked the rest of the way over to me, took hold of

my face with quite devasting precision, and kissed me. I tried desperately to work out whether I liked it or not, whilst trying to keep up and accustom myself to the texture of someone else's lips and skin against mine. It was a lot to think about. I had done the same with Alex once, of course. Had his lips felt papery? It was years ago, and I had sought his lips out rather than *being* sought. Yes, definitely papery to the touch, strangely thin . . . Malcolm broke away and his hands fell from my face.

"I thought your skin would be burning hot."

"Sorry to disappoint – cold as ice." Malcolm squinted into the dark. "It's a surprisingly cool night, isn't it?"

"I like your upper lip."

"Thanks."

"Hmmm. So, have I . . . have I gone over to the dark side?"

"Very much so."

He didn't ask what I meant – note that. Surely a normal person, or rather, not a diabolical being, would have been bewildered?

"Let's go, shall we?"

"Are you going to walk me home?"

"Yes, amongst other things."

I could feel Malcolm's smile even though I couldn't see it. I followed him almost blindly, taking short steps like a geisha so as not to blunder into anything.

I am definitely going to hell, I thought. And I'll never get a man like David Kessel there.

SUNDAY 4TH JULY 1982

"You see," I explained patiently to my bedroom ceiling, "people with Asperger's are born with a clearer logic and a lack of emotionality, which is unusual, and therefore seen as odd. *Actually*, we are far more reasonable than other people. Madness is referred to as 'losing your reason', but we have too much of the stuff. Therefore, I mean, ergo, Asperger's *can't* be madness, can it?"

"Oh, I *see*," said my imaginary listener.

I had formed and tested this explanation of my own condition through the early hours of the morning, repeating my spiel over and over again as Peggy slept in a dormouse-style curl at my feet and the sky turned the pale orange-gold of a ripe apricot. My eyes were sore, my head hurt: I hadn't had enough sleep, and I knew that however much I practised the perfect definition of Asperger's, the opportunity had come last night and I had missed it. I had failed to explain myself.

"There is no known cure, of course . . ."

Dr Gordner looked at me pensively, as Sigi shifted gently in the background. I was back at my assessment.

"I could just wake up one morning and not have Asperger's?" I suggested. "What happens later on in life?"

"We really don't know . . ."

"Do many women have it?"

"Well, we don't really know that either . . ."

"So why have I got it?"

"It is rather unclear . . ."

Dr Gordner and Sigi melted away.

My diary was really supposed to be a sort of therapy, but I subverted it, just as I subverted Asperger's with witchcraft. Post Dr Gordner and Sigi, I'd decided that Asperger's was only something that other people called me. So why did it matter now? Perhaps because other people, like the guests at Alex's dinner party last night, were suddenly beginning to matter.

My eyelashes scrunched against the cotton pillow. The cottage seemed to intrude on me. I could hear the walls and ceilings, the sound of the old wooden beams on the floor as they expanded in the accumulating heat of the morning. They were all living here, their soft but crowded noise pushing me out. I curled up, pulling my feet away from Peggy but still feeling the solid warmth of her animal weight, my T-shirt pulling tight across my back.

The thing is, I was pretty sure that I had lost my virginity last night. Almost sure – I mean, I must have. Malcolm had been quite determined. We had been 'fooling around', as American as that sounded. I was slightly experienced in this – having done various fooling activities with Alex before making up my mind and leaving him – but very out of practice. Then he tried to . . . you know, and I thought, *Oh God, it's actually going to happen*. My mind detached itself from my body and panicked. Although, actually, there can't have been that much detachment because it hurt, and he tried for a bit and then stopped. Does that count?

It feels oddly humiliating having to confess to a page of paper that I am a virgin. It is what I am supposed to be, of course, being Jewish and unmarried and all that. But it makes me less interesting to myself, and far more timid than I would like to be thought of.

So . . . Malcolm and Sex, albeit an abortive attempt. There has been none of this aforementioned Sex before now, not in this diary, and not in the real, physical part of me. Sex has always seemed like looking through the windows of a department shop without going in – you can see lots of other people doing it without any problems, but you remain on the outside. It happens a lot to Gentile girls, of course – they don't mind as much, not being God's chosen and everything. It is always vaguely intimated by Rabbi Guld that we should feel a little sorry for non-Jewish girls, lumbered as they are with such animal urges and lacking nice, Jewish options like David Kessel. But I have a very distinct feeling that Susie Leverson does it too, which clouds the whole issue from a purely logical standpoint as she doesn't have a husband to do it with.

I am still trying to work out whether it counted. The whole actual trying to get inside me lasted maybe a minute, ninety seconds. *Why* did it happen? That will have to be dragged into the light at some point; expunged (a rubbery word because I always think of sink plungers). At that moment, I was tentatively weighing up whether Malcolm succumbed to a growing and insatiable desire for me, or whether his insatiable desire was general and I just happened to be within short range. As for me, when I try to think about Malcolm, it feels as though I have fallen off a precipice – sudden silence, then the whistling of air rushing past me. Complete and utter blankness.

Have you ever seen pictures of those African tribesmen who wear metal rings around their necks that they gradually add to over time? I felt as though those rings were inside my body, stretching me unpleasantly. My own thoughts are giving me a headache, as I write them down.

So how to deal with this dilemma of Malcolm? Alex has crept into my mind as well, making me feel that he must somehow be connected to all of this, not to mention David Kessel. I must be mature and orderly – use the diary in a way that would probably make Dr Gordner proud, but my head throbs rhythmically like train wheels on a metal line.

Eventually, I made my way downstairs, cowering at the noise I made, and reached for the telephone, holding it as far away from my ear as possible.

Was I proud of myself? I listened to the rings of the phone, counting. I suppose it was rather exciting to be suffering. I mean, here I was, confronted with the sort of problem that independent adults face. Actual, grown-up women who work in offices with glass walls and wear stilettos and earrings and drink white wine in bars would face just this sort of conundrum. I realised, in a half-baked sort of way, that I was actually growing up. And what does an independent, sexually alluring woman do first thing on a Sunday?

"Evie?" Lizzie picked up, which was strange given that Dad was usually the first one up and about in the mornings, working in his study. I should have been annoyed, but by this point I was too confused to care. I was already packing; already making a mental note to check the name of the long-necked African tribespeople in my encyclopaedia before I left, just to know.

"Can I come home?"

FRIDAY 9TH JULY 1982

Whatever goodwill my parents had felt over my sudden return – Lizzie, in particular, taking it as an expression of dependence that she found very gratifying – had slowly evaporated over the course of the week. My gratitude at the provision of emergency respite at Hawthorns had similarly dried up. I hadn't set a specific length of time for my stay, telling myself that I 'would see', but the days had rolled slowly by and I was stuck, drawn into the familiarity of home as though I had waded into treacle.

Suddenly, it was the evening of Shabbat, and I'd found myself outside the synagogue in the creeping chill of the evening. I was fumbling with the strap of my new shoe, tossing my head compulsively to remove my newly cut hair from my eyes, and scowling.

"Hurry *up*, Evie!"

"I'm *coming*!"

From the distance of Thornlaw, the Asher Israel and its inhabitants had undergone a benign transformation in my mind. The familiar babble of voices, the patterns on the women's dresses and the deep voices of the men became affectionate. I imagined the throng in the synagogue car park like a murmuration of starlings and I missed it. It was nice to miss them, too – another voluptuous feeling. This evening, I watched the reality of the crowd with a sinking feeling that I may have allowed my memories to become a little rosy.

"I'm going in," I said to Aunt Mim, who hung back in the bushes.

"I'll leave you here, I think," she said.

"Coward."

Aunt Mim grinned and was gone.

I walked, squeaky in my new shoes, towards the light of the lobby. The men had rested hands in the small of their wives' backs, light but proprietorial. The wives rested their hands on their children or held their handbags – I had nothing to hold on to at all. Insubstantial as a ghost, I drifted alongside them. How much was being a wife turning yourself into an example of a man's materialism? I would have to remember to ask Aunt Mim.

The synagogue was lit even though the sun was only just beginning to set. Everything was golden and polished – it caught the ladies' earrings in a sparkle, illuminated the sheen of dresses and ties. I could smell perfume and aftershave; see the furrows from the teeth of the combs that had pulled long hair up and into place. It crowded too much into too little – too much to look at and listen to, and I started to think wistfully about the open space surrounding Thornlaw. The clean, pure air.

". . . Matthew Feld."

"*No!*"

"Apparently . . ."

I could hear the whispered voices of Sue Halpern and her friend Rebecca Levi behind me, twittering like urgent little birds.

"But his *wife* . . ."

"She's my aunt's second cousin, did you know that?"

"Is she? She said anything to you then?"

"Well, him and Susie . . ."

"Even though . . . ?"

"Mmm hmmm."

I glanced over my shoulder and conversation abruptly ceased. A fairly common effect of my presence; I was used to it. Sue Halpern and Rebecca Levi looked over to Susie Ishkowitz, in a peach hat with silk flowers that looked rather like something Princess Di would wear, talking to Susie Leverson. I stopped to watch them for a moment, in particular, Susie Ishkowitz. She smiled and talked, swaying a little in her high heels. She didn't turn to me, but I had the impression that she had seen me, nonetheless.

Had Susie Ishkowitz been doing something with someone named Matthew Feld, who seemed to come complete with wife? Alex was away so much, I thought quickly, and they haven't had a baby or anything. Perhaps . . . I went and stood beside the older people so that I could think more clearly.

"Jenkins, now, he's not so bad."

"All his ideas – civilised society indeed!" Sarah Leverson folded her arms and gave a rather masculine snort.

"Oh, hello Evie," said Mr Halpern genially. "How goes it in the sticks?"

"All right thank you, Mr Halpern." I looked at him, Mr and Mrs Ishkowtiz and Mr Altschul, before finally meeting Sarah Leverson's eye. I had prepared myself to meet her as an equal, but her eyes swept me up and down as imperiously as ever and I detected a little flicker of distaste at the corner of her mouth. She had chosen to forget our conversation in her kitchen, I realised, and was daring me remind her.

Wouldn't it be nice if Malcolm was here? He could smile

sardonically at Sarah Leverson. There had been a Jewish demon hundreds of years ago; I remember reading about it before Rabbi Guld had firmly but gently removed the book from me. His name was Asmodeus, and he fell so badly in love with a nice Jewish girl that he killed her seven successive husbands. One had to admire his persistence. I wonder if Malcolm would do that for me? Or perhaps Geordie demons are different . . .

"We were just talking about Roy Jenkins," said Mr Ishkowitz, to a violent sniff from Sarah Leverson. "I think Roy Jenkins is a decent fellow – you know he's just won his leadership contest?"

"Oh."

"I suppose that you don't get the news out there, do you, Evie?" Mr Altschul's eyes were so small and bright that he seemed always to be laughing.

"I happen to be on the telephone," I said. "And I buy a paper," I added, with affronted dignity. Actually, I hadn't looked at the news since Alex had arrived – it didn't seem to matter so much.

"Shabbat shalom, everyone!"

"Shabbat shalom, Valerie, don't you look well!" Sarah Leverson swooped majestically past me to kiss the air either side of Val's cheek and beam at her. "How's the little one?"

Val looked at me over the top of Tom's downy head; our eyes met and I resisted the impulse to take a step back. I was still afraid of Val, and I hated her for always popping up in places where I didn't want her. Then I would imagine Water Under a Bridge and feel guilty – and the guilt would make me hate her even more.

"I heard you're staying with your mum and dad."

"Yup."

"Don't you like the country any more then?"

"I do, it's just . . ."

"Lizzie said that it was poky – the cottage. Could have afforded something bigger, couldn't you? Nicer."

"We were not all lucky enough to afford a cottage at your age," said Sarah Leverson.

"Don't I know it," said Val. She looked at me.

"Oh, is this about the money that—"

"How are your Alex and Susie settling in, Miriam?"

"Oh, very well, I think. It is nice to know that you are there too, Evie." Mrs Ishkowitz looked very elegant in her silk printed dress and amber beads that evening, but it was her face and soft voice that I loved best. Her niceness cut through the atmosphere of hostility sharply, opening up a little channel between us.

"They've still got the flat in Leeds, haven't they? I mean, you wouldn't want to be in the middle of nowhere all the time."

"They've still got their flat," said Mrs Ishkowitz. An image popped into my head of Alex and me on the sofa in that flat, when it had been a bachelor pad, doing a similar sort of thing to me and Malcolm last week. I blinked.

"You should have let Alex find you a house," Sarah Leverson said, with palpable disapprobation of my own independence.

"Well . . ." I looked at Mrs Ishkowitz helplessly.

"Susie was telling me that she's got involved on the village hall committee and they do things for charity, you know, organising things."

"Well, she's like that," said Sarah Leverson. She glanced around. "I can't see her . . ."

"Over there look, Sarah, with *your* Susie. In the peach."

"Oh yes. She always looks so turned out. And orangey colours can be so difficult."

"Who is Matthew Feld?" I asked suddenly and rather loudly – I was pleased, you see, at having remembered that there was something I needed to ask someone. There was a deadly silence. Sarah Leverson's eyes seemed to grow narrower. It was so quiet that I could distinctly hear the rustle of the trees at the back of the synagogue, and the cars driving past the entrance. The air felt warm and used, a little dirtied. Then everyone started talking at once, very loudly.

"I should have called him William," Val was saying to Mrs Halpern. "I know it's not Jewish and everything, but . . . well, I didn't realise how nice it sounded until Princess Diana chose it."

"I'll still be watching the final tomorrow," said Mr Altschul. "Why d'you think we've come to the Friday evening rather than the Saturday morning – I need to do my pre-match preparations!"

"All the same, it isn't as exciting, is it? When we're not in it." Mr Halpern sighed.

"I've got a cousin who's Italian," said Mr Ishkowitz. "His mother came from Bologna, managed to get out in the thirties, then ended up over here. So, there's sort of a family connection . . ."

"Jenkins wants to do all sorts of things," said Sarah Leverson scornfully. "Making it easy for girls to get rid of their babies, not make it a crime any more for those awful men . . ."

"What men would they be, Sarah?" Mrs Ishkowitz raised her eyebrows innocently.

"You *know* . . ." Sarah leant in confidentially towards her. I watched her mouth, quite distinctly. "Homosexuals."

"Hey!"

"What?" I looked around and saw David Kessel beckoning. He was smiling broadly, as though he was genuinely pleased that I had come home. I stumbled over to him, my feet arched into the mould of my new shoes and feeling as though they didn't belong to me.

"Come over here." He gripped my arm and pulled me around the back of the synagogue.

"Shabbat shalom to you too," I said, stumbling after him and trying to work out whether I still thought he was handsome. 'Mrs Eva Kessel'. It sounded lovely and European, but it didn't sound like me. We were in the children's play area, a little tarmacked square with a wooden slide and two swings.

"Do you want to go on the slide or something?"

"Course not, silly. Look, it's a blank wall behind, so nobody inside synagogue can see us." He rummaged vehemently in the top pocket of his jacket.

"Oh." Was David going to propose, I wondered wildly? I wanted to jerk my arms and legs about, imitate that gulping panic inside me. But David pulled out a packet of cigarettes and offered me one. I accepted, as befitted my new image as an independent woman. I waited patiently for him to light it and took a deep breath, gradually inhaling the bitter taste.

"So, how does it feel to be back then? The wanderer returns."

I had read the description, 'boyish grin', many a time, but David's fitted the phrase so beautifully. "God," I said, holding my cigarette at a safe distance in what I hoped was a sophisticated manner and trying not to cough, "it's bloody awful. Everyone is staring at me. Or talking about me. Or both."

"Well, you don't have to worry about that with me. I'm talking *to* you. Nice, isn't it?"

"Very." We stared straight ahead over the cut grass, our view of whatever was further away cut off by the fenced perimeter of the Asher Israel. Here was Judaism, beyond it was the rest of the world, I thought. It was Shabbat, which further compounded the feelings of guilt that curled like my cigarette smoke, but I was getting used to doing things that shouldn't be done. Making a habit of it helped. "Everyone'll be talking even more if they notice we've both gone," I moaned. "You want to be careful – you'll have to marry me."

When I got home, I would pack my things, Peggy included, and drive back to Thornlaw next morning.

David laughed, exhaling a cloud of pale smoke which hovered in the darKevinng air. "Don't get your hopes up," he said kindly.

"Oh, because you don't find me attractive," I said. "Because I'm always saying the wrong thing, like when I compared shooting to bird-watching. I could see how ludicrous it was afterwards. But it was too late then. I see *now*. Why are you looking at me like that? Don't tell me that I've said the wrong thing to *you* too!"

"Well, you are right, in a way, because I *don't* find you

attractive," said David, with the same excruciating gentleness that Mrs Ishkowitz had used to me a few minutes ago. "But I don't find any woman attractive, if you get my drift." He stopped, and waited.

I could feel my face fall as I gradually understood what David had just told me. My eyes locked ahead, I wanted to turn towards him and stare and stare. Put my face close to his and really look at him for the first time. Silence was growing like a balloon as it filled with air. Before it burst, I had to say something, even if it was wrong. "Is that, I mean . . . is it allowed?"

David laughed again, a little harshly this time. "As much as this alarming thing that you have, I suppose. What's it called?"

"Asperger's," I said miserably. There it was again: Asperger's – alarming people, lurking in the synagogue playground. "I suppose that I don't really tell people. And I suppose that you don't tell people either, about . . . you being, you know, homo—"

"Gay."

"Gay," I echoed. "Happy and gay. Does it make you happy? Even when Sarah Leverson is rude about it?"

"Are you ashamed?" David asked suddenly. "I am sometimes, and then I look at all of those people inside those walls, at all the unthinking things they do and call it virtue, and I'm fucking glad that I'm not like them. Pardon my French," he added.

"I don't know whether Asperger's is shameful or not. Lizzie thinks it is, probably." It felt wonderful to be able to admit that, I realised, like a bird taking flight inside of me.

"No, she doesn't. She nearly got into a row with Mrs Guld

when she suggested that you needed to be put into some kind of home."

"Mrs Guld said that? God, what a . . ."

"Bitch?"

"Yes. Yes, those are the appropriate sentiments."

"Sentiments." David laughed. "Does this Asperger's make you talk like a ninety-year-old who has just swallowed a dictionary?"

"No! I mean, maybe. I don't know. Probably."

"You don't seem very clued up about the whole thing."

"I'm not," I said. "It's something that other people say that I have, but it doesn't really feel like me, you know? I mean, it's just a name."

"It's a mouthful. You don't need to be ashamed about it though."

"But I'm not sure. 'It isn't autism', that's what Dr Gordner said, and I think that you have to keep saying it, so as not to scare anybody. And if I don't scare anybody, I *shouldn't* be in a mental home."

"You shouldn't be in a mental home because you are all right, Evie," said David. "For God's sake, whatever this thing is, you are *you*. Why would you think that you should be shut away just because someone slaps a label on you? You're doing all right."

"Thanks," I said. I meant it too, not in the usual polite and automatic way. "I just call myself something else anyway."

"How would you describe the . . . symptoms? Characteristics? Erm, stuff?"

"I'm a witch," I said proudly.

"Are you? God, of course you are!" David smiled, but I don't think he was making fun of me.

"I am a *bit* ashamed though," I admitted. "Even when I am on my own and don't need to explain it to anybody. Do you think shame would exist without other people?"

"I don't know," said David. "But I do know this: shame weakens you, over time. It takes something that usually isn't that bad anyway, and makes it grow and chip away at you."

The sun was really setting now and David was barely visible, just a dark outline of himself. The service had started inside, and the doors had closed a while ago. I wanted to put my arm around him, but at the same time I was relieved that he hadn't touched me. "What are you going to do? With your gay?"

"Stick it out for as long as I can here, then, when they really start pressurising me to get married, I'll move to London, I suppose."

I could think of nothing to say. David smoked, I pretended to; we stared at the borderlines of the Asher Israel until they blurred and faded into darkness.

SUNDAY 11TH JULY 1982

Faithful Cottage is true to its name: it is exactly where and how I left it, which I take as some sort of compliment.

I finally arrived back today, lured into staying an extra night at home by Dad and Lizzie with the promise of roast chicken. Peggy did a demented grand tour, running the course of the cottage and garden whilst barking hysterically. I took my bag upstairs, dumped it in the sepulchral gloom of the second bedroom and made a vow to buy myself a wardrobe as well as a bedside table.

I had spent the entire journey alternating between intense concentration on the road and thinking about David Kessel. I was slowly learning the mysterious ways of the Alpine Sunbeam, but public roads – therefore, everywhere I drove – were still a huge problem. Swinging into my little uphill street, wobbly and emotional with relief at having made it without accident, I decided to let my emotions run riot about David, and cried. Peggy looked askance, and then climbed onto my lap, breaking wind loudly as she did so. I had been so stupid, I decided tearily, thinking that he wanted to go out with me and worrying and only thinking about myself. It must be lonely for David – I was lonely too, but I didn't mind because I was built that way.

A thought occurred to me in the Alpine Sunbeam: perhaps I spent a little too much time thinking about myself? I was odd, distinctly odd, and therefore worthy of further study. But sometimes I forgot that other people could be odd in an interesting way too.

I stuffed Peggy back onto the passenger seat and in doing so, caught a twitch of Dot and Vernon's net curtain. I turned my head away, dried my eyes and headed inside, jelly-legged from crying. Why does crying always effect one in the leg region?

MONDAY 12TH JULY 1982

"Hello, Joanie – it's Evie?" I don't know why I sounded so uncertain of my own name. I stared down at the Princess Louise Museum postcard that Joanie printed her number on with a neat, round hand, firmly resolved to be altruistic.

"Oh, Evie . . ."

"Joanie? Are you all right?"

"Oh, yes. But . . . not really. My heart is bad, I am getting chest pains. There's the WI social next week: a tour of Fielden Hall and sandwiches, but I don't think I'll be able to go."

"I'm . . ."

"My husband cancelled our hearing, just as I was about to set off."

"So. . ."

"The lawyer telephoned me. I didn't know what to do with myself."

"Sorry," I finally managed. "How's your list of words? I am adding 'fantasia' to mine . . ."

"Do you know, I really haven't thought. I am not much use at things inside my head any more," said Joanie. "The nice words seem to get pushed out by other things. Better on paper in my wordsearch books, where I can see them."

"I suppose most things are better where you can see them," I agreed. Then I thought, what would an altruistic person with a firm resolve do in this situation? A drawing of Florence Nightingale shining her lamp on wounded soldiers flashed through my mind, but maybe that was going a little bit far. "I'll come round," I said triumphantly, "to see you. And keep you company."

"I came round to see you," a faintly accusatory note entered Joanie's voice, "on Saturday. But you weren't in."

"Yes, I mean, no. I wasn't. I had to go home – family problems," I lied.

"Oh." Joanie gasped gratefully. "Well, I am in all the time now. So, if you want to come this afternoon, or tomorrow . . ."

"I will," I said firmly – possibly a little too firmly – and put the phone down with a happy bang. Joanie would be nursing her broken heart on the chaise longue, I supposed, with a fan and some eau de cologne. I could read to her perhaps, but nothing too romantic. It would all be so Victorian. Then I looked outside – it was a lovely day, and I thought of Joanie's stone house and its little windows with distaste. I could walk Peggy, I thought, get some sunshine and fresh air, and see Joanie another day.

In the end, I compromised and set off with an added possibility to call in on Joanie, knowing that I wouldn't. I let Peggy drag me along and half-closed my eyes in the sunshine, feeling how pleasantly familiar the paths were. I walked towards the centre of the village, entering a sudden patch of quiet – no cars or people and no reason for the lack of them, just a gloriously deserted stretch. I breathed more deeply – I always do when it is peaceful. I was alone, I thought, independent – if only Mrs Guld was here.

Was that Vi wandering along on the opposite side of the road, the broken strands of her grey hair catching the sun like a halo? "Sweet violets," she was singing, just loud enough to be heard, "sweeter than the roses, sweet violets . . ."

"Mrs Vi?"

She drifted around the corner and was gone. How odd, I thought. Vi should be in bed, shouldn't she? Perhaps I was having a vision, and if so, how exciting! I walked on towards the church as cars started along the road, and other people wandered into view – it had only been a few noiseless seconds.

Reverend Rishangles was leaning against the church wall, sleek and dark as a raven in his cassock. He seemed to be staring at nothing at all. I wondered whether I could pass him unnoticed, but he reluctantly dragged his glittering eyes from that invisible spot and straightened up to greet me. I was oddly pleased to see him.

"Mondays," he said, in his thin voice. "The day after the day itself, if you know what I mean."

"Sort of," I said. "I feel a little like that on a Sunday."

He nodded with resignation. "Everyone else occupied; your function becomes reduced, somehow."

"Did you have a . . . erm . . . a good sermon yesterday? I mean, sermons?"

He shrugged.

I had done such a good job at cheering Joanie up on the phone, I felt that I could continue my run of altruism with the reverend. "It's such a pretty church," I said, looking behind him. Actually, I found it rather a plain affair, the stone dull in the shade of the sun. It ran along in its rectangle, the tower like a child's wooden brick balanced at the end. I was offended slightly by its age, by its placid feeling of belonging, and thought of the Asher Israel and its newness that stuck out so sharply. "The tower is castellated."

"A vicar's home is his castle."

I had exhausted architecture, and it didn't seem to be having the desired effect. "Did you see Vi just now? She must have walked this way. It's nice to see her up and about, isn't it?"

"Vi?" Revered Rishangles frowned; his forehead folded into wrinkles. "No, no, no. She's bed-bound completely now."

"I was sure that I . . ." I tailed off, compressing my feelings of excitement. A real-life vision, I was thinking to myself – vindication for Evie!

The reverend's eyes seemed to penetrate the external cover of me. Feeling suddenly seen through, I began talking very quickly. "I rang Joanie this morning. I was worried about her, so, you know, and she isn't very well, her heart is bad."

"Ah. Joanie and her heart. Why do I imagine that she will outlive us all? Such a tiresome woman."

"But . . . are you allowed to say that? I mean . . ."

"Who heard me? Apart from you, and, of course, the dear departed." He indicated the graveyard with delicate fingers. "I will go round and see her."

"OK, well I must . . ." I indicated vaguely at the pavement and gave Peggy a surreptitious yank so that she didn't linger.

"May I offer you a little advice, Miss Edelman? Don't get entangled with Joanie, she'll only drag you down with her. And I say that out of kindness to you, rather than unkindness to her. I am sure you will understand – neither of us truly see the point of social niceties. I hear all sorts of reports of you, all sorts of charitable oddities. Beware of letting others think that you are charitable and exist to please them. This place is too small for anyone to disguise their true nature." He smiled at me with the corners of his mouth. "And come past this way soon. You are drawn here, aren't you?"

"I suppose that I like it, in a sort of foreigner way."

"Of course you do. 'A serious house on serious earth'."

"Who said that? Was it Jesus?"

"Close," said the reverend. "Philip Larkin." He turned on his heel and stalked back to his church.

I stumbled on a few steps, then, checking that he wasn't watching, quickly crossed the road and set off home. Aunt Mim, then Malcolm that day in the churchyard, now Vi – my visions were coming on apace. Except, I reluctantly had to admit that Malcolm was actually corporeal. Very corporeal. And Aunt Mim was family – did that count?

Distracted, I tried to process Reverend Rishangles' advice. His words were grey and smoky, wafting into one another and jumbling together in my mind until I couldn't make sense of them at all. "What did *you* make of it?"

"How should I know what to make of *that*?" Aunt Mim said tartly. She stomped along beside me in her green woollen dress.

"Why are you wearing that? Aren't you hot?"

"Boiling. But I didn't think it would be as warm as this and I'm stuck in it now, aren't I?"

"Can't you, you know, spin round three times, change your ectoplasm or something and get a new outfit?"

"It doesn't *work* like that."

"Sorry. I like him – the reverend. Even though I think he may have just insulted me in rather a gentle way. He was warning me about trying too hard to fit in, you know?" I pulled the strands of Reverend Rishangles apart slowly.

"Not really, no."

"Don't you like him?"

"Well, I don't think you should listen to anything he says," said Aunt Mim darkly. "I've met vicars like him before. Know-it-alls in black dresses."

"How've you 'met vicars like him'? You don't know any vicars! Do you?"

"Well, no. But I've read about one that he reminds me of . . . where was it now?"

"Not the one in *Jamaica Inn*?"

"Yes, exactly."

"But that vicar was a murderer and a smuggler and an out-and-out villain."

"Well, there you are, then."

"Hello, love!"

"Oh, hello, Edith." How had I managed to get home so quickly? Perhaps I should add flying to my increasing witchy prowess. But I suppose Aunt Mim and I had been marching.

"Are you all right, love?"

"Erm . . . yes?" I immediately straightened up and tried not to frown.

"I meant the other day, love. We all missed you, going away suddenly like that."

"Yes."

"Was it . . . *man* trouble? Only you looked so upset in the church that time I saw you, then you were upset when you came back . . ."

"Yes, I mean . . . no."

"You *do* look pale." Edith scrutinised me with a critical, feminine eye, her red hair gleaming softly. "The thing is, love, you have to give *them* the run-around, rather than running around after them."

Sometimes I feel as though I'm carrying a measuring jug inside me that fills slowly as I socialise with other people, gently but gradually reaching its fill. That measuring jug was now overflowing, having the effect of mixing up my senses, so the words were too bright for my eyes, the summer colours hard on my ears.

"Yes," I said. I flicked what was supposed to be a reassuring smile at Edith (although I suspect it was anything but) and hurried away.

*

Faithful Cottage had waited for me, small and discreet at the end of the little terrace. As I was fiddling with the key in the lock, Peggy shifting impatiently at the thought of seeing her armchair again, I heard voices getting nearer from the top field – a jumble of male voices. Alex, Malcolm and Dave appeared. Peggy immediately began to yip.

"Shut up," I hissed unpleasantly at her, "don't embarrass me!"

I stared at Malcolm, reacquainting myself. He wasn't as good-looking as I had thought. He looked too . . . too human. In my head he had become oddly elevated, with his dark hair and suit and his white teeth and glasses. I could see the shine of grease on

Malcolm's nose now, the stubble over his neck.

"I could murder a steak," Dave was saying. It was obviously a lunch break – they all looked a little sweaty, hot and tired. The pen in Malcolm's top pocket was askew. Nevertheless, I was possessed by the desire to open with something witty and intelligent.

"You should have brought a packed lunch with you, it would have been cheaper and more convenient," I said. I could *kick* myself, I really could.

"I'm not really domesticated," said Malcolm. "I have other things to attend to."

I smiled, thinking that he meant The Devil's Work. Then I realised that he could have been alluding to our . . . you know . . . and stopped smiling. I didn't want to be thought lascivious. Seductive, yes, but not lascivious. There was a fine line.

We hung about each other awkwardly, and I felt the intimacy we'd once had detach itself and float away. We seemed to hardly know one another. Alex had hung back and was suddenly deep in conversation with Dave. I watched Alex – he *knew* I wanted to say hello; something about the stiffness of his neck. He refused to make eye contact, and I felt like blowing a raspberry at him. *Then* he would stop pretending to be busy and manly, and treat me as though I was Evie and he was Alex.

"Are you going to . . . ?" Malcolm nodded at my door.

I held my breath, nodded, and felt that I was about to go up another level into adulthood. "Stay to lunch," I commanded grandly. Wondering what on earth was going to happen, I resumed fiddling with the lock and again opened my mouth to say hello to

Alex as he walked past. I felt that I needed the familiarity of him just then. He didn't look at me.

"Oh," Alex suddenly called back over his shoulder, "see you at the Fieldens' next week."

"What?"

"At Fielden Hall? Lunch? Susie said that she'd passed George's invite to you."

"Need a hand with that, love?" Dave called. He pointed at the lock.

"I am quite capable of doing it myself, thank you."

"Oooh, hoity toity. You want to watch her," Dave called to Malcolm. "Come on, Ishy."

A worried expression flitted across Alex's face as he made after Dave. Jealous, I thought. He's actually jealous. Feeling rejuvenated, I stepped aside for Malcolm to go first and then realised that I should have been ladylike and gone first . . . Lizzie would have known what to do. "Oh, I forgot about Joanie!"

"What?"

"Nothing." I shut the door. Too late now.

THURSDAY 15TH JULY 1982

I feel as breathless as Joanie – I'm so busy. Before now I have *felt* busy, but my business has consisted of going for walks, spells, learning about the acacia tree (I've moved on from poplars) and having to talk to people. Now, I am busy in the same way that *normal* people are, and it just feels so . . . so regular. It is wonderful!

List of things that I have learnt about Malcolm in the last three days:

1. He was born in South Shields. People from there call themselves 'Sandancers' – isn't that lovely and poetic? It must be such a romantic place. It sounds a little like 'Sandman' as well, doesn't it? I imagine that the more nightmarish connotation must be quite pleasing to someone of Malcolm's type.

2. He doesn't consider crisps and a banana to be an adequate lunch.

3. His fingernails are very pale and moonlike, and quite beautiful. I know because I checked for a 'devil's teat' – an extra fingernail that Anne Boleyn had, apparently.

4. He has shown me the plans for the modern houses and two blocks of flats in the top field. They are very square and blank, with plain sheet glass windows that look as open as staring eyes. "They look so ugly," I said. "If they were people, they would be short and wear cheap grey suits." He laughed and put his arm around me.

5. His star sign is Capricorn – he mentioned once

that he was born near Christmas, and I suppose that it would have to be something horned. I told him that I am a Leo, and I told him that technically we are incompatible because we are two such strong people, but that it *did* depend on rising signs and other planetary alignments, so it would probably be all right. "Are Capricorn and Virgo compatible?" he'd asked. "Yes, very. Why?" Then he said that it didn't matter.

6. He said that we would "take things more slowly" after the last time. I wasn't quite sure what that meant, but it seems to mean kissing and pressing up against one another most days. I am getting used to it all now.

I suppose that there have been other things besides Malcolm, too. And I can't really be bothered with books at the moment, except this one. My mind hops about like a frog between lily pads, always settling upon Malcolm. Malcolm McKay. Evie McKay. I sound as though I would wear cardigans and enjoy Joanie's WI social to Fielden Hall.

I have *thought* about Joanie, by the way: I am not a complete monster. But I haven't called in on her, and I haven't phoned her because I know that she would *ask* me to call in on her. Guilt almost makes me dislike Joanie, just as I dislike Val. I keep thinking of Reverend Rishangles telling me how tiresome Joanie is and wishing that I didn't agree with him.

Rather disappointingly, I've had no more visions. Vi has been the only one. I told Malcolm about it spontaneously, when we were up in my bedroom, sunbathing in the creamy afternoon light. He had teased me about my Adam Ants.

"Your chaperones for the afternoon, are they? They don't like me, I can tell."

"They aren't even looking at you!"

"They both are, their eyes follow me round the room like the Mona Lisa's are supposed to. The attraction of enigma, I suppose, in both cases."

"When you say both – both my Adam Ants, or both as in the Mona Lisa and my Adam Ants?"

"Whichever you prefer." Malcolm had sighed then, and there seemed to be a gap in the conversation, so I had told him about my vision of Vi and waited with bated breath. I thought that he would reveal something of himself, but he stared straight ahead, out of the window, perhaps regretting that he had shut himself away with me.

"I'm sure it was a mistake. Probably someone who looked like her. You only saw her once, didn't you?"

"Yes, but . . ."

"Well."

"Don't you believe in that sort of thing then?"

"Course not," he said. "There's nothing except what's real. Bricks and mortar – that's what you build from."

I stared out of the bedroom window too, sharply disappointed.

But gradually, I have come to think that no devil would believe in the occult – they are far too perverse for that.

SATURDAY 17TH JULY 1982

Dad and I were alternating the lines of a song. Something quick, light. The sheer joy of all the words – the charm, the civilised nature of the clever lyrics that have evaporated since and perhaps never existed. We were driving, the Ford was unusually spacious so the air almost whistled. Outside was green and sunny . . . but not home. I knew that, somehow, I wasn't close enough to home to be safe. The car jolted over a bridge, everything slowed down, my heart leapt and I woke up.

*

I had thought perhaps that Malcolm might have given me a call. The feeling of trepidation that I feel just looking at the telephone is unbearable. There's a little bit of longing, perhaps, and a strange tingling feeling that mirrors the one I get when he kisses me. Who knew that the telephone could become an erotic symbol? Is there no end to Malcolm's talents?

I did get a call, as it happens, at 10.23 a.m., and I rushed over and snatched up the phone. Joanie was at the other end, gasping for breath as usual, as though she was wearing a corset. My heart plummeted. I got rid of her as quickly as I could.

"You are kind," she had said, "to take an interest in an old thing like me."

"You aren't old," I'd replied automatically. When I put the

phone down, I wondered why Joanie had told me that she was going to the doctor about her heart – after all, it hadn't broken literally, only metaphorically. If only she would stop getting herself in a state. But then, I thought about the idea of her wearing a corset and thought that Mr Joanie must be the real-life corset: he was squeezing the life out of her, depriving her of air.

Malcolm, on the other hand, was beautifully independent. There was a coolness to him, a paleness that matched his white skin. This weekend was a perfect example of this attractive power of detachment: he had gone home, back up to Sandancer-land, only telling me yesterday morning and then off that evening, quite casually, because he must have known that I wouldn't mind.

"Shall I give you a ring?" I had asked, innocently enough. I thought that it was the appropriate response – after all, for those of us not deathly afraid of the telephone, it is normal to offer to give everyone a ring, all of the time. It was all very innocuous.

"No," he'd said.

"Oh," I said. I waited.

"It's just that I'll be busy," he said, frowning and folding something over his arm – I couldn't see what. I stared at him until he came and kissed me. "I'll come and see you Sunday night when I get back, all right?"

"All right," I said, thinking how daring it was that we sounded like lovers rather than boyfriend and girlfriend. Really, it was almost French.

I was sitting on the arm of the sofa now; it afforded me a better view of the phone. I kicked my legs in quick succession into the side of the sofa. Bump bump, pause. Bump bump, pause . . . The phone stubbornly refused to ring.

I should go out, I thought – then it would definitely ring. Perhaps Malcolm would see me as more unobtainable. My mystery, and therefore my allure, would deepen, and it would all be for the best. I needed some shopping anyway. What did I need from the village shop? More crisps, obviously, some cheese, one of those large Bakewell tarts in plastic packaging that, try as I might, always had most of the white icing clinging to the cellophane by the time I got home.

Perhaps the phone was broken? I picked up the receiver, just to listen to the line – it was there, steady. The plop of the receiver being replaced woke Peggy from the first of her many daily naps. She stretched luxuriously and came to me, planting her front paws up on my shins and scrabbling at them furiously. "We're on our own, aren't we?" I said. "Ow – stop it."

I still feel that being on my own is a treat – I haven't changed that much. Hearing my words fade into nothing – not everyone has that luxury. In fact, I have the best of both worlds. I have Malcolm, and I have my solitude. During that first waking when all the parts of me had not quite crystallised together, I had sensed that I was alone and was so happy. I could spend a pleasantly flat day without the upward spring and swift falls of Malcolm . . .

But Malcolm still hadn't rung – I'd been writing for fourteen minutes! *And* his face had faded. But I had the essence of Malcolm, I felt. I tried to think about Alex – just as an experiment, you understand. He seemed a little pudgy; it wasn't attractive compared to Malcolm's slim, straight waist. And Alex was messy – his figure came with thoughts and feelings that had accumulated over years. He had lovely eyes, but I couldn't remember them now. It was as though the imprint of Alex, although deeper, older, more necessary somehow, was a fact blurred by confusion. Malcolm's effect in my mind was immediate – shallow, but heightened by its novelty. Suddenly, I seemed to prefer him to everyone.

*

"Shopping," I'd said to myself, later that afternoon. Then, I heard voices outside my window.

"There it is," said one, the voice suppressed and low.

"What, *that*?"

"Yes."

"God. It doesn't look much, does it?"

"What do you expect?"

There was a short, mirthless little laugh. I couldn't see who the voices belonged to, just vague shadows thrown through the window, lengthening as they poured inside.

"Perhaps it's more attractive inside."

"Don't you believe it. Lizzie said . . ."

The owners of the voices wandered past, peering into the window of my main room. Their eyes met mine, and we all recoiled. It took me a second to realise that it was Val and Susie Ishkowitz. Even worse, I realised that I would now have to open the door. My movements were extra careful so that I wouldn't betray my reluctance to see them. When I opened the door, I noted two things: the first was that both Val and Susie had a sheepish look about them and were keeping a careful distance from the doorstep. The second was that Susie Ishkowitz was wearing jeans, only it didn't look the same as when I wore jeans. In fact, Susie Ishkowitz made her jeans look like a completely different piece of clothing. The denim sort of clung to her legs and nipped in her waist as neatly as a doll's. She had a thin, blue sweater on as well, and a gold bracelet.

"We thought that we would come and see you," she said.

"Did you?"

"Yes."

"Oh." I realised that I had to play along. "How . . . nice?" Nice was patently untrue, we all knew it, and I felt a moment of extreme exasperation. Rocking gently on my heels, I thought of what else I could lie about. "Hello, Val."

"Hello, Evie." Val's voice had a certain hardness to it that was shushed when she talked to men, or to Sarah Leverson at synagogue, but not to me.

"What are you doing here?"

Val had the grace to look slightly embarrassed. "I've come to see Susie," she said. "I thought it was a nice day for a drive into the country, and Susie was telling me about everything she's been doing, charity-wise, helping on the village hall committee and organising."

"I didn't recognise you at first."

Val raised her eyebrows and looked down at her cotton dress and tennis shoes. "I'm the same as ever."

"I don't doubt it," I said to myself. Outwardly, I said, "Haven't you done something to your hair?"

"I'm wearing a fringe now," said Val, combing the darker strands, sweaty under the sun, to one side with her fingers. It seemed to have been the right thing to say – she looked flattered.

"Do you think that I've changed?" I asked suddenly, on a whim. I realised that I knew the answer already. I realised, standing in my socks beside my front door, that I was different from the previous Alwoodley version of myself. I was leaner, my body felt harder and stronger, but I was leaner mentally too. It was as if the edges of me were firming up or coming into focus perhaps.

"Oh, no," said Val instantly.

"No?" I challenged her.

"No," she said. "You've got a bit of a suntan about you, and with your money now, you probably feel different. But you're always the same."

We stared at one another for a moment. Susie Ishkowitz seemed fascinated.

"Have you got Joe with you?" I asked eventually, reminding myself that I was, in some involuntary way, also the hostess.

Val's smile flicked off. "No," she said stiffly, "but here's little Tom."

"Oh yes." I hadn't noticed Tom before. I am not sure why, given that he was a fairly hefty presence with his pram and paraphernalia. Val drew back a cloth she'd pinned over the pram and waited. There was another silence. Susie Ishkowtiz turned and looked distantly towards the field.

"Aren't you going to say hello? To Tom?"

"What? Oh, yes." I leant forwards and patted Tom on the head.

His face immediately crumpled like a piece of discarded fabric, and he wailed.

"Would you like to come in?" I called, over the racket.

"We wouldn't want to impose," said Susie. "We were going to go for a walk, if you'd like to join us?" Val was already doing a three-point turn with the pram, her face thunderous.

"Thanks, but I am busy."

Susie nodded sympathetically, and I was relieved that she was playing the game too.

"Well, another time then."

"Yes." I said, and Susie smiled.

"Oh, just a minute!" I called out after her.

"Hmmm?"

"Alex said that you had an invitation for me, something about Fielden thingy? The Hall?"

Susie retraced her steps, head slightly lowered, looking as though she was thinking quickly. She took up an elegant stance opposite me, again at a safe distance. "Did he? I don't recall . . ."

"Something to do with Fieldens, this coming week."

"Oh, goodness. That. George has sold the field up there for development. You met one of the developers at the dinner party – Malcolm. You probably don't remember him . . ."

"Oh yes, I do! He's gone home this weekend, hasn't he?"

Susie gave me an odd a look. "Yes, well it is hard on him, being away for long stretches, even if it is a prestigious new development. Alex told me, but nobody is saying anything publicly yet. You don't mind keeping quiet, do you?"

"I wasn't going to tell anyone," I said proudly. It was nice for Malcolm and I to be secret for now.

"Good," Susie seemed relieved. "The village will have to know eventually, I suppose – if they haven't worked it out. Well, Wednesday, twelve-thirty for one, Fielden Hall. All right?"

*

I sat on a nearby stone wall, diary in hand, thinking of my old diary and shifting against the lumps of stone that were rough, sharp in places, but not unpleasant. I had catalogued every incident back then, faithfully recording everything that happened, just in case, writing the only power that I'd possessed. Every single time that Val had made the other girls laugh at me, had taken something of mine, had whispered something nasty in my ear as I had walked past her . . . how could I be so different to *them*, I had wondered?

Would I have to poison this diary by writing down Val's little gestures of nastiness again? It seemed that she had found me out; I hadn't been growing independent, I had just been hiding out here in Thornlaw and pretending to grow up.

No, I wrote, *no.* I wouldn't write about Val any more. "I trust myself to heal rather than harm," I said loudly. It was Saturday, after all, and that was my witchy phrase.

Peggy wandered out to see me, belatedly wondering what was going on. "Just us two again," I told her. She seemed relieved.

There was an unattractiveness inside of me, that some people just seemed to draw to the surface. Val and Susie were a part of my old life carried over; they smudged the line I had drawn between Alwoodley and Thornlaw. And they brought out a feeling of thunder, a darkness that made me feel trapped. I kicked against it. What would it matter if the village knew about me and Malcolm, anyway? I didn't have to keep secrets just because Susie Ishkowitz wanted me to.

Eyes closed, side to side I rocked, soothing myself and listening to the wind in the trees. The sound was different for every type of tree – a silvery swish for some, others softer, like the rustle of a silk dress. After a while I dissected the general noise, like the sections of an orchestra. There was the louder, thicker sound of the almost plastic oak leaves, then the birch leaves twinkling over the top . . . it became a pattern, and then it didn't seem so natural any more. My eyes opened. Why couldn't I just experience something as a whole?

But at least Susie and Val had gone.

WEDNESDAY 21ST JULY 1982

13.07 p.m.: "Now, red or white?" George Cuthbert had asked me in an avuncular manner, beaming at me but really pleased with himself.

"I rather think I am orange, actually," I said, smoothing out the lap of my dress. I was feeling particularly acerbic this lunchtime, having already had two glasses of champagne. My clip-on earrings were pinching my earlobes – I could feel the hot throb of my blood there like a second heartbeat. I had spent most of the previous night awake, imagining various scenarios and saying things like, "Oh no, George, I am inordinately fond of salmon", and, "What magnificent family portraits you have, Flora, is that a Gainsborough?" It never did, I thought, to be under-rehearsed.

We were currently in the wood-panelled dining room, soup had been served. There was a distinct absence of Gainsboroughs, only a few wishy-washy watercolours that were not worth mentioning.

George laughed, a tad uncertain. What George didn't realise, I thought, was that I was even more uncertain than he was. I had no idea whether I wanted red or white, and with a mounting feeling of hysteria, I realised that I couldn't focus on anything for more than a second at a time. My mouth felt dry and slightly scraped from the champagne. Champagne. "I think I'd like some more champagne," I said.

"Of course she would," said Malcolm. He hadn't come to see me on Sunday night. I had felt very small and abandoned until he had arrived on Monday morning with a box of Cadbury's Milk Tray and an apologetic smile.

"Right, erm . . ." George got up and appeared to be searching the sideboard.

"Champagne is about the last thing you need," said Alex. By some odd twist of fate or black art of wish fulfilment – I was too confused to work out which – he was sat beside me. David Kessel was there too, with a girl from the office named Sandra who would laugh and then tuck her chin in towards her neck as though she had just done something unconscionable. Then there was Jim, the estate manager, and his wife Jane, stoic and feudal.

"Pace yourself," Alex whispered to me under his breath.

"I'm positively fine," I said haughtily.

"Are you?"

"Course." Alex grabbed hold of my soup spoon and returned it to my bowl from where it had been, mid-flight, over my skirt.

"I'm not wearing the brooch that you . . ."

"The weather really is so changeable around here, isn't it?" Alex shouted.

"What do you care about the weather?" I asked. "This soup spoon is unusually heavy," I announced to the assembled company. David Kessel gave a kind of sneeze that sounded suspiciously like a laugh, but perhaps I misheard.

"Proper silverware is heavy," explained Flora, all the way at the top of the other end of the table. Her voice wafted over to me, as fragile as her chintzy dress.

Why was one earring causing so much more pain than the other? Did I have one very sensitive earlobe, and was that a medical condition? Was it part of the Asperger's, perhaps? I cautiously put my fingers to the back of my ear, cooling it for a moment.

"Of course, imitation is much lighter."

"We have the proper stuff at home too," I said, but Flora had turned back to Susie.

"This soup is very nice," said David.

"Oh yes, it *is*," echoed Sandra.

"Good idea to have it cold, wasn't it?" George sat back down at the table, having found me another champagne glass and filled it.

"I don't like it," I whispered to Alex. I mean, what was the point of cold soup? It seemed a tautology to me, and tasted of potatoes with something else vaguely interesting right at the end, just as you were about to take another mouthful. Like the soup, it was a cold room too. The wooden panels seemed to instantly absorb the heat. I would have to fill up on bread, I thought, only the butter was so far away. As I looked down the table it seemed to list like the deck on board a ship. "The *Titanic*," I said to myself, and sniggered.

"Aren't you having any bread, Susie?"

"No thank you, George."

"She eats like a bird," said Alex proudly, and gave Susie a look so blatantly affectionate that I found it quite nauseating.

"I wish I had sat next to David," I hissed in his ear.

"Susie does too," he said. "And so do I, for that matter. Now, shut up!"

"You shut up."

". . . the reverend running it all, or rather, he's supposed to be running it all . . ." Flora was saying to Susie.

"Reverend Rishangles?" I asked loudly.

"Yes."

"Do you know him?" Susie asked, with just the flimsiest overlay of irony.

"I've met him," I said, and then realised that didn't quite cover it. "I like him. He called one of my friends tiresome."

"He really is the strangest man," said Flora. "To be honest, I don't think he wants to be a vicar at all! When he first arrived at the parish, I paid a call, of course, and all he wanted to talk about was the north side of the church where all the criminals and suicides were buried. It was positively morbid."

"Morbidity in a vicar is a positive asset," I said.

"If you say so," said Malcolm gently. He was also at the opposite end of the table, 'away from temptation', as George had inexplicably put it. His face was as blurry as my defective memory of him.

"It is hardly our area of expertise," said David.

My ear lobes were burning even hotter, but I noticed that if I took a sip of champagne then it was momentarily distracting. I looked back down to my soup bowl but found that it had been removed. A whole salmon was brought in and placed in front of George.

"Ladies first. Evie?"

"Thank you, George, I am inord . . . ordin . . . ta," I said faintly.

"How are your renovations at Faithful Cottage going?" George deposited a quivering, fleshly pink mound of salmon on my plate.

"Oh, me? They're going . . . all right, I suppose. I need a new light bulb for the kitchen."

"Susie went into Leeds to buy new china," said Alex, "and she came back with plates and all that, but also a microwave oven and a Magimix blender thingy that looks like a modern sculpture. Last time I'm letting her shop for the house on her own."

"You were at work," said Susie pointedly. "And I thought that you wanted to enjoy your weekends."

"Wasn't all of that very expensive?" I asked. I thought of the dinner plates you saw spinning on sticks at circuses, the neat little spins starting to become loping and topsy-turvy as they slowed down. Goodness, my head hurt.

"Yoghurt and dill sauce, Malcolm?"

"He hates yoghurt," I offered instantly.

"For *God's* sake," muttered Alex. "I like her to spend money," he said to everybody else.

"I thought that if you were Jewish then it was the other way round," chuckled George.

Alex smiled quite charmingly. "But we own all those banks, George . . ."

"True."

"Some Jewish people like to spend money, and some don't," offered David blandly.

"What if being Jewish is nothing at all to do with it?" I asked, and everyone's eyes slid away from me. I was being tiresome, I finally realised, but instead of feeling sorry for the other guests, I only felt sorry for myself.

"Have some new potatoes," said Alex.

"That's the first kind thing you've said to me today," I said, and dug so deep into the dish that one or two outlier potatoes bounced onto the carpet. "It's all right," I said to George, "they didn't have any butter on them, so it won't stain."

"Did you read the papers this morning?" Flora asked. Her voice was becoming an irritant, I realised, hating it almost as fiercely as the gold clasps on my earrings. Why did it have to be so light and ticklish? I could feel the hairs on my arms lifting as it trickled down the table towards me. And why couldn't David be as amusing as he was behind the synagogue? Maybe smoking on the Holy Day of Rest in a children's playground had been subversive enough to create its own humour?

"You really feel for Her Majesty . . . it's awful."

"Perhaps he shouldn't have been dismissed," said David. "I mean, it doesn't make him any worse at his job."

"But the depravity of it," said George. "The least he could do was to have been discreet – now that it's come out, he deserves all he gets."

"You're right, George," said Alex.

"Do you mean the bodyguard who had the affair with the male prostitute?" I asked clearly. Flora put her fish knife down with a quiet clink. "I don't think that you are right, Alex *or* George. Since when did you have a problem with homosexuality? It's legal."

"Only just."

I looked across at David. "Could I trouble you for some more green beans, Flora?" He asked.

There seemed nothing more to say, suddenly. My head felt as though it was dragging itself round and round in circles. Everything was an effort. I tried very hard to remember what I was doing here. Slowly, through the fug of varnished wood and the orange sleeves of my dress and the delicate bones of the salmon in its dish, I remembered: George had sold his field. I decided to say something that was a) normal and b) complimentary. I would show them, I thought. "Congratulations on selling your field, George."

I held my breath; there was a moment of silence followed by a relieved murmur.

"Exactly," said Malcolm. "May I be the second to congratulate you."

"I'm very fond of that field," I said, as my plate was smoothly removed again. "I love the enormous ash tree in the middle. D'you know, it is so big that on windy nights I can hear the noise of the leaves. Also, did you know that ash trees span a sort of continuum between male and female? They are unisex, basically. Isn't that exciting?"

"I think that we may have had enough of sex for one lunchtime," said Malcolm. Flora shot him a grateful look. Then, as she turned away, he winked at me.

"Well, I didn't know that," said George stoically.

"In addition, 'ash' actually means 'spear' in Old English, so I was thinking that you could name your new development 'Spearfield', or perhaps 'Spear Ash Way'? It *is* only a suggestion, but you could think it over. Thank you," I added wildly, to the hand that had taken the remains of my main course away, but there was nobody to be seen.

"Those are good suggestions," said George, hand to chin pensively – even I could tell that he was only pretending to consider them – "but I am afraid that the name has already been decided on." He looked around the table. "We are going to call it Fairfield Place."

"Very pretty," said Susie.

"Oh yes, it *is*," said Sandra.

"It's all *right*, I suppose," I said, "given that it really is a fair field. But I still think that the name should have something to do with ash, otherwise what will people think when they see an enormous ash tree in the middle of everything?"

A large glass bowl had been placed in the centre of the table with a thick, beige syrup almost as shiny as the wood panelling. In a layer on the surface were discs of sliced orange, steeped so long that they had faded and wrinkled. My orange dress was brighter than these slightly warped, drunk-looking things. The table was too large for anyone to be able to reach forwards and help themselves. Nobody said anything.

"The ash tree isn't staying," said George. I looked into his face, saw his eyes slightly wary, his lips compress a little as he looked at me.

"But . . . you aren't cutting it down?" I looked over at Malcolm.

"You're so naïve, Evie," said Alex, trying to laugh. "What did you think? That we'd build an estate and leave a bloody great tree in the middle of it? I should think that the roots stretch for most of the field . . ."

"It stretches because it's so old," I said. "Older than you," I said to George.

"She just didn't realise," said Malcolm.

"Yes, but why? She's old enough to understand – she's nearly twenty-two, for God's sake!" Alex pushed himself back in his chair, and then leant forwards again.

"My birthday's in August. I'm a Leo," I said promptly. "They are typically generous and outgoing . . ."

"I don't think that age has anything to do with it. She has just formed an attachment to the ash tree." Malcolm didn't say that in a nasty way.

"Who does *that*?"

"Someone who loves and cares about nature."

"You make it sound like a virtue – you're the one who's going to be pulling it out of the ground, mate."

"But I can see something other than my own narrow viewpoint, Alex."

As the argument on the diagonal segued coldly back and forth, I suddenly realised something: Malcolm and Alex were arguing about me. I had two men arguing about me – it wasn't about the tree at all. Alex, sat beside me, wreathed in tension as he was, had lost his temper because he knew me well enough to be exasperated by me, and felt that he had a right to find me infuriating. As a single woman being argued over, I supposed that I had reached a sort of pinnacle of womanhood – it was supposed to be deeply romantic. But as it was actually happening, I just felt embarrassed.

"Well, things change, don't they?" George stepped in, all patrician features, speaking banal yet wise words from the head of the table. "Trees come and go."

"I don't," I said. I could feel my eyes blur with very illogical tears and thought that I should never have compared myself to a tree. The tree was far more special.

"Maybe that's the problem," said Alex, out of the side of his mouth.

"Things do change, don't they?" Susie was looking at me. "We all have to move on."

"Are we still talking about the tree?" David looked around with a superb mock innocence.

"I don't think that you should cut it down," I said to George, hoping to close the matter whilst still making my disapprobation felt. "Promise me you won't sell off any more land?"

George's face contracted again. "I really can't promise anything," he said stiffly. "It all depends on the finances of the estate, you see. Doesn't it, Jim?"

"I suppose it does."

"Jim doesn't sound very certain," I said.

"I like to hedge my bets," he said, and grinned.

"Shall we have a toast?" Flora called quickly. "To Fairfield Place."

"Fairfield place," we all echoed, and pushed our glasses up in the air and towards the centre of the table in an uneven oval. Eight wine glasses and my singular champagne glass. I suddenly thought of Aunt Mim. "Oranges," I said miserably. Everybody looked at me. "I just need the loo," I said.

"Try not to get lost," Alex whispered to me. Flora was expounding upon the virtues of a walled garden.

"You get lost," I whispered hotly, and reeled out. My skirt swished about, irritating my legs. I was moving too much, whirling uncontrollably. I pushed the dining room door closed behind me, yanked off my earrings savagely and leant against the wall. I was quite exhausted.

Footsteps grew steadily nearer and ascended the steps at the end of the corridor. They seemed full of purpose. Coming from the kitchen, I supposed.

"Making our way *through* the corridor, ladies, if I can just direct you to the door on the right? This section of Fielden Hall was added in 1785 by Ignatius Cuthbert, and comprises of a dining room, library and music room. You will see some magnificent mouldings in the music room – hung in ochre silk – and in the centre of the room, a case filled with the diary and letters of Wilhelmina-Jane Cuthbert-Clarke, a noted feminist of her time who rode a bicycle through Thornlaw on a Sunday, much to the scandal of its residents . . .'

The person attached to the voice glided through the corridor and into the music room as smoothly as if he were motorised. Margaret, Edith, Rhoda, Dot and many others I recognised vaguely from the village straggled behind him, looking up and around as though the concept of a ceiling and walls were completely new to them. Margaret had a posh jacket on, Edith's hair looked newly set, and she was wearing a string of pearls. I wrinkled my nose at the floral but slightly acrid smell of mingling perfumes.

"Evie! Nice to see you, love." Margaret gave me a hug. "My hands are bad," she said. "So I won't give you too much of a squeeze. We didn't expect to see you here, I thought you said that you were off to lunch today."

"Oh, she probably wanted to do a tour on her own, didn't you, love?" Edith carefully drew my hands out to their sides and looked at my dress. "You *do* look nice. All posh! Mind you, it is a posh place."

"Very posh," said Margery.

"Imagine *living* somewhere like this," said Rhoda, gazing out over the slope of the gardens.

"Imagine the heating bill," snorted Margaret. "We've seen it all before, of course – most of us know Fielden Hall like the back of our hands. But it's nice to wander around."

"Nice to work up an appetite," said Edith. "They don't do food, but they said they could 'accommodate us' in the conservatory, and we've brought some sandwiches and biscuits."

"Why don't you come and have something to eat with us, Evie?" Rhoda stared at my middle. "I'm sure you're losing weight."

"Evie?" The dining room door opened and George stood there. "We were wondering where you'd got to – come and have some oranges in Cointreau." My absence from the room had obviously given him a brief respite, and George now felt able to resume his hosting duties. He even smiled at me.

"I'm not sure that I should have Cointreau after all my champagne," I said, smiling weakly.

"Oh, the more alcohol one consumes in the middle of the day the better, on special occasions. Good afternoon, ladies – I do hope you enjoy your tour of the house." George stepped gallantly back, leaving the doorway free for me to pass through. I slowly, very slowly, pivoted back towards Margaret and her gang. I felt strongly disinclined to look them in the eye.

"Well . . . I suppose . . . I mean, I had better," I said, indicating the door awkwardly, and hurrying back into the dining room.

*

4.02 p.m.: "Alex was such a prat, wasn't he? Unbearably grumpy and all that."

"Was he?" Malcolm watched his feet as he walked. He seemed oddly pristine, as though he had watched the lunch at Fielden Hall from a glass case.

"Yes! He was so off with me, as if . . ." I tailed off. "As if he didn't like me very much," I added, and felt a little arrowhead of misery piercing me.

Malcolm and I made the downhill part of our walk, away from Fielden Hall and towards the village before the land started to rise up again as it led to Faithful Cottage. Our feet tripped pleasantly downwards, slapping against the pavement.

Perhaps lunch hadn't gone quite how I had intended it, but it felt conventional to be walking alongside a man and wearing a pretty dress – nice, even. The effect of the champagne had been very like seasickness, I thought to myself. But I was back on solid ground now. As we walked into the village, I pushed Margaret, Edith & co. to the back of my mind. They were one side of a scale, George and Flora Cuthbert were the other, and I was balancing somewhere in the middle, wobbling precariously. I tried to ignore that image and look out at the fields.

There was a gentle buzzing sensation around my temples. The patches of light across the ground that were shortening after the heat of the day seemed supernaturally bright. As I walked beside Malcolm, I wanted to flail my arms and emit a low, constant moan. I certainly didn't care what I said or did – the words came from a subconscious place and I felt that nothing bad could possibly happen as a result of them.

"Alex was all right," said Malcolm blandly.

"But you had that row . . ."

"Difference of opinion, that's all."

"Must just have been me then," I said. I looked at Malcolm and sought reassurance. "I can't think why."

"Alex and I don't exactly have your history, do we?"

"That was years ago."

"How many years ago?"

"Well, one and a bit ago," I said.

"Not long."

"It *feels* far away because it was then, and now I am here," I said. Surely Malcolm would understand? After all, his dark forces swirling around Thornlaw were a very different present to my past. Was I here for him, or . . . wait, did I believe that Aunt Mim's inheritance had drawn me to the light? Oh, it was all so confusing, and my ear lobes still hurt. "It's no explanation as to why he gets on my bloody wick."

"How long have you actually known Alex?"

"Since I was eleven. It was before my Difficult Stage, so I was quite short and my hair wasn't as wiry," I said. "I still remember the Ishkowitzs' first time at synagogue, Alex's dark head, everyone whispering about them. I thought how nice Alex looked, then he *was* nice, even after I entered my Difficult Stage. But now . . . now he isn't nice at all!"

"You've known him man and boy."

"I don't and didn't really think of him as either," I said. "Just as Alex. He was never overly boyish, and I suppose that I don't really think of him as a man, just as himself . . ."

"That might be the problem."

"But then I always suppose that he likes me because he retains that image of little, pre-Difficult Stage Evie," I went on. "*Why* am

I telling you all this?"

"Because you want to."

"No, it can't be that. Anyway . . . what did he tell you? About me?"

"That you two were once . . . friendly . . . and then you gave him the push."

"That's . . . I mean, I . . ."

"Alcohol makes you so articulate, love." Malcolm gave me an affectionate shove and I had to grab hold of a convenient low wall to steady myself.

"It makes me feel better than everybody else, to be drinking in the middle of the day," I said. I waved my hand across the village. "All these people having to carry on as usual and not go to Fielden Hall for champagne."

"Steady," said Malcolm, "you'll end up believing that you really are better than them. You know something that they don't, anyway, about the development. Are you scared of them?"

"Who?"

"All of those," he said. "The village folk."

"Course not!"

"You should be."

"What are you *talking* about?" It was my turn to give Malcolm a shove – he nearly reeled into the road.

"Just that convention and normality can be powerful in their own way. The villagers aren't as bright or odd as you, but they are in the majority."

I took a moment to consider this theory, but found it quite impossible. "Change the subject," I commanded.

"Yes, your Royal Highness." We wandered along in silence as, barely perceptibly, the ground started to slope uphill beneath our feet.

"*God.*"

"What?"

"I just can't get over what a prat Alex was at lunch."

"D'you know, I think it is a good thing that you left Alex all those . . . that year ago. Good for both of you. You have your independence; he seems happy with Susie."

"I suppose so, if you like that sort of thing," I said. Susie seemed so pale, I thought to myself. Bloodless, almost.

We reached my lane and walked up towards Faithful Cottage. Dot and Vernon were sat watching television, their faces stony with concentration. "Old Faithful," I said, when we arrived, and gave the wall beside the door an affectionate pat.

"Did that hurt your hand?"

"It did a bit."

"You see? You're not a match for anything round here." Malcolm kissed me, slowly, tasting of a blend of various alcoholic drinks and cigarette smoke.

"Why don't you come in?" I felt very flirtatious suddenly, and found that I was actually rather good at it. Several glasses of champagne had honed my technique.

Malcolm glanced briefly at his watch. "I can't," he said.

"Oh."

"Sorry."

"Going somewhere else?" I leant towards him in what I hoped

was the perfect combination of seduction and playfulness. "Going on another date?" As soon as I had teased him about this, I realised that I really wanted to know.

"Just . . . things to do." He kissed me again.

"You always do that," I said crossly.

"Do what?" Now it was Malcolm's turn to smile seductively – he was far better at it than me.

"Kiss me to end a conversation. It's sort of an amatory full stop. Why are you laughing? I *know* what you think of me. You think that I'm amusing and eccentric and precocious and naïve and irritating. All at the same time. So."

"Aren't you all of those things?"

"I don't think so," I said. "But what do I know? I'm just me."

Malcolm turned to go, perhaps aware by some form of devilish telepathy that I had finally had enough of the day and my brain had tipped into near incoherence. "Bye," he said.

"Bye."

*

Peggy was curled up on Aunt Mim's capacious lap when I came in. She peeled her eyes open, looked at me with a mixture of hurt and bemusement, and then went back to sleep.

"Peggy missed you."

"Did you mean that you missed me?" I asked gaily as I made my way into the kitchen. Once there, I realised that I had no reason to be, and promptly came out again.

"You do seem to be rather busy at the moment," said Aunt Mim. "You are taken up with that *male*."

"Rubbish," I said. "Apart from today, I've hardly been out."

"But you haven't been *here*," Aunt Mim complained. "You've been thinking about him, and it takes you away from yourself."

"I can't help it, can I?"

"I am sure that you could. You find him so fascinating, but if you knew everything there was to know, I think you would realise how dull he is."

"Bollocks," I said, succinctly.

"Then there's playing the friendly witch to all the villagers . . ."

"What's wrong with that? I *am* a friendly witch."

"The villagers saw that you aren't like them today," Aunt Mim said. "Things'll be different now."

"You don't know that, unless . . . you mean, you were there? At Fielden Hall?"

"I wanted to see the music room," Aunt Mim said haughtily. "And I happen to find the letters of Wilhelmina-Jane Cuthbert-Clarke most informative, if rather pedantic in style."

"I actually missed you when they served the oranges! And you were wafting about all along."

"I am far too robust to *waft* anywhere," said Aunt Mim. "Now, if you'll take my advice . . ."

"I don't want your advice," I said. "Actually."

We stared at one another. Aunt Mim's eyes were the prettiest pearlescent grey in the sun. "You used to care about my opinion," she said quietly.

"I can manage my own opinions," I said. "Malcolm, Alex, Reverend Rishangles – you just don't like anyone."

"I am merely trying to warn you . . ."

"You want me to become the next you."

"Nonsense."

"It's true!" I threw the words at her. I had not realised that I felt this way until the sentences formed, tumbling out of me. "You just want to stop me from being like everybody else . . . but I can be, you know. I can be normal. I had salmon for lunch and everything."

"But Evie, we *aren't* like everybody else." Aunt Mim almost wrung her hands. She wiggled with irritation, sending Peggy onto a sloping angle on her knees.

"Well, *you're* not for a start!" I said, "I mean, you aren't even real. You died three months ago."

There was a second of silence. The faint buzz leftover by the champagne cleared suddenly. There was nothing except the barely perceptible hum of my fridge from the kitchen and the particles of dust that floated between us in the sun.

"That was very hurtful, Evie."

"Look . . ."

"No! I see that I am no longer needed," said Aunt Mim.

"Don't be like that." I rubbed my eyes with my hands until I saw stars, trying to knock some sense into myself. How had I thought that I could ever be normal? My head ached, sealing the outside world off from me. When I took my hands away and opened my mouth to say something calm and sensible, Aunt Mim had gone. Peggy still hadn't opened her eyes. The leftover sunshine of the day was quite suffocating. It filled the room to bursting point.

"Oranges," I said to myself sadly.

WEDNESDAY 28TH JULY 1982

I set out on this grey, nondescript morning to the village shop, with a list that read:

- Apples
- Cream cheese?
- Lunch things
- Fanta

It wasn't the most inspiring of culinary prospects for me, but I cut my cloth quite happily according to what was at the village shop rather than drive into Barnsley for more nutritional and filling fare. Peggy didn't like Barnsley, I told myself. Not at all. She did, however, enjoy playing Orphan Annie outside the village shop, getting looks and cooing and pats from various other shoppers.

Speaking of Peggy's mental state, I had kept an eye on her to make sure that she wasn't distressed by my falling-out with Aunt Mim. She seemed absolutely fine, which made me wonder whether a five-year-old chihuahua was in fact far more resilient than me.

If this diary was a camera, you would have been able to see the little grimace I gave as I wrote the words, 'my falling-out with Aunt Mim'. You would be able to sense the little shivers of nerves running up and down my spine. A whole week since the lunch, and I have realised two things:

The first is that I had been rather drunk that day. The second is that, despite only having spent a paltry hour or two out of this week in the village or talking to other people, there has been a sizeable shift in atmosphere.

There is the space left by Aunt Mim, a heavy space despite the fact that she was, empirically speaking, unsubstantial. It was all air, I told myself crossly, but it didn't quite feel like that. I tried to replace Aunt Mim with real people, but silence has been keeping me company all week. Malcolm left for a few days – returned to his office. Then there was the telephone. It hadn't rung. After about thirty-six hours, I noticed how odd this was. Margaret had taken to ringing up when she wanted me to massage her hands; Rhoda had said that she would ring to make an appointment too. The situation grew so unnerving that I ended up making two phone calls of my own.

The first was to Hawthorns. I thought that Dad and Lizzie, whatever their failings, were not given to aberrations in routine. Lizzie would just be getting in, flushed and girlish, from some unnecessary social outing, or else in the kitchen. Dad would be working. The phone rang and rang, and eventually I replaced the receiver with a delicate click, feeling more defeated than I cared to admit.

The second was to Joanie. Again, the phone just rang and rang. I thought that she must be feeling better and had gone out, which I felt was rather selfish given that I had just decided to be charitable.

I have always loved silence, the changeability of it, the thick texture that it keeps around me. But now I was beginning to feel suffocated. Silence pushed me around the house – I banged and scraped myself against the walls as though the cottage was unfamiliar. Unnerved, my walks with Peggy grew shorter and I steered away from figures I could see in the distance. Silence enveloped me, and the more I wanted to break through its barrier, the more I was afraid to.

*

This morning marked a kind of watershed: I decided to go out like a normal person. If the village was avoiding me, then it was better to find out (I said confidently from the safety of my own house). After all, I wouldn't know until I ran into someone. Who knows? Perhaps Aunt Mim would make an appearance when I returned. It was coming up to seven whole days, and I had taken her point. After all, I said to myself, what else can Aunt Mim *do*? Go to an imaginary hair salon? Set up a bridge circle with the other deceased ladies of Thornlaw?

I remembered once that I had attended – reluctantly as ever, and in an absurd dress with pink bows down the front – a children's party when I was a little girl. There had been a bouncy castle, and I had abandoned myself to the delight of bopping up and down with the other children, unable to get hurt. Gradually, we stomped some of the air out of the castle, landing more deeply and making furrows out of the plastic. The other children had scrambled out. When I tried to follow, I became stuck in this wheezing, red-and-yellow-striped nightmare of looming plastic. I felt the same now. I was stuck, imagining that in seeing me at Fielden Hall, the village had realised that I was not one of them, and all my hard witching work to be accepted had been for nothing. I groped to get out of that thought, just as I had the bouncy castle. So, I grabbed my canvas shopping bag, put on a pair of clip-on earrings that were marginally less vicious than the pair I had worn to Fielden Hall, and set out into Thornlaw. The sun pressed the clouds as I walked along, unable to get through.

My feet seemed very audible down the lane. I passed Dot and Vernon's, Edith and Peter's, holding myself stiffly. I didn't dare to give the usual lingering stare through their windows. It was so quiet that I wondered whether everyone had gone away. No one seemed to take holidays in Thornlaw, I couldn't work it out. Sometimes one couple or another would go to the seaside for the day, but none of them stayed overnight or booked a hotel. Back they came after a day, tired and a little pinker than they were before, trudging inside with a cool box. As I walked along, I wondered if perhaps there had been some mass changing of minds and everyone had migrated to Southport Beach.

I was relieved and slightly anxious to see Margaret emerge from her house as I got to the end of the lane. She examined the anaemic yellow rose that grew in a spindly fashion near the gate and seemed peculiarly taken with one of its leaves, straightening up just as I reached her.

"Morning, Evie."

"Morning. How is it?"

"Hmmm?"

"The rose?"

"Oh, it's . . . you know." Margaret shrugged. "I'm not very good in the garden, but Paul can't manage it, bless him. Where are you off to?"

"Just to the shop," I said, grateful that I wasn't going anywhere near Fielden Place or Hall. "I thought I'd look in on Joanie too."

"Oh, love – haven't you heard? Joanie's had to go into Barnsley Hospital!"

"I . . . I hadn't heard." My insides gave a little lurch backwards, the kind that a car gives to right itself after a sudden stop. "How awful. I . . . I didn't realise."

"All this business with her husband. I'm sorry to say it, but he's a complete . . ." Margaret leant forwards and dropped her voice dramatically, "*bastard*. There," she added, almost proudly.

"You mean, it's her husband's fault?"

"He was the one that made her heart bad, wasn't he?"

I nodded. Apparently, it was possible for a broken heart to make you actually, objectively, physically ill. I would have to re-evaluate the entire cannon of romantic literature now.

"Should I go and see her?"

"That's sweet – you two are such friends – but she'll be out in a day or two, Margery said."

"How does Margery know?"

"Her sister's a cleaner at the hospital."

"Right."

"She's gone off today, Margery," said Margaret pensively. "Gone to see her dad in Skelmanthorpe – do you know it?"

"No," I said. I was thinking about Joanie, trying to imagine her in one of those blue hospital gowns that they put on everyone.

"It's on from Scisset," said Margaret disapprovingly. "And Scisset's a good four miles. Couple more on to Skelmanthorpe."

"Do you want me to come and do your hands this afternoon?" I asked. I'd had enough of Joanie – I needed time to digest what had happened to her.

"Oh." Margaret flushed slightly and looked away. "No, no thank you, love. The thing is . . . they are so bad now, especially on a day like today that's humid and all, and the doctor says they are only going to get worse, so . . ."

"Right." There were other things one could have said, I realised, but I was incapable of spontaneous persuasion. "Well, I might go up to Rhoda's then, see if she wants anything."

"I wouldn't, love, not now that she's lost her dog."

I remembered my biology lesson at school and the diaphragm, thinking that it sounded like a rather lovely girl's name and how fascinating it looked, like the pleated ceiling of a circus tent. Well, my diaphragm felt as though it had risen through my throat. The list of ingredients in the dog potion I had made scrolled quickly through my mind and then repeated itself.

"I must be going," I said mechanically. "It was nice to see you at Fielden Hall yesterday." That was one barrier that I could tear down, I thought. Best to get it out in the open.

Margaret didn't know what so say for a moment. "Yes," she said finally. "Them up at Fielden Hall – I didn't know that you knew them."

"I don't really," I said. "Honestly, I'm not sure quite what I was doing there." As soon as I had said that, I realised that it was uncomfortably true.

"It's that foreign chap at Fielden Place that you know, isn't it? His wife's on the village hall committee now. Watchful sort of thing. I've not spoken to her much. Very elegant, isn't she?"

"Yup."

"Bit too much for round here," said Margaret pensively, and I shot her a look of such abject gratitude that she raised her eyebrows. "Listen," she said, suddenly confiding again, "there's been talk about that bloke who keeps poking about the top field – you know, the one in the suit. Anything to it?"

"Nothing at all," I said quickly. Malcolm always entered my house from the field downwards rather than up the lane, 'so as not to give the neighbours something to talk about,' he'd said. Given that I hadn't spoken to him for days, I didn't think that it was quite the right time to unveil ourselves as a couple. I supposed that Margaret had seen him drop me home after lunch last week. Deciding to take Aunt Mim's advice and not tell the truth, I plastered a smile across my face. "There's really nothing to it."

"Nothing going on?"

"Nothing at all."

*

Trudging home from the village shop with lemonade instead of Fanta, some cottage cheese and an onion to be healthy, I was just about on an even keel, as long as I didn't think about Rhoda's dog or Joanie.

Edith threw open her sitting room window as I was walking back up the lane. I could clearly see a three-quarters empty packet of chocolate digestives on the coffee table behind her, and some crumbs.

"Morning, isn't it *terrible* about Joanie?"

"Yes, yes it is. But she'll be out in a couple of days," I said firmly.

"Will she? Oh, that *is* good. I'll bake her something and take it round. I suppose that you know all about it, given that you two are such friends."

"Hmmm."

"I saw you chatting to Margaret on your way out."

"Yes."

"It must be hard for you, with all you've been through in the last few weeks, love. A lot of *disappointment*."

"There certainly has been," I said fervently, thinking of Val's visit, Malcom's mysterious ways, a dead dog that I was perhaps *actually* responsible for, and that the village shop had not stocked Fanta for some considerable time. "Well, I'll let you get on."

As I turned the key in the lock, I had a witchy premonition that Aunt Mim would definitely be there, especially after I had applied her advice to Margaret in such a nifty manner. I swung open the door, lemonade bottle banging against my calves. There was nobody there.

THURSDAY 29TH JULY 1982

"Peggy?"

Peggy started up in her chair, pointed ears pricked, tongue caught out of one side of her mouth.

"Let's go for a drive," I said, in my faux-cheerful voice. There was at least one dog I could keep alive. Faithful Cottage continued to be Aunt Mim-less, and her absence was making me feel bereft.

I drove the Alpine Sunbeam away from Barnsley – I couldn't bring myself to think about Joanie in her iron hospital bed and nasty blue gown, let alone visit. We drove vaguely in the direction of Huddersfield – attractive simply because it was in the opposite direction. The clouds billowed up over my little yellow car as I drove.

A couple of miles later, I saw a figure walking along the side of the road that looked exactly like Alex. He was in his shirt sleeves, hands thrust in his pockets, head cocked at a proud sort of angle. I slowed down.

"What are you doing here?"

"Evie, thank *God*! Give me a lift, will you?"

"Awww, are you lost, little boy?"

"Oh, shut up," he said affably, and slid onto the passenger seat after a tussle with Peggy.

"What happened?"

"I went to value this house in Scisset," he said. "Jack from the office drove me there, I told him that I'd walk back to Fielden Place. It seems to be rather further than I thought."

"Scisset's ages away! It's a good four miles, everybody knows *that*." (Thank you, Margaret.)

"Well, I know that *now*."

"Does this make me more mature than you? I mean, driving in my car, I feel quite sensible compared to you, wandering along the road . . ."

"Oh, go on. Enjoy it."

"I am."

"You may have won this one, but you still have a silly dog." He eyed Peggy balefully.

"Hey! Well, at least I know the difference between a dinner plate and a microwave oven. Unlike Susie."

"Just leave her out of it, Evie! I was only joking about the dog. Why do you have to make everything so difficult?"

This had been said to me so many times before, usually by Lizzie, that I felt there was no comeback. It was evidently true that I *was* difficult, although it seemed to me a little unfair, given that I was only being myself and had no option to be anyone else.

We drove along in an increasingly awkward silence. Tiny spatters of rain began to fall across the windshield – perfect little marring circles of water. To me, it seemed that everything else was difficult apart from me: I had left Alex, he had got married. Now we were living at opposite ends of the same random place, like bookends. What if our fondness for each other was really a sort of remnant of what had gone before, like muscle memory? A subconscious response that didn't mean anything. Perhaps finding a familiar face in Thornlaw, albeit familiar for all the wrong reasons, had made us falsely close for a while, and now we were peeling apart again. Jews were clannish, other people said – we stuck together. Surely Alex and I were proof of it? But did we even like each other?

Alex decided to begin again. "Flora wrote me a personal note, after lunch last week, look!" He fished something crumpled out of his pocket.

"I can't look – I'm driving."

"We're on a straight stretch."

"No, Alex."

"All right, I'll read it to you. '*Dear Alex and Evie . . .*'"

"Huh?"

"I meant . . . I meant, sorry, '*Dear Alex and Susie. How lovely to see you for lunch. Please thank Susie for the pretty card she sent me! We are very pleased that you are going to handle the sales at Fairfield – George thinks that we are in very safe hands and it is nice to see a young couple living at Fielden Place. VBW, Flora.*' Isn't that nice?"

"What does VBW mean?"

"Very Best Wishes – you're so stupid, Evie."

"I'm clever enough to know where Scisset is."

Alex ignored me. "Flora and George have been so welcoming . . ."

"Why are you carrying it around in your pocket?"

"What?"

"Flora's note – why are you carrying it with you if she sent it last week? Does it give you some internal sort of glow to carry missives from the local aristocracy?"

I could see Alex tense in the corner of my eye. "You know, *I* value the fact that they include us, and you may turn your nose up at moving in exalted circles but some of us actually *care* about moving up the social ladder . . ."

"Evidently. Why do you care so bloody much though? We're Jewish, that means that we don't have to care . . ."

"You were the one who said that being Jewish doesn't have to mean anything specific. That was about the only sensible thing you said at that lunch – God, you were embarrassing . . ."

"I was nervous."

"You were drunk. And Jews have always been connected to estate owners, for your information, because they were often emissaries or land agents. So, there is a sort of kinship there and our ancestors obviously cared, despite what you think."

"Kinship, my bottom. Nothing has changed then: you're a land agent for a local squire. You've just set history back a hundred years, well done."

"George and Flora are my *friends*," yelled Alex.

"No, they are *not*," I yelled back. "They think you are *useful*. Are you really too big-headed to see that? What are you turning into, Alex? The sort of man who boasts about what his wife buys and sucks up to people you think will get you somewhere? You never used to be like this."

"It's called growing up."

"Well then, I won't be growing up."

"Evidently."

"Don't . . . don't say evidently, that's *my* thing."

"You must be glad you're out of it, then. With me. Anyway, you're the big head. You think that you don't need anyone, you think that you can get away with doing whatever the hell you want . . ."

"That's not—"

"True? Bloody is. You hide behind this Asperger's thing, and everyone has to make an exception for you because you're Evie Edelman and you know about fucking trees and remember things that people want to forget . . ."

Alex went on in this vein. My eyes filled with tears that seemed to drown out exactly what he was saying. Again, I felt that everything he said must be true, but it was so nasty, and it wasn't how I felt.

I did hear Alex say "careful!" and wondered whether he meant that I should be careful, if it was some kind of threat, or whether he was cautioning himself. It turned out to be rather more prosaic. There was an enormous, jagged pothole in the road that I hadn't seen – in a moment, the Alpine Sunbeam had crunched into it. Alex and I watched the expanse of primrose yellow hood jolt down steeply. Then came the bounce back up and the full stop with the nose of the car peeking into a layby hedge.

We sat for a moment, both of us breathing unsteadily. Whether the exertion was from surviving the bump or adrenaline from our argument was hard to tell.

"You know," said Alex conversationally, "I don't think that you should even *have* a driver's licence."

"I know. I shouldn't, should I?"

"I'll get out and see."

"See what?"

"You might have punctured the tyre."

At this, I scrambled out myself and headed round to the passenger side. Alex and I stood close for a second, staring at the front left wheel as the blanket of drizzle enveloping us changed to distinctly less welcome plopping rain that fell coldly down our necks. I crouched down and began feeling the muddy rim of the tyre. Alex sort of joined in, then we both straightened up stiffly.

Alex threw his arm heavily around my shoulders, but before I could even be surprised, he pulled me into his chest.

"Sorry," he said.

I looped my arms around his neck, and breathed great, hot breaths into the cotton of his shirt. When I lifted my head, we both squinted up at the falling rain, then I followed the rain as it fell onto Alex and trickled down his face.

We were growing up, our eyes told each other, and perhaps growing too far apart, who could say? Alex took my hand and suddenly our faces were very close. I could see the smallest marks on Alex's skin, his eyes were a kind of cloudy green and they were setting hundreds of little fires inside me. We stared, holding our breath. It would have been so easy . . .

A car approached, slowed down when it saw us, and uncertainly picked up speed again. My arms still around Alex's neck, I watched Margery and Derek drive past, Kevin in the back, brandishing a plastic toy. Derek's eyes were stoically ahead, Margery's round as she stared – at *us*. We watched the tail of Derek's car disappear, and quietly got back inside the Sunbeam.

"The tyre's OK, I think."

"That's a relief. We would have had to get it towed."

"Look at us though!" Alex exclaimed, pulling his damp shirt away from his skin with a lugubrious peeling noise. "We'll *ruin* the leather seating." I laughed at that, and luckily Alex started to find it funny too.

My laugh quavered, veering dangerously close to tears. Something that had opened up between us in the rain, a portal backwards to the way we were, had snapped shut again. With Herculean self-control, I started the engine and I drove gingerly, retracing my route home, miserable in a way that had a tinge of sweetness to it. "I'm turning into an old spinster," I said.

"You're a good girl, Evie."

"Don't be patronising, unless you want another fight . . ."

"Oh God!" Alex threw his hands up, laughing. "No! I can't take any more of it! I surrender."

"So do I."

"I could almost be a nice person, don't you agree?" Alex glanced at me, his eyes twinkling. "I am very nearly a very nice boy, but then I have to go and spoil it. I like getting my own way too much – trouble with being an only child. You know how it is . . ."

"Not personally."

"Hmmmm?"

"Joe," I prompted him.

"Joe. How did I forget about Joe? You *seem* such an only child, Evie. You inhabit your own world, as though you had to because there was no one else. Or perhaps Joe just is inherently forgettable?"

I went to slap Alex's arm, he dodged and laughed again.

"You shouldn't take pride in not being nice," I said severely.

"You can't have two negatives in a sentence."

"I didn't and you shouldn't. When you say that you aren't nice, it makes you unlikeable. And it disguises the fact that you are nice. That you care about people. Don't make yourself sound worse than you are: if you underestimate your own humanity then others will too, and you will lose more than just your image."

We drove along silently.

"Listen," said Alex. "I am about to be nice, and don't take it any other way. Whatever you are doing with Malcolm, stop. That's all I'm going to say."

"But . . . how? I mean, you can't . . . what?"

"You are straight-talking enough to know what I mean, Evie. I don't know how far it has gone, but . . ."

"Not very far," I said automatically. I shifted on the leather seat.

"Good. He should know better than to take advantage."

"He's not. I'm the one . . . I mean, *I'm* the one who is chasing him." I couldn't bear the thought of Malcolm feeling as exposed as I was at this moment, of him getting into trouble.

"Are you?" Alex sounded surprised.

"Course."

"What do you see in him?"

"Well, I like his upper lip," I offered. "And I don't see what the problem would be," I ventured, with a little onslaught of courage.

Alex cleared his throat. "Do you really not see the problem, Evie?" he asked gently.

"He *does* have rather a short nose . . ."

"The problem is that Malcolm is married."

"*No,*" I said, although it was more of an exhale than a word, the shock turning into a white ball in my mouth. "That can't . . ."

I remembered being outside Faithful Cottage, watching Malcolm in the sun as he looked at his watch after he'd walked me home. Of course, it was true; I had known that there was some nameless thing. There had been an obstacle, I just hadn't realised that the obstacle was another human being.

Alex was right, I thought. I was silly and naïve and the rest of it. I had one last go at piecing together my dignity. "They can't have been married very long? Malcolm isn't much older than us, is he?"

"Malcolm is thirty-nine," said Alex. He turned and gave me such a pitying look that I had to grip the steering wheel very hard.

Alex had never looked at me like that before, even in the cafe in Leeds. It had been a cold, wet day. February, one year, four months and . . . fifteen days ago, that was it. The muddy prints of customers' shoes covered the floor as delicately as a spider's web. Alex and I had sat at a table by the window. The glass was frosted, forcing us to look inwards to meet each other's eye.

"The thing is," Alex had said. He set down his coffee cup precisely in the central round of the saucer. The noise of other people splurged around us and the cash till rang open, loudly, and then was slammed shut. "I think it would be better if you said that you dumped me."

"Why?" I was numbed by the cold and the patterns of grey and green: grey sky, green walls inside. The chatter of the cafe was as thick as wool.

"Think about it: you get to say that you ended things, so no one'll feel sorry for you. You can walk into schul and everyone will say, 'there goes the girl who got fed up of Alex Ishkowitz'. You don't want people to pity you, do you?"

"And you won't mind them saying at synagogue, 'there's the boy who Evie Edelman got fed up with'?"

"I don't mind at all."

"Oh. That's surprising."

"Why?" Alex smiled.

"I thought you had more pride than that."

The smile disappeared. "I suppose it means that people don't call me a . . . a bounder, or whatever."

"A cad."

"A Khamer-eyzl."

"Donkey is about right."

Alex took that particular insult on the chin. There was silence for a moment as the talk around us thinned briefly. The owner of the cafe was eking out a pre-sliced piece of cake from the selection in the glass counter, watched intently by the customer.

"So you don't get to be called any of those things, donkey included . . ."

"I get to slink off somewhere."

"You mean, you get to slink off to someone else." I fitted together a very painful puzzle. "Are you really going to ask Susie Bernbaum out?"

"Who told you . . . ?"

"Susie Leverson said something. She took the particular time and effort to actually speak to me, so it must be true."

Alex looked uncomfortable and vaguely cross. Mostly uncomfortable. "Yes, probably."

"You're going to marry her," I said miserably.

"No . . ."

"Yes. Is it true love and everything?" The cash till slammed shut again with a rattle. "I bet it is. Well, she's so beautiful. She has lovely hair. Sorry, I mean, I suppose . . . you can't *like* her, surely?"

"Why not? I know that *you* don't like her, but you aren't me."

"But you can love someone without liking them. What's to like about Susie? She's all blank and cold. She looks like she doesn't smell of anything."

"Evie . . ."

"All right. Sorry. All I mean is," I said, thinking of Dad and Lizzie, "that sometimes couples have a sort of alchemy, and liking has nothing to do with it. That's all." I wondered whether I had said the wrong thing again, but Alex seemed pleased.

"Alchemy. I like it. So, do we have a deal? About the whole ending thing? You got fed up with me."

"Well, I suppose so."

Alex reached forwards and took my hands in his. The relief on his face was so painfully obvious that I drew back a little. I had felt very old suddenly, exhausted by other people and tired of myself.

"You're the best, Evie," he had said. "We probably would have grown tired of each other anyway."

"Look out!"

I had left it too late to accommodate an oncoming car and had to turn sharply towards a hedge. Branches musically scraped the paintwork. "You are the *worst* driver," said Alex, gripping the handle inside the door.

"Our second brush with the flora and fauna today," I said weakly, wondering why nature became so menacing when one was in the car.

"Christ alive, Evie."

"I know," I said sadly. "What have I got myself into?"

FRIDAY 30TH JULY 1982

I dreamt that I could see myself from the outside. Another equally long figure faced me.

"Who are you?" I asked.

"I'm Matthew Feld," he replied.

Then I turned and saw Malcolm. Rhoda was behind him, holding her dog.

"You . . ." I struggled, my brain misty and grey. Who was Matthew Feld? It was to do with . . . Susie. Susie Ishkowitz in the corner, head tilted like a bird. I made to run towards her, moving as though I was dragging myself through the sea.

Then I woke up.

Goodness, I was getting confused.

*

'*Village Hall Meeting – EMERGENCY situation arisen! All Welcome.*' said the flyer, crumpled from having been pushed through my door at top speed. By the time I got to the window, the messenger had gone, fleet-footed as Mercury (or perhaps on a bicycle).

My first reaction was one of abject relief at still being thought of as part of the village after my forays into aristocratic circles.

Dot was at my door like a flash, and we had walked down to the hall with Edith and Peter. Inquisitiveness can be the great leveller, and if Margery had chosen to publicise any sordid details of her encounter with Alex and me on her way back from Skelmanthorpe, the wave of gossip had not yet broken.

So, there I was, sat in the centre of things on one of the hard chairs that had been laid out in rows, tea urn gurgling quietly. The excitement in the air made a solid group of us; a swarm of bees buzzing around the hive. The murmurs swirled and enveloped me, becoming so insistent that I lifted my hands to swat them away. My own excitement tipped over into something more like panic. I was stuck – Edith on one side, Vernon, stolid as ever, on the other. But it was too late to leave, as a jowly sort of man with thick features and a striped shirt stood and cleared his throat.

"Ahem!" He seemed about to begin a monologue. "Shall we start?"

"Who's that?" I whispered to Edith.

"George Denton," she hissed, "Chairman of the Village Hall Committee. Busybody."

"Did you not want any tea, Edith?"

"Oh goodness no, love. I'm happy with my glass of water."

It was five o'clock in the afternoon. The summons had been so sudden, so swathed in urgency and mystery, that I felt it should have been at midnight at the very least, and we all should have been wearing a disguise.

"Can I open the meeting?" George Denton looked around him expectantly. "Now, first things first, sorry about all of this cloak and dagger business . . ."

I had a sudden thought and looked around for Alex. We had kept away from each other for forty-eight hours – a feat not unusual in itself, but one that was edged in confusion. My stomach turned an involuntary somersault when I caught sight of Susie Ishkowitz. I blushed slightly and turned away. She hadn't seemed to notice me, she just stared attentively ahead, as though George Denton was the most interesting man in the world, her head tipped appreciatively so that her bob opened on one side and lightly brushed her shoulder.

". . . but it has come to my attention – or rather, Jim the estate manager informed a friend of mine – that Sir George has sold the top field and there is to be a large housing estate there, with the possibility for the neighbouring fields to be sold off."

There was a murmur that rippled around the hall, lifting towards the rafters, and a couple of squeaks as people turned in their chairs to their neighbours with widened eyes.

"Oh *no*," whispered Edith.

"*And* they are going to cut down the beautiful ash tree," I whispered back to her indignantly. She didn't appear to have heard.

". . . a mixture of bungalows and houses, and I *think,* even some flats." George Denton paused for a moment to let the gravity of the situation take effect. I remembered Malcolm's plans; I tried to make the flat drawings real. But they remained one-dimensional, and I was conscious of the warmth of Edith's arm as it ran alongside mine, the smell of her perfume mixed with the deeper smell of tobacco from Vernon.

I'd begun to think about other things . . .

Few surprises were pleasurable, I felt, but I had actually enjoyed David's telephone call yesterday. He sounded reassuringly familiar on the phone, and the pattern of conversation that we made was as balanced and clean as the squares of sunlight through the windows as we talked.

"I thought I'd ring you up," he said.

"Evidently." I pushed my fingers onto the newspaper spread in front of me, examining my finger pads to see if there was backwards newsprint running across them. The pictures were mangled metal work of cars after the IRA bombings in Regent's Park. Thank heavens they were black and white – no red.

"I suppose that I wanted to see if you were all right? After the Hall, and that ghastly lunch."

I remembered being taken to Regent's Park on a sunny day very clearly, my memories all knee-high. Oma had taken me there to show me off, I could tell, and it was one of the happy times when all I had to do was walk along and be a child – that was all that was expected of me. We went to the rose garden; I pulled a branch of a pale pink rose down towards me, smelling it and wishing that I could eat its smell. Now that I was older, someone had set a bomb off there, in the middle of my memory. It felt like an attack on my home. Was part of me still in London?

"I think that I am still recovering," I said.

"I'm not surprised. It would have been better if we could have sat together, wouldn't it? More fun?"

"More fun in a less alcoholic way?"

"You were desperately drunk."

"Was it funny?" I asked. "You can tell me if it was, I won't be offended."

"I thought there was something magnificent about you," said David. "Magnificent and deeply uncoordinated."

"That could be my epitaph," I said. "How's Sandra?"

"What? Oh, you know."

"Why on earth did you bring her? Even Susie looked annoyed."

"One has to keep up appearances."

"Does one?"

"Don't tell me that you don't. You looked perfectly presentable in that orange dress. It suited you, actually. Suited your fierceness."

"Yes, I looked all right, and then I started on the champagne."

"Hmmm."

"And fighting."

"Hmmm."

"With Alex."

"Hmmm. Well, at least it never got physical. Keep the bread rolls in the basket, darling."

"Is that a euphemism? I think that there were some actual bread rolls in a basket somewhere, weren't there?"

"Probably, in between the soup tureen and the silver. It was all fancy schmancy, wasn't it? Far too much for a bunch of Jews from Leeds."

"Try telling Alex that."

"Oh, Alex'll get over it. The sheen of that lot'll wear off."

"What if it doesn't, and *we* wear off instead?"

"Never going to happen – we know him better than anybody else alive."

"That might turn out to be the issue."

Seven horses had been blown up by the bombs. What a mess they would all make, but I felt slightly sorrier for them than the guards. And the poor bandsmen – all their instruments, what a tangle. I had fallen asleep in my armchair, dreaming sunlit dreams of horses' legs and trombones when David had rung me.

"Oh, love. Is this because you had a snarky row?"

"Erm . . ." My arms around Alex's damp shoulders. I was sat in the Alpine Sunbeam with him, his face so close that it was almost painful. I hurriedly drew away, back to my sitting room. "Sort of."

"I've always thought that you and Alex communicate in a wonky sort of way, you know? Something gets slightly skewed or twisted from one of you to the other, but the sentiment is always there."

"Do you think that Susie was annoyed?"

"Probably."

"How do you know?"

"She blinked more than usual. And the bottom of her ear lobes went ever so slightly pink."

"You couldn't see them; she was wearing earrings like me!"

"I know, I know, I was just teasing you. Who knows what Susie is feeling? Maybe it's best not to know. Perhaps it's all very dark and subversive under the bob and beneath the manicure."

"All sweetness and light, more like," I said. "No wonder Alex married her – I could never be that gracious, or feminine, or anything."

"Oh, stop feeling sorry for yourself."

"Irish people have very similar surnames, don't they?"

"Do they? So do we, sometimes. What a weird thing to say."

"I was just wondering whether it would make it harder for the police to find the IRA men that did it?"

"What? Oh, the bombs. The police probably already know exactly who it was. *Anyway*, I have news."

"Exciting news, or melancholy news?"

"Exciting, of *course*. I'm leaving here."

"But you aren't here, you're in Leeds."

"Do try and *think*, Evie. I meant that I'm leaving Leeds." David paused, probably for dramatic emphasis, but it was long enough for me to take the receiver away from my ear and look at it quizzically. "I'm moving to London."

"*No.*"

"I am."

"How come?" London in my memory was a childhood place of permanently blue skies and bright green grass. But in reality, London was a frightening place full of far too many people – grey, grown-up. Everybody knew that.

"I've got a job in an estate agents there. Do you remember Lenny? He used to go to school with Alex and me, in the year above?"

"Vaguely . . ."

"Quite gangly. Always used to bring cream cheese sandwiches for lunch. Anyway, his uncle's cousin Hiram is an estate agent, and there's an opening. I'll have to interview for it, but Lenny said that the job's as good as mine. Can you imagine? London? I won't have to be anything that I don't want to be there. Not straight, or Jewish, or anything."

"You'll have to be straight if you are working for Lenny's Uncle Hiram, and I never heard such a Jewish way of getting a job in all my life!"

"I suppose that's true. I won't be free, but I'll be . . . freer." He laughed.

"Freer is a start though. David?"

"Hmmm?"

"Have you ever actually had a boyfriend?"

There was a split-second silence, and I thought that I was going to have to check the receiver again. "You mind your own business, Evie Edelman. And come with me."

"What?"

"*Susie* would have said, 'pardon?'. I said come. To London. What have you got to lose?"

"It does sound very exciting," I said dubiously. I looked at the field opposite the house. Earlier, I had seen a deer wandering through the grass and had felt that to be the pinnacle of excitement. Maybe my standards were too low? "You are already getting more camp," I noted.

"Get away with you," David laughed, and put the phone down, leaving me inky fingered, tangled again in a flare of a metal parts, horses keeling to the side like pushed cows, part of me in London.

*

". . . the issues that this development raises are threefold." George Denton consulted his sheaf of lined paper. "Firstly, our amenities are not equipped to deal with this influx . . ."

I had the bizarre urge to giggle at the use of the word influx.

I am not sure precisely why. "In-flux," I whispered meditatively. Edith stared at me.

"Secondly, there is the aesthetic look of the village – too many modern houses will detract from our picturesque appeal and change the façade of the whole place. And, of course, there is increased traffic, as the inhabitants will have to commute to and from work. In summary . . ."

"In summary, George, what the bloody hell can we do about it?" A male voice called out, to an uncertain chorus of laughter.

"Well," said George, peering over his half-moon glasses and going slightly pink, "in reality, the situation is such that, errr . . ."

"That we can't do anything about it," said Margaret tartly. "Is that what you were trying to say, George?"

George found a second wind. "There are of course official channels for complaint, and we could contact the developer in question."

"He'll just tell you to get knotted," said Margery. "Evil, they are."

"But, when the chips are down and the cards are on the table, it is Sir George's land to do what he likes with," said George Denton. "And if he is determined to sell it, well, it'll go to some developer sooner or later."

"Bloody man," muttered Vernon under his breath. I couldn't tell which George he was referring to.

"Hold on a minute," said Margaret. "There's somebody here who knows Sir George *intimately*. Perhaps she could have a word . . . Evie? Where are you, Evie? There. Stand up, love."

I got uncertainly to my feet, wishing that my outfit did not consist of mint green leggings and a sweatshirt with a sheep on and a small but perceptible toothpaste stain just above the right breast. I looked around at everyone, unsure whether smiling was called for or not. I really should have brushed my hair today, I thought.

"I . . ." My voice sounded low and flimsy in the hall. "I really don't know him that well."

"Why would he listen to *her*, Margaret?" A faceless voice spoke up.

"Yes, exactly," I said. "I mean, we all toasted the deal weeks ago, and he seemed relieved to be selling the thing off . . ."

"Hold on a moment," said Margaret ominously. "I thought that you didn't *know* about any of this developing nonsense. That's what you said the other day."

"Oh no," I said. "I knew all about that. Malcolm – the developer's name is Malcolm, he's a Sandancer, don't you know – showed me the plans, and Alex told me last month that he was hoping to be the agent to sell them . . ."

"You mean you didn't tell us?"

"What were you thinking?"

"Evelyn . . ."

"Oh, for *God's* sake . . ."

The voices layered up on top of each other, like that of a Greek chorus. It was a sort of song to my own shortcomings – all about me. My legs shook gently, but I didn't dare sit down.

"She's probably all for it, that's why she didn't say anything," said Vernon suddenly and loudly, addressing the front of the hall. He didn't look up at me. "Thinks she'll get a job."

"Yes," said Margery, swivelling in her chair, "because her and that foreign bloke who bought the Place – they *knew* each other before, she said so. They've been in cahoots all this time . . . I saw them *kissing* by the side of the road, up to Skisset."

I instinctively looked to Susie, who suddenly became very interested in her fingernails. She splayed her hand in her lap and looked at them coolly. I couldn't quite see, but I bet myself that they were painted, unchipped. Probably a subtle, pretty colour. Although that was the least of my problems, for some reason the thought of those perfectly manicured hands made me insanely angry.

"I *didn't do anything*," I shouted at Susie, but my voice seemed to stay inside me.

"No, it's because she wants work," said Vernon. "That's why she came here, because she was unemployed in Leeds . . ."

"Made redundant," someone whispered clearly.

"No, Vernon, I'm sorry but that's not it," said Edith. "I'm afraid to say, it's even sadder than that. You see, she *came* here because of a love affair that went wrong – she was jilted, weren't you?"

"I . . ."

"I saw her, sitting in the churchyard crying, and then she went away for a few days, and when she came back, she looked quite peaky and a lot thinner, if you catch my drift . . ."

"Disgraceful!" Someone announced. George Denton shifted in his seat and looked quite embarrassed.

"You're imagining things, Edith. As usual. So are you, Vernon."

Vernon automatically opened his mouth to contradict Margaret, but seeing the austere look on her face, snapped it shut again. "Tell them, Evie. Of course, she has work. She came here to set up one of them homeopathic, massaging businesses. She's fully trained, aren't you?"

"Umm . . ." Aborted, jilted, jobless . . . All those words crept up to me and stared. I should answer Margaret, I told myself hastily. But then, what could I say that wouldn't cause even more consternation? Could I even speak any more?

"Fully trained, my arse," said Rhoda, her eyes glinting. "She killed my dog!"

There was another collective gasp. I saw that the chorus was turning out to be the chorus to a tragedy. I would have to say something so mature, so articulate, so similar to the speeches that I had addressed to my bedroom ceiling, that I would win them back. "I'm a witch," I said instead.

"Oh, don't be *funny*," said Rhoda.

"I am," I said, my voice cracking like a teenage boy's. "I had a vision of your mother, of Vi, walking past the church, and you said that she was completely bed-bound."

"Oh, we don't want any of that," said Dot.

"You must think we live in the dark ages," said Peter. "Just because we aren't city people with stereos and things. I don't know."

"She isn't completely bed-bound, if you must know, she gets up and she wanders," said Rhoda. "So that's what you saw. Visions, indeed. The idea."

"Can we get *back* to business?" George Denton called feebly.

"Hold on a minute," said Margaret. "You said that there was nothing going on. What was this other thing that you didn't want us to know about then, with the developer? More secrets?"

"He and I were . . . were . . ." I knew that my mouth was open and my cheeks were bright red. I felt white inside, so bright that I couldn't feel anything at all. Then, a woman stood up. I didn't know her. She had a hard face, and dyed blonde hair so you couldn't tell her age. I crumpled a little as the attention was momentarily lifted from me. My ears felt full, as though I was listening to everyone's anger through a glass wall.

"The thing is," the unknown woman said, "whatever she says she is, I heard it on the charity board, from someone who knows her, and knew her before, that she's got a *mental condition*."

There it was, Asperger's, knocking my witchcraft down and trampling upon it. It wasn't a mental condition, I wanted to say, but it was . . . something. Something that I wouldn't be able to describe properly, the lack of words ruffling my insides with panic. In a stranger's mouth, whatever Asperger's was became hostile, menacing.

There was a flurry of murmuring, and then the hall fell deadly silent. I felt as though someone had reached inside me and was dragging out my deepest, darkest secret with their bare hands.

"She's got this condition, haven't you? Had to see a psychiatrist and everything. Why else do you think that she's living here, telling every single one of you something different about herself? Another lie? Why else would a young, unmarried girl be living away from her parents like that? I doubt her family even want her. *She's dangerous, and she should never have come here.*"

The last few words were muffled by my hands over my ears, reflected in an echo that I had created, rather like holding a shell up and hearing the sea. I screwed my eyes shut so tightly that it was painful, and, amidst the neon dots and black and the tunnelling sound of the stranger's voice, I screamed. Even through my own fingers, I could hear that it was quite unearthly. Silence after, but nothing went away – all the people were still there, ready to assault my senses again, crowding me, their harshness bouncing into and off my body, covering me with invisible bruises. Before I could start crying, I stared down at the varnished wooden boards of the floor, which melted as the tears came, pushed my way to the end of the row of chairs, and ran away.

AUGUST

Gladiolus – Peridot – Leo – Fire

"August brings the sheaves of corn,
Then the harvest home is bourne."
SARA COLERIDGE

"Vague misgivings about my character began
to spread through this limited society . . . it was
said that I was an immoral, an unreliable person.
These two epithets are happy inventions designed
to suggest things we are ignorant of, and leave
people to guess what we do not know."
BENJAMIN CONSTANT

"The pure hand needs no glove to cover it."
NATHANIEL HAWTHORNE

(He knew a thing or two about unpopular women. I have so many layers of gloves that you can't see the shape of my hand, metaphorically speaking. Oh dear.)

Horoscope for August:

Leo: Has your magnetic presence been ruffling a few feathers, Leo? With Pluto retrograding into your Six House of Daily Work, it is time to get your house in order.

SUNDAY 1ST AUGUST 1982

The combine harvesters have been out for a few days. I pretended not to be annoyed by the dull, industrialised roar of them as they ground down the fields. The spiked furrows that the harvesters left in their wake were vast and rich, chocolate brown. They darkened the landscape around the village, absorbing the sun.

Lammas Eve. Lughnasadh if we are being pagan about it – halfway between Litha and Mabon, a pagan holiday even though I call it by its Christian name. The season turns at this time, looking away from summer and preparing for autumn. But Christians took it and called it Loaf-mas, from the bread of newly harvested corn that they blessed. Or maybe Lamb-mas, as they did in the Cathedral of York, where lambs were born out of season in the province.

I supposed that Reverend Rishangles would be busy blessing bread, perhaps even travelling to the bakeries himself. I imagined the gentle cynicism on his face and clouds of flour on his black robes. He was too clever to be unaware of the paganism of Lammas – that knowledge would lurk under a flimsy layer of respect for his own religious observances. He would know that it pertained to the earth: brown, clodding and distinctly unspiritual.

Christianity was a gossamer layer over the reality of it all, a bastardisation of what was really meant to be.

So, it is a holiday – a time of jollity, forced or otherwise. But I stared at my own reflection, wondering what I looked like even though I could see myself.

I looked, as objectively and kindly as possible, at my own face. It was a severe face, handsome if you were being kind. She hadn't been sleeping well, this girl, and there was a sheen over her eyes that it took me a while to work out. Finally, I realised that it was fear. She/I was afraid, partly, I think, of herself. I liked her long mouth and nose, but her eyes were too dark to have any expression at all.

"Me," I said to myself.

I had come to realise that I had a little house inside of me that I walked into sometimes and shut the door. It was a fairy house, with latticed windows and red, curved tiles lining the roof like the scales of a fish. Whenever I was confronted by somebody else's emotions, or expected to do something impossible for me but easy for everyone else, I would walk into that little house without a backwards glance. I would shut myself away in a silence so pure that it was clear, uncoloured. I thought that, after the village meeting, I would have been able to spend time in that little house until it was safe to emerge, but had found to my consternation that I couldn't. I was locked out. Faithful Cottage had been my initial refuge. I had successfully locked myself in, but I couldn't retreat any further away from what had happened. Instead, I found myself stuck, physically inside, safe, tucked away, but not able to put enough distance, another set of walls, between me and that evening.

From the cottage, I watched sunshine picking out the tips of the leaves and the top of the grass. The lane and the fields mocked me by being open and inviting. I didn't feel good enough to go and join them – it was as if the sun would shine on the ugliest parts of me.

The nights got dark a fraction earlier – 'drawing in', they said, like a cloak. I felt a miserable sort of contentment at the thought that the days had, almost imperceptibly, been getting shorter since Midsommar. Early evening now – in another hour or so it would be dark. The outside would finally catch up with me.

I thought of all the options that I had been given by the villagers: looking for work, pretending to be a witch, actually being a witch, running from a broken heart, or mad? Perhaps all of them were true, depending on the angle you took me from. Perhaps they were all right in their own way. The idea of truth being so subjective made me uncomfortable. But then why had I felt that it was so unfair and wrong? I had actually seen Vi, as opposed to her phantasm, I must remember that. Susie Leverson remained un-hexed . . . I was a bad witch.

Tap, tap, tap.

I must be going mad, I thought. I was imagining someone was trying to get my attention.

What percentage of me had been ashamed when I had told the entire village about my affair with Malcolm in a manner so inarticulate that it was more expressive than words? I decided that pride was around the four per cent mark; five would just make me sound arrogant. The rest, the remaining ninety-six per cent, was mostly comprised of shame.

What could be done, I asked myself. I sat down on the sofa and pulled Peggy onto my lap, but she pulled away from me as soon as she could. She didn't seem to enjoy sitting on me any more – were my thighs getting bonier? Aunt Mim had comfy padding.

Tap, tap, tap.

Again. I wasn't going to look round. Try and focus on material things, Evie, I told myself sternly. I really must stop thinking that I see things that aren't there. I'd lost my job – I was no longer a career witch. I was as redundant as, ironically, Vernon believed that I was.

Malcolm had gone back to his wife, I was sure of it. Of course, he had never really left her. It was already over – the fragile, tentative connection between us that Malcolm had been so careful never to make too visible or strong. I hadn't thought about him for forty-eight hours: did you know that you can push somebody down in your mind, refusing to acknowledge them, and it actually works for a bit? Only now, in the diary, am I about to let him out a little. Everything is safer between the pages of a book. Perhaps he had shut himself away in that inner cottage of mine I'd been writing about, locking me out and leaving me to face the world. Malcolm had taught me a lot, I thought. He had taught me how weak I was, how important it was to make things look a certain way. All bad things. But then, hadn't Aunt Mim tried, kindly, to teach me the same?

Tap, tap . . . oh, for God's sake!

I whirled around. When I saw Malcolm, smiling his devil smile and motioning to let him in through the kitchen window, I asked myself quickly whether he was actually there, but he knocked gently again and made a sad face as I stared. I smiled in spite of myself, drew up the window and took a precautionary step back as, to my surprise, Malcolm immediately propelled himself through the little window, squeezing from side to side, coming out over the stainless steel sink and the curled corpse of my yellow sponge (I'd forgotten to eat, so there had been nothing to wash up).

"What are you doing? I have a front door, you know."

"It's romantic, isn't it? Like *Romeo and Juliet*, this."

"No," I said soberly. "I don't recall Romeo actually shimmying up the balcony. Didn't he just stand below it?"

"I was trying not to be seen," Malcolm said, smoothing down his hair and adjusting his tie. I took a cruel pleasure at seeing him squeezed and messy.

"Oh, very romantic. And it's too late for that," I said. "I told everyone. The day before yesterday. It just came out."

"Oh, *Evie*."

"Don't say it like that. You don't have the right to say that."

"OK, OK." Malcolm thought for a moment as he changed tack. "You were looking so beautiful at the window just now, with the sunlight streaming behind you . . ."

"It's too late for all *that* as well. Alex told me about your . . . your wife." She was really real now, I thought, now that I had said the words. It was a quite The Disappointment. "She was the Virgo, wasn't she?"

"Alex told you, did he? The *bastard*."

"Never mind that now. What's her name?"

"Eh?"

"What's her *name*? Your wife?"

"Sharon."

I am afraid that I snorted. Snobbism tends to be unforgiveable, except in this particular instance.

"Well, there's no need to be like that about it."

"Well, there's no need to have had an affair with me, was there?"

"It's complicated."

"Marriage isn't that complicated as a state, is it? I mean, either you're married or you're not."

"Give me a break, Evie. I can explain . . ."

"And you thought that you would *shimmy* into my kitchen in order to do it," I remarked haughtily. Now that I looked at him, I realised that of course Malcolm wasn't in his twenties, or anything like. He was thin and pale, that was all. His eyes twinkled, I suppose. His determined character made him ageless. All of those things fooled me, just as layers of transparency end up taking on colour that isn't really there. He was smiling now, looking preternaturally (wonderful word, pity its first diary usage is at this point) youthful.

"I just came . . ."

"Yes?"

"To ask how you are."

I narrowed my eyes. "That was all, was it?"

"Yep."

"Oh."

"How are you?"

"How am I?" There had been nobody to ask me that for a while. "I feel like, like instead of having a body, I've been drawn by a child who has crayoned very hard over and over in a circle. I'm like a bad drawing with no lines. That's how I am. Inside, I mean."

"That doesn't sound good." He came towards me. "You must have been to hell and back, what with all this."

"I certainly have," I said grimly. "My status in the village has changed from oddity to pariah. Quite the downgrade."

"But why didn't you just lie? You didn't have to tell everyone about us. No one would have found out if you hadn't said. Or did someone realise? You could have denied it . . ."

"I don't mind lying, except that I would have been lying for you. I lied for somebody else once, to make his life easier. I am not going to do it ever again."

"Goodness," said Malcolm softly. "Well . . . I thought we were in this together. I suppose that the villagers'll get their knickers in such a twist about the new development that eventually they won't see me and think of you."

"That's all you're really worried about, isn't it? Getting over what everybody else thinks."

"Well . . . it is something to consider, isn't it? You care what they think of you, don't you? Oddity to . . . whatever it was."

"I'm not sure that I really care what I appear like, just what am."

"Yes, yes, yes. I know. And you think that *I* am selfish and dishonest and sexy and unprincipled."

"Aren't you?"

"I don't know. I don't think so, but what do I know? I'm just me."

"You should have just said yes," I said.

Malcolm kissed me and it felt at once familiar and foreign. There were vague echoes in my memory of his lips, but the physicality of it felt like an imposition. His hands snaked lightly around my waist and he began to walk me backwards towards the sofa. I put my hands against his chest, to stop him or to touch him, I couldn't be sure. I'd thought that Malcolm was Satan himself, but that old incarnation of him was hazy. The present Malcolm was far more compelling, and had the advantage of actually being tangible.

The phone rang, suddenly, as phones always do. Malcolm's teeth scraped my lip as we both jumped, and I wondered why nobody had invented a telephone with a ring that gradually built up in volume.

"I have to . . ."

"Leave it . . ."

"No! It might be important." I dragged myself away from Malcolm's lingering hands and heard him flop on the sofa with a theatrical sigh of dejection.

"Evie? Is everything all right?" It was Dad's voice, dry as ever down the line, worry making his tone only marginally more strident.

"Errr . . . yes?" I looked over at Malcolm doubtfully. Was Dad somehow telepathic? I very much hoped not, else he would have had a difficult few days. "Why shouldn't it be fine?"

"You rang."

"Did I?"

"A few days ago. Saturday the twenty-sixth, to be precise, at fourteen-oh-two."

"Oh, that." Thirty-Six Hours Post Row with Aunt Mim. "Well, I'm fine now. Why didn't you pick up?" I just *knew* that I had forgotten something – I had forgotten to worry about where Dad and Lizzie had got to.

"We were away," said Dad, sounding mildly affronted. "I had my meeting at the Università di Milano, discussing the possible sabbatical. I took the rest of the week as a holiday, a jaunt if you will. I left Clive in Leeds with some research . . . it *is* the vac, of course, but his mother lives somewhere really quite inclement – Mold, I believe – so he stayed. Clive is quite promising, you know . . ."

"Did you have fun?" I realised that I couldn't bear for Dad to ask me if I was all right again – I might have to tell him the truth, and I had a sort of pushing feeling in my throat that signalled crying. The Venn diagram of two parts of me were overlapping. Malcolm and Dad were – unbeknownst to one another – in the same room.

"Fun? I wouldn't quite use that adjective, dear. My meeting took up a lot of time and preparation – I was rather nervous, actually. But, of course, there are so many parallels – historical parallels – between the industrialisation that took place in northern Italy and northern England, underpinned by the morality of the Enlightenment . . ."

"Are you doing a lecture or just talking to me? I really can't tell."

Dad sighed deeply. "I was merely expounding."

"Oh," I replied, not entirely sure whether that answered my question or not. "Did it go well?"

"Oh, I think moderately well. The head of faculty and I seemed to think similarly. He came back from his holiday in the Lakes just to see me."

"Did Lizzie enjoy it?"

"Your mother did a great deal of shopping," Dad said grimly.

"Dad?"

"Yes?"

"Was industrialisation really progress?"

"I think that it can be termed as such. There was a great moral weight attached to industry, so it was certainly considered the right thing to do at the time. It pushed society forwards, it created demand and supply, and employment. . ."

"But it created low-wage employment, and a middle class that exploited a lower one . . ." Malcolm popped his head over the sofa and made a face at me, before flopping back. "And it created all this stuff that we don't need, like chinaware and microwave ovens. What is so moral about that? Isn't there an immorality about people destroying the countryside, putting up houses that no one can afford, just to create work?"

"Who're you talking to?" Malcolm sounded worried.

"Shhh. Isn't that a by-product of the earliest industrialisation?"

I listened to Dad sigh again, and Malcolm was listening – no noise from the sofa.

"Hindsight is a wonderful thing, Evie. If we knew the consequences of everything we did in advance, we would never do anything."

"I know," I said.

"Evie . . ." Malcolm's hands were around my waist – he had crept up on me. I kicked him, sharply in the shin.

"*Shit!*"

"Pardon?"

"Nothing, Dad. Is that how you decide whether you have been a success or a failure? By weighing the bad things you cause against the good?"

"It is one way of doing things."

"What about everyone saying how moral it was? Doesn't it just show that people judge things to be moral if they understand them, or if it coincides with something similar happening at the same time?"

"Well, yes. You may have hit upon something there. Morality is not quite the fixed notion we all think it is. Any judgement can be accepted by huge swathes of people and turn out to be quite unethical."

Malcolm hobbled back to the sofa.

"Like when people think that you are immoral because you are different?"

"Evie, are we still talking about industrialisation?"

"Not really. I have to go," I said.

"Oh, right," said Dad. "Well, you'll call again, I suppose. Oh, and some news from your mother: The Halperns have bought a little dog, and they have named it Jezebel."

"Oh . . . why?"

"I don't know. It seems a deeply unfortunate name to me."

"I meant why did Lizzie ask you to tell me that?"

"I really haven't the faintest idea," Dad said. "Perhaps she thought that you would find it entertaining. You . . . you are all right?"

"Yup."

"Well, I will tell your mother and she will be pleased. You sound different. But then, I suppose that is an outcome of independence," he said wearily. "You know, my dear, you really should try and go to university. Otherwise, it's a waste. Of yourself, I mean."

"Bye, Dad."

"Bye," he said briskly.

The tall streak of Dad flickered in front of me. His mind would have flicked back to work now – reading, checking on Clive's progress. There was a fastidiousness to Dad that made him oddly vulnerable. It would be so easy to ridicule that tweedy, spare figure with spectacles, his academic approach to the most instinctive things. I thought how much I loved him, in a painful type of way that pulled my stomach in and closed my throat. Something that isn't necessarily good but has pushed things forward, I thought. Progress.

"Is it over? What on earth was that? Some sort of dial-a-tutorial?"

"I think that you should go," I said clearly.

Malcolm got to his feet. He rubbed his shin and looked at me archly. "Are you sure you want me to go?"

Being arch was an unattractive quality in a man, I decided. "I am pretty sure I do."

"Are you angry?"

"I don't know that either."

"But you still have feelings for me? You must have *some*, somewhere?"

"I don't know. But I don't think so, actually."

We stared at one another. I felt hollow, a quiet hollow, insulated from him.

"Help me get back out through the window, at least?"

"You can go out through the front door," I told him. "There's nothing to hide between us now, is there?"

I followed Malcolm out into the golden blaze of the mid-afternoon. He was tawdry-looking in such a beautiful light, and far too human to be a devil. Devils were glamorous things, I realised. There was a purity in their devilish ways, or at least a singularity of purpose. They would never have allowed themselves to get caught out.

Still, Malcolm wavered. "I'm coming back in a few days. For work."

"It's my birthday in a few days," I responded automatically. How much older I felt – far more than a year had passed in the last few months.

"Lammas Eve," said Malcolm. "Today, I mean. You'd suit having a birthday on Lammas Eve." He looked at me, and for a moment there was understanding between us again.

"Juliet's birthday was on Lammas Eve," I said.

"Juliet as in *Romeo and*?"

"Yes. It's a plot device, you see. She dies before her birthday, before she gets to reap the rewards of the harvest. So, she sows, but never reaps – all part of the tragedy. It's metaphorical."

"Oh."

"I'm definitely reaping," I said. "I think that it's turning out to be a tragedy in itself." We stood at the door.

"You know a lot of strange things, don't you?"

"Yes," I said immediately. "They are like tiny pieces of jigsaw that never fit together. I had always thought that a facility for facts was my most attractive feature."

"Actually, I think it is your eyes."

"Really?"

"And your mouth. It is wide. Generous."

"Yours is your upper lip."

"I'll come back for your birthday."

I shrugged. "If I asked whether *you* had feelings for *me*, I know that you would say yes. You could easily be lying – people do, people who cheat, and then they laugh at the people who believe them." I showed him out grandly, feeling that it was better to quit while I was ahead. Then he turned, about to say something, and I cut him off quickly. "I know, we're nothing like Romeo and Juliet," I said. "It was nowhere near as romantic."

*

Writing all this down, I relived Malcolm yet felt safe between my sheets of paper. Do you know, I had forgotten why Dr Gordner ever wanted me to keep a diary? I have a feeling that it wasn't to write down witchy phrases of the day. Or to turn a book into my only friend because the pages were blank until I wrote on them. And I like that. I have bastardised my diary. Taken its intended use and twisted and warped it until the diary suited me.

Why can I never fit in with what other people want?

Malcolm has taught me a lot, I'm beginning to think. He has taught me that I am strong; strong enough to turn my back on a person if it is right. And he has taught me that, just because I couldn't make things look a certain way doesn't mean that I deserve to suffer. Perhaps . . . perhaps all good things.

Progress, of a kind.

THURSDAY 5TH AUGUST 1982

Three days until my twenty-second birthday. Then I will tip the balance from just-about-adult into full-blown twenties maturity. I don't mind adding another year to myself, because I've realised that I feel older too.

I've always loved being an August baby: an orange-and-gold month, a lazy month where everything becomes tawny. The light mellows; the hay bales look like pagan offerings to the gods. The flower of my birth month is poppy (also gladiolus, but I could never get on with those) – but they'd splashed the fields and sides of the roads around Thornlaw in June, folding like handkerchiefs in the breeze, becoming redder as they doubled up. Those splodges of crimson have vanished now, giving way to the long, drying wild grass. My birthstone is peridot, a yellowy-green, either sickly or invigorating depending on what mood you're in when you look at it. I had always asked Dad and Lizzie for a peridot bracelet for my birthday. Each year, they were unable to find one and gave me something else.

They say that your world broadens with each passing year – or something like that, anyway. Mine had shrunk in the past few days, reducing to Faithful Cottage. I hadn't gone out much – the thought of anybody else produced a grey fear, rather like footsteps slowly walking up the stairs towards you. The limits of my own world solidified: upstairs, downstairs – the little rooms that tumbled into one another. The garden with its bleached, crisp grass and wrinkled remains of flowers. Even the air felt different, harder to breathe freely. I'd always preferred to place restrictions upon myself, it felt so much safer. But the feeling that I *couldn't*, that invisible block across the front door, was the truly debilitating thing.

Peggy was bored. Yesterday afternoon she had begun to lick, then pensively chew, the leg of her armchair. I shot fearful little looks at the phone, missing the harshness of its ring. Aunt Mim continued to stay away, although the thought of her seemed to be fading too. I had told her that I could deal with things by myself – I realised now that I had to stay true to that promise.

I stood listlessly in the centre of my main room. 'Listlessly' was entirely the right word. I knew exactly what it conveyed: restless, bored, unhappy and fidgety, all rolled into one. "Genius," I said softly.

The painting of the Thornlaw Saw Mill was incongruous above my fireplace in its gold frame. Strangely enough, it had never really fitted in Thornlaw. I remember standing and staring at it in Alwoodley, watching the bubble and swirl of the painted stream, admiring the feathery leaves of the trees that were edged in yellow as the sun touched them. It had seemed so exotically rural, beautiful in a way that was simple.

"I could go out," I said to myself, in an experimental way. My voice sounded fragile, unused and flat. "I could go there," I said, a little more loudly this time. I had located and memorised the exact location of the saw mill on the map before I had even arrived in Thornlaw, but I had forgotten to actually visit it.

Before I could change my mind, I slipped a lead on Peggy and stepped outside, savouring my freedom. Then I dived back into the house and got hold of the map, remembering that the last time I got lost in the environs of Thornlaw, I had stumbled straight into Malcolm.

I marched down the lane, ignoring the voice inside telling me that I could go and see Joanie. She must be out of hospital by now, I thought, probably on the mend. But I was too raw for her chatter, and there would be plenty of time. Looking left at the fields (and definitely not right at the other cottages), I swung off into the countryside. Peggy ran ahead, delirious with pleasure at finally being freed.

I was glad that the sounds of the village softened away. The birds and branches and leaves quickly took over and I tramped along, my thoughts making a curved wall around me that took me away from the sky and fields. I was there, but I couldn't step outside of myself.

The beat of my own walking became a song, a tinny beat that was a combination of every Adam Ant song I knew. For all the lyrics I had ever memorised, I couldn't think of any words. There was no next line, just one foot in front of the other.

Only the necessity of pushing the hair away from my cheeks reminded me that there was an outside of myself. Eventually, I had to look up. I had to pull the map out of my pocket. I was still going the right way, I thought. I just hadn't got there yet. Patience.

*

I wondered if I was truly myself, or whether another Evie existed as created by the villagers. How much easier it would be if everything they said was all a lie, or all true. All or nothing – so lovely. But the real truth was disturbingly half-grained. There were parts, segments, half-truths that were then twisted and turned, taken alone or taken badly that described me a little, yet not fully. It felt as though I was made of clay, helpless as fingers were poked into me. I was twisted and moulded knowing that I was infinitely twistable, mouldable.

I tried to envisage Margaret, Edith and all the others, but the very word 'envisage' implies that you can see their faces. They had become a mass, part of the brown floor and orange light of the village hall. "Mad," they had said, because they were behind the times and didn't know that it was indelicate to call people that. They didn't know Dr Gordner. How could I be mad? I was *me*, sane enough to myself.

One foot placed itself forward into the grass.

Another foot placed itself forward into the grass.

There was a thought, edging delicately around the back of my mind: how had the villagers known about my Asperger's from a charity committee? I hadn't told anyone in the village, I thought, running through my conversations at high speed. I had definitely never mentioned it. There was the handful of them up at Fielden Place and Hall, obviously, but they didn't mix with the village, except for . . . Susie.

Susie had told them. Of course she had. It was her revenge for Alex, and her distraction from Matthew Feld.

One foot forward.

Other foot forward.

Both my feet. "Best foot forward," I murmured. Which was my best foot?

It was a cold, vicious sort of revenge – as cold as Susie herself. No wonder she had looked embarrassed in the village hall that night – she had planted the seeds against me and was about to reap what she sowed. Perhaps Alex had been party to it – that thought made me slow one foot, letting it hover above the ground. Perhaps, all the time, Susie and Alex had been laughing at me. I couldn't forgive them – not for telling everyone, but for making me dislike the people they had turned against me. I hated Susie, and no doubt she hated me for supposedly (although not actually) kissing Alex. If she's been having an affair too, I hated her even more . . . I marched ahead, swinging my arms.

Left, right.

Left, right.

Left, right.

It felt as though a huge wave was about to break inside me – already I could feel the retreat of the tide, dragging the sand and stones inwards in order to push forwards in a great wall of water.

I was alongside the river, but I had seen nothing resembling a mill. Finally, I stopped, turning in a circle. I saw that, from an empirical point of view, there really was nothing to see. I had walked past a sort of crumbling square of a building – was that it? I checked the map – I was exactly where the river curved. Why couldn't I see it? Maybe it was me, not them, after all.

*

I heard a whistle, the confident sort that a shepherd gives to his dog. The person coming towards me waved. I hesitated and waved back, not being able to make him out. Finally, he got close enough for me to see that it was Paul, or Mr Margaret, as I called him in my head.

"You have sharp eyes," I said, as he drew up to me.

"You have one of them figures," he said. "Could tell it was you a mile off."

"Oh."

"What are you up to then? Hello, little dog, hello. She's a yappy one, isn't she?" He seemed pleased enough to see me. Perhaps a little embarrassed at being alone with me without Margaret – he wasn't the sort of man who would ever seek a woman's company.

"Oh, just – just walking."

"Me too. The wife's gone into Barnsley, so I thought I'd take the opportunity, you know? Shall we?" He sat down, facing the river, surprisingly limber. I sat beside him and stared at the white pattern of the sun on the water. We sat in a silence that I could only hope was companiable. There was a paternal air pouring off Paul, and I braced myself for some plain-speaking, homely, Northern advice.

"My mum and dad lived in Thornlaw too. Not in my house, in one of the ones they pulled down. I used to come out here when I was a lad."

"Did you? I was looking for the saw mill."

"You've found it." Paul motioned over to the shack.

"That thing? I thought it was a labourer's cottage. Where's the wheel?"

"Oh, fell into rack and ruin years ago," said Paul. "They should have kept it up, made it into a museum or one of them heritage sites, but they aren't too bothered about us out here. Must be a disappointment, if you came out all this way to see it."

"It is a bit. I have a picture of it that is so pretty, and I thought . . . anyway, I suppose that you saw it in all its glory when you came out here as a boy?"

"Oh, yes. I was the middle of three boys, you see. Alan, he was the eldest, always off with his friends. And Henry, well, he used to cling to my mother. Everybody loved Henry. Being the middle one, you're the odd one out, you see. Sometimes it felt like everything I did was wrong. So I'd come up here." He laughed softly. "Didn't want to go back, sometimes. Have you got brothers and sisters?"

"Just an older brother."

"Well, there we are then."

I wasn't quite sure whether I had proved or disproved whatever point Paul had been trying to make. Joe hadn't figured much in my thoughts for the last few days. He hadn't figured very much in general since I had moved out here. I'd seen Joe as part of a life I'd left, inextricably linked with Val, with respectability. I'd wanted to leave him behind. I'd done what Aunt Mim wanted . . . except that it was only what I *thought* Aunt Mim wanted me to do, I realised now. Was I really supposed to be here, witching? I had ended up tangled and messy and unhappy.

I would give Joe the money for his new house, I decided there and then. My creation from Aunt Mim's inheritance was crumbling. Perhaps Joe could take some of the money and create happiness in his new flat or bungalow? I didn't want to be unkind, or withhold anything from anybody – even Val.

"Did it help? Coming up here?"

"Do you know what, it didn't at all," Paul said sadly. "When you have all this beauty around you, but you can't appreciate it, you just feel even more filthy, don't you? All this nature, it's overrated when you're wrestling with your problems. And it makes the going back all the more difficult. No," he looked at me, "no point running away from it all really, is there? Well, I must be getting back – she'll be home soon. I'll leave you to it, love." He pressed my shoulder and I listened to him walk away. When I was sure that he had gone, I started to cry.

I must have cried for a while. It all got rather melodramatic and self-indulgent in the end – great, gasping sobs that rolled into one another, tears trickling and staining the top of my sweatshirt. All of that. By the end, I cried automatically, my mind divorced from the situation, clean and blank.

If this was another story – if I was a romantic heroine or had been born in another time – I would have found my suffering unable to be borne. I probably would have died, a Thomas Hardy-esque martyr of womanhood. I would have become a warning, a cautionary yet glamourous tale of loss. But, of course, things aren't like that. It started to rain, actually – a stormy little late summer shower. It cooled the air and splashed into the river. The rain chilled me and my teeth chattered.

Slowly, my physical suffering outgrew the spiritual. My grief burnt itself out. I got stiffly to my feet. Peggy and I went home.

On the way, I saw Vi. She tiptoed towards me.

"Out wandering again, are you?" I said cheerfully, my eyes red. She smiled at me and wandered on without saying a word.

SUNDAY 8TH AUGUST 1982

7.04 a.m.: "Aren't you going to wish me Happy Birthday, then?" I pulled the duvet tighter around me and stared at my Adam Ants. "Just one of you? No? Oh, *go* on. It won't kill you."

The Adams stared into the distance. My full-length Adam still cut rather a dash, but both of them looked flimsy somehow. They were becoming transparent and brittle; I looked at them and noticed the thinning of the paper rather than their faces.

"Are you cross with me? For betraying you with real men (and

I use the term loosely) like Malcolm and Alex?"

Still no response. I had another thought. "Sorry, about all the stuff you had to see. You know – me and Malcolm on the bed, and everything. We were only messing around."

I remembered that Malcolm had said he would come and see me on my birthday. I knew straight away that he would not, and felt only relief. I was thoroughly insulated from the knowledge that he would let me down by now. Malcolm had retreated in my mind to a sort of symbol, a black-and-white manifestation who only appeared to tempt me, to the dark witch that I didn't want to be. Perhaps, in that way, he had truly been a devil.

Still, the Adams wouldn't look at me. One of my windows was open on its narrowest setting. A little breeze blew into my bedroom, and the Adam with the rose flapped a little, detaching from his lower right ball of Sellotape.

I was out of bed and, feeling the momentousness of the occasion, solemnly took them down. "That's better," I said to myself.

I would still love their music, obviously; I would never, ever, ever stop loving that part of my Adam Ants. Ever. But they were just paper, after all.

*

8.12 a.m.: Card count. (From the ones that arrived yesterday lunchtime, of course. Perhaps more to come tomorrow?) In no particular order, we have:

- A kitten looking out from behind a jug of flowers, signed from Sue Halpern. Sweet of her, although she knows that the cat should have been a chihuahua, surely?

• A shiny postcard from David Kessel. 'LONDON', it says on the front, in the colours of the Union Jack, with Big Ben, Covent Garden, Charles and Diana, and somewhere else with a round bit placed into quadrants. It read: '*Happy Birthday, you old witch – come and live here. You know you want to! Xxxx*'.

• A splodgy, depressing landscape, clearly chosen and written entirely by Val, although she had put Joe and Tom's names as well. It is now in my bin. Val, I thought, had invaded Thornlaw and therefore was a traitor. An enemy of slightly odd women, or witchcraft, which may well amount to the same thing. And I was going to buy her a house nonetheless, because I had realised that only kindness would insulate me from my own hatred of her.

• A large card of *Witches' Flight* by Goya. It is mostly black except for the levitating bodies, and I love it to bits. This is from Lizzie and Dad, and there was a little package in pink tissue paper (it should have been black, to match the card, but I suppose you can't have everything). Inside, there was a peridot bracelet, a circlet of tiny stones on a very thin gold chain. I held it up to the light and watched the green/yellow of the stones. I understood why peridot wasn't popular – the colour is as bright as limeade – green was supposed to be unlucky, its brightness was almost irritating. With some struggle, I managed to put the bracelet on all by myself. It reminded me of the green and yellow trees of the painting of the saw mill, and the green water.

*

11.45 a.m.: "Delivery for Mrs . . . Mrs Edell-man?"

"That's me," I said cheerfully. "But how come you deliver on a Sunday?"

"I'll do anything when the price is right," the delivery man said with a laugh. "We're not supposed to." Whilst I signed my name, he took his cap off and rubbed his head. "Going to be hot today."

"It already is. Well, thanks."

"Thanks."

Peggy was terribly interested in the large carboard box that now stood in the middle of my main room like a misshapen obelisk. I paced around it for a moment, getting used to the thing, before giving in and ripping the tape across the top with a pair of kitchen scissors. There was yet more packaging inside – weird little plasticky bits and paper. Peggy began to bark ferociously.

"All *right*, Peggy".

Eventually, I took out a television. Not a big one – a sort of smallish, ladylike one. A 'little telly', to go with a little car, and the little job that had thankfully never materialised. Still, inexpert as I was with anything technical, I began to admire its nattiness. It was rather sweet, actually.

"I name you Arnold," I said solemnly. Peggy sniffed at it and looked disappointed.

I imagined that Dad and Lizzy would have put a label or a note somewhere. Perhaps Joe had contributed, in which case a house in a cul-de-sac was the least I could do. I must sort out the money for his house, I reminded myself, as I rummaged through the plasticky bits. There was something underneath all the padding . . .

'*Dearest Evie, Happy Birthday! Have a lovely day. VBW (only kidding!) Alex & Susie xx*'.

As I read Alex's chirpy, shallow little note, I was consumed by something – and for the first time, it was red in colour, like a spray of blood. I had often heard anger being described as a red mist, and I had never quite understood it. A mist seemed too ephemeral; anger was surely something that was physically there. Anger was not coloured red, either, it was orange and bright blue. Surely everyone knew that?

"Stay there," I commanded Peggy, who sat down and looked vaguely worried. The next thing I knew, I was charging through Thornlaw looking neither left nor right. The village didn't exist anymore, it was merely the line that connected Faithful Cottage to Fielden Place. *Left, right,* my brain called enticingly, trying to make a beat as I tramped along, but I ignored it and stayed firmly in the present.

Alex would most likely be at home, in residence in his country house, playing the country gentleman, I thought, with his wife who had messed around with another man and helped blacken my name without even messing up her hair or losing an earring. And who exactly was this married man that they'd all been gossiping about in the synagogue, linking her name with his? I wanted Alex and Susie to explode, I realised, to combust. I wanted to tear them apart and then walk away. The patronising note, the superiority inherent in their joint gift to single me had balanced atop the tinder of the witch trial at the village hall and set alight.

Furious as I was, part of me hoped that neither of them would be home. However angry I became, confrontation held too many unknown variables for my liking. Still, I marched up the driveway, each piece of gravel annoying me separately, feeling as though I had lost a game that I thought I had been playing according to the rules. Nothing was fair, I thought. Here I was, back at Fielden Place, looking in. I had nothing left to lose.

I banged the knocker very assertively, and possibly for three or four bangs too many, then felt a cold little shard of fear as I heard someone actually coming to the door.

Susie opened up, gratifyingly underdressed in a pair of jeans and a pale pink blouse. I noted that, as usual, she was still prettier than me. Then I noted that I no longer cared. Her prettiness would make it easier to hate her now. She looked at me, mouth open a little, and we both took our metaphorical gloves off.

"I want to see Alex."

"Erm . . ."

"I want to see him," I said, a little more loudly. Alex materialised as if on cue, trotting down the stairs.

"Here's the Birthday Girl!" He got to the foot of the stairs and his face slackened as he saw my expression. I imagined that I was rather red-faced at this point, and Susie's expression as she turned to him was unimaginable. Alex quickly assumed the fearful expression that a man can only have when he is about to be caught between two women arguing. "Are you girls all right?"

"I want to talk to you." I barged past Susie. "I know about what you did," I whispered to her as an aside, and went into the living room.

"Evie," she whispered, "don't tell him—"

"What on earth—"

"*Why* did you buy me a TV? And put that stupid little note with it?"

"I thought you'd like it," said Alex, who looked completely bemused. "Evie, is this really happening? Are you actually angry because we bought you a birthday present?"

"YES!"

"There's no need to shout."

"Yes, there IS, because we are *having* an argument. Right now."

"On a *Sunday*?"

"Oh, stop being so Gentile."

"On your birthday? When I bought you a present?"

"I didn't want a present!"

There was a silence. "Shall I take it back?"

"No." I sat down in one of Susie's chintz armchairs. The bounce of the new upholstery nearly threw me right back up onto my feet. "It made me feel . . . it made me feel like you didn't care any more."

"How can you . . . Evie, how can you think that? I bought it especially for you."

"But that's just it: it was a *gesture*. It was as if you wanted to plaster over something, or felt guilty. That's the trouble out here. Something honest happens between us, and then two or three things happen where you are just pretending or trying to cover up the honest thing."

Susie leant against the doorframe and folded her arms. "What did you buy her?"

"A . . ."

"A what, Alex?"

"A television."

"I suppose that I should be relieved," said Susie. "I was really imagining all sorts of things. Don't forget you promised to mend that bathroom mirror this morning," she said, turning on her heel and leaving us to it.

Alex sat down beside me and we stared into the middle distance together. Had I overreacted a tiny bit?

"I don't know what to do," he said.

"You could have told her that you'd bought me a telly," I said, anger subsiding. "The note was signed from both of you. I thought . . ."

"I told her I'd get you *something*. What did you think?"

I could be being ridiculous, I realised – it was a definite possibility. I was here, angry about . . . what, exactly? What was

Alex supposed to do? I had lost him because I wasn't like other people, but I suppose that wasn't exactly his fault.

"I thought that you were both laughing at me," I said. "You know, as a couple . . ."

"God, Susie and I barely get time to have a glass of wine together in the evenings, what with being in Leeds and then down here and all the stuff to do with the house and keeping up with everybody."

"Oh." Perhaps, in being like other people, Alex had even more to lose.

"I liked having you here," he said suddenly. "It's been . . ." He tailed off.

Finishing other people's sentences was almost a hobby of mine, but this time I didn't know what to say. I also noted Alex's use of the past tense and I remembered that sometimes Alex seemed to know me better than I knew myself. I heard gently remonstrating noises of china that Susie was washing up in the kitchen.

"It's OK. And . . . the TV is very nice. Lovely gesture."

"I thought you said that you never lied, because there was no point."

"Well, I go back and forward on that," I said. Alex's drawing room could be called the living room now, because it was well and truly lived in. There was a warmth left by human bodies, a fraying of the edges and untidiness of objects picked up and put somewhere different. Only the books were untouched, gathering the faintest film of dust. "You like having me here in the same way that you like having your mother's books here. It's a possession that you can look at sometimes, a reminder. But I'm not really happy to just sit and wait to be taken down, Alex."

He nodded.

"Do you remember when this room was empty?"

"Yes."

"It all started then really, didn't it? Or when I saw you through my kitchen window?"

"What started?"

"The game."

"I wasn't . . ."

"Yes, you were. We both were. Cat and mouse. I was as much to blame as you."

"Mouse and cat then."

Susie came in, cool and unobtrusive. "Is there some sort of problem that I should know about?"

"Suse—"

"No, let me. The thing is," I interrupted, "Alex bought me a telly for my birthday, and I didn't like it at first but I do now." I looked at him. "It was kind of you, really," I said, and watched Alex's face flood with hope. He looked ironic and kind and pathetic all in one go, and I realised how possessive I was of him. I owned a stake in all those expressions that flitted across his face, however fleetingly. "I am going to watch loads of stuff on it. Loads," I announced.

"What are you looking forward to watching?" Susie asked carefully.

"Cartoons," I said immediately. "*Scooby Doo*, and *Willo the Wisp*, and all that."

"Right."

"Best be off," I said. To reach the door, I would have to walk past Susie, and I had the sudden idea that she was going to hit me. I edged past, eyes forward, trying not to cringe. She didn't move – it was like walking past a ghost. I still hated her, I reminded myself as I walked away, because she'd told everyone about the Asperger's. But that seemed oddly impersonal now. Its colours were faded, and with it the very mettle of the thing. Even the married man . . . what business was it of mine, I asked myself wearily.

Had I just broken up the odd triangle that had formed between me, Alex and Susie since we had ended up in Thornlaw? It felt as though we had all lost something. I had separated Alex out from myself, certainly. I had demanded something of him – it hadn't been about the telly at all – and he couldn't give me anything in return. I had shown myself, he had hidden – hidden behind Susie and Fielden Place, and . . . that was just the way it was now. Susie had handled the situation superbly, because she knew that all she had to do was stand and watch as Alex and I finally realised that our bonds were broken.

As I rounded the corner past the church, I saw Joanie sat on one of the benches across the road. It was nice that she was out of hospital, but I hurried onwards. Really, I had been meaning to call round, and of course I would. I kept thinking about it at odd times, and making a resolution. But I wasn't in the mood to cope with Joanie right now – all I could think about was trying not to think about Alex and Susie.

Now Margaret was heading towards me; I saw her for the first time since my trial at the village hall. Before I even had time to be apprehensive, she waved at me and trotted forward. I had never seen Margaret move herself urgently and it was a sight to behold. I realised that this was either going to be a wonderful reconciliation or another row. In the remaining milliseconds before she reached me, I tried my best to be philosophical about it.

"Oh, love." Margaret rooted in her handbag for a handkerchief. "I'm so glad I've caught you."

"Me too. Look, I think that there's been . . ."

"Have you heard the news?"

"What news?"

"Oh, love," Margaret said again. She drew in a shaky breath. "It's terrible. Joanie's dead. She was taken back into hospital yesterday morning and had a massive heart attack."

I opened my mouth but no sound came out. Margaret pulled me into her for a hug. Being taller than her, I sort of rounded my shoulders and dropped my head to fit on Margaret's shoulder. We remained there for some time.

TUESDAY 10TH AUGUST 1982

I hovered nervously behind Margaret as she extracted Joanie's spare key from under a pot of wilted geraniums and rattled it in the lock. "Are you sure we should be doing this?" I wanted to ask, but the hospital and the solicitor and Joanie's sister in Scotton had said that we could – nay, *should*. Besides . . . we were doing it. We were letting ourselves into a dead woman's house. Still, I hung back. Margaret valiantly battled the lock, but I could sense her own misgivings.

The door creaked as it opened and I gingerly stepped over the threshold. Welcome to Brambledene.

Shouldn't a witch be *au fait* with death? Why was I scared? The word 'witch' had suited me when I came to Thornlaw; now it seemed the wrong shape and size, and just not very sensible. But when had I cared about sensible?

Margaret and I took in the white plastic phone on the mahogany table and the fraying, brown and orange stair carpet with mutual distaste. The whole house seemed to be pausing, drawing an in-breath as it waited for us to speak.

"I've never been in here before. Dropped round some magazines once, but . . . where shall we start?"

Dust. Faded, eaten meals, thumbed magazines, I was thinking. Everything trapped inside, sealed by the locks on the windows, hanging in the air.

"Upstairs, d'you think?"

Margaret and I silently padded up the stairs, the plastic carriers we had brought crackling. The stair rail was invitingly smooth but I wouldn't touch it.

"Well, they could have made the bed up." Margaret tutted. "These ambulance people."

"I suppose that it isn't really in their purview," I said weakly.

"Well, it must have been in view," Margaret said. "They were the ones that got her out of bed."

We both looked at the stout wardrobe. Curve-fronted, a thin

sheen over it, it reminded me of Joanie. Should I tell Margaret that the wardrobe reminded me of Joanie? It might comfort her . . .

"Wardrobe's as good a place to start as any."

"All right."

"You do the drawers. Or the dressing table, look. That wants doing."

"All right." Inanimate objects are so deeply pathetic when they have been abandoned. Far more so in my opinion than animals or people. Inanimate literally means without a soul, but there is a soulfulness in something so still, so left behind. I looked at the delicate, pattern-less fans of creases spattered over the bed where Joanie's body had been, and I wanted to rewind her into in. I wanted to go back to the time when she was alive. "Back," I said.

"What?"

"I just . . . nothing."

"I hope that wasn't some spell or incantation or other," said Margaret grimly, clouds of pastel cotton blouses draped over one arm.

"It wasn't."

"Because we don't want any of that."

I picked up a matt china cherub from Joanie's dressing table. His little cheeks, coloured with a painted circle of blush, puffed mischievously at me. If I had seen it when Joanie was alive, I would have wanted him to sit on the mantelpiece with my china rabbits and cause mischief. But it looked so silly now. I wouldn't want someone to pick up one of my china rabbits in the middle of baking her pie and turn it over in their hands after I had gone.

"D'you know, I am not sure I should have brought you," huffed Margaret. "I've already filled two carriers and you've not even started."

"I'm not sure that you should have brought me either. Margaret?"

"Hmmm?" Margaret turned, hand upraised in valediction towards a coat hanger.

I had to quickly formulate a question that I hadn't known I had wanted to ask. "Do you . . . do you think I'm weird?"

"Well, you're a bit of a strange one, aren't you? Why didn't you just say? About the development?"

"I didn't think that it was very interesting."

"You've got a lot of growing up to do," said Margaret. "All that money and books and no sense."

"I know that now," I said miserably. "Do . . . do *you* think that I'm a witch?"

Margaret narrowed her eyes at me, appraising. It was too much for me, so I studied my tennis shoes for a while.

"Well, you're certainly not quite like everybody else," she said.

"Because I'm posh?"

"Well, there is that. No, I meant that . . . well, you look at things differently. You're not like other people your age. That's it, actually. You're old, an old soul, but without the experience." Margaret stared at me triumphantly. Under a new lease of life, she whirled around and began to yank pleated skirts from their resting place. *Snap*, they went as they left the clips of their hangers.

"The question is, what do you want to call it? I wouldn't go on too much about witches and all that if I were you. I mean, it's daft advertising yourself like that. Don't you know what they used to do to witches round here?"

"Yes. But witches can be friendly, can't they?"

"They can be as friendly as they like, folk still don't trust them. They use them when it's convenient, that's all."

"You mean, they *used* them."

"What?"

"You used the present tense."

"What's wrong with that?"

"I suppose that it sounds a little strange if you don't believe in them."

"Who said anything about not believing in them?" For the briefest of seconds, I thought that Margaret winked at me. I must have been wrong – a tic, perhaps, or nerves or something. "Folks don't change that much, whether we live now or in the past. You'll find some jewellery in that drawer there, put it out nice for Joanie's sister. Or for that new bint of her husband's . . ." She sighed and shook her head.

"How did you know that Joanie kept her jewellery in there?"

"You don't always have to *know* to see things with your two eyes. You of all people should know that, Evie. There'll be some posh underthings in the third drawer down, we'd better pack them away."

I turned back to the dressing table, inhaling the sickly smell of face powder, looking at the thumb prints on the bottle of lily of the valley talc, the smears across the glass tabletop. I tried to sense whether this had been a happy or unhappy house, but all I felt was stifled. The air was clogged by Joanie – by her desperation, by attempt after attempt at failed self-sufficiency. This house was a pretence at being all right, and something unfolded and expanded inside my throat, pressing me, blocking the words. The sadness I felt was too deep to cry, far deeper than the one I had felt beside the saw mill. It was proper, adult grief. I felt as though I had been stretched upwards into a new space.

I turned round to Margaret.

"I'd best get at these shoes," she said. "Some poor beggars will want them, I suppose, even if they are cheap leather."

FRIDAY 13TH AUGUST 1982

Of course, the date is dreadful, I know that better than anyone. But the day itself is mild and ineffectual. Poor Joanie, though – fancy being buried on the unluckiest date in the year. Just her luck, really.

"Though he were dead, yet shall he live: and whosoever liveth and believeth in me shall never die," Reverend Rishangles had said in a solemn boom. In the midst of his congregation, he removed himself from us, addressing the ceiling and floating with these dead souls that circled the churchyard. Only occasionally did he deign to give us a glance.

We processed into the churchyard, towards the grave wedged between the split trunk of the tree. Why did Christians talk so much about death at a funeral? I almost missed Rabbi Guld – he would have said that Joanie was sheltering under the wings of

God's presence, and that would have made us all feel better.

I had somehow been absorbed into the procession and the service. Very little was required of me, I now realised, other than doing what everybody else did. The church was dimly lit, I was wearing a black dress – I blended in physically if not spiritually. Now I was processing, measuring my pace to that of the others, my head bowed so that I could feel the back of my bare neck absorb the air. As we passed the tree curled around that upright little tomb, either as though it had been dropped from a great height or had sprung up from the ground, I shot it a conspiratorial glance. The thick tangle of branches stared back at me, reaching out like tentacles covered in stiff, dusty leaves.

I didn't wear the polka dot dress that I had worn to Aunt Mim's funeral. This dress had a waist, and sleeves with thick silk cuffs that lay lightly on my hands. Lizzie had dropped off her black hat with the wide brim, and I had pinned my hair back behind my ears. I wasn't exactly Princess Louise, but I had made an effort to be as feminine as possible because I knew that Joanie would like it. It was the last favour that I could ever do for her.

The service had been a constant battle not to notice all the prosaic little details that leapt forwards. The pressure to be considering death and eternal life made me smell the woody dampness of the church all the more strongly, made me aware of the noise I made as I shifted on the bench. It made me feel the fabric of my new dress, and my stomach rumble because I'd had no breakfast. But every now and again, I felt the discomfort of something other than myself as I wrestled with Joanie's passing.

Little bubbles of grief floated innocuously to the surface and then burst with a surprising amount of pain.

There were so many 'Christ have mercy's and 'Lord have mercy's and sinnings, I thought to myself. It was all so strange. I am not sure that us Jews really expected God to have mercy – we just waited for the worst and were far more practical about the whole thing. And this was God's House, I had thought, looking up at the timbered ceiling and the slightly discoloured plaster. He actually lived here. He was here now. He didn't live in synagogues, only at the temple in Israel, where I imagined the climate to be far more clement than Alwoodley or Thornlaw.

We had reached the graveside, ranging around the horrible dug hole. Loitering so as not be in the front row, I watched Joanie's husband position himself carefully beside the vicar. He was a good-looking man, short with heavy features. His hair was greying but had a slight curl to it. He looked sensuous and selfish. His girlfriend ("Nicola," Edith had whispered to me, imbuing the syllables with a disgust that I didn't think possible) stood respectfully behind his shoulder, her hand reaching forward, holding his. Simultaneously holding back and pushing herself forward, I thought. She wasn't large and pale like Joanie, nor did she overdress. She was slender, older than she would like to be thought, and would age further into nondescription.

"You were the better woman," I told Joanie, hoping that it was true.

"For as much as it has pleased Almighty God to take out of this world the soul of Joan, we therefore commit her body to the ground, earth to earth, ashes to ashes, dust to dust, looking for that blessed hope . . ." Reverend Rishangles swayed gently in the breeze, his voice beginning to build momentum and his eyes shining. "When the Lord Himself shall descend from heaven with a shout, with the voice of the archangel, and with the trumpet of God, and the dead in Christ shall rise first," he cried, his voice carrying like the call of a bird.

I watched him, fascinated. It was almost as if he was possessed, I thought. Then I shook myself. That was entirely the wrong thing to think.

How was I supposed to take comfort from Joanie's death if the Reverend insisted upon talking about dust, as though Joanie was something to be hoovered up? I thought of the Kaddish, with all its talk of abundant peace and blessing and kingship – it soared over the earth and concerned itself with the life of the soul. There was something triumphant about it. As I stood in the graveyard, watching the coffin being lowered, I felt like an imposter again. My feet felt heavy and cool, as though all Reverend Rishangles's talk of dust and earth was pulling me downwards, anchoring me into the earth.

I looked around. Nobody was crying. Joanie's husband stared at the coffin so penetratingly that I wondered if he was trying to check that Joanie was still in there. Nicola clung to him and gave an experimental sob – Margaret shot her such a filthy look that she dried up immediately. On the other side of the vicar was Joanie's cousin Barry, who had travelled up from Salford. The rest of the congregation politely ignored the Lancastrian interloper.

I felt very much alone, and realised that Joanie would have stood beside me, possibly linked her arm through mine. All those times that I had assumed her 'bad heart' to be a romantic ailment, when it had been a disease, classifiable and eating away at her. I felt so silly. Silly and alone.

But then, hadn't I felt alone when they buried Aunt Mim? At least this time I was alone because I was an individual. I was no longer a child, sheltering behind my parents and disapproved of by my community. I was here as an adult, because I had befriended a woman on my own, without any religion or culture to bind us together. Thornlaw had judged me, but at least it judged me as an adult. I may have spent parts of the service wishing that I was back at the Asher Israel, but that would be trying to turn back time. I couldn't ever go back to Alwoodley without regressing into a teenager again and clipping my own wings. And I liked being able to fly.

"May the Lord bless you and keep you," intoned Reverend Rishangles. He seemed to be winding back down now, his momentary flare of passion spent. "The Lord make his face shine upon you and be gracious unto you; the Lord turn his face toward you and give you peace." He petered out, suddenly his usual, frail self again.

"Amen," everybody chorused.

"Amen," I mumbled, a moment later. I thought of the Lord's enormous, shiny face. It sounded endearing. Almost as nice as his wings that people sheltered under.

The meandering circle we had formed around Joanie began

to break apart. We dispersed uncertainly, watching one another. Edith gave my arm a squeeze as she walked past. "I know that you were close, love," she said. Margaret smiled at me.

I trod ground until Rhoda came up to me. She didn't realise that I was waiting to speak to her, or perhaps didn't want to realise. "I'm sorry about your dog," I blurted out, interrupting whoever it was talking to her.

"Oh!" Rhoda seemed surprised. "That's all right – doesn't matter so much now, I suppose. He was old."

"Well," I said tentatively, "as long as you are all right. How's Vi? I saw her . . ."

"She had a fall, couple of weeks ago. Been over in Barnsley, in the hospital."

"Like Joanie was," I said automatically.

"Yes. We'll have to find her a home, you know: I don't think she can stay here, but how we are going to afford it, I don't know."

I nodded, and Rhoda moved on. It was expiation of sorts, I supposed: no wonder Vi hadn't answered me the last time I'd seen her. I'd only seen her as a vision, which I felt made up for the time before when she'd been disappointingly real. Perhaps I wasn't completely useless in terms of cosmic power. Apparitions of the dead were vaguely comforting, I felt, but I had better focus on the living for a bit.

I scanned the thinning groups of people, wondering who to try and make up with next, before my eyes rested on Susie. I hadn't seen her at the funeral service; she seemed to have materialised out of nowhere, dressed respectfully in navy. We saw each other, or rather she looked through the pale blue transparency of her eyes in my general direction, and we made our way over to one another as if on cue.

"Hi . . . hello," we both said at once.

"I didn't see you in church," I said.

"No. I would have loved to be there, of course, but I spoke to Joanie's friends and Reverend Rishangles and made them aware that I couldn't really attend something Christian like this. They were very understanding about it."

"Uhm hmmm." The gap that we were delicately trying to bridge was as wide as ever. Panicking slightly, trying not to look down into the chasm, I tried to focus on the things I wanted to say instead. "I wanted to apologise . . ."

"That's all right."

"No, no I . . . I haven't done it *yet*! Sorry. There. You can't like me very much, and I don't blame you."

"It is difficult in our situation, isn't it?"

I looked at Susie. How much did she know, I wondered. Could she have guessed everything I felt for Alex because she felt it too, or did she assume that her experience was deeper, or better, because she had won him in the end? All the time I had thought of Susie as a thing rather than a person, like an object one skirted round, just there to block my path. But what twists and turns had she been through along the way, as Alex and I pulled back and forth?

"I . . . I mean . . ."

"Oh, *Evie*," she said, "did you think I didn't know how much you loved him?"

"I thought that you didn't care much," I said. "You are his wife, after all. You're the official one."

Susie smiled and shook her head.

"And . . . and Matthew Feld," I offered shyly. "I mean . . ."

"I'm sorry?"

"They said . . . I mean . . . I thought . . . at synagogue, they were talking . . ."

"Oh, Matthew Feld – the man that Susie Leverson was seen with when she should have been somewhere else."

"Susie *Leverson*?"

"Yes."

"But I thought . . . oh, God." I covered my face with my hands and went all hot between my cheeks and my fingers.

"Sorry to disappoint you," said Susie wryly.

"But when I came round the other day, and you said not to tell Alex . . ."

"Oh, I didn't think you meant anything like that! I was talking about, unfortunately, the charity committee . . . your Asperger's."

"Well, I understand why you told everyone about the Asperger's. I would have done too, in your position."

"Actually," said Susie calmly, "I didn't. I am afraid that Val told everyone when I took her to meet some of the committee that Saturday."

"Oh, God."

Susie shot a slightly ironic look towards the church.

"Sorry again, then. I thought that it was you."

"I was responsible in a way, albeit indirectly. But I would never have talked about it otherwise. I don't even understand it, to be honest."

"I'm not surprised," I said. "Neither do I."

There was a pause. "I suppose that Val will always be a thorn in your side."

"I'm going to buy her a house," I said miserably.

Susie's face lit up, gently, into a smile that made me feel rather special. "That's kind, Evie."

"It is, isn't it?" I agreed magnanimously.

"You know, Evie, I do feel bad about all this. But I want you to know that I would *never* have an affair with a married man."

"Neither would I," I said firmly. "Not a real affair, not when it actually came to it." We both pondered this for a moment. "So . . . what happened with Susie Leverson?"

Susie leant closer, and for a moment I almost liked her. "She was *seen* at about eleven o'clock at night, parked near the golf course with Matthew . . . Mr Feld, in his Cortina. Apparently, things were . . . very animated."

"No!"

"Yes!"

"Hah! How Sarah Leverson must be fuming . . . oh, sorry," I said, as I sensed Susie withdraw. "How you must hate me, with all my chaos and melodramatics."

"It is rather a sleepy village," said Susie. "At least with you around, it is never dull. And at least you are you." She paused for a moment, then looked at me clearly for the first time.

"I suppose . . . I suppose that I never really knew what you were like," I said. "I still don't. I always wondered why Alex liked you, because I don't know how you really are."

"Well, men never know how we really are, do they?"

"Don't they?"

Susie shrugged. We looked around us. Then I looked down at my shoes instead, and turned red. "Bye then," I said, as bashfully as if Susie had been my date for the evening.

"Bye," she said quietly, and I fancied that she was also awkward. We had both been a bit silly.

Was that the problem, I wondered as I headed out of the churchyard, that Alex knew exactly what I was like? Oh, I was too much myself for Feminine Mystique. I glanced right and left just before I turned out of the gate and saw the arc of Reverend Rishangles leaning against the church wall, clearly taking a moment off work. He straightened up at the sound of my footsteps, but on seeing me relaxed again, and I was reminded of the cigarette I'd shared with David Kessel in the synagogue playground.

"How was that?" He scuffed at the gravel path with his shoes, sending a little cloud of dust that evaporated into nothing. "Your first Christian funeral, I suppose."

"It was . . . all right," I said.

"Damning with faint praise, is that the expression? I suppose it must be rather odd to be the stranger at the gates." I glanced at him, at Reverend Rishangles' inscrutable face. To me, he seemed expressionless, and that made everything he said something of a surprise. But I remembered that some people could see extra colours and I immediately felt stupid, realising my own limited sight to be the only standard I knew. What if everybody else understood his face perfectly, and I couldn't see? What was I missing?

"I should have been kinder," I said. "Everybody thinks that Joanie and I were such friends and now they are being kind to me, but I neglected her terribly."

"We should all be kinder."

"But . . . but that is *general*," I exclaimed. "And this is specific. I should have been kinder to *her*. To Joanie."

"Did you like Joanie? Really and truly?"

I thought for a moment. "Yes," I said.

"Well, that is all that matters now, as she is not around to be tended to. And next time, perhaps, you will be kinder."

"Is that the standard Christian advice?"

"It is the only advice that is available to give," said Reverend Rishangles. "Nobody can travel backwards through time. You came to the funeral. And it *was* rather odd for you, I could see it."

"Religious people have more in common than pagans though, don't they? Even if they are different religions? Or do they? Don't you ever do pagan things, like on Lammas Eve when you bless the bread?"

"I suppose so. It makes me uncomfortable."

I nudged him, and he turned to me in surprise, as if shocked to learn that he existed in a physical way. "Go on," I said. "I bet you enjoy it."

"I do, exactly," said the Reverend. "That is *why* it's un-comfortable." We looked ahead of one another peaceably. Suddenly he roused himself. "Have you decided what you have to do?" His silvery little voice jangled like bells in my head.

"I think so," I replied.

"Hmmm." Reverend Rishangles nodded his approval.

"We should probably both be smoking a cigarette at the moment," I said, "it would help with the atmospherics."

The Reverend heaved himself off the wall and dusted his cassock down. "What a strange girl you are," he said. He smiled at me and walked away.

*

It was evening. Having recorded Joanie's funeral so carefully, as if that would make a difference to her, I was exhausted. But there was one other thing I'd done in the gloam of the night:

"Could I speak to Gavin Stephens, please? It is Aunt Mim's niece." I waited, listening to the sound of my own breathing in the mouthpiece. Gavin Stephens came to the phone surprisingly quickly.

"What a pleasure to hear from you again, Miss Edelman . . ."

"I wondered if you had gone home to your supper," I said.

"You are in luck; I am working late, as is my indefatigable secretary, Joyce . . . how is The Country?"

"Not at all what I expected, and rather awful in some ways," I said cheerfully. "The thing is, do I have to live here any more?"

"Excuse me?"

"What I mean is, can I move out now?"

"Well . . . yes, if you like."

"I want to get as far away as possible, to the biggest city."

"Ah, well there are property agents who specialise in overseas sales, I believe . . ."

"Oh, I meant London, of course."

"Ah."

"And I need to sign some money over to my brother Joe, and his nasty wife. But *how* does one do that?"

"Are you absolutely sure that you *want* to do that, Miss Edelman? If you have a difficult relationship with the spouse . . . you haven't been coerced in any way?"

"Her name is Val, although perhaps I should think of her as The Spouse," I said. "It is more that, if I didn't help Joe buy a house, I would feel coerced, but by my own meanness. Does that make sense?"

"Ermm . . ."

"And I think it is better to be nice, if you can," I said, "especially when people haven't been nice to you, and you know what unkindness feels like. It is a little like sandpaper, isn't it? Only on the inside."

"Would you excuse me a moment, Miss Edelman?"

"Yes, all right," I said, bewildered. What was I supposed to be excusing? Was he about to hang up the phone? I heard the click of a button.

"Joyce – forget that paperwork for now, would you?" I heard Gavin Stephens say. "Coffee and biscuits. I have some very important business with a valued client to attend to that may take some time. Yes, yes it's her."

FRIDAY 20TH AUGUST 1982

I have just got back from a positive witching session, slightly flustered and covered in dry leaves, but otherwise peaceful.

I went into the woods, you see, to cast my healing spell. It had to be done, although it was my first spell since . . . you know . . . the village hall, and Joanie, and everything. For a while, everything had crumbled around me whilst I stood, uncomprehending and hysterical, in an array of inappropriate sweatshirts. As I stumbled in the cool shade, finding a spot to cast my spell and trying not to trip over branches, I felt an uneasy mixture of hope and embarrassment. But you must never be embarrassed when you practice magick. Always be sincere, always believe, I told myself crossly, or else there is no point.

I carried with me a pentagon drawn on a piece of paper, and some mint stolen from Dot's garden last Sunday when she and Vernon went to church. Slightly floppy, dry mint now, but it's powers of healing would hopefully be undiminished. I sat cross-legged on this piece of paper, trying not to feel the uneven, dry texture of the twigs below, and visualised white light.

You were supposed to send the white light to the place you wanted to heal. I saw myself, not just one part of me. My whole self, Evie, the witchiness I had been so sure of until recently, the Asperger's which reared its head and rendered me mute sometimes. Perhaps I wasn't so much separate parts, just because there were things I didn't like about myself. I held myself in my mind – all of me. Slowly, the white light drained away, fading as I came back and sat in my own body with what I could only hope was elegance and dignity.

Did I feel any better? I wasn't sure, and gave myself a tentative poke in the arm. "I'm a witch," I'd said at the village hall, but I was uncertain whether I suited witchcraft any more – I had become too aware that I didn't have to be a witch, or anything at all. Maybe in dividing myself up into parts and sticking labels on them, I was deliberately fragmenting myself. Wasn't I me? Perhaps, I thought, I felt a little freer.

"Why don't you ring up George? He might ask you out fishing today." A cool, familiar voice drifted over to me from the path running parallel to the place I had chosen.

"Too late to go now. Anyway, I can't just ring him up and invite myself."

"I'm sure he'll invite you."

"Perhaps."

I stayed very, very still, and watched Alex and Susie walk along together, arm in arm. My human statue impression worked – I wasn't noticed.

"She's going, I suppose," Alex's voice said across the distance between us.

"Yes." Susie's voice wafted softly.

"I mean, I saw the 'For Sale' sign outside Faithful Cottage."

"Yes," said Susie again.

"Do you think that I should have passed it on to her?"

"Hmmm?"

"Malcolm's letter. To Evie," said Alex. "I promised him that I would give it to her . . ."

"No."

"I think that he's left his wife . . ."

"Alex," said Susie, little threads of steel running through her voice, "you did the right thing by throwing it away." The twigs crackled under their feet.

"I suppose that I could always ring her . . ."

"Better just to let Evie go," Susie said. "Don't you think?"

I watched their backs moving further away from me. They walked together in comfort, mutual comfort. Quietly used to one another, I realised. Alex and Susie had a calm sort of love which allowed them to sync their walk, and probably much more. I had wanted more.

*

Draft of letter to Dad and Lizzie:

> *Dear Dad and Lizzie,*
>
> *I am going to London, not moving back home like you wanted – sorry. I think that I will be happy in London, or I hope so. You two must have been happy there once, and Oma, and I think that Aunt Mim ~~will~~ would be pleased. ~~I do actually like you quite a lot. I am very fond of you both, although especially Dad obviously.~~ I love you.*
>
> > *Evie (and Peggy)*
>
> *P.S. How is Clive coming on with the research, Dad? You can tell me about looms if you wish.*

P.P.S. Thank you for coming up this weekend and helping me with the cottage. I am writing this on Friday, so you haven't actually come up yet, but I am assuming that you do and it is great.

P.P.P.S. Now that I think about it, I really do love you, actually.

*

Draft of a letter to Joe:

Dear Joe (and Val and Tom),

I have arranged with Nice Gavin Stephens and Joyce (she doesn't have a solicitor's power, nevertheless she does appear to do paperwork and make coffee very efficiently) to give you the money for a deposit on a ~~"nice"~~ nice house. No need to pay me back.

Say hello to Val, and tell her that I hope she will think of me every time she unlocks her new front door and goes inside. Tell her to get Lizzie to help her with the decorating.

~~I love you,~~

VBW,

Evie and Peggy, and also, I think, Aunt Mim

SEPTEMBER

Aster – Sapphire – Virgo – Earth

"Warm September brings the fruit,
Sportsmen then begin to shoot."
SARA COLERIDGE

"Is it all a game, then?" she asked.
Anthea looked sadly back. "Only if you win," was her reply.
"If you lose, it is far more serious."
ANITA BROOKNER

"Ridicule is a weak weapon when pointed at a strong mind."

(Which is all very well, Martin Farquhar Tupper, but it seemed a pretty strong weapon at the Thornlaw Village Hall. Maybe I do have a strong mind, though – I like to think so.)

THERE HAVE BEEN MOMENTS THIS SUMMER WHEN I have been tempted to disagree with Mr Ant, but it turns out that he was right all along.

Horoscope for September:

Leo: The autumn will bring new horizons. Having finally worked out who you can trust, be prepared for rewarding change.

WEDNESDAY 1ST SEPTEMBER 1982

I wish that there was something pagan or witchy about the first of September, some deeper symbolism. I definitely feel that there *should* be. But Mabon, the Autumnal Equinox, isn't for another three weeks, and the calendar is surprisingly blank. No symbolism, no hidden specialness to today. Nothing. All that exists is a strange back-to-school feeling as the weather turns cooler and the leaves curl. Perhaps it is better that way – things can't always mean something else. "Everything is what it is," I had once read in one of Isiah Berlin's philosophy books. It seemed oddly unphilosophical, but very true.

"Magick flows through me, as it has flowed through each witch in time." That was Wednesday's phrase, and it feels oddly appropriate as I sit here in a layby with Peggy, looking back over Thornlaw. The phrase itself flows – flows and moves me onwards, forwards, into what I hope is progress.

As I navigated the village, I told myself that I would come back one day, but I still had a smooth, disc-shaped feeling of desolation in the pit of my stomach. I'd navigated the Alpine Sunbeam carefully around the dips and curves of Thornlaw's centre. Past the church, following the road through. In these last weeks, the knowledge that I was going had focused Thornlaw clearly for the first time, as though I was already removed from it. Thornlaw wasn't a bad place, I decided. I just didn't belong there – something that Reverend Rishangles had perceived straightaway. A couple of old ladies ambling along the pavement together caught my eye as I drove – one stout and curly-haired, in a kaftan, talking vivaciously, and the other one pale and large, a little unsure, pulling her scarf with nervous fingers. Before I knew it, I had driven past and they were out of sight. I looked at Peggy, watching out of the passenger seat window calmly.

"Joanie's finally found a friend," I said to her. Perhaps Aunt Mim would keep Joanie company and make her laugh. They must have come to see me off, I thought, then got so caught up in their gossiping that they missed me. I would miss them, but Aunt Mim had her own existence of a kind (perhaps 'life' would be going a little far), and I had to pursue mine.

"Goodbye," I said loudly, over my shoulder. Peggy looked back too.

*

It is surprising how little I have. There were my suitcases in the boot, some cardboard boxes and bags on the front seat beside and below Peggy. My books, my china rabbits carefully wrapped up in kitchen towels. Almost the same number of things that I had taken to Thornlaw. And this, of course. My diary, the extension of myself *and* an external object I thought of as a friend. Both things at the same time. I had brought my diary to Thornlaw and covered the pages with my growing up.

It had been so easy to sell Faithful Cottage that I felt like a will-o'-the-wisp, barely having existed in it. I wafted about in between packing my things, expunging myself from the place. Dad and Lizzie came to help me repaint the bedroom wall cream; the sugarplum pink was quickly gone. Dad had accidentally trodden on the violet brooch that Alex gave me and crushed it. Now that sturdy little building was under offer, waiting to be faithful to someone else. I seemed to have accrued nothing material when I lived there except Arnold (Alex's little telly), and he was going to be raffled off at the next village hall event.

After my little stop here, I would continue heading south to London. David would be there, and so would Oma, in spirit. I'd tried to put down witchy roots when I left Alwoodley for Thornlaw, and found nothing that had rooted me here. Those thick, claw-like roots of the trees in the churchyard had ossified in the ground – no space for me. I was as rooted magick somehow, different from the inside out – but my past lay in the centre of the capital, in grey and smoke and bustle. No longer the blue and green London of my childhood – I could use a bit of grey. I expected London to be older, wiser, a little rougher and grimier, the edges frayed. Hopefully, we could grow even older together.

The roads had widened as I left the village. "I make my peace with the you," I said to Thornlaw now, small and manageable from a distance. But I don't want to get too sentimental. It never does to think too much about leaving anything.

"Gonna get going then?"

I could hear Alex's voice so clearly it made me ache, and I

tossed my head to drive him from my mind. "Stop distracting me," I told him crossly. Still, I turned to the passenger seat to smile and slap his arm as he reached for the steering wheel, but he wasn't there – he was living his real life, back in Thornlaw with Susie. Not a ghost, just a voice summoned up by the vividness of my own memories.

Switching on the windscreen wipers to bat away little spots of rain, I thought about loving Alex – the fact that my feelings lingered was inconvenient at best, cruel at worst. Nobody else could make me dislike Alex, not even Alex himself. However badly he behaved became irrelevant in comparison to those feelings running underneath anything that happened. Moving away would only make matters worse in the beginning – it would be easier than ever to love somebody from far away, their face blurred. But in the end, I would grow forgetful. Alex would fade, his blurred face replaced by new blurred faces.

If I was a different kind of person, perhaps Alex would be sat beside me now and we would be leaving for London together. I suppose that, for a truly happy ending, love would have triumphed, and all of that. I would be happy. But then, Susie would have lost a husband and been unhappy. Dad and Lizzie would have felt embarrassed going to synagogue and hearing me gossiped about – even Susie Leverson in the Cortina couldn't distract from that. Alex would irritate me profoundly, sometimes. I would probably throw ornaments at him.

The engine running, I began to edge out of the layby with deliberate care. Back on the road, I thought of Dr Gordner suddenly. I was sat opposite him in his office, Sigi blinking at us.

It was almost the end of our session, and Dr Gordner had taken the merest second to glance at a spot behind me that I guessed was the clock. I felt the helplessness of someone guided inexorably to the end of something.

"What do I do now?"

"I'm sorry?"

"Well, do I take tablets? Or have therapy, or have to tell Dad and Lizzie something specific, or . . . ?"

"You don't have to *do* anything," Dr Gordner had said, looking amused, which I thought was a tad unprofessional. He cleared his throat hastily. "There is no cure for Asperger's. It is the way you *are,* not a disease, Evie. We can meet again if there is anything in particular you need to talk through, or you need help with?"

Sigi winked at me. "I can't think of anything I need," I said. It was how I had felt at the time, although I wondered now if I had said that because I hadn't known what I needed.

"Right. Well, I think that the best thing is for you to just carry on," he had said, as though *not* carrying on was an option.

I would never see Dr Gordner again, I thought now. There was no reason to visit that dusty office, and I would be miles away, living another incarnation of my life. He'd handed me a different interpretation of the way I was – one that I had resisted, but had forced me to know myself better in its own way. Everything is what it is, but am I a witch? Was I Asperger's in human form? In the last few weeks, I felt as though these labels had peeled away and left me with myself, which was more complicated. All I could be, I thought, was my own mixture of differences.

"So, everything is normal," I'd said, "but now I know that my normal is mine alone."

Dr Gordner had smiled. "Got it," he said. His kind, tolerant face faded, leaving the rain-spotted road through the windscreen. I drove on and on, smiling to myself as the Sunbeam picked up pace.

There's really no such thing as a happy ending, largely, I think, because there's no such thing as an ending itself.